MORE THAN A TOUCH

"Then, it's settled," Darien said⟨...⟩ng her legs under her and leaning on one ⟨...⟩e professional, be friends, make ⟨...⟩ share an occasional bag of ⟨...⟩

"You'⟨...⟩color of her skin und⟨...⟩ou can't keep up a pro⟨...⟩cue sauce on your face."

She laug⟨...⟩cked her thumb, dabbing at her chin. "Oh, w⟨...⟩r You let me sit here all this time with my face dirty—that ain't right!" When she started to stand, he touched her arm.

"Don't go yet. Leave it. Let me get it." He reached out in reflex and found the tiny splatter mark with the pad of his thumb. Maybe it was when she'd licked her finger again that had been his undoing or the playfulness in her wail that had been the final straw that unraveled him.

Whatever it was, he was glad that she relaxed, sat down easy, closer, and allowed him to run his finger over the crusty surface of her chin. But just touching her made his hand tremble. Her skin was like satin; the offending splotch had to go, and before long, his thumb had found his tongue, only to return to her chin. As he did it, he knew it was too familiar a gesture, way too intimate a thing to do, but it was either that or draw her in hard to kiss it off her chin—and he wasn't sure if he'd stop there.

BOOK YOUR PLACE ON OUR WEBSITE AND MAKE THE READING CONNECTION!

We've created a customized website just for our very special readers, where you can get the inside scoop on everything that's going on with Zebra, Pinnacle and Kensington books.

When you come online, you'll have the exciting opportunity to:

- View covers of upcoming books
- Read sample chapters
- Learn about our future publishing schedule (listed by publication month *and author*)
- Find out when your favorite authors will be visiting a city near you
- Search for and order backlist books from our online catalog
- Check out author bios and background information
- Send e-mail to your favorite authors
- Meet the Kensington staff online
- Join us in weekly chats with authors, readers and other guests
- Get writing guidelines
- AND MUCH MORE!

**Visit our website at
http://www.kensingtonbooks.com**

LESLIE ESDAILE

Sister Got Game

DAFINA BOOKS
KENSINGTON PUBLISHING CORP.
http://www.kensingtonbooks.com

DAFINA BOOKS are published by

Kensington Publishing Corp.
850 Third Avenue
New York, NY 10022

All Kensington titles, imprints, and distributed lines are available at special quantity discounts for bulk purchases for sales promotions, premiums, fund-raising, educational or institutional use.

Special book excerpts or customized printings can also be created to fit specific needs. For details, write or phone the office of the Kensington Special Sales Manager: Kensington Publishing Corp., 850 Third Avenue, New York, NY 10022, Attn: Special Sales Department, Phone: 1-800-221-2647.

Dafina and the Dafina logo Reg. U.S. Pat. & TM Off.

First Printing: September 2004
10 9 8 7 6 5

Printed in the United States of America

Acknowledgments

I come from a long line of *hey-mon*, work five jobs, got a *side business* type of people . . . a family of "in your DNA," *to the bone*, entrepreneurs. Everybody in my family had something going on, along with a day job or two or three. They used every gift the good Lord gave them, everything from burning hair in the kitchen, to carpentry and a little jack-leg plumbing, to selling weekend-caught fish out of a station wagon, to taking up hems, or selling dinners out the back door. Name it, they did it: multitasking, wearing many hats, and creating plenty of hilarious escapades in the process. They were in denial about being so-called workaholics. Their motto: God bless the child who has his/her own. These folks, no matter what era, kept cash, opened family businesses, and had much drama going on at all times. It was a lifestyle—just the way things were done—and they embraced each new day for the new opportunity it presented. This book is dedicated to them and all who have that same gene, as well as for the brave souls who weather the storms that come with side business adventures.

Therefore I must especially give my loving thanks to my husband, Al, and all our children: Helena, Michael, Angelina, and Crystal for understanding that the author/consultant/speaker they live with is genetically predisposed to entrepreneurial pursuits. These dear folks live with a serial entrepreneur, and as this crazy, zany story will attest—a family business affects everyone in the equation. Thank you, family.

Special thanks and acknowledgments also go to my editor, Karen Thomas, who shares my vision and makes me laugh; to my agent, Manie Barron—who, as an entrepreneurial spirit, is probably worse than me; to my film agent, Katy McCaffrey—who is a bright, creative spirit that puts up with my wild adventures; Nicole Bruce for her patient efficiency and calm voice; to Monica Peters of GritsnCheese PR, for all of her wonderful efforts; to Tony Nottingham, Charles Holmes, and Crystal Weston, for getting my "paper" straight; to John Milligan and his fine staff at Milligan & Company, LLC go my deepest respect for their integrity, professionalism, fairness, accomplishments, community commitment, and for creating an environment at the firm (despite their resounding success) that is very much like a large, warm, close-knit family. That says something about who they are—great people!

Chapter 1

Philadelphia, present day . . .

"What!"

"That's right, baby," the night security guard who was sweet on her said. "Brotherman just called here and said he had a pass from the super to let them tow your Diamante from the garage. Now given how fine you are, and all . . . I just wanted to hook a sista up—ya mean?"

Yeah. She knew what he meant. Later for that.

"Thank you sooo much," Darien said, her feet finding her red Prada mules in a flash as she hoisted her barrel Louis Vuitton bag over her shoulder and snatched on her full-length mink coat to cover her red silk teddy. What was the world coming to? Damn repo man vexing a struggling sister at four o'clock in the morning! "I'll make it up to you later, I promise," she hedged, speaking quickly into her metallic flip cell phone that matched her nails, having no intention of doing some brother she hardly knew. Not over *a car*.

"That's what I was countin' on, baby."

"Yeah, well, can you stall him while I go down the service elevator?"

"The brother has to come past me first and show me the letter before he can be running through the property and hooking up a vehicle to take off prem—feel me? I gotchure back."

She blew out a sigh of relief and flavored it with a loud kiss designed to melt the guard. "That's what I love about you, Akeem. You're cool people."

Darien slammed her door behind her, dashed down the hall, and tapped her foot as the elevator gears engaged. Everything around her felt like it was moving in slow motion while she was the only one in the universe on fast forward. Not only would she have to discreetly drive out of the complex and then find a good place to hide the parked vehicle, but then she'd have to flag down a cab in a thong and teddy under her coat. The whole escapade was so ludicrous that she laughed. Finding a cab would not be a problem, if she let the coat breeze open a little.

Mischief on her mind, she stepped into the elevator. It was all a game. Shoot, the big boys had been scamming for years—so what was wrong with a sister getting a little reparations? Whateva.

All she knew was that she was supposed to be young, gifted, and black. This was the age of the black woman. But how in the world did she manage to amass nearly $60,000 in student loans, $10,000 in credit card debt, and a backed-up car note, with no high-powered media job like she thought she'd have by age twenty-five?

The reality was sobering as the elevator made its slow descent to the lobby level. Now all she had to do was slip off her heels, sneak down the long back hall, and go out the delivery side door, tiptoe barefoot across the clearing to the garage, then make a beeline to her numbered space, fire up her engine, and be out. Never mind that it was twenty degrees outside and she'd just had a pedicure. Darien shivered at the thought of putting her bare feet down on the grimy street. *Eeeew.* This didn't make any sense!

But she needed her car to get around and continue to look successful. Only if one presented oneself a certain way could one get ahead. It was the American way. And riding a bus to a job interview was out of the question, especially when the most coveted PR jobs were out in the burbs. No. A sister needed her ride.

She couldn't worry about shoulda, woulda, coulda. No matter that her landline to her apartment was disconnected due to lack of bill payment. Besides, this was only right, she reasoned. After all, she'd played by all the rules her parents had told her to follow—namely, she didn't have a baby yet without a husband, had pursued her career to the nth degree, and had managed not to get involved with any "loser" type man . . . albeit, she didn't have any man these days. In fact, she hadn't had one in more than a year, and *that* was not her normal routine. But she'd left all that man drama behind when she'd fled Atlanta and had taken an apartment in the plush Spring Garden Museum complex.

As the elevator came to an abrupt halt, she flattened her back against a side wall, peeping around it, one shoe in each hand, before jettisoning herself out of it and around the corner. No repo man. *Whew!* She only saw the back of Akeem's head and his discrete, under-the-desk wave for her to hurry up while he stared at the monitors on her behalf. Cool.

Wasting no time, she was down the hall and out the back door in a flash. Her feet hit frigid concrete, and the change in temperature set her teeth on edge. Oh no, this was no way for an educated sister to be living.

And how did this happen, anyway? That's the thing that kept nagging at her as she tried to still her heartbeat and half run, half hop to her car, avoiding glass and oil grime puddles in the process. Oh, this was nasty!

Every pebble, every minute piece of gravel, and un-identifiable hard piece of debris seemed to have found the soft flesh of her feet, making her limp the last ten yards to her pretty, candy-red, custom-fitted car. But she'd beat the repo man at his own game. Salvation and a sense of victory filled her as she deactivated the alarm with a little *beep-beep*, stuck the key in the lock, jumped in, and slammed the door. She could hear another vehicle approaching. It sounded heavy, like flat-bed-truck action. Man . . .

Okay. All she had to do was start up quietlike. She peered at her shoes. She'd have to figure out how to clean up the insides later after she put them on. Right now it was about motion.

Darien eased the car into drive and crept down the ramp, flashing her magnetic badge at the gate's electronic eye. As soon as the garage barrier arm lifted, she heard a commotion, and in her rearview mirror caught a glimpse of a tall, burly nemesis followed by Akeem.

Without a second thought, Darien put the pedal to the metal, screeching out of the garage nearly on two wheels. She laughed out loud, raised her middle finger, and sped around the corner, disappearing into the night.

Now the question was, what garage should she take her baby girl to? All she knew for sure was it was going to be a pain in the butt trying to move her vehicle around to various indoor lots—not to mention, expensive as all get out. She let out a little sigh, trying to think of the name of the nice brother who worked the overnight shift at the indoor lot at the Doubletree Hotel. What was his name? He might let her park there for a couple of days, sans charge, as long as his boss didn't catch on or sweat him. For a moment she wished her Diamante wasn't quite so custom detailed and quite so recognizable. No matter. It would all work out.

"Is Nate around?" she asked sweetly as she pulled up into the garage entrance.

The old man working with Nate just nodded. "Lemme get him."

"Thank you sooo much," Darien cooed, trying not to giggle as the old man cut her the evil eye.

As soon as Nate rounded the corner, he smiled. He loped toward her; his lanky form would have pegged him for an NBA champion were it not for the parking garage uniform. For a moment, Darien looked at his chiseled features set in a handsome burnt almond face. What might he have become with the right opportunities? she wondered.

"You still up to tricks and games I see."

"Who? *Moi?*" Darien laughed and batted her eyes at him. "I'm just in a real jam. *The man* tried to take my car. Do you believe it?"

"It ain't yours until you pay for it, suga," Nate replied with a wider smile, "but I might be able to help a sister out, if she'll act right this time."

Darien allowed her expression to become forlorn, as though she'd lost a puppy. "You aren't still holding a grudge against me, are you? I told you what happened and why things got mad-crazy, and why we couldn't hook up . . . and, and . . . see, what happened was—"

"What happened was you played a brother who ain't stoopid. You coulda at least called." He waited, creating a stalemate.

Oh, man . . . she was gonna have to think fast on her feet. Her feet!

Responding quickly, she jumped out of her car, barefoot. "Look at me," she said, allowing two big tears to well up in her eyes, sniffing for dramatic effect. "My feet are all black," she added, showing him her grimy soles. "My cell was cut off, my landline was jacked by the phone company . . . and this old man who works security was nice enough to come upstairs and bang on my door to tell me the repo man was on his way."

"Damn, baby," Nate said, his voice slow as he appraised

her, sensing for fraud. "I didn't know it was all that. A sister as fine as you shouldn't have to live like that." Then he rubbed his jaw, as he appreciably looked her up and down. "But I thought there was this young buck workin' over there."

"He got fired," she lied, shaking her head. "They put some old dude on his shift at half the salary—you know how they do us."

Nate nodded, buying her story. "Aw'ight, but you gonna hafta start treatin' a brother a little better than you been."

"I know," she said in a soft voice. "I've just had a lot of things on my mind—issues. I've been moving here and there, sleeping at my friends' houses, and—"

"Now, see, that's the problem. You don't listen. I told you before you could crash with me." Again he waited and offered her a wink and a lopsided grin.

"Can I?" she asked, not even trying to consider that option. "I thought you were just playin'."

"Hell yeah you can crash with me," he murmured, coming much closer to her than she wanted.

"Well . . . listen," she hedged again. "Let me sneak back to my place, get some stuff . . . and, uh . . . if the coast is clear—like if my landlord hasn't locked my door on me, I'll be back either tonight or tomorrow. But can I leave my car parked here for the night? I only have twenty dollars to my name until my UE check comes. . . . and you know how slow unemployment checks can be."

"Yeah," he said, stepping in closer. "It's cool. Leave your keys with me and—"

"Um, see, that's the problem." Darien glanced around quickly, getting ensnared by her own game. "I might have to come in during the day, get my ride, so I can go on a job interview . . . and, if I have to try to work on some angles, you know, a sister has to stay mobile. I gotta be flexible."

"Don't play me, Darien," he warned. "I ain't trying to lose my job over no dumb stuff."

"I'm not playing. I'm trying to get my thing right so I won't be a burden on you. We both know that after a minute I'll need to contribute to the refrigerator, at least. Right? I'm just being real."

Again Nate rubbed his jaw, but eventually nodded. "Aw'ight. I'll drive you back to your place—wherever that is, and—"

"No, no, no," she interrupted. "It's best that you stay here so *the man* won't get wise. Plus, if that old dude at the front desk sees me with you, he might get all attitudinal, thinking I had somebody to pay all my bills . . . so . . ."

"Yeah," Nate conceded. "I feel you. How about if I park your car in the VIP spaces so you can come in and out at will? We'll keep our thing on the down low—that's best for now. Cool?"

She gave him her most brilliant smile of appreciation. This was why she liked the guys from around the way. They had *real* resources—not just fancy dinners—and did more than talk a buncha rhetoric. Conversely, brothers in the suits had no real power and couldn't even help a sister get a job—and were just as cash strapped as she was. But brothers from the 'hood could fix a car; could feed you on the sly in the best of restaurants; could valet-park a girl for free; held the gatekeeper keys to the gas company, the water department, the electric company, theaters, movies, airlines; could activate a cell phone on a hookup . . . and if all men were equal, wanting more than a bright smile for their time and talents, then why not go for the guys who could really hook a sister up? Albeit, she knew she was pressing her luck, and one of these days she was going to have to put up or shut up, but it wasn't tonight. She wasn't hardly trading booty for a parking space—brother, *pullease*!

Darien stepped closer to Nate, stood on her tiptoes, and kissed his cheek. "Thanks sooo much."

"Oh right, and you didn't tip her off?" Maxwell Ferguson was beside himself with rage. He'd been trying to get this car back for a month so he could get his commission.

"Man, I told you. All my tenants are execs and VIPs, some artists, and they all keep strange hours. All you got is the right to tow her car, not arrest her. Up here in Philly, ain't no sister going to jail for owing a car dealer. The po-po got better things to do with their time."

Maxwell eyed the lean brother who sported shoulder-length locks beneath his security guard cap, his uniform pants so baggy that he looked like he belonged at a hip-hop concert, not protecting a building. Maxwell pegged him to be about twenty-two years old, tops. Maybe it was the pierced tongue that Maxwell couldn't help watching as the kid spoke. The little silver ball in it jumped as the guard lied to him between his teeth. This was a setup, if ever he saw one.

"You know I'll be back," Maxwell finally said in disgust.

"I know you will," the young security guard said with a sneer. "And, just for the record, tow man, I hope she slips your money-grubbing ass again, too."

This didn't make no kinda sense whatsoever. Darien stared out of the cab window, her feet freezing in her red mules, feeling like a hooker after a bad night. She was supposed to be the smart one in the family. The youngest and most educated of all her siblings, she was also the most in debt, and only had a great figure, courtesy of her expensive athletic club membership that had now lapsed, and a to-die-for wardrobe to show for it. For some un-known reason, earnest tears rose to her eyes.

Sure she was good at dipping and dodging disaster, but the real fact of the matter was, she didn't have a neat little house filled with loving, rowdy children and a stable, blue-collar husband. She didn't own her own car; the Diamante was a lease that came with a hefty note that was currently past due. Before long, the new apart-ment landlord's office would catch on to her fast-mov-ing financial shell game. This month, rent was going to be late, if she could pay it at all. The credit cards were maxed out, and it was only a matter of time before the dealer would find her car hidden in the private tenant-parking garage—if she could ever park it there again. Plus, she'd have to extricate herself from Nate, Akeem, and several corporate-type brothers who all wanted the same thing . . . a fair barter for a hookup, on which she'd never delivered.

And now that her parents had passed away, she didn't even have them to secretly fall back on in tough times like she'd always had.

She paid the cabbie with the ten-spot Nate had given her. This was crazy. She needed to talk to somebody, but her three older sisters didn't want to hear it. Louise, Brenda, and Cynthia all said she was selfish and spoiled rotten and always had been, which they asserted was her chief problem. Although they loved her, Darien knew that she wasn't exactly welcome to live with them either.

Darien let out her breath hard as she trudged back toward the apartment building lobby, half of her mind reflecting on the past, the other half trying to devise a way to again avoid Akeem's misplaced libido. Darien stopped walking and pulled her cell phone out of her bag and stared at it.

If she called home now, right at this moment in the

apartment building courtyard, with an SOS, she knew what her sisters would say. They all felt her cavalier, self-absorbed lifestyle, as Cynthia always argued, would be disruptive to the calm of their homes. They would say that they could understand a real emergency—tough times befalling someone who was being responsible. But then they'd also tell her that this self-induced financial mess that she'd created didn't qualify as an emergency. It was simply comeuppance. Time to take the weight, time to pay the band after a long, expensive dance. The Jackson sisters had convened a kitchen conference on the matter earlier in the year and weren't having it anymore.

They had coalesced against her, reminding her that none of them had had the opportunity to take luxurious Caribbean vacations, spree at the hottest concerts and clubs, buy fashionable clothes, and eat at will at the finest restaurants. They'd lamented about how they'd been tethered early to husbands, households, and children, and had diligently paid off their student loans, credit cards, or whatever other debt they'd amassed—without parental aid.

Plus, Darien knew in her heart of hearts that her sisters considered her to be snooty, and petty jealousies always arose between them. She could almost hear Cynthia's saying, "The problem is you think you're cute, just 'cause you were the one born with hazel eyes and long hair." Then Louise would chime in about how much money Darien spent on keeping a French manicure or some other outrageous color on her nails. Then Brenda would add the final blow, yakking about how Darien never had to really exercise, and that she'd been born with flawless, caramel skin—and the real truth was that she had to abstain from so much to keep her figure, worked hard to keep all the outer appearances up . . . hair, nails, skin took work!

Darien thrust her cell phone back into her purse. No

matter what was going on, Darien's looks and her sisters' claims of the unfairness of it all—that she'd been the one blessed with all the family's best physical attributes in one package—was sure to mar any prodigal homecoming. Just like they always threw the fact that she was the baby in the family in her face and reminded her of all their hard work versus all of her devil-may-care ways.

But they never gave her credit for the fact that she'd attained a master's degree with nothing but hard work, or ever gave her props for the fact that she took on her graduate student loans and everything else that went with a corporate lifestyle, on her own. *That* they couldn't take from her. And she surely wasn't the only person in America who had been downsized from a glitzy job. Darien shivered hard and wrapped her arms around herself, deciding whether it was safe to go inside. Her sisters needed to get over it—old, fat, judgmental heifers.

"You will not fail," Darien whispered to herself as she slowly walked across the courtyard. "And you will not call them—not like this," she murmured, trying to convince herself while knowing full well that, although they were concerned about her joblessness in general, a part of them had been waiting for her fall for a long time to teach her a little humility, to make her have to get her hands dirty with what they considered *real* work. After all, they'd come up before their parents had enjoyed the affluence they showered on the "accidental" gift of a menopause baby in the family, Darien.

In Darien's mind, being born at the right time wasn't her fault, either. No more than it was her fault that she'd been born as the prettiest girl in the family or the fact that the economy went tilt or that she needed to keep a certain image for her one day successful profession. With a fifteen-year gap between her and her next eldest sister, Louise, and even older sisters before her, all the Jackson girls had to scrap for any gains in life, except Darien.

That wasn't her fault. None of this was *her* fault. Well . . .
maybe a little of it was, but not the whole kit and caboodle.

As Darien neared the entrance, she could see Akeem's
wide grin when he recognized her through the plate-
glass window of the lobby. With the holidays looming, her
rent about to be past due, creditors haranguing her telephone until her telephone was disconnected, while she
also dodged the car repo man, she might have to go home
to the family gathering at her eldest sister Cynthia's house
and fall on her sword. Their mother always used to say,
"Pride goeth before a fall, baby." For Darien, this was
going to be more than a fall or "taking low" as Grandma
called it. This was going to be a proverbial crash and
burn. Being humbled like this before her sisters was almost enough to make her scream.

This was total bull! It was also a matter of principle,
now . . . especially since the woman had the gall and au-
dacity to lower her custom-tinted windows and flip him
the bird. Never in his life had he been so outraged. People
didn't have any moral fiber left in this world. No discipline, no ethics—no common, daggoned sense! Who
takes on a bunch of bills they *know* they can't pay?

Nobody was gonna scam Maxwell Ferguson. Oh no.
He'd come up the hard way from Macon, Georgia, by way
of Atlanta. He didn't deal with games or good-looking
gold diggers, and definitely didn't suffer fools. He didn't
have time for that, or any woman looking for a free ride.
It was about being disciplined, he reminded himself as
he circled the block again. He kept in shape, kept his
mind free and clear, and his pocket well guarded. Hadn't
been out in the world losing focus with women in a coupla years—unlike his brothers. Instead of getting snagged
like them, he'd put all his energy into building the business.

So, Miss Thang was gonna give up the car tonight

'cause what she didn't understand was that he'd worked hard as the eldest son to help his parents raise his five brothers and two sisters. He'd set a solid example for his siblings and had self-financed his way through college with a stint in the military.

Miss Jackson needed to take a page out of his book and stop trying to front with possessions she could ill afford. If the lady wanted nice things, then she could work for them, like he had—using his veteran's resources and saving every dime to start out with a coin-op Laundromat that his second oldest brother now ran. He didn't "get over" on people. He'd done it the straight way, expanding the Laundromat into a corner store that another of his brothers currently operated, until he'd gotten enough resources to hook up a credit dodgers service that his sisters ran, and a string of small apartment duplexes and tiny enterprises from Alabama to Virginia—all family-run operations. A sense of pride swept through him, muting his anger. He'd accomplished a lot by age thirty-five. True, he wasn't filthy rich, but he wasn't hurting, either.

Maxwell let out a long, weary breath as he sat in an obscure parking spot down the street from Darien Jackson's building. His latest expansion with his credit dodgers business led him to the fat contracts available on the northeast corridor. While New York and DC seemed a little too fast-paced for his liking, Philadelphia was perfect. Philly was more like a big down South. It had a solid African American community of homeowners, a progressive black mayor, and he could tolerate the pace. All he had to do was set up a tow yard as a minority firm in a city that was entrepreneur friendly. The black mayor there was pushing for neighborhood transformation and revitalization, which meant he could also get a portion of the abandoned car-towing opportunities, too.

Not to mention, in some neighborhoods he'd scoped out, property was cheap and real estate on the rise, and much more reasonable in price than in the big cities that bordered Philly. Here, he could buy what looked architecturally like a Manhattan brownstone for a fraction of the cost, and there was a steady flow of student population from the more than twenty-two area colleges and universities.

Setting up a tow business here would be akin to killing two birds with one stone and would keep his shop running at full capacity without waste. He could tow deadbeats, like the sly Darien Jackson, at night, and remove abandoned cars by day. Once the operation was rolling, he could turn it over to his youngest brother to run, and then go back home to the South. That's the way he'd started all his businesses, by working them for a year, then turning the enterprise over to a sibling, and just taking a management-investor cut off the top.

That made sense, anyway, since he was the only unmarried one in the bunch of Ferguson kids. His brothers and sisters all had a bevy of children, and most of the Ferguson clan had put down solid roots. So, in his mind, he could afford to take the risk, would spec out a new opportunity first, then if the operation could fly, he'd find one of his siblings who wanted to run it. Everything was decided by family committee. That's the way his parents would have wanted it—the Fergusons were tight, and the family motto was: the blood is thicker than the mud. So no big-city, fast-talking, slick-as-dishwater sister was gonna take bread off the family table by hiding from her obligations on his watch.

"Aw, man, sis. You should have been in here," Akeem said, laughing. "The brother was all puffed up, looking like his head would explode when he heard a car motor and went running to the window. Dude ran out the doors before I could say anything, just in time to see your middle finger flash out the window. It was beautiful!"

Darien had to laugh, even though she covered her mouth. "Oh, Akeem, it was too crazy!"

"I know. But I had your back, right?"

Darien nodded, covering her concern with another round of laughter upon hearing the change in Akeem's voice, which held the tone of a quiet, but hopeful demand. Time to pay up. Dang, she wished he didn't have her cell number. She forced herself to laugh harder. Before it had been necessary, but now that he was trying to make a booty call, he would probably think the temporary amnesty he'd bestowed upon her gave him the right to blow up her phone. No way. Didn't people just help each other anymore without always trying to work a deal? Geeze!

"Look at the bottoms of my feet," she said, still laughing as she dropped her purse on the security desk, snatched off her shoes, and began hopping on one foot to show him the damage on the other, all the while wondering if pneumonia would set in and save her from it all. "That is so foul."

"Don't bother me none," Akeem said, tilting his head and giving her body the once-over-lightly. "I'll wash 'em for you."

"See . . . that was TMI. Way too much information."

They both laughed, both knowing she was stalling.

"Nasty! Uh-uh. Before I do anything else tonight, I have to—"

"Watch your back, is whatchu gotta do—*now,*" Akeem said, all playfulness gone from his voice as his head jerked up.

"Miss Jackson?"

By the crisp way her name was said, Darien knew it was either the police or the repo man. Damn!

Akeem gave her an apologetic shrug for watching her instead of his monitors. It wasn't his fault, though the situation piqued her to no end. Who would have figured the man would be so dogged to double back? The only saving grace was she didn't have her car.

"Yes," she said as curtly as she'd been addressed. She straightened her back with an extra ounce of pride and turned around slowly.

It took a moment for his mind to catch up to what his eyes soaked in. There was no way around it, the woman was fine. She looked like a mischievous gypsy . . . her long, auburn hair windblown, like she'd been running from the law—and had been. Her pretty cheeks were flushed and her big hazel eyes glittered with pure defiance. As he glanced down her svelte body, he shook his head, wondering if she'd even had time to fling on some clothes beneath the fur before making a break for it. She thrust her chin up, as though that would make her look more authoritative. But how could a woman hold credibility with a red shoe in each hand in a plush apartment building lobby, with dirty, bare feet in the middle of winter? The sight of her was both mesmerizing and comical. For a moment, he forgot what he was going to say.

What was wrong in the world? she wondered. No repo man was supposed to be six-two, built like a linebacker, and as fine as all get out. See, now, she knew she wasn't living right. This was God's way of punishing her, offering her total humiliation served raw. And it didn't help any that the man had a triumphant smile on his face. She could feel her nails dig into the butter-soft leather of her shoes. But if she flung one at him, she could be arrested for assault. And dressed like she was, he probably thought she was a streetwalker, anyway.

"You know there's this matter of the leased car."

"Really?" she said, forcing her voice to be even and not sarcastic.

"Let's not play games, Miss Jackson. How long do you think it's going to be until we find it, tow it, and be done with this little charade?"

"I don't know what you're talking about." She dropped her shoes and slipped them onto her feet.

"Oh, so you never got any notices from the dealership?"

He had a very nice voice, even though the brother needed to stop being so tense.

"No," she said, looking thoroughly shocked. "I have been . . . moving. A lot. Even though this is my so-called address."

He folded his arms and stared at her, becoming more annoyed as each moment passed. Then she did something that temporarily disarmed him. She walked toward him, put her hand on his shoulder, peered back at the security guard, then looked him dead in the eyes.

"That good brother at the front desk has been helping me. He's been keeping stalkers away from me." She sidled up to him closer and spoke in a low, conspiratorial tone. "Can we step over there, so all my business isn't in the streets?"

Maxwell nodded. He could appreciate how embarrassing handing over the keys would be, and would allow her that ounce of dignity. If he would, God forbid, ever find himself in the same predicament, he'd die a thousand deaths if the whole thing were made a public spectacle. He walked with her to stand far enough away from the security guard's desk so that the nosy brother couldn't overhear what she had to say, and then he gave her a look that told her, *make it fast.*

She let out a well-timed sigh, drew a deep breath, and rambled on as fast as her mind could concoct the tale.

"My ex-boyfriend was sorta nuts. I mean, I haven't dated a soul in over a year because I just couldn't deal with a toxic relationship like that ever again . . . and I would never want to put another man in harm's way. You just never know about people—I mean he was educated, came from a decent family . . . but he was absolutely out of his mind. That's who I thought you were, and that's why I flipped you the bird."

She looked off in the distance and spoke in a soft tone. "I lost my job because of all the personal drama . . . that was a year ago. Then I fled my hometown, Atlanta, trying to rebuild my life, get a new job, and just pull my life together. Then . . . I found out that *he* found out where I was—so I kept moving." She peered up at him, tears brimming. "I know this is no concern of yours and doesn't change the fact about what you came here to do, but I just wanted to let you know that, everybody who is behind on their bills isn't playing some game. You seem like a very nice, hardworking sorta guy . . . and for whatever reason, I don't want you to walk out of here with my car keys thinking less of me."

"Miss Jackson, really . . . it's not my place to cast judgments or aspersions on anybody's character. I just need to get the car, you know? It's just business." Guilt lacerated him. He had judged her a near prostitute, a deadbeat, and a few other words he didn't want to acknowledge while peering into her big hazel eyes. Man, had he been way off base.

"It's been horrible," she pressed on, instinctively finding the crack in his hard façade. From the corner of her eye she saw a disappointed Akeem skulk away when the older morning guard replaced him for a shift change. She'd tell him whatever, later. Just like she'd give Nate the slip and get her car by day when he wasn't around. If she could get out of this, she'd pack in the dead of night and leave Philly and head for California, Canada, Chicago—anywhere but here where she'd played her hand out. Right now she had to keep talking her way out of her jam.

Darien glanced over her shoulder as though someone might overhear her, building dramatic tension into her theatrical performance. "They disconnected my telephone, which was my lifeline to safety . . . my sister had to get me a cell on her family plan. I only come back to the building at off hours once a week to get my mail, and half the time I'm so down, I don't even read it. You have no idea how horrible it's been. Both my parents are dead, and my sisters have children . . . they work hard and don't have much to spare to bail me out. I used to have a wonderful corporate PR job I loved— that's how I qualified for the car in the first place, and you can see from my credit report when the trouble began a year ago, and now all that hard work and education has gone to hell in a handbasket because I hooked up with a crazy person. If I could start all over again, I would." She paused partly for emphasis and partly to draw a breath, and because it was the only truth she'd spoken thus far.

When the man before her gave her a sad nod, as though he could identify with that feeling, she continued, but with less conviction. It was oddly becoming hard to lie to this kind soul, this guy who really was only doing his job. Truth slipped out in increments, mixed with all of her tall tales of woe. "I didn't even realize how many months had passed. I was just trying to keep myself from losing it—running scared all the time makes one day just slide into the next." That was as honest as she could risk being. The whole situation had her closer to the edge than she'd wanted to admit. The stress of ducking and dodging was perhaps worse than having everything she owned packed and dragged away.

Her voice became quiet as she thought back on how all of this came to be. "I had no idea somebody was actually out looking for me to take my car . . . I've never had anything so humiliating happen to me in my life." The first part of what she'd told him was a lie—she knew the moment the notice came. But the other half of what she'd said was the stone-cold truth. The thought of poverty terrified her. Having everything she'd worked for stripped from her nauseated her. There were days when she would wake up and just start crying, wishing she could yell out, "do over," and have someone in the world hear her.

With that she swallowed hard and glanced away, drawing shaky breaths.

"Didn't you try to get a bench warrant on the man . . . an order of protection for stalking you and intimidating you?"

She shook her head as two big tears rolled down her nose while she hung her head in true shame. This was beyond bad. She should have never used such a compelling excuse. You didn't play with something like alleged domestic violence, when there really were women in the world who struggled against those true horrors. Guilt was making her lungs feel like they'd collapse.

"The police are so overworked, and creeps slip through the cracks all the time. I just gave up trying to get help like that, and figured if I could just pull myself together . . ." She waned to let the subject die. She'd gone down the wrong path and needed to wipe the slate clean.

Her voice trailed off on another shaky sigh. God forgive her. But it wasn't just about a car; it was about fighting for the last vestige of her lifestyle. It was about feeling stripped naked and rendered helpless by twenty-nine percent credit card debt that had mysteriously escalated during the night because of a couple of late payments. It was about fees upon fees, building strategically designed late fees that one could never seem to conquer. It was about scamming the people who were scamming you—that's all. Just like they didn't care about her, or put her face to an account number, she likewise didn't put a face to all those collection agents and customer service reps. The whole thing was an impersonal game of Survivor.

But this man before her had a face—a kind, handsome one—and was indeed a person. She tried her best to remember that the whole issue was about having to lease a vehicle and not be able to buy one, and rent an apartment instead of being able to buy a home, because no one ever showed a poor black girl from down the way how. Throughout all the things that they'd taught her, all the rules and regulations heaped upon her, the critical thing they'd neglected to teach was how to manage capital. They'd thoroughly explained about being the last hired and the first fired, but why didn't they tell a sister what to do financially when that happened? And how come it was okay that the Enrons and WorldComs got to do the same things she was guilty of, using billions, but have it written off as a bad corporate move, whereas the little people like her had to pay the piper until their stomach linings wore out from worriment?

Darien peered at the man before her, her gaze seeking, searching, begging for one person in the world to just back off and give her a break to make good on her mistakes. Didn't he understand that? *Have a heart, brother . . . please . . . have a heart.*

Damn. This just didn't make sense for a pretty, educated woman to have to deal with the aftermath of an abusive knucklehead like that. If that had been one of his sisters, he and his brothers would have probably dealt with the punk the old-fashioned way—Southern comfort justice. Now how in the hell was he supposed to take girlfriend's vehicle, probably her only means of escape if a lunatic cornered her? Over just a few months of a backed-up lease? His mother had raised him better than that. It just wasn't Christian. Maybe she could go to the bottom of his tow list.

"You're four months behind on your payments, and your insurance has lapsed, which means the car's registration is all jacked, and it also means that the dealer's asset is sitting out there uninsured . . . there are a lot of issues here—even though I can fully appreciate your circumstance, ma'am."

Did he just call her ma'am? Was that a tone of re-

spect in his voice . . . a change from the initial self-right-
eous indignity that he'd affronted her with? Guilt
stabbed her in her side, but this was about survival.

"I know," was all she said for a moment. "When I get
my next unemployment check . . . later this week, I was
going to have the car insured again, then try to sort out
the registration. Then, with what's left, I'd pay for food
and rent, and hope the utilities will hold out through
the winter. I'm starting to go through my jewelry now to
pawn a few items." She looked down at her coat and
sighed, unbuttoned it and slipped it off her shoulders.
"Can you take this as a payment, sir? If you resell it, it's
gotta still be more than I owe, even used."

He pushed the coat back toward her, trying to keep
his focus on her eyes, lest he offend her. But his peripheral vision was as sharp as a laser. Standing there in a red
silk teddy with goose bumps making every part of her
come alive before him was asking a lot for a man to ignore.

"Ma'am, you put that back on, and you hock it for
food if you need to, all right? And don't be risking your
life running out in the street like that anymore, hear?
There's a lot of crazy people out in the world. More
than that loser who treated you badly."

She glanced down. "Oh my God . . ." She quickly put
the coat on and covered her face with her hands, breathing into them deeply. "You see how terrified I was? Do
you think I would run out of my home dressed like this
just to get away from a repo man? It's come to this!"

"It'll be all right," he said slowly, not sure why—also
not sure why he had the urge to hug her.

"If I could just find a job in my field . . . I would work
hard, would work off all my debts, and could get back
on track. But where am I going to find something like
that overnight?"

She looked up at him slowly, her gorgeous eyes glistening with tears as she wiped her nose with the back of

her hand. Then, without a word, she reached in her coat pocket and simply handed him her car keys.

"This is not your problem."

He was slow to accept her offer. Truly, this was not his problem, but why did he suddenly feel like it was? And why was his mind scavenging for ways to help her out? What was wrong with him, standing there, not wanting her to turn away from him and go back into obscurity again? And what made him reach for her wrist, turn her palm over, and put the keys squarely back in the center of it? Was he crazy?

"You used to work in PR?"

She looked at him wide-eyed and nodded.

"I might know someone who needs some marketing and public relations consulting."

She covered her mouth.

"It's not a large firm; it's more like a small family enterprise, but the pay would be decent for a decent day's work. And, uh, there may be a way to work an honest barter—PR work from a real professional for half the price, but with the back-up lease bill wiped out, as long as the insurance is up-to-date by the end of the week. The CEO might even be able to show you how to restructure your debt, get on a credit repair plan . . . might even be able to help you get a clean, safe, but inexpensive apartment, but they're located down in Macon. I don't know how you feel about being back down South."

"Are you serious?" This time she wasn't playing games. Her palm covered her heart, and she walked away from the guy she only knew as the repo man in the lobby, needing space, air, and a place to sit down before she passed out. God forgive her . . . she'd come up with a long, convoluted story—had lied to this nice, charitable man . . . had treated him like he was any other brother, all of whom, she'd thought had more games in them than Milton Bradley. She glanced up, waiting for a bolt of lightning to strike her through the lobby ceiling. Her momma was probably turning over in her grave.

"Yeah, I'm serious," he said, coming to sit across from her.

He'd always prided himself on being a good judge of character, and her openness, a ladylike decorum when cornered meant everything. It gave her credibility, in his mind. She could have cussed him out like a Dutch uncle, could have went off and acted ugly. But she didn't. She hadn't lied about her education; he had seen her résumé and pay stub details from her lease application. Her credit report showed she was in good standing before her life was turned topsy-turvy. It wasn't much of a stretch, he reasoned, as he waited for her to make a decision. And it wasn't as though he was giving her a free ride—she'd work hard for the money, and it would be a win-win situation.

About the most he'd do for her would be to try to show her how to restructure her debt, come clean, and reprioritize her life—*that's it.* After all, odds were that the sister came from a good family, and it was a shame that she'd gotten herself into a world of mess. Besides, his firm needed a real hotshot PR consultant to brand his multiple enterprises and reshape his corporate image—right? A little guidance could help her get herself together, and then Miss Darien Jackson could be on her way. At least that's what he told himself as he sat there convincing himself that he hadn't lost his mind and that his family wouldn't have a conniption.

"I have to ask you this," she said, her tone humble but firm.

He already knew what a fine woman like her would be worried about. "No strings attached," he said fast.

"The reason I haven't found a real job yet, even though the economy is slowly recovering, is . . ."

"You want an honest paycheck for an honest day's work."

She nodded, holding his gentle gaze. "I don't want to be used."

"How about if I have them draw up a contract, you read it over, then sign on for the job. That way, if there is anything untoward, which I guarantee you there won't be because that CEO doesn't roll like that, then you have a legal shield. At least they can't just turn around and tow your car because you didn't do something that's not up and up."

"That's mighty fair of you, sir. More than fair. I never wanted to make my way in business by getting there on my back. I didn't go to school for that, or take out sixty grand in graduate school loans for that."

"Understood," he said, standing and offering her his hand. He wasn't sure why, but her last statement sealed the deal for him. "Let's start again. I'm Maxwell. Maxwell Ferguson."

"Although you already know my name from a deadbeat list," she said with a smile, standing to shake his hand, "I'd like to start again, too. My name is Darien Jackson, public relations professional."

Chapter 2

Darien walked in a circle with her cell phone pressed to her ear as she waited for her best friend to pick up the telephone.

"Mavis," Darien said fast, almost breathless. "Oh my God, girl. Wake up!"

A sleepy Mavis laughed through a yawn. "You gonna have to stop calling my house at wild hours on a drama mission, chile. What's the matter with you? Do you know what time it is?"

"Yeah, girl. I know, I know, I know. But I have to move to Macon, Georgia, girl, and see—"

"What!"

Darien had stopped walking in a circle. She was now pacing.

"See this brother—"

"Wait. You finally get caught for check kiting or something?"

Darien laughed, knowing that it really wasn't funny. "Oh, chile. See, my car payment was late, and the repo man was chasing me . . . and—"

"You gonna have to give up this life of crime, girl-friend. You ain't handlin' your business. See, ya shoulda had some suit-wearing negro front you the money, then you could roll that cash over to the car dealer, tell him some old mess to blow up his head, then—"

"No, no, no, no, no! I can't be living like this anymore."

Mavis let out a long, weary sigh, followed by the distinctive sound of a sister sucking her teeth. "Girlfriend, it's the American way. Men try to play us, you've got to play them, and things stay in perfect balance—karma."

Darien pulled the telephone away from her ear for a moment and stared at it. Did she actually sound like that—crazy—when she was explaining her antics to her sisters? If so, no wonder they did an intervention.

"Yeah, you're right," Darien said in a much-subdued voice. It was time to get off the telephone with Mavis. But another part of her wanted to share the whole adventure with her wild girlfriend. They'd had *a lot* of fun together. They had been thick as thieves together since high school. Mavis was the only other woman with whom she'd ever been tight, and her girl was the only one who understood this crazy life they were leading.

"Of course I'm right," Mavis said, chuckling through a deep yawn. "Now tell me what happened. We'll come up with a strategy. Let me pee and get a cup of coffee. Dang, girl."

Darien laughed as she heard Mavis moving about in her apartment. Now *that* was a true girlfriend—someone who would go to the bathroom while still talking to you on the telephone. Through the process, Darien filled Mavis in on all the juicy details of her recent scamology amid whoops of laughter that had them both in stitches.

"Oh, noooo . . . you did *not* run into the streets half naked to get away from the repo man!"

"I did, and he was *fine*, chile. That's what made it so bad." Darien had to shake her head. "And he turned out to be a really nice guy." She could almost see him as she described him to Mavis. Tall; nice pair of broad, muscular shoulders; clean cut; deep-set, honest brown eyes; the body of life covered in a tow-truck mechanic's uniform—gun-metal gray, it was. Looked good against his chocolate-brown skin . . . but his eyes . . . so warm, yet, intense. His manner of speaking, intelligent, perfect timbre in a rich, baritone southern drawl. A shiver of interest passed through her. Darien had to remember that she'd sworn off the male species. Like Mavis said, they were just playthings, and a sista couldn't afford to get it twisted or her head all crooked over some man.

"Chile, don't believe the hype. There's no such thing as a really *nice* guy. Pulleease," Mavis scoffed, breaking Darien's reverie. "Stay focused."

"Okay," Darien said, her voice filled with dejection. "But here's what I've gotta do. I have to pay rent . . . fifteen hundred, and get all my utilities caught up—call that another five hundred, and—"

"Stop," Mavis said, her tone like that of a schoolteacher. "Why you gotta do all that? When's the rent due?"

"In a couple of days, and—"

"So move. Take the brother's offer, get some fine men to pack your mess up in the dead of night, and be out. There's no reciprocal agreement between the state of Georgia and Philly. The utility companies down here won't know."

For a moment, Darien said nothing. She wasn't sure why this sounded like a bad idea, especially since she'd moved on the lam before. But for some reason, when she took this new position, she wanted her business to be right. "Yeah, I can do that," she said halfheartedly. "I mean, I know a lot of brothers with bulk and can get the security guard to let me slide out under radar."

"Plus, you have a ten-day grace period before the management gets wise and starts watching you, right?"

Darien nodded, even though Mavis couldn't see her.
"Right," Mavis said again with conviction.

"Yeah, that's true . . ."

"Don't go down there all cash strapped. A sister always needs to stay fluid, liquid, gotta have a little something in her shoe, correct?"

Although Mavis was making perfect sense, something in Darien's gut just didn't sync up with the concept. "That's what I'll do," she said. "Thanks, girl. That's why I called you."

"All right," Mavis said, slurping her coffee in the process. "Holla when you're on your way to Georgia. I love you, boo. Stop freaking, it'll be all right."

"I love you, too, boo. I've gotta go."

Darien closed her flip phone and glanced around her plush apartment. She looked at the sumptuous cream-colored leather sectional sofa, the expensive black stereo system and high-definition TV she owned, courtesy of MasterCard and Visa. All of her African print accessories that blended into an elegant collage of brown-and-black-toned pieces could fit in a mid-size U-Haul truck—but she couldn't rent one of those without plastic. All of her black plates and gold flatware; all of her matching black Krups kitchen appliances; fluted crystal, long-stemmed champagne glasses; and her bedroom furniture and even her flat, black, high-tech office systems were light freight in comparison to her wardrobe. It didn't make sense.

Pacing quickly through the one-bedroom apartment, she glanced out the penthouse picture windows at the Philadelphia skyline. Tall buildings rose through the mist as the morning made the city come alive. All of her life she'd wanted to be on top, live on top, enjoy the finer things in life—but this wasn't any fun. This was only an illusion. Real fun was living like this, if you could afford it. Fronting was nerve-racking, and she'd had enough.

Her hand went to her throat as another chill swept through her. Her mouth was dry, throat raw, and head was beginning to get stopped up. The last thing she could afford was to get sick on top of everything else. She had to keep moving. Her apartment could get packed up in a matter of hours—that was the thing that made her sit down slowly on the side of her bed. For all this drama, her life could easily fit inside a half-sized truck and be carted away.

Yet, her parents, who never had much at all, had a home that her sisters were still breaking down and taking things from after two years, as though it were some mystical genie lamp with an unending wellspring of resources. Momma had everything. Even dead, she still did. Beautiful scarves, lovely old dishes, priceless family photos, history, love, warmth could still be gleaned from the little house down South that none of them could bear to sell or live in.

Darien sneezed twice and stood, going to her closet, which would be the hardest part of the apartment to break down. The linen closet would be a cinch, as would the bathroom. Plush, designer terry towels, a few over-the-counter medicine items, and her Egyptian cotton sheets were housed there—two boxes, max. But her closet . . .

Just looking at the array of shoes made her tired. Then the handbags. Darien did a quick assessment. "That's at least three thousand dollars right there," she muttered to herself, fondling the strap of a Gucci pocketbook with sudden disgust.

She shut the closet door and went to the drawer of her vanity, opening velvet box after velvet box of tennis bracelets, one-carat diamond-stud earrings, rings, pendants, pearls, until she almost got sick.

Darien flung her mink on the bed and paced to the bathroom, dry-heaved twice, and turned on the shower. Her feet were freezing, and her soul felt like it was frozen, too. Dropping the sweaty red teddy on the floor she plunged herself into the warm spray and lathered on the expensive emulsion she'd acquired from Bath and Body Works.

"Enough," she shouted against the tiles. She knew what she had to do.

"You get that car?" his brother Otis asked as he entered the small tow office at dawn.

"No," Maxwell said, too weary for words. "But I worked a barter."

"Aw, man . . . she worked you, didn't she?"

He would not dignify his brother's comment. Otis was the second eldest in the family, and the one always challenging any decision he made. He wished he'd had a chance to talk to his younger brother, Jovan, first. Jovan was cool, understood shades of gray when negotiating deals, and would have understood, even if he didn't agree.

"The sister is a PR consultant," Maxwell said, his back turned to his brother as he poured a cup of coffee.

"And?"

He could feel Otis's eyes boring into his back. "She got downsized, had a crazy brother chasing her around, and got behind in her bills. But she has the capacity, I think, to—"

"You *think*?"

"Yes, I think," Maxwell said very precisely as he added sugar to his black coffee, stirring it loudly. He turned around to stare at Otis when Otis didn't comment. "So far, my thinking has been working just fine for all of our family businesses—don't *you* think?"

Silent tension crackled between them as neither brother spoke. The issue that had always been there stood in the middle of the floor like a referee.

"What's the barter?" Otis finally asked, backing down, but not cowed by Maxwell's unspoken authority.

"I'll send her a public relations contract to work off the debt, and she'll do corporate branding, an image uplift on the firm . . . maybe wrap some innovative marketing around all these disparate pieces of business we have. I'm not totally sure about what all I'll have her do for the firm, but that's the gist of it."

Otis was on his feet. "You're not sure? Is that what you're telling me? All you know is some sister with plenty of game gave you a long story, and because you haven't had any tail in a while, you—"

"Don't go there with me, Otis. I'm in no frame of mind—"

"You should have brought this back to the family, to the board, before your mouth wrote a check that your ass can't cash!"

"What?" Maxwell set his coffee down so hard that it sloshed onto the blotter on his desk. "My ass can cash a lot of checks, trust me! I've been cashing checks for all of y'all since the beginning, so I don't have to take *jack* to the committee, the board, whatever. I made a spot decision, given the circumstances I observed, and I do not expect a lot of grief about it."

"Oh, so now we're just moochers, some strays you brought in off the street like a charity case? Like we don't work, put in as much time into the businesses as you do?"

"I didn't say that." Maxwell sat down hard in the metal chair and slurped the too-hot coffee, wincing as it scorched the inside of his mouth. This didn't make any sense, and the same bull always came up between him and Otis. Doreetha would probably have the same reaction, knowing her. Then he had to contend with all the spouses who would weigh in with their two cents.

"Then what are you saying? I thought that the blood was always thicker than the mud with the Ferguson clan."

"It is," Maxwell said, rubbing his face with both hands. He was so tired that's all he could say.

"Then how you gonna give some chick a job to work for *us*, without getting a hiring sanction from *the family*— and determine her salary and what have you?"

Every muscle in Maxwell's back knotted as he looked up slowly from his palms. "Because, no matter what, Otis, you need to be clear—I'm the CEO of this firm, and I run this joint." He stared at his brother, dead-locked. "Tell me if I need a better reason than that?"

Her heart was beating fast as she made her way onto the bus, her large Coach barrel purse gripped firmly to her side with her elbow. Her destination—Jewelers' Row.

There was no sense in going to the pawn shops. Their payout was low, and she wasn't coming back with a claim ticket to collect what she parted with. This was final.

She could feel her face growing hotter with fever as nausea set in. The flu was deadly these days, but she had to make this right. Lying in bed with everything she had to do looming before her would only make her feel worse.

Darien stepped off the bus, weaved, and began walking down Eighth Street from Market, back to the scene of numerous overspending crimes.

She stopped in front of her favorite jewelry shop, where she could count on custom-made, one-of-a-kind, eclectic pieces to tantalize her. Without fanfare, she drew a deep breath and pushed her way through the glass doors.

A tall, exotic blonde with her hair twisted into a classic chignon greeted her with a smile. They knew each other well—that is, as well as a sales rep can know a regular, foolish customer.

"Hi, Anne," Darien said through a sniff.

"Oh, hello, darlink. You don't look well at all."

"I'm not, Anne. Don't hug me," Darien said through a scratchy voice. "I might be contagious."

The blonde drew back and gave Darien a forced smile. "Then whatever are you doing in here, when you obviously feel so ill?"

Darien gave Anne a little nod with her chin to indicate the need for a private chat. Anne, in full ebullient style, came around the counter with flourish and bid Darien to sit down on a light blue velvet chair away from the few shoppers in the store.

"Talk to me, darlink."

"I've had some relationship drama," Darien said in a quiet voice, hating that she had to lie to get this thing done. But it was the only way to save face. What else could she tell the woman—I've been stupid, spending money on clothes and jewelry like a crack head, and now I'm trying to clean up my life? Never happen.

Anne nodded and leaned in, despite the threat of the flu. "Many of our clients, people who you'd never *dream*, have fallen on difficult times, and come in . . . so, don't be ashamed. It wasn't your fault, love."

The woman patted Darien's hand quickly, making Darien feel worse.

"I have some things I bought a while ago . . . and, I was wondering . . ."

Anne only nodded, her line of vision glued to the items Darien slowly extracted from her purse. As she popped open each midnight blue velvet case, Anne just shook her head.

"That much? I remember when you purchased this piece," Anne murmured, fondling a diamond tennis bracelet. "It was stunning on you." She looked up with a sad smile and held Darien's gaze. "Are you sure? Even the emerald ring?"

Darien just nodded as her vision became blurry from tears. "I have to, right now."

Anne sat back and sighed. "You know, jewelry has a five hundred percent markup. Just like clothing, etcetera, has about a one hundred and fifty to three hundred percent markup . . . you never buy retail, love—only wholesale. So, I don't want you to think I'm gouging you, but we have to buy this back at what we, as a jeweler, would have paid for it. Understand?"

Fury coiled within Darien. She was half mad at herself for being so stupid and half angry with the woman before her, not exactly sure why. But she did know one thing: Anne was working her, even though most of what she'd said was probably true. It was all in the way Anne's too-sad expression belied a hint of anticipation. Darien knew from scores of negotiations before this one that if you see vulnerability in an opponent, exploit it. That's what Anne was doing, simply leveraging the fact that she obviously needed money badly, and fast.

"You're right, Anne," Darien said after a moment, letting out a long sigh. "I guess because I don't feel well and was overwhelmed, I panicked." Darien slowly folded the cases closed and smiled. "I'm in no rush and should probably just sell these on eBay. Thanks so much, Anne, just for listening."

"Now wait," Anne said, standing and touching Darien's arm, no longer appearing concerned about catching the flu. "Maybe you should talk to Jacob, our owner. He is always interested in helping our best customers and will work with you." Anne's eyes darted nervously between Darien's face and the back of the shop. "Hold on, and let me get him. All right?"

Darien sighed. "Oh . . . all right. If you think he'll be able to help. But at this juncture, I'm just not sure of anything any longer."

"Just one moment," Anne said, again patting Darien's arm, but with nervous energy, not consolation. "Jacob," she said, raising her voice loud enough for the elderly man in the back to look up. "I need your help on a value question."

She hated standing in line. As a taxpayer—and taxes were about the only thing she did pay since they came off the top of any check she'd ever received—she felt it was an outrage to have to slowly file to the only few windows open in the post office. But she had no other option but to wait.

When it was finally her turn at the window, Darien blocked out the disgruntled, signifying, long breaths and huffs that the other patrons offered when she pulled out a wad of bills and began rattling off a ridiculous list of money order requests. So be it. With each money order she placed, she felt lighter, as though another brick of burden was lifting from her shoulders.

Barely able to breathe through the congestion that was now full-blown and making a sinus headache pound in her temples, she thanked the lady at the window and made her way to the Doubletree Hotel.

"Hi, sir," she rasped to the elderly man at the window. She wondered how someone his age could work all night and be there the next morning. Darien glanced over at her car. "Is it all right if I take it now?"

The old man shrugged, not even looking at her. "Ain't my bizness."

She knew what that meant by the judgmental way the offhanded comment had been said. Reaching into her purse she produced a small envelope. "I owe Nate a few dollars that he lent me last night, plus for the night at the garage. Can you give it to him when he comes in . . . and tell him I said thank you for everything?"

The old man accepted the envelope from her with a scowl, but the look in his eyes had softened. "You needs ta go on home and git some tea in ya. I'ma tell Nate you

came, and you was lookin' sick . . . I know he'll 'ppreci-
ate the payback, too."

"Thank you, sir. That's where I'm headed. Home."

By the time she'd gone to all the utility companies to
square up her past and to give them a shut-off date, and
had gotten her tags, car registration, and insurance
right, the late afternoon sun was turning the sky a deep
orange-streaked hue. Fever was sending chills through
her that made her teeth chatter, but she had one last
stop to make—the rental office.

As expected, the office secretary was in. Darien peered
around looking for Isaac Kramer, glad that he wasn't
there.

"Miz Smith," Darien said, wheezing, fatigue finally
making her native southern drawl spill out, "I came
with the rent, and I'm gonna have to leave soon."

The older woman was on her feet as Darien weaved
and held on to the desk. "I know I'm always late, and always have a long story, but I just have to go somewhere I
can afford to live, and—"

"Chile, sit down before you fall down," Mrs. Smith said,
her firm voice warm and filled with worry. She glanced
around the abandoned office. "Now listen, baby. You
take yourself on upstairs, lie down, and call a doctor."

"I'll go lie down, but first I've gotta give you a money
order, and I have to leave here before another rent is
due, and—"

"A money order?" Mrs. Smith shook her head and
went into her drawer for the receipt book. "You know,
darlin', I been watchin' you."

Darien just hung her head. She felt so awful that she
couldn't even defend herself with a witty lie. She plopped
into a chair with pure defeat. "I'm sorry," was all she
could say.

Mrs. Smith wrote down something in the receipt book and then tore off a yellow copy for Darien. "Baby, everybody might not 'xactly speak on thangs, but they ain't blind."

"I know," Darien rasped, her throat feeling like razors had cut it. "But I'm trying to make good now."

"I ain't talkin' 'bout what you owe or don't owe this old codger in here." Mrs. Smith rounded her desk and came to lay a hand on Darien's shoulder. "You done tol' me so many long tales, girl, I could braid a rope with 'em. But I also know you have a good heart . . . was always pleasant and nice to me, had respect. Then when you would git ready to tell a lie," Mrs. Smith said with a deep chuckle, "you'd look away, shamed, then take a deep breath and tell me some ol' mess, like I was born yesterday. And I would say a little prayer for you and just say, 'Uhmmm-hmmmm.' So I was always asking myself, how this sweet, young thing git herself all tangled up in tryin' to be slick?"

Darien looked up into the aged brown face that was etched with lines that implied years of hardship and wisdom. For a moment, the kind face blurred, and it made Darien look away. She reached into her purse and pulled out the one pair of pearl earrings that she couldn't come to agreement with at the jeweler's. "You were always nice to me, Miz Smith. I just want you to have something nice in return. Thank you for not telling on me all those times when you could have."

Mrs. Smith smoothed Darien's wind-mussed hair and then put a gnarled finger gently under her chin, all the while refusing to take the small midnight-blue velvet box.

"Now, you listen here, baby girl. My receipt book says you sent in a letter thirty days ago that you needed to move, like the rental agreement requires, so you don't have to pay for an extra month, which we both know you ain't got. That way you ain't gots ta be gouged by them greedy bastards that charge folks too much for rent no how."

"But Miz—"

"Don't be arguing with me," Mrs. Smith said, her eyes fiery with determination. "I'm old and done worked here low onto 'bout twenty-somethin' years, and I forgets where I can lay my hand on things from time to time. Forgets to mention little details to the management now and again. You understand me? But I bet your computer could make another letter print off right quick, dated . . . ummm, last month, that could quietly find its way to my office before you has to go, couldn't it?"

Tears rose in Darien's eyes and streamed down her cheeks. It was no act.

"Now, you go on up to your apartment and call a doctor, like I said. We'll worry about all this other moving business, later, when you feel better."

"I can't," Darien whispered. "I don't have medical coverage. I'll take some Theraflu, and—"

"You ain't got *nobody* to care for you?"

That's what did it. The sudden realization that there was nobody in the world to care for her made the dam against her sobs break. Darien covered her face with her hands; hard, bitter sobs of remorse and heartbreak came from a place so deep in her soul that she couldn't stop. "My momma's gone, my daddy's gone, my sisters think I deserve whatever happens to me . . . none of the men I've ever dated would do for me or care if I was sick . . . my best girlfriend is all the way down in Atlanta. Ain't nobody to care for me, Miz Smith. I can't even pray because I done told so many lies that even—"

"No, no, baby. Shhhhhh," the older woman said, drawing Darien up from the chair into a tight, motherly embrace. "*He* always cares. Don't you forget that—and you best start calling on Him when you need Him."

"Oh, Miz Smith, don't," Darien protested, trying to wrest herself away. "You'll get my cold."

"Uh, uh, honeychile. I pray. Jesus got me covered . . . just like He got you covered, no matter what you did. All you have to do is take the first step of trying to get right. Let Him carry you for a little bit of the way, chile. Anybody with plain eyesight can see you tired of running."

The statement made Darien hug the older woman tighter instead of extricating herself from Mrs. Smith's hold. And the harder Darien held her, the harder she cried, until all that was left were stuttering sobs.

"Now, chile, let me tell you," Mrs. Smith said, stroking Darien's wild rush of hair. "We all have to help each other in this mean old world—other folks do it all the time. That's why I'ma help you." She held Darien back from her and looked at her with a gentle gaze. "The lady that cleans the penthouses is my old-time girlfriend. Says you can eat off your floors, place is clean as a whistle and you ain't never home, so your security deposit will be at the top of my list of checks to write out to you. Okay?"

All Darien could do was nod.

"Now. That part is settled. I already knew you was leaving, anyways 'cause old man Phillips, the morning security man, said he seen some young feller come in here and give you a little grace. That was a sign. Time to get right with the world, make a clean break. An angel was smiling on you."

Stunned, the tears abated as Darien opened her mouth then closed it.

"See, chile, I know why yous mad at the world . . . 'cause it ain't fair. Truly, it's not. And, yes indeedy, Lord, rich folks use every trick in the book and help their own, then turn around tryin' to preach to folks about fairness and bootstraps and all. Coupla so-called VIP folks in here ain't paid no rent in a loooong time, but they ain't gettin' put out—but we ain't talkin' 'bout them, we talkin' 'bout you."

She let out a weary sigh as she cupped Darien's cheek and shook her head, her wise old eyes never leaving Darien's. "But, baby, you can't do like them and expect to have peace. And, at my age, you'll learn, peace of mind is worth a mint. Young folks gots ta learn that, in this world, all you gots is your good name. A helping hand, a barter, is one thing—always remember that's how we got from slavery to today. But never forget the honorable thing, and all this stuff y'all young folks buy for show ain't worth a plug nickel when it's over. All that glitters ain't gold. Enrich your spirit, and abundance will come in very unexpected ways."

Darien covered the old woman's hand and closed her eyes. The truth of what she said seeped into her bones like medicine.

"You burning up with fever, honey. So, I'ma shut down this office, come upstairs with you, and you gonna take something. Then I'ma make you up some old-time remedies to flush your system and break that fever. You got potatoes and socks, maybe some onions, plus a little sugar for a good plaster?"

"I think so," Darien murmured, thoroughly grateful for the loving care Mrs. Smith was so freely willing to bestow on her.

"You got a neighbor that might have some, if you don't?"

"I don't know my neighbors," Darien whispered, feeling more isolated with each diagnostic question Mrs. Smith asked.

"Well," Darien's elderly benefactor said, sighing, "I gots neighbors and chirren, too, who will bring me what I need to work on ya. But I don't claim to be no doctor. I can pray over ya and give you some of what my grandmomma taught me, but if the fever ain't broke in a day or two, you and me is goin' to the emergency room. You hear me?"

In that brief exchange, Darien knew why she was

headed south. She knew what she missed, knew the sound of that place that had neighbors and ministers and shopkeeps and postmen who knew your name. New tears rose to her eyes as she slipped the pearl earrings into Mrs. Smith's hand despite the older woman's earlier protest. "Give these to one of your children if you don't want them . . . just as my only way right now to say thank you, ma'am. I needed to borrow their momma today."

"Arnetta, I need you to do this for me today, without going into details with Doreetha."

"Oooooooh, big brother, I ain't never heard you like this. Now, why we gotta git a contract all squeaky clean and FedExed up to this lady in such a hurry?"

"Arnie . . . I don't know. Gurl, listen . . . Otis has been on my back about it all day, and I just have this feelin' I can't explain." He walked in a tight line between the window and his desk, almost tangling himself in the cord in the process.

"You know Doreetha is gonna have a cow," Arnetta said, laughing. "But as the vice president of human resources, I guess I can pull rank. Would serve her right, any ole way, since being the CFO and comptroller, she thinks she controls everything and everybody in the family."

Maxwell had to chuckle. "Her title fits her, though."

They both laughed.

"You tell Jovan?"

His sister's question gave him pause. "Not yet." Maxwell sat down slowly.

"She's that pretty, huh?"

Maxwell shot out of his chair. "From what I gather, she's been through a lot . . . and I don't want Jovan cornering her and making her feel uncomfortable."

"Oh, she must be *fine*," Arnetta said, giggling.

"Whooowee! Drama is 'bout to turn this family upside down."

"No, it ain't gonna be no drama, Arnie. Can't be. Nobody has the time or patience for that. Jovan is—"

"The director of marketing, the youngest of all the brothers, and loves him some fine women. Plus, if she's a public relations *consultant,* she has to deal with Jovan, right? Ain't PR supposed to work hand in hand with marketing?"

For a moment, he couldn't answer his sister. Arnetta was right, and the fact that she was laughing hard in the telephone disturbed him. Truth was, he hadn't thought of all that. Truth was, he wasn't sure why he was introducing drama into his family, his business, or potentially his life.

"This is a fat contract, though," Arnetta said in a sheepish tone. "She know all the terms and conditions in it yet?"

"I didn't discuss all of that with her, only about how she could work off her debt to our firm and—"

"Ooohhhh . . . so it's like that."

"Like what, Arnetta?" His sister was getting on his nerves.

"Like a nice surprise." Arnetta sighed. "Is she sweet, Max? 'Cause if you like her, then I'll love her . . . 'cause you don't like nobody—least not lately, you haven't— and I'm worried about you."

"It's not like that, and you don't need to worry about me."

"Daddy had a heart attack, and Momma had a stroke working themselves into the ground, and never did anything to have real fun, so it's my right as your baby sister to worry about you if I wanna."

Maxwell closed his eyes. "Arnie, would you just do the contracts?"

"Yeah . . . bet she's gonna have a fit when she sees all the nice perks in it. This is a great surprise."

He began doodling on his blotter, annoyance making his pen etch bold, black strokes across it. "There should be nothing surprising about an executive type package being offered for executive level services offered by a true professional with a solid educational background and a very strong work history." He forced Darien Jackson's image out of his head, mentally kicking himself for remembering what she looked like with her hair all mussed, tears glittering like diamonds in her big hazel eyes, wearing nothing but a skimpy teddy under a mink coat and standing in the lobby with dirty bare feet. Maxwell Ferguson let out his breath hard.

"My bad," Arnetta finally said after she'd stopped laughing, her tone patronizing and gleeful. "You done went all corporate on me so I can only take you at your word—girlfriend must be all that and a bag of chips."

Mrs. Smith's diligent ministrations had been better medicine than any doctor could have prescribed. Even though she had a smelly salve greased across her chest, a bandanna of skinned potatoes plastered to her forehead, and socks filled with raw potatoes, too, she felt much improved.

The scent of potent, nasty teas sat on her nightstand, along with a recognizable white, purple and orange oversized envelope.

Mrs. Smith was hovering in the doorway when Darien sat up.

"Think you can keep down a little mint tea and toast?"

"Mrs. Smith," she said, coughing a bit, "you've done enough. In another day or two, I'll be fine. The sleep was the bulk of what I probably needed."

The older woman smiled and took a deep sip from her coffee cup. Then she gave a curious nod toward the Federal Express envelope. "Might as well see who that's from. If you have to pay the piper, best to know how

much, so you can make arrangements to pay little by little."

Darien nodded and sighed. "You're right," she conceded. "Sooner or later I've gotta deal with them all."

It didn't bother her that Mrs. Smith had come close
and was eagerly watching her open the envelope. After
someone had seen you vomit in a waste can at the side
of your bed and even dumped it for you, what secrets
were left?

"It's a job offer," Darien said, shocked. "The guy who
came to get my car actually delivered, like he said he
would. I thought for a while that he was blowing smoke—
after I paid all my utility bills . . . I thought . . ."

"Well, suga, he gave you his word, and he came
through."

Obviously, Mrs. Smith wasn't getting it. Darien stared
at her, producing the contract for evidence. "Most men
I've dealt with don't *come through,* much less like this.
Their word isn't worth squat. They'll tell you anything
to get what they want, but this is signed by some lady
named Arnetta James, vice president of human resources for Allied States, LLC—a *real* company."

"Do tell," Mrs. Smith said casually, glancing at the paper
and donning a pair of reading glasses that had been in
her apron pocket. "Looks legit to me, suga."

"But read it, ma'am. It says that I get full medical and
dental on a temporary plan, even as a consultant."

"Uh-huh," Mrs. Smith said, appearing unfazed. "Also
says you get to live in one of the apartment complex
suites while there for a four-month period to develop a
public relations campaign for them, and that your rent
will be made to the dealership you owe in lieu of rental."
Mrs. Smith let out a slow whistle after reading the sentence in the contract. "Plus," she added, flipping the pages,
"seems like they own a trucking company . . . must be
where that feller worked who was gonna tow you. They
say they'll move you with an eighteen wheeler." She

looked up at Darien and smiled. "Part of the relocation services, I suspect."

"But, they're still gonna pay me . . . How did a repo man hook up something like this?"

"They're going to pay you, from the looks of things, a modest salary that's fair. You've gotta eat and still have to pay off your credit card bills, and I suspect student loans. But truth is, this ain't a bad deal, so don't go looking a gift horse in the mouth, baby."

"But they hired me without any references, with my bad credit, too."

"You don't know who they called," Mrs. Smith said with a sly chuckle. "Believe me, they did their home-work."

"If they called my old job, then they would have found out that I had a good record and was laid off after a cor-porate merger . . . the new company already had their people in place and—"

"And if they called your landlord, they would have gotten me on the telephone." Mrs. Smith folded her arms over her chest and gave Darien a wink. "Mighta heard some very good things about a young lady who al-ways struggled to pay her rent on time and always had a cheery disposition and a kind word to say. Somebody coulda just put in a good word or two with a little extra polish on it when Ms. Arnetta James called."

Darien stared at Mrs. Smith, not knowing what to say for a moment. "God bless you . . . but how did a repo man—"

"Now, listen here. You don't know *who* that man knows, right? Might be family, an old college friend . . . folks down South is tight with one another. So, he saw a damsel in distress and tried to make a way out of no way . . . a way for you to come clean, go straight, and be honest." Mrs. Smith looked at her hard, but a smile was tugging at the corners of her mouth. "Now, if you go on down there and work real hard and honest, the fact that that man took a shine to ya ain't no skin off your nose."

Darien could feel her eyes get wide with shock. "Miz Smith!"

"Baby girl, I might be old, but I ain't always been old . . . so if that man got a cousin or brother or somebody that helped ya, no harm done. And you don't hafta do *nothin'* you don't want to—especially since you're gonna take that job and treat it no different than if you was working for some big company, right? You don't owe him like that."

"No . . . I guess I don't," Darien said, relieved, her confidence slowly returning. She looked at the contract again as Mrs. Smith thrust it back at her with a wide smile. She read and reread every line, her mind turning over the facts quickly as she scanned the document. "And I am going to work hard, *really hard* and honest, Miz Smith."

"I know, baby. Your stuff in the other rooms is already packed. Me and my girlfriend done tagged and boxed everything but your personal effects in here."

Darien struggled to swing her legs over the side of the bed. "I couldn't ask you to do something like that—that's so much work, and you've already—"

"Been paid by the company that's moving you . . . I did take the liberty to tell them that we was on service hire for you . . . if you don't mind."

Darien's shoulders slumped with a new wave of relief. She stared at the rug, wondering if angels really did come as people in disguise. Something unfathomable was moving obstacles out of her path and delivering blessings that she didn't feel like she even deserved.

"Get back in bed, chile. When you feel up to it, all you have to do is let us know and we'll work with you on this room." Mrs. Smith fished in her apron pocket and produced a letter that she slipped onto the nightstand.

"Sign this so it can find its way into the file. . . . Remember, you told me thirty days ago in writing that you were leaving." She chuckled and clucked her tongue. "And darned if I didn't accidentally put it in my coat pocket instead of the files. I was so harried that day and on my way out to lunch. Mercy me."

Darien glanced up from her pillows as she sank back against the warmth of her bed. But she held the older woman's gaze, conviction lacing every word. "For real, Miz Smith, I'll work hard and do you proud . . . you gave your word on me, which is worth more than gold."

"Just be well and do right, that's all I ask," the older woman said, leaning down to kiss the top of Darien's head.

"I'm going straight, Miz Smith. This time I'm not playing."

Chapter 3

With hope of a fresh start in her heart and Georgia on her mind, Darien was on the road the same day the huge moving van carted away her life. Armed with a stack of her favorite CDs, a full tank of gas and a wad of cash, Pennsylvania, Delaware, and Maryland were a blur as she passed through each state, partying in her shiny, newly washed car all the way to DC without stopping once.

The odd thing was, she wasn't even hungry or fatigued. Nervous anticipation pushed her forward as she gassed up her ride again and kept going. But the long, two-lane, unending highway through North Carolina wore on her. Eleven hours straight, and she knew she had to stop and eat.

Her mind raced, albeit her body didn't follow suit as she got more gas and contemplated her future. If she could just make it to Atlanta, maybe she'd bed down at her sister Louise's house overnight and push forward. That way she could be there by Thursday.

Darien sat in the local Waffle House simply pushing the food around on her plate, another six hours of travel staring her in the face. Going to Cynthia's was out, despite how much she loved all her rowdy nieces and nephews. Her eldest sister *always* had a lecture in store for her. If she went to her second oldest sister, Brenda, she'd call Louise and Cynthia for sure—and then they'd all swoop down on her with conviction.

Each bite of waffle and eggs made Darien more and more weary, until she could barely hold her head up. Yeah, she would have to make a pit stop—but where?

A sudden sadness filled her. Why wouldn't she have thought to immediately go to Mavis's house? That was her best girlfriend in the whole wide world.

Darien slowly set down her fork and sipped her coffee, deep in thought. What was different about this escape from a city than any other she'd pulled off—and more importantly, why was she keeping everyone who was close to her at arm's length? she wondered.

Shaking the disturbing thoughts, Darien reached into her purse for money to pay the small bill, spying the business card that had come with her moving instructions. Miss Arnetta James seemed so nice on the telephone, a real peach. There was warmth about the woman's voice that Darien had rarely heard, especially not directed toward her. She fingered the business card, a new wave of excitement coursing through her as she extracted her money and snapped her wallet shut.

No, this was something she had to do alone. She didn't want advice or he-say, she-say opinions about how to play this whole thing. She'd promised Mrs. Smith that she'd go straight, and that was gonna take a whole lot of personal concentration. Maybe she'd just find a cheap hotel on the outskirts of Atlanta then call Miss James when she woke up. Besides, she wasn't due for twenty-four more hours. The instructions had said for her to show up on Friday so she could get settled into her home, and then on Monday she'd come into the offices for orientation to the firm and would get started.

Darien stood with a bone-weary sigh and stretched

the kinks out of her legs. But there was that one nagging question that again sent butterflies free in her belly. Who in the heck was this Maxwell Ferguson?

"My goodness! She's not due here until tomorrow, Max," his sister said with a wide grin that irked him. "No, for the fifth time, she hasn't called."

"I was just wondering if she'd scammed us, or what. That's the only reason I'm asking." Maxwell straightened his tie and spun around in the high-backed leather swivel chair behind his wide mahogany desk, trying to ignore Arnetta.

"You know that doesn't make any sense, big brother. The woman sent in her contract, and our boys done picked up her whole life in a truck, so for her to just send us all her belongings and not show makes no sense."

He would not look up at what he knew was Arnetta's smile of triumph. The logic of her statement tore at his embattled brain. Even though he focused on a stack of files on his credenza, he could feel his sister standing there, arms folded over her chest, a victory in her grasp.

Unable to avoid her any longer, he looked up at her cheerful expression. It was mocking, but also tender as she crossed the room, shut the door to his office, and returned to his desk to sit before him.

"I'm on your side with this," she said, her deep brown eyes twinkling as she pushed a thick curl behind her ear.

Maxwell's shoulders relaxed, and for the first time since he'd met Darien Jackson, he felt himself smile. "Thank you," he said quietly. "This isn't what everybody in the family is making it out to be."

"I know," she said, leaning in close to him and reaching for his hand to pat it. "I think Darien Jackson is just what this firm needs."

He nodded. "We need a change. Some new life to

bring new energy, a new perspective . . . someone to shake things up and help us grow."

His sister sat back, placing a finger over her frosted lips. "Yes, we do," she said after a moment.

"She's really got a strong background, Arnetta. You've seen her résumé." He stood and walked to the window, looking out at everything and nothing. "Why the rest of them are fighting me on that is beyond me." He turned and looked at his sister, searching her face for under- standing. "Why do they always fight me on everything?"

Arnetta sighed. "Maxwell, you know folks hate change."

He nodded, suddenly glad that she was in his office this morning. "Yeah, I guess you're right. Change is hard. It requires doing things differently, and people hate to give up old ways. But like you always tell us, if you keep doing the same things the same way, then turn around and expect different results, that ain't nothin' but crazy."

Her smile broadened, yet it almost seemed as if she were trying to swallow it away. "Yep," she said, standing. "That's all it is, Max. Don't take it personally. You know how family can be."

"I guess I've sorta had a raw nerve about this, haven't I?"

She opened her eyes wide, pure mirth glittering within them. "I guess you could say that, but you didn't hear it from me."

As always, just like when they were kids, she'd made him laugh.

"Okay, okay," he finally admitted. "I guess I've been a little edgy." Then he straightened his tie again and tried to sound serious. "But that's only because I'm tired of being challenged by everybody."

"Yep. Understandable. And that's why you flew from Philadelphia, left Otis up there to manage things, and are back in HQ now instead of staying where you were. You had to come down here, even though you haven't been here for the past two months, to handle your business, get folks straight, and set the tone."

"That's right," he said, reminding himself why he'd come back to headquarters. "It's important to set the tone and re-establish a baseline from time to time."

"Yes, it is," she said, a chuckle resonant in her voice. "You can't be playing when you're serious about something like this."

"That's what I've been trying to tell everybody. I'm tired, and I'm not playing."

Arnetta cocked her head to the side. "You've been tired for a long time, Max." Her gaze was playful, yet gentle. "I totally understand that."

"Girl, I have been working like a dog for years," he admitted. All joviality had left his voice. "No vacations, no time for me . . . not that I'm complaining—I did what I had to do to make sure this firm was on solid footing for us all. I did no less than what Mom and Dad would have wanted." He smoothed the front of his navy suit and pulled his white monogrammed shirt cuffs down so that they showed at the right length.

"Daddy put all that weight on your shoulders," she said, her voice tender like balm. "And you bore the weight well, Max. I'm proud of you . . . and know how exhausted you have to be." She looked at him and walked toward him slowly. "Big brother, even iron wears out, if you don't coat it right, if it's been out there exposed to the elements night and day, if'n you don't put a little time and attention to it to keep the rust back."

He let his breath out hard and sent his gaze back to the window. God, he loved Arnetta—the only one in the bunch who understood him. "Sis, there are days—"

"And nights," she said, a slight chuckle lifting her voice.

"Yeah . . . I work nights, too."

"Uhmmm-hmmm, but you need to take a few nights off."

He could feel a slow smolder of anticipation run through him, just thinking of the night he was working and ran into Darien Jackson. But it wasn't about all that. She owed him money now, and owed the firm. He had to keep that reality in the proper perspective. This was just a reasonable workout situation, that was all. He buttoned his jacket and jammed his hand into his pocket. "There's too much going on right now with all the expansion for me to take any time off," he said, but without real conviction in his tone. It came out more wistfully than he'd intended, but he wasn't sure why.

"You're only thirty-five," Arnetta said quietly. "You've made your first several million—and have taken *good* care of *all* of us. We can part with you for a couple of nights. But what we can't do is have you fall down with a heart attack or stroke."

They both stared at each other, remembering the sudden loss of their father. Maxwell soon looked away, not wanting to think about how his dad worked like a Georgia mule to provide everything he could from the labor of his expert carpenter hands. It wasn't fair. The man didn't reach his biblical promised age of several score and then some. But then, what was promised? His father had been blessed, had a bunch of sons who could do well. It just hurt his soul that no matter how much they'd all bought their mother or tended to her, the woman gave up and died anyway, allowing the results of a stroke to finally take her. Perhaps it had all come down to missing her husband so much that there was no consolation. None of them would ever know until they passed on to glory. But if loving somebody that much could steal the breath out of one's body, he didn't need that much love in the world. So, it was settled. Why he had even thought about that was beyond him.

"Once I get this new consultant oriented into the firm, maybe I'll take some time off."

His sister only nodded and went closer to him, brushing invisible lint off his shoulders. "You look great . . . and as soon as she calls, I'll hit you on your cell phone."

Before he could answer her, Arnetta pecked his cheek, turned on her heels, and headed out the door.

The weather had been kind to her. It was cold and brisk, but the sky was a brilliant blue. Sweeping white clouds etched the sky, and Arnetta James had sounded so excited on the telephone that she'd dressed quickly, donning her best corporate gear.

Darien glanced down at her chisel gray, muted plaid duster, which matched the square-necked dress that stopped mid-thigh. Her silk stockings added a professional polish to her legs, and the black, understated Fendi pumps were perfect. She went to reach for her pearls, then realized that almost all the jewelry she'd owned had been sold or given away.

Banishing despair, she found a tasteful pair of large clip-on oval-and-onyx costume earrings, cringing that they were faux pearl. But at least they matched her outfit. Her silver ladies' Timex made her sigh, but hey, she was going straight, she reminded herself. This was a first impression. No need to appear too flashy. This was a corporate job, and as long as she was well put-together and presentable . . .

She stared in the mirror trying to decide whether or not to wear her hair up in a classic chignon or let it fall about her shoulders. She could also pull it back with an onyx barrette. There were just too many decisions to make as she applied a light gray shadow to her eyes. Makeup had to be impeccable—not too much, not too little, just a hint. Her hands were shaking. Macon was two hours away. Arnetta James had keys to an apartment that she'd never even seen. What if her stuff never made it? What if everything was damaged? What if they hated her on this new, but temporary consulting job?

What if Maxwell Ferguson was the boss's son or something and was expecting a physical down payment for the debt she owed? What if she'd just made the biggest mistake of her life?

She pulled up to the quiet little street expecting to see a big apartment building, but was instead greeted by a quaint yellow-and-white Victorian duplex that was bordered by a neat lawn. Darien adjusted her black wool coat as she slid out of the car, her gaze now focused on the smiling woman who'd come out of the front door.

If this was her new neighbor, it was a good sign because she looked pleasant, seemed to be her same age, and had a little pixie face filled with mischief.

"Hi," Darien said brightly. "I think we're gonna be neighbors." The wide smile that greeted her in return made Darien's cautious climb up the stairs not feel so daunting.

"You must be Darien Jackson," the woman said, coming to her with an outstretched hand.

Darien laughed. Boy news traveled fast in the south! "Yep. That would be me. Do you work for Allied States, too?" She was hoping her new neighbor would say no. She wasn't sure she liked the idea of being the new girl in town, and the new employee, and nearly having to room with someone from the job—just in case things didn't exactly work out. That's all she'd need was for her business to be circulated around a water cooler somewhere. But she kept her smile beaming as she accepted the woman's outstretched hand.

"Yes, I work for Allied," was the woman's reply. "Arnetta James."

Darien opened her mouth and closed it, and immediately wrapped a professional cloak around her speech. Oh my God! It was *her.*

"Miss James. I'm so sorry. I didn't—"

"Expect me to be standing on your porch in jeans and a sweater with my hair all over my head," Arnetta said, laughing as she dispensed with the handshake and slung an arm over Darien's shoulder. "Girl, you've been traveling," she added, looking Darien up and down from a sideline glance. "Tell me you *did not* drive all the way from Philly in heels."

Whatever reservations Darien had were instantly shattered. Laughing as they entered the building and walked up a flight of steps to the spacious parlor on the second floor, Darien could feel her shoulders drop two inches.

"I thought I was to come here and meet the realtor, then I was going to check in at the office," she admitted.

"Chile, pullease," Arnetta said with a wave of her hand. "Number one, I am the realtor." She winked at Darien. "I'm in charge of HR and temporary housing, putting up guests, setting up meetings, you name it, falls under my job function—and you'll soon find out that all of us who work for Allied wear about a zillion hats."

Arnetta shook her head and walked deeper into the apartment. She opened her arms, adrenaline ricocheting through her like she was an excited puppy. "You like it?"

Darien stood in the middle of the floor and covered her mouth. All of her boxes had been deposited in the right rooms, each piece of furniture set and arranged the way she probably would have.

"Your people did all this?" she asked in an awed whisper.

"What people, chile? Them moving men get on my nerves. They would have just come in here, left everything wherever, and you'da walked into a nightmare, so I brought my nosy self here to make sure everything was the way it should be." She covered her mouth and laughed hard. "Whooo boy, they was mad at me! I kept changing my mind, making them set your sofa up at different angles—I hope this works for you until you can sort yourself out."

"It's fabulous," Darien said, truly meaning it. "Thank you so much, Miss James—"

"Arnetta! I'm not old enough to be no Miss James to you. Besides, we all go on a first-name basis. We're not that formal at work, even though we all work hard."

Almost too overwhelmed to speak, all Darien could do was nod. Again, another angel had come into her midst, and for a moment she was so filled up that she blinked back tears. "This is so nice," she said, her voice trembling with emotion as her eyes assessed Arnetta's wonderful handiwork.

"Come on," Arnetta said. "Take a look around."

Darien gaped at the expansive parlor that two rooms within her old apartment could have fit into. It had a huge bay window overlooking the front yard, with crisp lemon-yellow paint that was still fresh to the smell. The high ceilings and crown molding gave it an air of genteel splendor, and on the coffee table sat a lush green houseplant with a big pink bow.

"Y'all brought me a plant, too?" Darien rushed over to it and took up the card, her eyes on Arnetta.

"You back home, girl. You know how we do—hospitality."

Indeed, Darien remembered, and without any reservations left she went to Arnetta and gave her a big hug.

Arnetta hugged her back hard, then held her back. "Welcome to the family!"

"Thank you for having me," Darien said as she paced behind Arnetta, but could only cover her mouth when she saw the fireplace in the living room and another, much larger leather sectional in front of it.

Totally confused, Darien's line of vision shot between Arnetta and the foreign furniture. "But ... but ... this is not my stuff."

"I know," Arnetta said, rubbing her jaw in a way that gave her tiny, heart-shaped face a comical expression. "But see, that had been bothering me all day. When your little bit of stuff got here, it was enough to fill up the parlor for an entertainment center, and the dining room don't need much, even though your table looks like a postage stamp in there ... some plants could help that, I wasn't sure whether to put your little sectional in the front, so folks could come in, hang their coat, and sit and watch TV—with the living room being for more private company—and then, again, I thought about putting your office in there where there's good light, the fireplace ..." Arnetta sighed, letting her sentence dangle. "I might have overstepped my bounds a little, putting your things in here for you, but—"

"No, no, no," Darien said, quickly, not at all wanting to offend. "It's ... just so ... expensive and not mine."

"Company property," Arnetta said, seeming relieved. "Don't worry about that. We've got stuff in storage; move furniture around our various locations all the time. But you like how I've arranged your desk by the window, with a little walking space and a sofa by the fire—just in case you're up working late at nights ... and, uh ... may need to relax?"

"It's perfect!" Darien said, her eyes again scanning the room. "I don't know how I'll ever be able to repay you."

"Just keep the boss happy by doing a good job, and all will be fine, you'll see."

Darien nodded. If this was how they treated consultants, how in the heck did they treat permanent employees? she wondered. "Done," Darien murmured, following Arnetta, who was off again like a bouncing ball and walking fast into the next room.

"This is your bedroom," she said, with a sweeping arm. "But you probably need every closet in this place," she added, laughing.

Before Darien could muster an apology, Arnetta had dashed into the adjoining room, making her gasp.

The master bathroom was as big as her old bedroom, and the pretty ferns that had been added surrounded antebellum period-fashioned fixtures, complete with a walk-in shower and a large, oval Jacuzzi tub. A fresh set of lemon-yellow towels had already been hung with a new bar of Dove soap, toilet paper, and a sealed toothbrush and toothpaste set out on the sink—just like she'd landed in a five-star hotel.

"Stop gawking," Arnetta said, flipping her wrist. "On move-in day the last thing a woman wants to do is be rooting around in boxes to wash her face or to find toilet paper so she can pee. I call this our productivity improvement process."

"Oh, Arnetta . . . you are too much. You've thought of everything. God bless you."

"He already has," she said, issuing what Darien had learned was her trademark wink. "Now let's go check out the kitchen," she added. "The lady who cleans for us has been through here once, but if you're like me, I know you'll go through it again—just because it's the kitchen."

They both laughed as they made their way back down the hall, through the dining room, and toward the kitchen. But Darien was floored as she passed the beautiful floor plants and ficus trees Arnetta had put in the dining room to make her furniture not appear so lonely.

"You cook?" Arnetta asked casually as she opened cabinets and prattled on about the various merits of the large, black-faced appliances in the room.

"I can," Darien said, her confidence weak. "But to hear my sisters tell it, just 'cause I'm the baby—"

"They don't think you can burn."

"Right!" Darien exclaimed, becoming indignant as she made the admission. "You're the baby, too?"

"The last of eight."

Darien shook her head. "I know they must be on you, especially down here."

"Uhmmm-hmmm," Arnetta said, with one hand on her hip. "Girl, please." She cocked her head to the side. "What's your specialty?"

Darien had to think for a moment. It had been so long since she'd tried her hand at anything or had anyone to cook for that she almost couldn't come up with a response.

"I do all right by peach and walnut cobbler," Darien finally said.

"If you mentioned peach and walnut cobbler, then you do more than all right by it. Tell the truth."

Again, both women laughed.

"Okay," Darien said. "I can put my big toe in some cobbler, girl—and it makes my oldest sister, Cynthia, sooo angry because she's the first one who got married, and is supposed to be the ruler of the whole Jackson clan. You know, the keeper of all Jackson women traditions."

"Don't I know it!" Arnetta shook her head. "My older sister is *just* like that, too. Runs everybody crazy."

Laughter rang out in the kitchen and before long, Darien could hear the twang edge back into her voice, along with a familiarity she couldn't put her finger on. This was like family—long, lost, and dreamed-for family. It made her bold, gave her a confidence level that she had forgotten she had, and totally endeared Arnetta to her. No matter what happened at Allied, she only hoped that she and Arnetta would become real friends.

"I can throw down on macaroni and cheese, but Louise makes a better ham than me—although I can hold my own, now. Brenda got the greens, hands down, and nobody disputes that," Darien said, going to the large double-door refrigerator and opening it, loving the camaraderie and the fact that a light lemon scent of cleanliness wafted out of it toward her. "But I make this specialty sweet iced tea with peach juice and chunks . . . and can tear up bread pudding—and can't nobody in the family touch my roasts."

"I hear you," Arnetta said. "Me, I'm the queen of pecan pies."

"You can make pecan pie?" Darien gasped as she put her hand over her heart.

"I'll bring you one, only as a trade for some real cobbler—from scratch."

"You're on," Darien said, laughing as she gave Arnetta a high-five.

"I might hafta bring you some of my oldest sister's lemon-butter pound cake—she gets on my nerves, but that's her thing."

Darien briefly shut her eyes. "Dang, Arnetta. Y'all gonna make me gain twenty pounds down here." She looked at the short pixie before her, and her tone became wistful. "You know how long it's been since I've had any real fun . . . or food . . . or family?"

Arnetta just smiled and looked away like she had a secret. "No, but I can guess. Lot of that going around lately." She sighed and walked toward the door. "Where are my manners?" She clicked her tongue and pushed a thick, dark brown curl behind her ear. "Why don't you hang up that outfit you have on, save it for work, and put on some jeans? I'll take you to go get some food and will drive you around a little bit. Then you can come back here and rest, unpack a few things and get settled. Okay?"

The mention of food made Darien's stomach growl, and both women laughed hard.

"I told you for the last time, Arnetta, I do not want to meet her outside of a business setting. Monday at the board meeting is fine. Then—"

"Then why was you all jumpy this morning, fixing and refixing your suit like you're going to a prom?"

Maxwell pulled his cell phone away from his ear and stared at it for a moment, before returning a sonic boom response to Arnetta. "You need to stop playin', Arnie! I told you why this woman was here, and—"

"Oooo-kay. Dang."

Why he was breathing hard or so angry at Arnetta was incomprehensible. His little sister would bait him to no end when they were kids, and today he was in no frame of mind for it. He had things to do, business to tend to, and there was no reason in the world why he should stop doing what he'd planned for some impromptu dinner with Darien Jackson.

When Darien came into the parlor, Arnetta had an expression on her face like a cat who'd eaten a canary. She couldn't wait to find out where they'd go to eat, especially having just talked up home cooking.

"Now don't you feel better?" Arnetta asked, referring to Darien's flat shoes, jeans, and casual knit top as both women pulled on their coats.

"Much improved," Darien admitted, accepting the door keys from Arnetta. "Where to?"

"Oh, let's just drive and see where the road leads us."

Darien followed her benefactor, almost skipping. Regardless of the hunger, there was nothing like a road trip. As they made their way out to the street and climbed into Arnetta's white Escalade, all Darien could think of was how lucky she was that Maxwell Ferguson had cut some deal instead of towing her car.

Edging close to the subject that brought her shame, Darien watched as neat southern homes and manicured front yards gave way to sprawling estates, sweeping verandas, and white-columned mansions. Instinctively she knew this was where magnolias, wisteria, and lavender grew wild. The taste of pecans; fat, succulent strawberries; and homemade ice cream danced through her mind, along with melons so sweet and ripe that there was no dainty way to keep the juice from running down one's face.

"Here in Macon, we got us a black mayor, too," Arnetta said with pride, "and the director of the Economic Community Development Department is also a brother. That's how our CEO got his start, was and remains his mentor. You should know that's why he's so tied to the area and building businesses for us folks who might not otherwise have a prayer in corporate America."

Darien nodded, soaking in all that Arnetta was saying. The insight to what made the CEO of Allied tick was crucial.

"I respect that," Darien said, remembering the company data that had come with her package. "I promise that any marketing campaign and public relations strategy I come up with will highlight both his accomplishments and community commitment."

"Aw, shucks, he's gonna love you," Arnetta said, a giggle rippling through the SUV. "Now, you know all those boxes on the organization chart?"

"Yeah," Darien said slowly, hoping she wouldn't be quizzed.

"Well, let me set the tone. The director of marketing is fine, and you might get the wrong impression that he's a player. Don't judge a book by its cover just because he's a young, *GQ*-type. Don't believe the hype. He might get all up in your face to test you, but ignore him. Don't let him make you get all nervous and what-not. He's really a gem and don't mean no harm . . . loves his wife dearly, too."

Darien laughed, her eyes roving the landscape. "Seen his type before, and trust me, I'm not about to cry sexual harassment—this is my big break, if that's what you're worried about."

"No, I wasn't worried about that," Arnetta said with a chuckle. "I was more worried about his crazy-ass wife busting into the office starting drama, if you must know. She ain't having no females in her man's face, so make sure she never gets that impression. Feel me?"

"Oh my God . . ."

"Yeah," Arnetta said, laughing as she shook her head. "Now the other male directors are cool, too. They run various divisions and pretty much will go along with the get along, if you know what I mean . . . all except the VP of Operations. He's been bucking to take the CEO slot since the company was founded, but he mainly works out of the Philadelphia office these days. You pacify him and get him on your side, then the comptroller will chill. But she can ride you like a witch rides a broom, if she doesn't like you."

"Whew," Darien murmured, slumping back into the leather seat. "Thanks for the heads-up on all these personalities." For a moment, neither woman said a word. "The CEO . . . what's he like?"

Arnetta smiled, glanced at her quickly, but kept her eyes on the road. "Tough, but fair. Got a good heart. Needs a vacation in the worst way, but too danged stubborn to take one. He's complicated—can be generous to a flaw, then turn around and be so frugal he'll make an eagle scream to get off a quarter. But we can't fault him though. He's seen how folks had to work hard, pinch pennies, and have discipline to build what they built, and he probably doesn't want to mess up. He's so concerned about making a mistake that he won't take a real risk. In business, he has the Midas touch but then second-guesses himself and is such a control freak that he sometimes micro-manages things he could leave up to someone else, but he's a good guy."

"Tough but fair. That's all anybody can ask for," Darien said after a while, feeling Arnetta's gaze boring into her as though she'd burst if Darien didn't respond.

Finding neutral topics to restore the laughter and previous ease between them, Arnetta seemed to sense that talking about the new job was making her tense again. With ebullient hospitality, Arnetta rambled on about the Ocmulgee River that followed Route 16, describing the bridges, pointing out the highlights of Macon-Bibb County. Her human resources tour guide told her all about the historic Hay House, the shows of culture and music one could see at The Douglass Theater, gave her a glimpse of glamour as they passed the Georgia Music Hall of Fame on Martin Luther King Drive, then went on and on about the merits of the Sports Hall of Fame— who was in, who wasn't, and who should have been, and even got into a long diatribe about the Cherry Blossom festival and the Georgia State Fair. When Arnetta started giving her historical recounts of Macon's history, Darien held up her hand and laughed.

"You sure you don't work for the tourism bureau and not Allied?"

Pulling up to a little house that doubled as a restaurant, Arnetta giggled. "I'm selling Macon hard, ain't I?"

They both laughed.

"Okay, I admit it. I hope you'll like it here and stay longer than four months, 'cause your contract says that if you do, you can be offered a permanent position, so, yeah, I have an agenda."

Darien smiled as Arnetta put the gears in park. It was the nicest compliment she'd ever received.

"If everyone is as nice as you and Maxwell Ferguson, then I can't see why I wouldn't want to leave."

Arnetta covered her chest with a flattened palm, leaned back in her seat, and briefly closed her eyes. "Then, Lord, my prayers have been answered."

It seemed a bit melodramatic to Darien, but then again, to get someone to move from a big metropolis down to Macon might be harder than imagined. That was all she could think of as they got out and began walking. But the question of how Maxwell Ferguson fit into the equation still bothered her.

"Arnetta, can I ask you something?"

Maybe it was the tentative tone of her voice that had made Arnetta come to a full stop to look at her just outside the restaurant door.

"Sure." Arnetta's eyes searched her face.

"Mr. Ferguson . . . he was real nice to me, even though we met when I was having a problem." Darien sighed and closed her eyes. The truth was in the center of her throat, choking her. But the last thing she wanted was for someone as nice as Arnetta James to think poorly of her. "Your repo man . . . can you tell him thank you for me for recommending me for this job?"

"Our *repo* man?" Arnetta's eyes opened so wide that the corners of them seemed like they would split. Then she covered her mouth and turned away laughing. "Oh, Father God."

Pure humiliation made Darien's face burn. "I know you probably think I'm a total dead—"

"No, no, no. I'm sorry," Arnetta said quickly. "It ain't you. It's just that Maxwell Ferguson is a trip, but he's a man of his word."

Relief swept through Darien, and she didn't bother to hide it. "You'll tell him thank you, though?"

"I will," Arnetta said, recovering slowly and wiping tears of laughter from her eyes. "But it would be better coming from you, trust me."

"I just met him once and don't know how to reach him," Darien said in a far-off tone.

"He'll be at the staff meeting Monday." A sly smile tugged at Arnetta's cheek.

"But, seriously, as HR . . . I have to tell you, I'm qualified, I am *not* going to sleep with him just because he helped me get this job. That's never been my style,"

Darien said, her tone firm as her spine straightened a notch. There. She'd said what had been worrying her since this whole adventure began. Money or no money, she had her standards, and she wasn't just trading booty for dollars or a car. "And you all have been so overly nice," she added, everything spilling out of her at once, "that I'm getting scared, like I might owe more than—"

"No, don't even go there," Arnetta said in a gentle tone, placing her hand on Darien's arm. "Your résumé speaks for itself, and if I thought you were some scamming hoochie, trust me, I would not have signed off on the contract hire." Arnetta paused, the twinkle in her eyes softening to what Darien could only compare to genuine concern. "Max and I talked about you at length, and I trust his judgment."

It took a moment for Arnetta's words to sink in before she could accept them. Not because she didn't trust Arnetta, but simply because no one had ever really vouched for her before. "He seems like a very nice man," was all that she could say.

"He's the genuine article, and I think the world of him."

Darien stared at Arnetta hard, allowing her easy spirit and gentle way to fill her. It was almost as though her eyes were playing tricks on her, because in Arnetta's eyes, even in her tiny face, she could see traces of Maxwell Ferguson's features. The man had been on her mind, nonstop, perhaps to the point where she was psyching herself out. She shrugged off the eerie similarity and forced a smile, giving a little nod toward the restaurant.

"They look like they can burn in there," Darien said to lighten the mood.

Arnetta laughed and gave her a tender out. "I am trying to show you the *real* Macon that's not in the brochures.

Honey chile, they make homemade ice cream, fried chicken that'll make you wanna smack yo' momma, snap beans, candied yams . . . smothered pork chops—come on in and act like you know!"

Chapter 4

On Monday morning, Darien's eyes opened before the alarm clock sounded and before dawn broke. It didn't matter that she'd stayed up half the night unpacking boxes or that she and Arnetta had eaten until they thought they'd burst and had laughed until they'd both literally cried. All of the crazy family antics that Arnetta had described in her big, loving, and off-the-wall family didn't matter either. Today was the first day—the moment of truth.

Moving through the duplex with military precision, Darien Jackson readied herself for inspection. This would be the most important public relations job she'd ever undertaken. She had to sell the top brass at Allied States, LLC, on her competency.

As she snatched her purse and hoisted it over her shoulder, heeding Arnetta's wise advice, it suddenly dawned on her. Through all the conversation, she hadn't asked the critical question—what was the CEO's name!

Stunned to a stop, Darien covered her mouth with her palm. *"Oh my God."* She closed her eyes as she whispered the horror. Not only didn't she know the CEO's name, but the organizational chart that she'd memorized only listed functions, not names with each function. She didn't know anybody's name!

Desperate for information, she tried Arnetta, knowing even before the vice president of human resources's voice mail came on that it was too early to reach her.

What had been on his mind? He'd changed suits three times that morning, and for what? This wasn't a fashion show; it was a senior staff meeting. Maxwell Ferguson hit the intercom with impatience.

"Peg," he said brusquely, "is the conference room set up with the overview and presentation of Allied?"

"Yes, Mr. Ferguson," his secretary efficiently replied. "Plus, I ordered the coffee, tea, juice, fruit, and Danish and sent a voice mail reminder to everyone Friday evening before I left."

"Good. Thank you," he said, fidgeting with his pen as he disconnected the open line. He just hoped that everybody would get there before Darien Jackson so they could caucus first. He knew his family well enough to know that timing was everything. Folks had to be talked to eye-to-eye, face-to-face, and any landmines and issues hashed out at the table while breaking bread to clear the path.

Maxwell shook his head. It was about more than clearing the path. This was akin to cutting a swath through dense jungle where old dramas would tangle things up just like vines. It wouldn't be a simple matter of whether or not Darien Jackson could do the job. She was an outsider who had gotten inside through unorthodox means, which would send his siblings into a tizzy about her motives, his motives, and everything else in between.

And, ironically, if someone asked him his motives, today he wouldn't be sure. Every move he'd made had been predicated on an indefinable gut hunch, just like every solid business venture he'd undertaken. But why this particular scenario gave him a case of the willies still disturbed him was a lingering question. And going into a family free-for-all unsure was a sure way to get sucker-punched with a question he couldn't and didn't want to have to answer.

He didn't have time for deep contemplation. There were a hundred tasks on his desk as well as business appointments calling his name. But all he was doing was moving files and pink message slips from one side of his desk to the other. His attention was so scattered that after a while, he just simply gave up and stared at them with total disinterest.

A light tap on his door made him nearly jump out of his skin. It took him a moment to form the words to summon the intruder to come in.

"Yes," he said, annoyance clear in his tone. When he saw Arnetta peep in, he relaxed. "Come on in, girl, and stop playing."

"I was gonna toss my hat in the door, first," she said, giving him a jaunty smile before slipping into his office and closing the door behind her.

She appraised him slowly, keeping her voice confidential. "Doing the gray Armani this morning with the black Cole Haans . . . I *definitely* approve."

"Arnetta . . ." he warned, snatching a stack of files to peer at instead of her. But the compliment was not lost on him, and her approval meant the world at that moment.

"She's really, *really* nice, Max. She's no fraud, and you know I would know."

He briefly glanced up at his sister. "Yeah? That's good to know."

"No. I mean she's *really* nice. Seriously."

This time when he looked up at Arnetta, he held her gaze.

"Maxwell Ferguson, you did good. I like her—*a lot*. She's one you coulda brought home to Momma."

He was speechless. His sister had never liked anybody enough to say that before.

"She's warm, funny as all get out . . . has a crazy family like ours. She's a Baptist, too."

He smiled as his sister came farther into the office and sat down.

"I'm not interested in her religion, just that she comes in here and does a good job."

"I'ma invite her to church so—"

"Oh no." He was out of his chair like a shot. "That's a violation of people's personal space, EEOC laws, probably, and—"

"And she has to do the circuit to pass by Rev so she can—"

"Are you crazy?" He just stared at his sister in disbelief.

"Maxwell, all the wanna-bes who are always sweatin' us about who you're seeing and what-not have to be sent a message that the most eligible bachelor in Macon is off the market. Plus, if she can't cut the mustard in church, you know Doreetha will never allow her into the family."

"The family? See now you are trippin', sis—and you need to cut that mess out long before everybody else gets here. Not a mumblin' word about any scheme you have going on in your head. No games. You are not to get into my business like that or start deciding things that aren't even gonna happen . . . and, and, you ain't even asked the woman if . . ." He stopped mid-sentence, horror lacing the question as his corporate diction disintegrated to down home. "Tell me you didn't say—"

"Pullease. What do you take me for, an amateur? I wasn't trying to scare the chile."

He let his breath out hard with both fury and relief. "One word, Arnetta—*stop.*"

"But she's sooo nice, Max. So what you need," Arnetta cooed, sprawling in the large leather chair.

"What I need is for *everyone* to be on the job, be professional, and for her to do her job and to stay professional so that this company gets a good strategy put in place and—"

"Oh, a good strategy is in place, trust me. And she's more than professional. The po' chile is scared to death that some repo man might be trying to work her out of booty that she almost didn't come down here."

Maxwell blinked twice, cocked his head to the side, and rubbed his jaw trying to fathom where his sister got that.

"Max," Arnetta said with a giggle, "she doesn't know who you are."

They stared at each other for a moment, and he sat down very slowly.

"I don't understand?"

"I sent her all the corporate information, sanitized, without anyone's name on there. She knows this is a family-run business, the relative size of the holdings, and whatever, but she has no idea that the man who actually tried to repossess her car is the CEO. And she also doesn't know that the VP of Operations is our brother, Otis, or that our other brother, Jovan, is the marketing director, or that Montrose runs the trucking division, or that Odell runs all the real estate stuff, or that Lewis is in charge of storefront holdings, and she definitely doesn't know that Doreetha is your chief financial officer and comptroller . . . or that I, Miss James, with a different last name, am in charge of human resources."

"Oh, . . ." Maxwell closed his eyes then leaned forward on his elbows, raking his fingers through his close-cropped hair. "Why didn't you tell her? I thought once you sent the documents to her . . . I mean, after she got the contract and had agreed to come down here . . . Arnie . . ."

"Because I wanted to know if sister got game." His sister looked at him hard, holding his stricken gaze without apology in her tone. "You did this thing so fast, without any reason that I had to be sure some Philadelphia hoochie with a long story hadn't gotten her claws into you and blew up your head while you was tired, big brother. And I was dang sure not going to let her know you are worth millions until we got that straight. And if I found out she'd slept with you while thinking you was a repo man, just to keep you from towing her car that woulda told me everything I needed to know. So, at the moment, she thinks some old man owns this enterprise and is shaking in her designer shoes about possibly losing a good job because she won't trade sex for money, which made me feel so good that she was ready to pack her bags and bolt at just the thought of it, so I said, *Arnie, this is a solid sister.* Yeah, I played her, but for good reason . . . and found out how much I like her, so once we get tighter, I'll tell her, but for now, I'll just say everybody was moving so fast that we didn't realize how much she didn't know."

His sister sat back in her chair, straightened her spine, and folded her arms over her chest in triumph. Arnetta hadn't even taken a breath as she'd delivered the world according to Arnetta. Women were so treacherous it was frightening, as brilliant an interview process as it was. But he still didn't like it.

"Have you ever considered that, let's just say for the sake of argument, hypothetically speaking, if I was remotely interested in this woman, and she comes in here this morning to see me as the CEO, totally blindsiding her, with all my immediate relatives in key positions, that she might think she's been hired for a booty call? A complete set-up."

When Arnetta opened her mouth and closed it quickly, he stood and paced between the window and his desk. "This is why I don't like games, Arnetta. You didn't think about how she'd feel or react. While I know you were only trying to help, all you did was make matters worse. I assumed that things would be clarified in the paperwork you were supposed to send her, but my distance to her and her job scope would also send a message of honorable intent."

He stared at her hard, choosing his words carefully and delivering them slowly for impact. "Don't you think that's why I didn't call her? Don't you understand that that's why she only has a business number in the Philly town office for me? Because I was trying to come at her straight—with a fair financial workout plan, not to make her my woman!" He had to catch his breath and lower his voice, which had escalated on its own accord. "Don't you realize," he said, finally collecting himself enough to continue, "that's why I wouldn't join you all for dinner Friday night? Don't you understand that's why I put her through *proper* channels and made sure contracts and the right paperwork were in place, because—"

"Oh, Max—"

"No, sis. This time you let me finish talking before you come up with a cockamamie workaround to this disaster." He looked at her so hard that he was sure she'd stopped breathing. "While Darien Jackson is here, I am not going within twenty-five feet of her without a legitimate chaperone. While Darien Jackson is here—if she elects to stay here—there will be no church, no dinners, no private chats."

Maxwell rubbed both palms over his face and strode to the window, willing himself to calm down as the worst-case scenario played out in vivid color within his mind. This was a mess!

"As it is, I'll have to apologize, as will you, and fall on my damned sword to probably keep her here doing her job for the next one hundred and twenty days, working off her car note. And, Miss Arnetta Sophia Ferguson

James, if she goes ballistic and wants to immediately move home, which would be well within her right under the twisted, crooked circumstances, out of all fairness because of the drama you have set in motion, I'll have to move her back to Philadelphia and probably eat the lapsed car note— just to keep me and the firm out of some sort of litigation!"

Arnetta had stood up to go to him, but the door swung open with a bang, forcing their attention toward it.

Doreetha stood with hands on both hips, filling the entrance to his office with her ample form. "You all mind telling me what in Jesus's name is going on!"

Darien stood on the white marble steps in front of the mansion and just stared up at the splendor of Allied States's corporate headquarters. Sure, she'd seen the photo in the information packet, but the fact that a black family owned what was once surely a plantation and had turned it into a business empire, was truly blowing her mind.

Awed, she picked her way carefully up the stairs, passing the huge white columns that gave her the feeling that she was walking into the White House. This morning she was going to meet the president and CEO who'd turned what had been a tragic history of her people into the Promised Land . . . right in the middle of the Deep South.

She was more than awed, she was proud. As she entered the spacious lobby, electricity passed through her. She glimpsed the period antiques, high ceilings trimmed in gold gilded crown molding; tasteful, muted moss and mauve surroundings that matched the tapestry; velvet drapes; and looked at the professionally polished receptionist. Class . . . to the nines. Man, what she could do with a place and family like this in *Black Enterprise* magazine, *Essence, Ebony* . . . *USA Today, Business Week* . . .

Adrenaline shot through her as she waited for Arnetta to fetch her. She was gonna do so good on this job. A prayer came to her, and she recited it over and over.

Jesus, Lord, let them like me. Father God, forgive me for anything wrong I've done. I'll make it right this time, just let them like me, like my ideas, and let my work help promote this family the way it should be. In all my heart, you know, Father, that I never really cared about doing a good job, just getting paid. But this time, for real, Lord, I'm not playing. These people have done so much, came from nothing, and they've smiled upon me, have shared their grace. Please don't let my past ways haunt me or mess this up.

She nearly jumped out of her skin when Arnetta came up to her and said hello.

"Oh, hi, Arn—I mean, Miss James," Darien said, not wanting to sound too familiar on the job. She knew Arnetta had been kind to her, but this was work, this was business.

But the stricken look on Arnetta's face worried her. What had she done? She'd only been in the building less than five minutes! Darien's grasp tightened on her portfolio. Maybe she wasn't dressed appropriately? But that was crazy. Arnetta had said to wear what she'd worn on the drive down from Atlanta.

"It's gonna be all right," Arnetta assured her as though reading her mind. But Arnetta was also patting her arm nervously, the way ministers did family members when someone was about to die. "We gonna lean on Jesus this morning and say a prayer before we go into the boardroom."

If Arnetta was calling on the cross and a prayer was in order, this was really bad. Darien felt her mouth go dry, and all she could do was nod and follow Arnetta up the sweeping spiral staircase.

As they entered the outer office, a pleasant-looking older woman greeted them.

"This is Peg Jones," Arnetta said stiffly. "She's the CEO's administrative assistant."

"Welcome," Mrs. Jones said, seeming to want to say a whole lot more. "Can I rest your coat, sweetheart?"

"Thank you, ma'am," Darien said in a squeaky voice. She needed water so badly that she would have gladly slurped it from a faucet, but she was afraid that if she went to the ladies' room at this juncture, not only might she be late for the meeting, but she might actually go in there and puke.

Without much room to do more, she followed Arnetta into the boardroom. Her gaze swept the room as every male at the table stood, anticipation making her heart beat so fast and hard that her ears rang.

Then she saw him. Her benefactor. He was as clean as The Board of Health, all decked out in a cold-smooth charcoal gray suit, quarter inch handkerchief showing from the breast pocket, platinum Rolex, matching cufflinks on monogram, no doubt custom Oxford-style shirt, corporate paisley tie, platinum collarbar beneath Windsor knot. No-nonsense expression. Chocolate-brown complexion, flawless. Body, to die for. Countenance, strictly business. Fine enough to make her wanna slap herself, much less her momma . . .

The assessment took all of three seconds, but she could have stared at him for three hours. Instead she offered him a professional nod of recognition and let her gaze take in the other members at the table. Funny thing was, they all looked alike.

"Our vice president of operations, Otis Ferguson."

He didn't speak, only nodded as she approached him and extended her hand.

"Darien Jackson. Pleased to meet you," she said as confidently as was possible, given that she'd just learned that the VP of Operations was related to Maxwell Ferguson somehow. But she tried to banish the questions that were zinging through her brain as she exchanged a handshake with what could have been Maxwell Ferguson's body double, just a few inches shorter and without any hair.

As Arnetta made the rounds, Darien's brain worked like a fire engine, alarm bells going off with each introduction and as she assessed the features and body structure of every Ferguson at the table. But when Jovan Ferguson held her hand a little longer than seemed appropriate and started in on small talk about her trip down from Philadelphia, she truly panicked while smiling pretty and diplomatically extracting her hand.

From the corner of her eye, she watched her benefactor, as well as Arnetta who looked so much alike, once in the same room that, she was about to pass out. But the one that kept her on her feet and stone lucid was Doreetha Anderson. The old broad never blinked, and the look she'd cast in Darien's direction could have cut steel.

"And, uh, of course you've met our CEO, Maxwell Ferguson."

Darien held on to the back of a chair to play off her knees buckling. She nodded. "Mr. Ferguson, thank you for this opportunity." Oh, no . . . What was she supposed to say? Later. She'd blast him, later. Later, she'd pack her bags. Later. Not now. Not in front of all these people—the freakin' CEO was out towing cars? *Oh my God. Jesus, give me strength.* This was a *real* player. Brotherman had worked her so hard she'd moved! All her stuff was in an apartment he owned, probably had keys to. Oh my God!

"So why don't we all get some breakfast then have a seat and go over where Allied States, LLC, has been, and where we want to go in the next five years," Maxwell said.

The woman looked like she was about to fall out, faint dead away—if she didn't cross the room and slap him first. She'd literally blanched. All the color had gone out of her pretty cinnamon face the moment Arnetta had announced him by title. He knew this was going to happen!

Maxwell tried to focus on the task at hand, noticing that Darien Jackson had only made a paltry attempt to put a slice of melon on her plate and a strawberry, and her hands were shaking as she brought it with a cup of coffee back to her seat. This was bad. Real bad.

What was worse was the reaction he had to just seeing her again. No denying it, the woman was fine . . . *Jesus.* By day, all done up, maybe Otis had been right. Maybe he'd worked so hard for so long that, when he'd just seen her, he'd actually lost his natural black mind. Arnetta had a point—he needed to pray on this one. Wasn't about looking at her sideways, under these circumstances.

But, Lord have mercy, sideways was just as awesome as frontways and definitely backways. *All right, all right, Ferguson, focus,* he told himself. Long legs in sheer silk . . . pretty auburn hair all on her shoulders, eyes that drank a man in, gorgeous face, million-dollar smile, curves to stop traffic on I-16 . . . definitely needed to be riding in a nice car . . . definitely shouldn't have to be running from no crazy man . . . somebody oughta keep her safe and in whatever style she'd become accustomed to. *Oh, damn . . . focus, man.*

Darien barely heard a word that was said during the presentation. Half of her mind was developing the verbal beat-down she'd give Maxwell Ferguson while the other half of it was both denying and processing how flattered she actually was. That a man went to such lengths to get in her drawers was an awesome acknowledgement, and as a recovering game player herself, she had to hand it to the man. As she watched him describe his holdings with pride, she had to admit that the brother had worked his entire life to the bone. There was no denying that he'd built the company from the ground up and was a shrewd businessman.

"So, Miss Jackson, that's where Allied has come from and where we want to go. Your take on it?"

Oh no he was *not* going to ask her to participate in this meeting, under the shock, and with it just being the first hour on the so-called job—to digest all of this? Okay. Fine.

Darien drew a deep breath and made a tent with her fingers in front of her lips. She glanced around at the table, remembering all that Arnetta had told her about each family member and each corporate officer, which she now knew were one in the same.

"I only have one question," she said, pausing for theatrical effect. "Why isn't this firm featured on the cover of *Black Enterprise?*"

Shocked expressions greeted her as Maxwell Ferguson returned to his chair slowly and sat down. Good. Just what she'd wanted. Shock value.

"Frankly, we never really thought of it," Jovan said. "We've been out hustling business, working hard, and nobody was really focused on the press."

"That's your job," Doreetha snapped. "If we could have done it, we would have, but each one of us has been overwhelmed just keeping the lights on in here. Do you know how much it costs to run an operation like this?" Doreetha folded her arms over her chest and glared at Darien.

Unfazed, Darien nodded. "That's precisely my point. You all have worked hard to achieve nothing short of the phenomenal," she said, truly meaning it. She watched Doreetha slowly unfold her arms while the others sat up taller. She stood and watched them watching her from her peripheral vision as she made her way to the front of the boardroom. "May I?" she asked Maxwell, not looking at him or waiting for his response as she took up his laser pointer and went back a few slides in the Power Point presentation.

"You began here," she said, bringing up the appropriate slide, "and you are now here—and you did it as a family—have invested back into your community, have created jobs during an economy when businesses are failing, and are all educated, but were not born with silver spoons in your mouths. That's a story. An inspirational one." She set the pointer down beside Maxwell Ferguson without looking at him as she walked back to her chair, her gaze holding each of his top officers. "If I wanted to become an entrepreneur, I'd be impressed and want to learn how each one of you did it. If I were an investor, I'd want to learn how you navigated around all the financial potholes to snag solid contracts and keep the company flowing in the black. If I were a politician or community activist, I'd want to hear—for once—a story of good news about how doing the right thing did not have to work cross purposes with being a profitable enterprise, and if I were a parent, teacher, minister—pick a profession—I'd want the picture of this family hanging on my inspirational bulletin board or wall of fame."

When no one spoke, Darien sat, leveled her gaze at the group and allowed her voice to drop to a dramatic whisper. "So, I'm going to ask you again. Why hasn't this family been on the cover of every African American national magazine in the country?"

The woman was making his palms moist. There hadn't been that much electric energy in his firm, or in his life, since the early days of starting the firm. Darien had even shut Doreetha up. Otis was wiping his bald head, and

Jovan was nearly trembling. Arnetta had gone slack-jawed, and poor Odell was holding his cup of coffee mid-air while Montrose and Lewis just gaped at her. How was a man supposed to answer a question like that ... damn ... how was a man supposed to deal with a woman like that?

Jovan suddenly laughed and shook his head. "You're hired. Daaaayum, Maxwell. You're always right. She's awesome." He issued a megawatt smile at Darien and leaned in. "Arnetta said you were qualified—hands down, that's obvious. You and me ought to work together to develop a strategy ... so that what we're doing in the marketing department coincides with your PR strategy—feel me?"

From the corner of her eye, Darien noticed Maxwell bristle. She could have sworn Doreetha had puffed up two dress sizes as Jovan was speaking, and Arnetta was now looking down and doodling on a pad. Otis had his arms folded over his chest, and the other brothers appeared to have come down with a case of lockjaw. Darien almost laughed. Naw ... these folks were not going to run her out of town. Hell naw, Maxwell Ferguson wasn't going to play her and then scare her out of the best chance she had at getting a plum assignment in her portfolio. Oh yeah, she'd take this business to the top, along with her own reputation as a stellar PR maven—but on her own terms.

Darien chose her words with precision, diplomacy oozing from her lips on a balmy, homespun drawl. "Sales is indeed the engine bringing in revenue to the operation, Jovan. Much respect. But we have time to do your already front and center department. First things first, though. To best shine light on anything, even a room in one's home, requires a multiple lighting schematic to highlight everything just the right way ... all the important facets to give the room a larger look and feel. To create the illusion of being bigger requires some re-

cessed lighting, some direct lighting, some torch lamps—
do you follow?"

Blank stares returned. Darien smiled. Good. Disarmed.

"Doreetha Anderson's department is the infrastructure of this whole operation. She is a female CFO and should be positioned for *Essence* magazine's career section. Next, we look at how biological brothers have come together to do the heavy lifting, to appeal to the magazines targeted to predominantly male audiences, and then you and I can talk about how that should translate into sales efforts."

"We always said the blood is thicker than the mud," Otis murmured toward Jovan.

She tore her gaze away from Jovan's, thoroughly satisfied by the way Doreetha's glare had softened to flattered humility, and reassured by the nods and murmurs of approval coming from Otis, Odell, Montrose, and Lewis. Arnetta's head was bobbing up and down with agreement so hard she thought the poor chile's head might drop off. But Maxwell Ferguson was stoic. That concerned her.

Darien nodded in Maxwell's direction. "That's your lead hook. Save the best till last. The man behind the machine. He's the one who we pitch as *BE* cover material. Meanwhile, he needs to scale back on some of the day-to-day operational activities that can be delegated." Darien paused, her message to him almost telepathic— *what the heck are you doing out towing cars, brother!* "I want him on the chicken circuit, doing ribbon cuttings, charitable banquets, anyplace the press and the typical who's who will be so we can get buzz created about the maverick behind Allied. He needs to run this next phase of growth like he's running a political campaign." Darien sighed and sat back in her chair. "I want him to be in so much ink that the phones here are ringing off the hook with both press and clients for every operation you have. Understand?"

"Now hold on," Maxwell said, feeling his life getting ready to be reordered without his consent . . . very much like one Darien Jackson had just awakened his libido without his consent. "I'm used to having my hands in the clay. I like to be sure that the operations are solid and—"

"You have to trust your officers to do their jobs and stop micro-managing them so you can grow this business. Period. You cannot be in two places at one time, and you cannot be out doing things like towing cars," she said with emphasis, her gaze narrowing on him, "or cleaning buildings with the crew—even if it is a new contract. No, you cannot be reading inventory levels on every store shelf, nor can you worry about the paint job in every apartment." Darien folded her arms over her chest. "You keep doing that, and you'll not only stay where you are, growthwise, but you'll burn yourself out while making your firm seem like it's a small town mom-and-pop operation."

"We've been telling him that for years!" Otis said, slamming his hand on the table. "I like your style, Miss Jackson. You tell him."

"Ain't said a mumblin' word," Jovan said, reaching over to shake Darien's hand. "Welcome to the family."

"Amen," Doreetha said, nodding like she was in church. "Been telling him for years that the accounting is the backbone, and he don't need to be arguing about the cost of one plumber over the other and gettin' into everybody's hair with minutia."

"Boy gonna have a heart attack if he don't slow down," Lewis added in, nodding.

"I been telling him he needs to act more like a CEO than a plow horse," Montrose agreed, slapping five with Lewis.

"But took somebody from the outside to come down here, sit for five minutes, and tell him what should be as plain as the nose on a man's face." Odell stood and went for more coffee while Arnetta just shook her head and laughed.

"That's just the thing," Arnetta said. "You can't see your own nose on your face—you either need a mirror or for somebody to tell you what it looks like. Right?" She gave Darien a warm smile. "Like I said. We needed you to come on down here to help us out. We're good at what we do, but you're good at what you do, so we hope you'll stay and work with us—even for a little while."

"I thought she had a contract," Doreetha said, standing fast and leaning across the table in Darien's direction, but looking at Maxwell. "Gettin' paid good money, too," she added, her hot line of vision searing Darien.

"I do, ma'am, and I intend to honor it. Thank you for having me."

Doreetha settled herself, fluffing her dress and straightening her lavender polyester suit jacket like a mad hen smoothing ruffled feathers as she sat down. "Fine, then," she said after a bit. "Then you needs to be coming to everybody's department to learn, *from them*, what they do." She scowled at Maxwell, triumphant.

Maxwell looked around the room with deep concern. What had he done? It was the best PR snow job he'd seen in all his born days—the whole family played like a violin. Now that the genie of hope, high expectations, and a shot at fifteen minutes of magazine fame was out of the bottle, there was no stuffing her back in. He could see Doreetha now, peacocking around the church with an *Essence* magazine under her arm, and if Jovan got in some media spread, he'd have to file for divorce for sure. And all this because he was trying to be a good Samaritan . . . trying to help a sister out.

He and Miss Thang needed to talk—privately—so he could usher her and her crazy ideas back to the Georgia border. Who did she think she was, with her fine self, telling him how to run his business, or where to spend time managing the things he was always used to managing . . . needed to manage, in fact, to keep things on track! Did she have any idea what it took to keep all those operations afloat? And she wanted him out doing the chicken dinner circuit? Never happen. Not in a million years—no. Uh-uh. No woman was gonna blow into town and have him change his ways just because folks around the table got stars in their eyes.

But it had all happened so fast, right before his very eyes. Darien Jackson had come to town, created a family mutiny, and had practically turned his whole life upside down.

Chapter 5

"You wanted to see me after the meeting, Mr. Ferguson?" Darien smiled with triumph as she and Arnetta stepped into Maxwell Ferguson's office. She glanced around at the masculine furnishings as she tightly clasped her purse and portfolio. This was definitely the power suite, and she knew she'd bested him at his own game. The brother was positively undone and had hesitated to answer her immediately. There was also something about the frown he gave his sister. What was that about?

"Yes," he said after a moment, suddenly wishing that he hadn't asked Arnetta to be a constant chaperone. "There are a number of things we need to get straight—"

"Absolutely," Darien said brightly, strategically cutting him off. "I'm so excited about this major opportunity. Your firm has fabulous potential, and with the right campaign, I know I can put you all on the map." She nodded as though reconfirming the facts to herself, and she glimpsed Arnetta's sly smile. Oh yeah, this brother was going down. "Now, with that said, this week I'll need to drive up to Atlanta to make some contacts with a few friends I have in the media, then I'll get in touch with a solid photographer to line up your company photo shoot.

I'll also do some competitive analysis . . . I'll develop a SWOT grid, too."

She was pleased when Maxwell tilted his head with an unspoken question.

"Your firm's strengths, weaknesses, opportunities, and threats—a SWOT grid. From there I can best determine what PR buttons to push, and—"

"I don't want to do the chicken dinner circuit. That's out," he said, his tone sounding final as he sat down hard.

He motioned to the chairs facing his desk as though bidding them to sit. Arnetta complied; she didn't. Instead, Darien dropped her matching purse and portfolio on an empty seat and then folded her arms over her chest, letting out a long, weary sigh.

"Mr. Ferguson, how do you expect me to do my job in the most effective manner if you resist the simplest request? That's not in keeping with the spirit of the agreement, whereby you gave me carte blanche to develop—"

"I know, I know, I know," he said, clearly annoyed. "But I'm no politician. I hate wasting time, rubbing elbows, doing functions and . . . well, frankly, I'm just not good at it. I've always worked behind the scenes." He looked up at her, hoping she'd understand as much as he wished she'd just sit her pretty behind down. There was just too much coming at him all at the same time, and the fact that his sister had a wide grin on her face didn't help matters in the least.

"Yeah . . . behind the scenes," Darien scoffed, allowing the double entendre to hover in the air between them as she sashayed over to a chair, carefully lifted her portfolio, and sat. "Well, now that you've hired me, all that's about to change. I don't do behind the scenes or the down low. I'm about broadcasting positive information—and Mr. Ferguson, you've got one helluva story to tell."

Although it was a stalemate, part of him liked her

spunk. He was truly flattered that she thought he had something newsworthy to tell. He just didn't like the idea that he had to be involved in the process.

"It just seems like such a waste of time . . . I could never do what Bill did." He shook his head as he thought about his mentor.

"Bill?"

Darien opened her portfolio, slid out a burgundy marble-hued Mont Blanc pen, and began to jot down notes as though she were a physician writing a prescription.

"William Jones," Arnetta said quietly. "He was there when—"

"My father worked a lot," Maxwell interrupted, not wanting his sister to go too far in her explanation. This wasn't a therapy session, it was business—and Darien Jackson didn't need to be all up in their family business and taking notes on it, nor did she need to know how much his mentor had stepped in to cover his father's quality time deficits with his children. "Bill Jones showed me everything he knew about running and building a business. But the man did the circuit like no one I'd ever seen. He used to take us to every charity function, every baseball game, every ribbon cutting, and was the one who ran the whole economic development scene— even cosigned for the first loan I took out with the Small Business Administration so I could buy my first multiuse building . . . the one you're living in on Cherry Street."

"That was our corporate headquarters in the beginning," Arnetta said, filling in Darien as though imparting juicy gossip. "We operated out of the first floor, and the second floor was Maxwell's apartment so he could just get out of bed and run downstairs to work day and night. Then we moved in here, and Max kept an apartment up there on the second floor and installed the gym on the first floor. But Mr. Jones gave him—and I guess. us—a start."

"He sounds like a wonderful man," Darien said, her tone reverent as she looked up, slid her pen back into place, and closed her portfolio. The facts arranged and rearranged themselves in her mind as her glance landed on Maxwell's handsome face, then slowly went to Arnetta. Her intent to simply work this brother out of everything he had was beginning to get shaky. It was something about the way he'd described his mentor, and she wasn't sure what that was. Maybe it was the tone of his voice, which had dropped an octave. Or maybe it was the gentle quality it held, she just wasn't sure.

"Then, if you saw how he did it, used well-positioned public relations to further his cause, which sounds like it was admirable—namely, helping people—why are you so opposed to it?"

Her question felt like a bee sting, and it hung in the air just over his desk while he tried to formulate an answer. How did one explain to a woman—and in front of his sister—that he'd never measure up to Bill Jones's gregarious, warm way with people? The man was almost like a minister. And how did one try to wrap one's brain around the fact that he could never seem to work hard enough to ever measure up to his father—a man who did for eight children and a wife, using his bare hands, no education, and sheer sweat to keep his family better than fed?

"I just don't like it, that's all," he said after a long pause, once it was clear that both Darien and Arnetta were just going to sit there waiting for an answer. "So, start with the others and work me in last. At least let me warm up to the idea, first."

"That's fair enough," Darien replied, but her eyes glittered with mischief. "How about if I start with Jovan, then work around to Doreetha's department, and—"

"Start with Doreetha," Maxwell said, wishing he hadn't spoken so quickly or cut her off. "I mean, Doreetha is very excited about a possible women's magazine piece," he added, catching himself and recovering. "Not much gets her excited, and once you win her over, the others will follow."

He could have kicked himself. That's not what he'd meant to say. Darien Jackson didn't have to win anyone over, per se. Her mission was only supposed to be to elevate the company profile, not to win some family popularity contest. But the more he stared at her, all of his intentions became fuzzy. She had so much energy and was so gorgeous . . . and she thought so highly of what he'd built that it was hard to keep everything separated.

"Okay," Darien said, a bit of singsong in her voice.

He frowned. She reminded him of Arnetta when Arnie was trying to be smart.

"I'm serious." He gave Darien a warning glare.

"I know," she murmured. "Duly noted."

"Well, I'm glad we got that straight," Arnetta said as she stood, swallowing a smile. "I guess I'd better get Miss Jackson oriented to where each department is located. We can start with accounting and review the merits of our customer service and billing area, then go over to meet with the guys in the various operating units while they're here in town."

"Good," he grumbled, not sure why everything was irking him.

"Sounds like a plan, then." Darien stood and clasped her purse and thin leather portfolio.

He glanced at her slender, manicured hands. God she was awesome. He tried to wrest his attention away from sweeping down her body as she turned to leave. He forced himself to look at the stack of contracts on his desk, the same stack that he'd been moving from side to side for nearly a week. He had to get back to work. He needed to concentrate. But Jovan's presence at his door made him bristle. Even though his younger brother had never run on his wife to his knowledge, he wasn't sure why he always had that reaction around him when it came to the ladies. Probably because Jovan was always the life of the party, and the women gravitated to him, but for some reason, today, he didn't feel like being upstaged by his dashing younger brother.

"Hey, great meeting," Jovan said with a suave smile as he entered Maxwell's office and openly appraised Darien.

She smiled shyly at him, offering a coy, "Thank you."

He didn't know why that grated him so, the fact that Jovan had made the woman blush, but it did.

"I hope the boss wasn't too hard on you for your first set of marching orders." He glanced at Maxwell dismissively and returned his full attention to Darien. "After Arnetta walks you around the departments, how about if we do lunch . . . so, uh . . . you can get to know what's going on in marketing a little better?"

"She's got a full schedule, and I'm taking her to lunch," Maxwell informed him in a brittle tone. "From there, we're driving up to Atlanta to meet with her media contacts and to set up a photo shoot. Her schedule is booked."

Darien opened her mouth and then quickly closed it. Arnetta looked positively stunned, but then glanced down at the floor, a smile contorting her expression.

"He's the boss," Darien said with a shrug. "What can I say?"

"Think he bought it?" Arnetta asked as she peeped out of the window.

"Hook, line, and sinker, but, girl, why you always get me involved in doing your dirty work?"

Arnetta put her hands on her hips, laughing as she defended herself to Jovan. "I do not know what you are talking about."

Jovan shook his head and raked his fingers through his hair, chuckling. "See, you're gonna get me in trouble with my wife *and* my brother."

Feigning innocence, Arnetta covered her heart with her hand. "Me get *you* in trouble—you need to stop playing." She stole over toward the window again, watching her brother walk toward his navy-blue Lexus, head held high and back very straight. "You think he likes her?"

"Why you in the man's business?"

They both laughed.

"You didn't answer my question," she said, her gaze riveted on the parking lot below.

"She's a knockout, Arnie," Jovan murmured. "How come you never hooked me up like that before I got married?"

"Shoot," she said, waving him away. "You never gave me a chance, with all them hoochies on you."

"Oh, so now my wife is a hoochie?" His tone was indignant but also filled with an easygoing dose of sibling humor.

"Now don't get me to lying—I didn't call the girl nothing. You know she's my heart, that's why I'm so hard on you."

"Okay, Miss Butter Wouldn't Melt in Her Mouth. And why you gotta be hard on me? I don't do nothin' I ain't supposed to—"

"That's you talking, not me. Don't be putting words in my mouth. I'm not saying what you do, all I do know is you better treat my sister-in-law right, hear?" They both laughed.

"Arnie, for real, you know I love that girl. My wife is fine as she wanna be, admit it. You're just trying to make sure big brother gets one like I did."

Arnetta started walking away from him quickly, giggling as she got out of his play-box range. "But you still didn't answer my question," she said again with emphasis. "Think he'll give her a chance?"

"Lord knows I would," Jovan said wistfully, his gaze going to the window.

"I'm not talking about you. I'm talking about Max." Arnetta waited, her gaze seeking.

"Yeah," Jovan finally muttered. "But why you have to get me in it?"

" 'Cause you know our big brother. Got standards, wouldn't even talk to the chile without an escort. Always paranoid that some sister is gonna get in his pocket. And the onliest way to get him to move off a dime was to throw a little competition in the mix. You the only one who could've made him get all territorial . . . I just wanted to know if he had any fight in him."

"Yeah," Jovan said, running his hand over his jaw. "You needed the brother with finesse and suave for the job. I feel you." He laughed as she gave him a love tap on his shoulder.

"Uhmmm-hmmm. All right, GQ. Just remember, this was just to get Maxwell out of here—with her. Don't be gettin' no fishy ideas."

"Me?" He gave Arnetta a shocked expression as he straightened his tie, then laughed hard as she arched an eyebrow.

"All of y'all is crazy, and Maxwell is as stubborn as a damned mule and about to look a gift horse in the mouth."

Jovan sighed as he glanced at his brother's car leaving the lot. "And what a mouth . . . Dang, Arnie, if he don't go for it, we'd better check his pulse."

This was *not* in his plans. This didn't make no kinda sense at all! He had things to do, places to go, and people's phone calls to return. But he wasn't about to allow his brother to create an EEOC issue in the firm or chase the sister out of town on some dumb junk. At least that's what he told himself as she sat across from him picking at a Caesar salad.

He watched her take delicate bites and chew each

one slowly, her lush mouth working the wrong side of his brain. It had been so long since he'd been alone in female company . . . but then again, she wasn't really female company—she was a temporary employee. A consultant. He had to remember that.

"So, tell me about all your hopes and dreams," she said after a sip of iced tea.

He almost choked on his iced tea as his brain processed the question while he watched the way she licked the moisture from her bottom lip, trying not to become hypnotized by her beautiful hazel eyes.

"Not much to tell," he said, forcing a chuckle, then bit into his burger. "I wanted to be an entrepreneur. Runs in the family."

"Oh, come on, Mr. Ferguson. You wanted to be more than an entrepreneur. Be honest. For once."

Her smile was intoxicating, and he laughed at the way she arched one eyebrow. He was so glad she wasn't going to tongue lash him about the way she got down to Macon, or get into a full fit about Arnetta's potential deception. She was a good sport, he reasoned, as she leaned forward, made a tent with her graceful fingers before her mouth, and looked at him.

"Max, okay?" he said, unable to resist her charm.

"Only if you call me Darien."

He nodded, glad that some of the formality was peeling away, yet worried as heck that it was.

"I wanted to show my father that a man could be educated and a businessman, and do for family and the community without being soft," he said and then immediately took another sip of his iced tea to wash down his inexplicable confession. He glanced around the posh restaurant, wondering how in a few moments this woman had siphoned the bare truth from him.

"From what I can tell, your father worked hard," she said, her tone gentle. "But he didn't appreciate that you could, too."

"Yeah," he said after a while, abandoning his lunch. "I kept trying to tell the old man that he was working himself to death . . . needed to work smarter not harder. He sent us all to school—well, he sent *them*. I went into the service and did my stint to pay my own way, but then he fussed and complained every day about how we had opportunities he and Momma never had, and always went on and on about how we didn't appreciate all they'd sacrificed for us. Told him there was technology and ways to leverage his carpentry business to expand it, get more workers to help him out, but he wouldn't listen. Loved him dearly, but he was as stubborn as a mule."

"Hmmm . . ." she said, her smile soft and her eyes twinkling with mirth. "Must be something in that Ferguson DNA."

He laughed with her. It was a hearty, honest, cleansing laugh that they both seemed to need.

"What about you?" he asked out of the blue. He wasn't sure why, but at the moment, genuinely wanted to know.

"Me?" she said with a nervous laugh.

He watched her retreat a bit from the direct question, and her sudden withdrawal baited his interest even more. "Yes, you."

She sighed and put down her fork. "My mother had four girls, okay. I was the last one. They tell me my father kept trying for that boy, and when I came out, my mother looked up at him and said, 'Willie, that's it. You git what you git, but I ain't having no more babies.' "

Her smile had become so sad, despite the cheerfulness in her voice that he just wanted to reach out and touch her face. "How old was your pop when he had you?"

She chuckled softly, her finger tracing the condensation droplets on the side of her glass. "Daddy was fifty when he made me. I was his trophy, I guess."

Maxwell picked up his hamburger and took a huge bite. "Well that explains it," he mumbled while chewing.

His comment made her bright smile come out of hiding.

"How's that?"

"If I had a pretty little girl, big ole hazel eyes, looking up to me at *fifty . . .*" Maxwell shook his head. "Shoot. I'd have her on my shoulders, would be taking her to show her off to all my boys. And smart, too? A real go-getter. Any man would be proud of all a that. Please." He took another bite of his burger, wondering how and why he'd commented on how fine she was. "It's a man thing."

She looked at him sideways. Part of her mind was trying to grapple with what he'd said about the way she looked, and the other part was repeating the words, *and smart, too.* The last part of his compliment warmed her the most. Maxwell Ferguson had called her a go-getter, not a gold digger, and the difference between the two meant the world. And the fact that he looked like he'd said too much made it all the more endearing.

"My mother and my sisters couldn't stand how he used to act," she admitted, no longer interested in her salad.

"Bet they couldn't," he said, his tone so casual as he munched and sipped his tea between mouthfuls. "I know if I were him, and you were my last, I'da spoiled you rotten."

"He did," she admitted, laughing as she watched his mouth work his sandwich, noticing every facet of his even, brown face. There was a kindness in his eyes that made her line of vision drift away toward the other tables. His eyes held a gentlemanly sort of elegance that was also working her resolve to stay aloof. "When I was a little girl, he'd whisper in my ear when he thought I was asleep. He'd say, 'Princess, don't you let no knuckle-head treat you no different than me. Promise me, 'cause dead or alive, you remember you always got me.' " She looked at him suddenly, as though remembering he was there. "Then he died." She took a sip of iced tea, wishing she'd never let him into that quiet space within her. She neatly folded her napkin beside her plate as though it were her private life, and then tucked it away into her subconscious again, needing space to merely breathe. They were way off the subject. "Like I said. Not much to tell."

Oh, but she was so wrong. What she'd disclosed told him everything.

"How long ago did he pass?" Maxwell waited, gently pushing his plate to the side.

"About two years ago," she murmured. "Still miss him. Miss them both," she added. "I loved my mother, but I was Daddy's girl."

He nodded. "My dad passed a few years ago, but my mother was my heart. She's been gone two years now. No way to get used to it . . . just take it all one day at a time."

She nodded in agreement, and a companionable silence fell between them, along with the irony of their shared losses.

"Must be a lot of weight on your shoulders," she said after a bit. "Seems to me, though, that you've more than filled his shoes. Bet he's proud as punch, looking down from Heaven . . . know your mom must be telling all the angels, 'That's *my* boy.' I know I would be."

She smiled when he looked away, seeming embarrassed. But it was the stone-cold truth. It was also an olive branch that she was extending, her comment an act of appreciation for understanding a little bit of her past. "It's a woman thing," she added, glad that he'd bashfully smiled. "To have a stand-up, do-right son . . . one that probably escorted his momma to church, took care of all his brothers and sisters, and probably a host of nieces and nephews, cousins, and what-have-you . . . plus, gives to his community. Uhmph," she said, shaking her head. "God rest her soul in peace, and I do appreciate the loss, but at least she went on to glory knowing she had a son—one son in the whole bunch— who would do her proud. She could count on you. That, I'm sure, meant a lot to her."

He didn't know what to say. The woman had rendered him totally speechless while also giving him a sense of renewed purpose. All he could do was hail the waitress for a check. In her brief statement, Darien had imparted to him the same gentle brand of confidence that his mother always offered, no matter how much his father derided his efforts. If his mother were still living, he would have brought one Darien Jackson by to meet her.

"Let me tell your story, man. Please. At least let me do that in return for all you've done for me."

"I didn't do anything special," he said, covering the bill with his credit card. "I hired the best PR consultant currently available. The firm needed it, so it made sense."

She watched him humbly minimize his efforts, wondering if Mrs. Smith had been right and if the angels really did have a hand in orchestrating her chance meeting with one Maxwell Ferguson.

"So, where to first?' he asked, standing and going to her chair to help her out of it.

For a moment, she was stunned. Never in a business setting had a man actually helped her out of her chair. This was old school—real old school—or was it something more? She had to check herself, lest she forget that he was a client.

"Well, I was going to go to Atlanta during the week. Uh, I haven't called my contacts there yet."

"Call 'em, and let's go today. No time like the present, right?"

Flustered, she almost dropped her bag as she dug into it for her cell phone. "Sure. No time like the present." Oh, boy, this was bad. A long drive, alone with him? Darien depressed the speed dial button to connect to Mavis's office. She kept her gaze forward as Maxwell escorted her from the restaurant. "It's me, Darien Jackson," she said, unnecessarily adding her identity to make Mavis know she wasn't alone. Mavis's response was a laugh that she ignored. "I'm with a VIP client, and we're on our way to Atlanta. If your schedule permits, I'd like to bring him by your office to see if we can work out a spread for the magazine."

She ignored Mavis's squeals and hoots. Darien kept her face poker-rigid, answering her friend in monosyllables. There was no way she could just break for the ladies' room and fall against a stall to tell Mavis that this might be *the one*. Then again, what was she saying? *The one*. Oh, this was not good at all.

Between the butter-leather seats, soft jazz, and the rich tone of his voice, not to mention the wondrous scent of him that filled the interior of the car, by the time they pulled up to Peachtree Plaza, Darien was almost liquefied. No this man did not make her laugh till she almost peed her pants, telling her all of the childhood antics he and his brothers pulled. It just wasn't fair. He was supposed to be arrogant and so full of himself that by the time she got to Mavis's, she could mentally blow him off. But as she pressed the elevator button, her hands were practically shaking. Why did he have to humbly tell her about how he'd built each division with so much passion lacing his voice? When the doors opened on the correct floor, she hesitated.

"Everything all right?" he asked, giving her a puzzled look. "Hey, I know this was abrupt, and I wasn't testing you . . . it's just that it was a beautiful day. I didn't feel like going back to the office, and—"

"No, no. Everything is fine," she said fast, stepping off the elevator and into the long corridor. "I was just thinking of the angle, the hook, for the story. I haven't really researched, and—"

"I didn't give you a chance," he said, following her, and wondering when he'd taken leave of his senses. Not only was he overstepping his bounds, he'd pushed her into a meeting with a media source unprepared and even admitted that he didn't feel like working today. Truth was, he just wanted to continue to listen to the melodic sound of her voice and to spend more time alone with her, but admitting that would be disastrous. And how was he supposed to admit that he loved the way she smelled and the way the sunlight danced in her eyes and off her caramel skin . . . and bounced off the golden highlights in her hair?

He loved her laugh and the way she described her crazy sisters . . . the fun they'd had as children, and how she was always the one in trouble. He could almost picture it as she'd spoken, her warm laugh entering his very bones. How was he supposed to explain that it had been years since any woman had made him belly laugh down to his soul, especially when he was just coming to terms with some of those realities himself?

She said a quiet prayer—*Mavis, do not start. Don't embarrass me, girl.* Darien opened the door to the office with a flourish, almost bumping into the glass and chrome as she did so. This man was frying her brain. Mavis would see it all over her face. *Oh, Lord, girl, please, do not start.*

"Mavis Williams is expecting us," Darien told the receptionist, her tone succinct and strictly business. She turned to Maxwell and kept her expression grim. "She's a bit unorthodox, but she's extremely good at what she does," Darien warned.

He only nodded.

Darien briefly closed her eyes while her back was turned to him. *He had no idea what he was in for.*

"You may have a seat," the receptionist said, motioning toward a large beige IKEA-type sectional.

Darien glanced at her watch as she and Maxwell moved toward the lobby furniture, both electing not to sit. "She said she could give us an hour."

He again nodded and glanced around the white walls and stark gallerylike outer office, noting the framed covers of *Urban Professional.* Never in a million years would he have imagined Darien Jackson could get him on the inside like this, and so fast. Duly impressed, he tried to seem nonchalant, the whole time wondering what he was in store for.

"Darien, how are you, lady?" Mavis said, breezing into the lobby.

The two women exchanged an air kiss, and Darien scanned Mavis's fire-engine–red power suit with approval.

"I'm fine, love. You look well," Darien said, her tone light despite her nerves. *Please let her like him* . . . She wasn't sure why, but at that moment it was important.

"I see the move hasn't harmed you a bit," Mavis said, her gaze nearly undressing Maxwell as she spoke to Darien. Jutting her hand out quickly, she held his gaze. "Mavis Williams. Pleased to meet you."

Darien thought she'd die a thousand deaths. How could she have forgotten to introduce the man! "Oh yes. This is the CEO of Allied States, LLC—Maxwell Ferguson."

Mavis boldly straightened his lapels and beamed up at him. "Oh yes, we can definitely do him."

He'd heard what she'd said, but had to rerun the comment through two mental filters to be sure he'd heard it right. Had this woman just propositioned him . . . or was he tripping? He glanced down at the petite woman and over to Darien for support.

"Yes, I thought you could," Darien said, but her tone was somewhat brittle. "Your office?"

"Definitely," Mavis said, her bright red mouth turning up at the corner to issue a lopsided smile. "Thank you, Darien. I might have to bump a spread for him."

She was gonna kill Mavis the first chance she got. Maxwell looked like he was afraid to follow her as they left the lobby and walked down the long white hallway to Mavis's office. A hundred ways to strangle a girlfriend came to mind. All Mavis was supposed to do was be cool, look him over, and help her get some ink on him and his family—not out and out drool over the man!

Darien watched as her dramatic friend flounced into her corner office, offered them a seat with a sweeping wave of her hand, then sat down on the sofa and crossed her legs—allowing more thigh than was necessary to show. And as always, Mavis's face and hair were beat to the nines. She made no bones about raking her red talons through her short Halle Berry wipe-away curls, and began toying with her tennis bracelet as she merrily chatted.

"So, *Maxwell* . . . tell me about yourself."

What was with these media types? he wondered. Was the whole "tell me about yourself" thing their basic come-on line? Ten minutes, and he was out. This was definitely a bad idea.

"Not much to tell," he muttered, wishing he were back in Macon. Perhaps he should have sent Jovan on this mission. At least his smooth brother would have survived the assault.

"Well, I can't do much with *that*, can I?" Mavis said, shaking her head and opening her arms toward Darien who'd fallen unusually quiet.

"What he and his family have built is fantastic," Darien said, her tone guarded. "Mr. Ferguson is just a very private man and isn't used to our media probes." It was a warning shot over the bow, which she hoped Mavis would heed. *Tread lightly; this is a delicate situation. Do not mess with him.*

"So, talk to me," Mavis said, her tone becoming more subdued as she glanced at the clock. Appearing utterly disappointed, she stood and walked over to her desk and put on a pair of reading glasses.

Aw, girl, don't be like that.

Darien glanced at Maxwell, who was now looking out of the window.

"From an SBA loan, they amassed over ten million in assets," Darien said with pride. "This man single-handedly built businesses that are run by he and his seven *brothers* and sisters, and the business is debt free."

Mavis looked up from the photo contact sheets that she'd been appraising on her desk, her gaze locking with Darien's. "Do tell?"

Silence fell between them as their telepathy engaged.

"Do tell," Darien said flatly, wondering if Maxwell was hearing all of what hadn't been said. "Maxwell Ferguson is the eldest."

"Really?" Mavis stepped from behind her desk and leaned on the edge of it. "I thought Allied was owned by—"

"An old man?" Darien said, her tone low and controlled. "Not."

"That's a story," Mavis said with a wide smile. She reached over and pressed a button on her telephone console. "Any photogs available this afternoon?" Her question sounded more like a command as she paced away from her desk, regaining Maxwell's attention. "Where are your businesses located?"

Before he could respond, a voice from the console drew her back to her desk. "Well where's Ted?" Mavis snapped. "I want the best on this. I might have to pull the McCoy farm story and push it back to Black History Month. Tell Ted to get up here. I've got a CEO worth ten mil waiting, and I need a spread that can slug in for our holiday issue."

"You'd do that?" Darien looked at Maxwell. "It normally takes four to five months to get on a magazine's print schedule."

"Yeah, girl. For old time's sake—why not? What's power unless you use it wisely?"

"Thank you. Think you can help me place a few calls so we'll have a ripple drop? I want waves of ink—one mag a month, if we can swing it."

"I know what you need, Darien—*trust me.*" Mavis eyed Maxwell, making him look away from her hot glance.

Please, girl, stop. Later. I'll fill you in.

Mavis smiled, as though reading Darien's mind. "I'll call my girl at *BE*—you know Darlene?"

"Yeah, I know Dar, well." Darien stood, her nerves wound tight enough to pop. But she was glad that Mavis had chilled, if only for a moment.

"She owes me," Mavis said with a wry smile. "Which means, *you'll* owe me."

"Done. January issue . . . say, something about how to plan a family budget around the time of year when folks are all recovering from their holiday shopping madness?" Darien began pacing, and she tried to ignore the way Maxwell was looking from her to Mavis as though observing a tennis match.

"Just what I was thinking," Mavis concurred. "Then, for February, you do the black history circuit—you pitch him as a second-generation wonder."

"March, I have to get the sisters in a spread. Who's up at *Essence?*"

"Lonette," Mavis said, going to her Rolodex to jot down the number. "You call her first, and I'll follow up with a beg pitch—but I want the exclusive on Maxwell. I want the homestead, shots of where he grew up, how his mind works. I'm pressed for time, Darien, so you'll have to write the article and let one of my people put the by-line on it. Top it off with a group shot."

Darien nodded, quietly ready to fall down on her knees and kiss Mavis's spiked, snakeskin-covered feet. "Thank you," she murmured. "Just give his CFO a sidebar as the one managing the numbers—who's-the-power-behind-the-throne type of thing. For political reasons, it's important that Doreetha get more than passing mention in the piece."

"It would make matters easier within the firm," Maxwell finally interjected, standing slowly and choosing his words with care, but not sure if he should have done so.

Mavis threw up her hands when Darien glanced at Maxwell. But her smile had broadened as she gave Darien a wink. "You're in debt up to your eyeballs—you know that, right?"

Both women laughed. "Don't go there, but true. I love you, too."

"I suppose each Ferguson wants their own little special section within the piece?"

Darien grabbed her hair down to the scalp with both fists and pulled it to make Mavis laugh harder. "It's a *family* business, Mav."

"That's why you're writing this one," Mavis said, closing her eyes on a weary sigh. "You have the local rags covered."

"Done. I'm right on it," Darien said, closing her eyes, too. At least Mavis was in good humor about it all. "Press releases will be written all week, tailored by department in the firm and local. Philly, DC, Atlanta, Baltimore, my newspaper contacts are strong, then I'll get him on the VIP circuit so we can get some regular ink in the society pages, ribbon cuttings, charities, flood the airwaves with interviews after the various ink drops. They already live in the papers in Macon—I don't need to go there."

"My article needs to be on my desk in a couple of days."

Darien stared at Mavis. "Oh, Lord . . ."

"Boo, it's gonna be all right—but don't miss my deadline. Don't have my boss looking at me sideways, hear?" Mavis glanced at Maxwell Ferguson. "We'll take a few studio shots downstairs, then my man will trail you back to Macon while there's some good light left—maybe catch a sunset shot of you standing on your porch, whatever. He's good. Call your family; have them gather around the fireplace. Can you get somebody to hang Christmas stuff or place a few ornaments on the mantel?" Mavis waved away the suggestion. "I'll send a bag of junk back with Darien. She knows what I want—a tree is too much drama. You do have a fireplace? Oh, the McCoys are going to freak . . . might have to give them the cover to make up for it. Darien Jackson, you owe me, big time. Oh yeah, how's your family? You gonna stop in and see them this trip?"

"Girl, are you crazy? Did I not just tell you what the schedule was?" Darien looked at Mavis with complete disbelief.

"You oughta at least call them while heading out with Ted."

She'd heard Mavis loud and clear. But she was not exposing herself or this wonderful man to family—yet. "I'll call them after the shoot," Darien promised. "Business first."

Mavis nodded.

It was like an out-of-body experience. Several questions collided in his mind at once. How did they know each other's families, when did they meet, they were obviously tight, but how tight, had he been discussed before, and to what extent? It was one giant run-on mental sentence.

Her girlfriend was all barracuda. Was Darien a shark, too, and was he bait? But that sweet, innocent-looking thing that was Daddy's little girl had just transformed into a media maven right before his eyes. It was both electrifying, and way too profound for words. He kept to the sidelines and let Darien Jackson do her thing— next question was, just exactly what was she doing? He'd seen negotiations go down, but the pace and the way the women in the room with him operated was unnerving. Yet she'd delivered, in a major way. He wanted to throw her across a desk and make love to her— hard—as much as he wanted to get as far away from her as possible. Now she was going to invade his home, his sanctuary . . . visit his momma's house and his, with a photographer in tow?

He hadn't said another word, remaining spellbound just watching these sisters work.

Chapter 6

During what had strangely become a tedious drive back from Atlanta to Macon, Maxwell was so quiet that drawing conversation from him was like hunting for hen's teeth. Try as she might, he would only give her one-word responses. So rather than allow the uncomfortable lull, she filled in the gaps with incessant conversation about what to expect on the photo shoot, almost giving herself a headache.

But the nervous energy winding through her made her press on. She knew she was babbling, yet that was a better alternative than jumping out of her skin. Not really knowing the man, she couldn't tell if he was annoyed, disappointed, or bored. In an odd sort of way, she missed the man who'd made her laugh, keeping her in stitches about his family. Now, he'd gone behind his corporate shield and was driving, stone-faced, as though on his way to court. She watched the muscle in his jaw work, and finally gave up with a sigh.

"What's the matter?" he asked, after an interminable silence.

"I was gonna ask you the same question." There. She'd said it, and it was on the table.

"Nothing. Just thinking about all the things the guy trailing us wants to take pictures of."

Okay, she could deal with that. Progress. "What part of this is freaking you out?" Darien asked with a smile.

"Freaking me out? Be serious, Darien." She had no idea. Maxwell reached for the hands-free cell phone unit and depressed the number to Peg. He wasn't about to dignify Darien's question. Ferguson men weren't afraid of anything.

"Peg," he said as calmly as possible, "get Willa Mae on the line for me, and ask her to be sure the front yard to Momma's house doesn't have chickens running out there . . . and tell her I've got a man coming to take some pictures—have the mess off the front porch. Now you know how my mother's sister is, so you're gonna have to sweet-talk her for me. Maybe even get Arnie to call her, if she gives you flack."

He kept his eyes on the road and rolled his shoulders, trying to release the building tension in them. "Let everyone know to stay put at headquarters. We're coming to get some shots in there. See if the girls can get the desks in order, tidy up the stacks of paperwork back in billing . . . you know, we've got company coming." He peered in his rearview mirror at the old Ford Taurus that was following them. "From the office, we'll probably go by my house, so everyone should be ready to move fast so this photographer can do what he has to do as quickly as possible."

Darien listened as Maxwell's assistant crisply took down a laundry list of calls to make. Immediate understanding washed through her as she waited for him to complete the call.

It was reflex when her hand extended and her palm landed on his forearm. She could feel the tight, steel-cable network of sinew even through his coat. "Maxwell, it's gonna be all right."

For a moment he glanced at her, and she could feel his grip loosen on the steering wheel by just a hair.

"I hope that guy brought a wide-angle lens," Maxwell muttered. "By the time we get to Macon, every niece, cousin, nephew, and distant relative will be standing on the front porch of my momma's house." He wiped his palm across his jaw. "This was a bad idea, Darien."

She chuckled, but didn't remove her hand from his arm. Something about touching him, even in a platonic way, just felt so right. "You know this photog is from Atlanta and used to that, otherwise Mavis wouldn't have sent him. You think the McCoys didn't have a huge turnout? Shoot, a farm family, too?"

He glanced at her and chuckled. She had a point, and he certainly liked that she'd touched his arm in the soothing way she did. When she sat back and removed her hand, it left a slight ache from the absence. "I just don't want them to do a magazine spread about some big, country bumpkin who got lucky."

Her eyes widened with pure shock. "What? Are you crazy?"

He gave her a long glance then sent his line of vision back to the highway.

"Yeah, maybe I am—to have allowed you to talk me into this."

She folded her arms over her chest, appearing indignant. "First of all, *I'll* be writing the story." Darien shook her head as she stared at him. "Second of all, I hope half of Macon shows up on your parents' porch."

He let his breath out hard. "Now why in the world would you want—"

"Because I want to show just how many people are standing on your shoulders," she said, interrupting him. "I want the photographer to show where you *really* grew up, then juxtapose that against where you are now and let the photograph speak for itself. I want people to see a man who came from humble means, who pulled not just himself up by his bootstraps—but an entire clan."

When he glimpsed at her again, triumph made her sit up taller in her seat. "That's right. I want everyone to see all those generations, all those babies and spouses and extended relations that have a job all because you did yours well . . . and I want them to see seven brothers and sisters, each made young millionaires because of the fair profit-sharing arrangement you have going on. Think of it, Maxwell, not a soul in your family gotta worry about how their kids are gonna eat, go to school, have a roof over their head—one man did that. If you ain't proud, I am."

Again, silence befell them, but this time it wasn't a strained quiet; it was a deep, contemplative calm. He'd never really considered his life that way, or really thought through what he was doing in terms of what it represented.

"But I didn't do it all myself," he admitted in a low voice. "If my family hadn't pulled together and gone along with my ideas . . ."

"But that's the thing," she said, arguing her point. "You had vision, ideas. That's what makes a leader. And from what I can tell, you've never asked anyone in your ranks to work harder than you—plus, you're fair, Maxwell. You didn't line your own pockets and keep all the profit and let your family go begging, did you?"

What could he say? The woman had a way with words that turned him around and messed him all up inside. "Family is supposed to stand by family," he said bluntly, trying to dull the warmth she'd sent through him.

"Not every family—or person—does that. You and I both know it, so give yourself some credit." She sent her gaze out of the window. "Dang, you are so hard on yourself, Maxwell Ferguson. Guess it's gonna be my job to drag you kicking and screaming into being nice to yourself, for once."

She made him smile, and as many times as he tried to swallow it, the daggone muscles in his face wouldn't obey.

"All right, all right," he finally conceded. "So, you're gonna meet my aunt Willa Mae, and about a hundred Fergusons and Atwaters. Get ready. It's an experience."

Maxwell hadn't lied. As they pulled up to the yellow-and-white aluminum-sided house, all Darien could do was gape. They couldn't even get the Lexus close to the house, as both sides of the street were filled with every type of vehicle imaginable. Between friends and family, neighbors and relations, it looked like an outdoor concert was taking place. People slapped Maxwell on the back, hugged him, smudged his face with all shades of lipstick, and rattled off introductions so fast with such deep drawls that she could barely remember a single name. Folks mistook her for kin and just hugged her up anyway, trying to remember whose child she was, and then made wedding pronouncements that made her blush when she tried to explain that she was new in town and worked for the firm. Chickens ran amuck, scampering away from children. Babies wailed, and the photographer sighed.

"One shot, then we head downtown, I'll do some interiors to get the family at work, then we do his house—and I'm out. Mr. Ferguson, I need a bullhorn," the photographer admitted, patting his Army fatigue jacket as though he might be carrying one on him.

Maxwell smiled. "Lemme get Doreetha."

Darien watched in amazement as Maxwell waded through the crowd and commandeered his sister. She stood on the top step with a cast-iron pot and metal spoon in her hands, and began to clang them loudly. From some deep reservoir of power, her voice stilled the group as she bellowed orders. "Listen up, y'all. We gotsta do this fast—one shot, then this man gonna be on his way. So everybody jus' sidle up to somebody, hug in, squeeze up, and say cheese."

It got quiet. Even the babies stopped crying. Children came to a skidding halt. Ted looked at Darien in awe and tightened the leather strap holding back his shoulder-length Nubian locks. "That's the damnedest bullhorn I've ever seen," he whispered then turned his attention to the restless group. "Okay, all brothers and sisters of Maxwell Ferguson in the front row—even balance with him in the middle, and then everybody else get on in there wherever you can fit. Little ones sit down on the steps. I'll take three like that then—"

"We all gonna get a picture—a copy, right?" Doreetha yelled.

"Yes, ma'am," Darien assured her. "Wouldn't have it any other way."

She was so happy that Maxwell had returned to his former jovial self. She watched him practically bloom under the attention the photographer paid to his siblings as the group shots were taken around the headquarters office. When they all lined up on the winding staircase and Ted went down on one knee to capture the ornate chandelier as well as the executives, she'd covered her heart with her hand. But the way Maxwell stood tall on the front steps of his empire with his arms open, then posed with one foot up on the base of a column, one knee bent, his jacket unbuttoned, leaning forward with a dashing smile, made her weak in the knees. She wanted a copy of every print. Right then and there she made up her mind to get him plastered on the front page of every rag with whom she had any influence. Her brain scavenged for resources . . . she had to contact a website designer. Maxwell Ferguson needed to be launched into cyberspace, too.

"Okay, the final frontier," Maxwell said, casually slinging his arm over her shoulders as the group walked toward the parking lot. "You're going to hang early Christmas ornaments in my junky bachelor pad, and then maybe, just maybe, we can call it a day, right?"

They all laughed, but the fact that his arm was draped over her shoulder sent a shiver through her. He'd relaxed enough to hug her in like kin. Although it was a short walk to his car, she cherished every moment of the close physical proximity, and when he removed his arm to fish for his keys, she wrapped her arms about herself to stave off the sudden loss of his body heat.

Damn, this man was under her skin.

"I should drive and follow you," she said, trying to regain her professional distance. She glanced in the direction of the tall, lanky photographer who was leaning on Arnetta's car. "Once Ted is done, I'll need to get back to my desk and start writing—if I'm to meet Mavis's draconian deadline."

"Oh yeah, right . . . the article to go with all these fancy pictures. That makes sense, because he may need a while over at my place." Floored, Maxwell watched her walk away from his car to find her own. This woman was under his skin. She was right; after the photo session, she had work to do. What had been on his mind? True, it was the start of the week, and normally he worked nonstop all week and through the weekend . . . but . . . he was hoping to ride solo with her for a little while longer.

The sudden loss of her beside him made him temporarily morose as he climbed into his vehicle, listening to his siblings' engines turn over. He'd only met Darien Jackson a little over a week ago, and really just got to know her in the less than twenty-four hours she'd been with him in Macon, then to Atlanta and back. But for some odd reason, it felt like he'd known her all his life—as though she were family.

He mulled over that feeling on the long, silent drive to his home. The inside of the car still had her sweet scent in it, and he missed the sound of her voice within it so badly that he almost hurt.

Nothing could have prepared her for what stood before her. She was glad that she'd been driving alone and could gasp aloud as her car followed the navy Lexus up the long gravel drive. She was on a road, not a driveway. A private drive. One as long as a city block, with land around it . . . trees, and what looked like some sort of manmade lake. This was the *junky* bachelor pad? "Oh. My. God . . ."

Quickly camouflaging her surprise, Darien parked along the circle and jumped out of her car. "Okay, folks. Last stop," she announced. She glanced at the marble fountain and geometric-shaped hedges, but didn't miss a beat. "Now, Ted, what do you want to do?"

"Work for him, or be adopted by him . . ." Ted rubbed the stubble of goatee on his chin and simply shook his head.

"Ted, come on. Seriously," Darien quipped, needing to sound unfazed. She grabbed the bag of ornaments, keeping her focus on the family that was exiting the cars.

"You think I'm playing," Ted said, still gaping. "Man, you've got a photographer's dream out here." Ted glanced around, apparently unable to decide. "This is like a Hollywood set . . . you know what you could do out here?"

"Well it's cold out here," Doreetha announced. "I say we go inside, let this man make up his mind, and I'ma fix me some tea. All of this hullabaloo on a work day evening, when we had to get bills out. Pulleease." She sucked her teeth and strode before the group, leaving Maxwell, Darien, Arnetta, and Ted to straggle behind the brothers who had followed her initial lead.

"Don't mind Doreetha," Arnetta told Ted with a smile. "She don't stand on ceremony with anybody."

Darien could hear the voices of the people walking beside her, but couldn't comprehend a thing they were discussing. Her brain was still trying to wrap itself around the alabaster veranda that rimmed the house, the double oak doors that led into it, housing stained, leaded beveled royal-blue glass and brass knockers, twenty-five-foot ceilings, a crystal chandelier in the foyer that looked like it belonged in the White House, and the Roman marble floor. No, she could not hear a word of small talk as she followed the photographer led by Maxwell through the expansive house, and Maxwell's siblings flopped on velvet period furniture swathed in navy tapestry fabrics without a care in the world. Who *was* this man?

"Upstairs is a mess," Maxwell said, seeming embarrassed. "You ain't taking pictures in my room or in the bathroom. If you ask me, the living room or sitting around the dining room would be best."

"I like the living room," Ted said with awe in his tone. He looked around and pulled out his light meter, testing. "Fabulous light, sun's going to go down soon—but from the bay window, with the fireplace behind you all . . . if we move the sofa . . ."

"You can move whatever you want," Maxwell said with a shrug, going to the piece of furniture.

"Wait, wait, wait," Ted admonished. "The dining room is calling me, too. Decisions, decisions," he said, swiftly walking through the archway. "I love this polished mahogany beast that seats twelve. Looks like a boardroom table inside a freakin' house."

"You want to take shots of the real boardroom," Maxwell said, laughing, "then you'd better keep walking toward the kitchen—and Doreetha is the CEO in there."

"Dang, no Skippy," Doreetha yelled from the other room as the team of venue scouters crossed the kitchen threshold. Impatient to begin, she continued stirring her tea as the others rummaged for grub.

"You ain't got no food in here, Max?" Jovan complained, leaning in the refrigerator and looking disgusted. "Why didn't you have Willa Mae fix you a plate back at the house?"

Darien was mute. She stood in the doorframe of what looked like a restaurant galley. A huge center island made of whitewashed granite took up the middle of the floor, with sparkling copper pots of every size and dimension hanging above it. The large oval oak table in the cut-out bay window nook had a padded light blue and lemon yellow built-in bench on one side and six matching chairs on the other. Darien's gaze swept white oak cabinets, stainless steel and wood trimmed appliances, then shot toward the double glass doors that led to the deck. She couldn't fathom why a man who lived by himself or who seemed to walk with such humility, would have built a palace like this—with such feminine colors and detail, unless there was a significant female in the equation. It didn't add up.

Otis's suggestion returned her from her momentary mental lapse as he argued the merits of taking the group shot in the library.

"No, that's all junky in there," Maxwell replied. "It doesn't look like a library should, lined with books and stuff. My computer is in there, junk all over the table, papers everywhere, exercise gear is in there . . . naw."

"But it has such pretty wood in there," Arnetta fussed. "He don't have to show your messy side. We can put a couch in there." She turned to Ted for support. "Maybel, when she cleans, keeps the wood in this place like glass. And there's a fireplace and a beautiful blue Oriental rug in there, plus—"

"Come on, y'all, we're burning daylight," Maxwell said to end the dispute. "Let the man decide. We're all tired, and it's been a long day—plus, he still has a drive back up to Atlanta ahead of him." Maxwell shrugged an apology to Ted. "Man, I can cover you at a local hotel for all the effort. This was spur of the moment, and my people ain't easy to work with."

Doreetha offered an indignant snort, which seemed to make Ted smile harder.

"Much obliged," he said, looking at Maxwell, but also glancing at Arnetta then down at the floor. A slight tinge of red color crept into his almond-hued face. "A place to crash and some grub would definitely make me not have to rush."

"I'm going to go put a few ornaments up on the living room mantel, as Mavis suggested," Darien said softly, finding her voice. She had to do something, move, walk, use her hands to fidget with placing things to recover her blown mind.

Maxwell watched her quietly exit the room, wondering what had come over her. She'd seemed so genuinely happy that he was coming around and had dropped his resistance to the whole concept, and now she looked as though she'd lost her best friend. "Let's take Darien's lead on this, since this was her idea," he said, hoping that's all that was wrong with her. "We'll do this final sequence in the living room."

But as he followed her through the house, his comment had only seemed to make her sadder. He moved mechanically, abiding the photographer's instructions, jostling his position, switching seats ten times with various siblings until they got repositioned, and allowing his tie and jacket to be straightened, but his mind was a million miles away throughout the ordeal.

"Okay, one last shot, and that'll be a wrap as they say in Hollywood." Ted beamed and stroked his huge lens. "I got some good stuff, people. I think you're all going to be happy." He looked at Darien. "Thank you, lady, for setting this up. I'll make sure you get all the shots so folks can choose, too."

The photographer glanced around the house again, his gaze settling on each sibling, but landing on Arnetta. "You ever need a freelancer, holla. And, one thing you might consider is getting shots of all your operations on location. Philly, Baltimore, DC . . . you know, my man Otis out on the trucks—in one of the tow jauns or one of the eighteen-wheeler moving vans; Odell with a hardhat on, doing the construction oversight piece when y'all break new ground on a new strip mall or apartment complex, maybe get a shot to show Montrose and Lewis behind the register counting cash from one of the Winn-Dixies or Laundromats you own. And I could definitely show Arnetta standing in front of your real estate sign. Just a thought."

Darien watched the males in the room study Ted hard, very hard, and she tried to quell what could become unnecessary tension between them and the photographer. Ted's attention toward Arnie was obviously making her blush, but Arnetta's big brothers clearly weren't having it. "You know, Ted has a point, folks," Darien said, trying to rescue the moment. "In your corporate headquarters, at the very least, but especially for the new brochures and website, a wall of fame is in order."

For once Doreetha agreed. "That makes plenty sense, Darien. But you be sure he takes shots of the customer service area."

"*Commitment, value,* and *quality* should go on the brochures and website right under your department image, Doreetha."

"Now, see, this girl is on the ball, fellas." Doreetha folded her arms over her ample chest. "Mr. Ted, I suggest you take your last shot in here, then you call Peg to get on everyone's calendar and send me an invoice for what your services and stay in all them cities is gonna cost. And don't be sending me no unnecessarily high bill. Hear?"

"Done," Ted said, practically genuflecting toward Doreetha as he edged toward the door. "The last shot is Mr. Ferguson . . . uh, outside."

Doreetha shook her head. "There's several Mr. Fergusons in the room, son."

"Uh . . . the CEO," Ted said quickly. "If you don't mind, I'd like to catch you on your back deck, overlooking all your land as the sun sets."

Maxwell sighed. "Sure. Let's get it over with."

Darien stood quietly in the open doorway, watching the sun cast crimson and rose-gold against the side of Maxwell's face. The sounds of Ted's camera magazine going off fused with the distant low call of the whippoorwill and the gurgle of a stream, and it sent her gaze out as far as she could see. Yes, she'd heard him explain how he'd done it, created all of this wealth in such a short time, but as she stared at him, a profound reverence overcame her.

"That's a wrap," Ted said, hugging his camera like it was a new girlfriend. "Man, I have pure gold on this baby."

"Thanks, brother," Maxwell said, shaking Ted's hand. "I'ma like working with you. Get up with Doreetha so she can put your stay here in Macon on our corporate tab. No need for a working man to be out of pocket, then have to wait for reimbursement."

"You're all right, Ferguson," Ted said with appreciation, then shook Darien's hand on the way back into the house.

"You're awfully quiet," Maxwell said with a sheepish grin. "I don't know if I can get used to that," he added, teasing her.

Too undone to come up with a witty response, she opted for the truth, her gaze carefully roving the expanse before her. "I can't figure it out . . . why would you build all of this, to be alone in it . . . as beautiful as it is?"

Her reply made him go still for a moment. "Because it wasn't for me."

Her gaze held him until he was forced to look away.

"I didn't think so," she murmured, and began to walk back into the house.

"It was for my parents," he said, stopping her retreat. "They just never got to live in it."

She turned slowly, and he was glad that she did. He wanted more than anything for her to understand that no other woman had lived there, but wasn't sure why that mattered as much as it did.

He looked at her windswept hair and brushed a wisp away from her cold-flushed face. "I got so caught up in the architectural plans, asking Momma what her favorite colors were, what things—if she could dream of anything in the world—she would want in here for her and Dad . . . and every day I'd come watch the men build, add stuff she didn't even ask for."

Maxwell chuckled sadly and looked out toward the horizon. "She'd always say, 'I just want my children to be happy, and I've got all the house I need, Maxwell. See, I have a home, son. You can't buy that.' Then Daddy died around the time the foundation was poured, and even though I showed it to her, she wasn't about to move in here alone. None of my brothers or sisters could bear to be here, knowing it was for them, just like nobody would live back in the old house, either." He let out a long, weary breath and returned his gaze to her. "It was a waste of effort and time . . . so, I just carried my stuff up to the second floor and decided to move in. I have a lady come in every now and then to clean, but I'm not here much. Maybe one of the kids in the family, who don't remember, will want this one day. But, truth be told, it's too much house for me to really ever enjoy."

Darien nodded, not knowing what to say. In her former life, she might have jumped for joy to know just how available this wealthy bachelor was. But a deep hurt for him filled her instead. Touch, rather than words, seemed much more appropriate, but neither one of them were exactly ready for that, either.

"It was built with good intentions and love in your spirit, Maxwell. That can never be a waste." She paused, knowing that it was time for her to leave when Doreetha appeared in the doorway. "The photos, I'm sure, will be wonderful—and I want to thank you both for trying this out." She glanced at Doreetha and then back to Maxwell. "I had a great first day . . . thanks so much. So, I'll get to work now on writing up a good article that I hope does you proud."

He couldn't even play it off for Doreetha as his line of vision remained on Darien's retreating form. He could feel the others glancing at him as they said good-bye, and he couldn't move or speak. All he could do was watch her leave his house, one that she'd briefly made to feel like a home as she'd lit it up with her presence, added life to it, put up little doodads and Christmas or-naments. He no longer cared what they thought; this woman had him hook, line, and sinker.

She'd been lonely before, but never to the point of wanting to cry like a baby all the way home to her strange, sterile, new apartment. As she pulled into the driveway, Darien leaned her forehead on the steering wheel and wept. She missed her momma so badly that the tears just wouldn't stop. Then she thought of her daddy, and the tears became deep, agonized sobs. Arnetta had invited her to church one Sunday, and she'd casu-ally accepted without committing to when that would be, but she hadn't set foot on holy ground since they'd closed the lid on her father's casket and the white-uni-formed nurses had almost had to carry her out of Mt. Zion.

"I can't go in there," she whispered into the empty

cab. "Lord, don't let Arnie take offense, but I can't do it." The thought of breaking down, sobbing, wailing, screaming, shot through her. Ezekiel Tabernacle was not just a church; it was Maxwell's home church, which was connected, by way of extension to her job and her public image.

Darien flopped back against the seat and wiped her face with both hands, not caring that her makeup was ruined. She would go inside, take a hot shower, put on some exercise duds, and work out this depression on the StairMaster. Whatever. She'd only been in Macon for a heartbeat and her whole life was flashing before her eyes. Every wrong she'd done, all the work she'd left undone.

A new wave of sobs throttled her. When she'd looked into Maxwell's eyes and he'd admitted building a mansion for his parents, one that they never got to enjoy— all because time ran out—the pain in his expression connected to her own and made her need to cover her mouth to keep from shrieking. Oh, God . . . how much time had she wasted on this planet in the pursuit of foolish things? First Corinthians 13 came to mind: "When I was a child, I behaved as a child . . . but when I became a man, I put away childish things."

A sob broke past her cupped palms, and a crying jag close to hysteria overtook her. What if she'd been the child in the family who had done right? What if she hadn't wasted all that time fighting with her sisters, their jealousies notwithstanding? Why did she give her parents the blues, always being fresh, sneaking out to parties, just totally going left when they said go right? Spending money on trite baubles . . .

And what she wouldn't give for just five minutes in their arms right now, or to sit with her mother over a cup of coffee to tell her all that she'd just seen. And to snuggle up against her daddy so he could pet her hair and laugh with her over her latest adventure . . . What if she'd tried half as hard as Maxwell Ferguson to make a better life for her momma? All her sisters were married, had children, and would go on for generations like all those wonderful, rowdy Ferguson children that ran in the front yard. Somebody would hug them always because they were somebody's momma and had stepped up to the sacrifice . . . had built homes of good intent. Plus, she'd lied to this man, told him some crazy mess about being stalked, which was the only reason he had pity on her and gave her a second chance to dig out of debt. How was she going to make *that* right? Ever? What if, what if, what if kicked her butt while guilt lacerated her until her shoulders shook.

The sound of silence was deafening. For the first time in his life, he couldn't stand it. Silence followed him around the house like a haint, room by room, right on his heels, over his shoulder, laughing at him, echoing off the walls, making him put on his jeans and a sweater, making him find his loafers and leather bomber, driving him away from his vacant home and into the night.

He felt like a complete fool, standing on the porch with a bag of ribs and a six-pack. He was so out of line that he'd walked up and down the steps three times before he could dredge up the nerve to ring the bell. No one had given him the woman's private home number, and he certainly didn't ask for it. How Arnetta kept her filing system in the office was beyond him, and Darien wasn't even listed in the book. With Arnetta on the lam somewhere, the only other person who might have known was Doreetha—and God knew he wasn't calling her.

Noticing that the first- and second-floor lights were on, Maxwell hesitated. How was this gonna look? All right, at least he'd brought food, and he could tell her what he'd convinced himself of—namely, he felt bad that she didn't have a chance to stop in and see her people when they were in Atlanta. He'd learned the hard way that, when it came to family, time waited for no man or woman. Plus, he'd worked her all day, on her first day no less. They hadn't eaten since lunch, so the least he could do was bring her some food—especially since she probably hadn't had a chance to learn her way around town, yet. Right? Right. Made sense.

Maxwell took a deep breath to steady his nerves and rang the bell. What was the problem? Bringing food was . . . it was . . . uh, hospitable. He could hear the stereo blasting as he waited in vain for her to open the door. Okay, maybe she was on the telephone. Or maybe she didn't open the door at night, unless she got a call in advance, which was wise, given these days and times for a single female. But how in tarnation could she think while the music was so loud it was pulsing the porch boards?

Part of him was ready to give up on the third ring. Maybe if he just left the food offering on the steps, then called Arnetta to have his sister let her know it was there . . . He let his breath out hard in annoyance. That was so high school! All right. Think.

He banged his fist on the door, and then went to the front bay window. He could see a shadow moving throughout the first floor. Disgusted, he hurried down the steps and along the side yard with every intention to tap on the glass, hoping she'd hear him, but then froze.

Mesmerized, he could only stare at her through the glass, clutching the bag of ribs with one hand, and cradling the six-pack under his arm.

Every instinct in him knew it was wrong to just stand in the yard like a lovesick puppy, but daaayum. She was bopping to the music, a pair of black tights on that seemed like second skin, her long ponytail bouncing as the muscles in her firm, round behind clenched and released to every step she pushed out against the Stair-Master. Her shoulders had a coil of muscles working under her perspiration-sheened skin . . . itty-bitty tank top showing the rest of her long spine that dipped down at the base and gave rise to a butt that would stop traffic. Yeah, he'd been out of circulation for a long time, but he hadn't gone blind—at least not yet.

It had only been a few moments. He could judge that from the verses in the song. But it felt like he'd been standing there for an hour, and something was definitely making him breathe short sips of air in through his mouth. He tapped on the window, his ears ringing, wondering if his blood pressure had elevated high enough to produce a stroke.

She turned around quickly, and his mouth went dry. Her damp, midriff orange tank top clung to her breasts, held high by a visible sports bra. Her waist seemed like it was small enough for him to encircle with both hands. Her belly was so flat, with a cute little belly button that he could barely smile back at her. But her legs . . . Jesus . . . long, willowy, graceful—have mercy! She pointed at him and slapped her forehead, put her hands on her curvaceous hips, laughed, and then raced for the door.

He didn't move for a moment, watching her breasts bounce, absorbing her in profile, and nearly forgetting all his excuses for being in her yard, pining at her window, at night . . . a CEO . . . dayum.

"What in the world?" she asked, laughing as she flung open the door and he came up the walkway.

"I didn't want you to think we'd lost our Southern hospitality down here," he replied with a grin, thrusting the food before him as evidence. "You worked hard all day, and I wanted to let you know I appreciated what you did."

She graciously accepted the bag, and he almost dropped the beer as he clumsily handed it to her and stepped back from her.

"Maxwell, you should have called. I'm looking crazy, hair standing on my head, all funky and sweaty."

She'd obviously misread his step back. It wasn't because she was funky, it was to check himself. He laughed. "I couldn't call 'cause I don't have your number."

"Oh," she said, taking a whiff from the bag. "We can rectify that."

Her smile made him back up two more paces. He had to get away from her before he said or did something that would make her uncomfortable, he told himself. But God help him, as he looked at her flushed face and the way her chest heaved up and down from the recent exertion . . . and the way the cold air had made her nipples sit up under her shirt . . .

"Are there ribs in here? I can smell barbecue!"

"Yeah, I wasn't sure what you wanted, but, uh—"

"Thank you!"

She jumped up and down and laughed, clutching the bag to her. He thought he'd pass out.

"You're gonna come in and share them, aren't you?"

"I could—I mean, I didn't call. I've interrupted your evening routine and—"

"Generally, I don't let anybody see me like this. Not a lick of makeup on, looking like a hag . . . but, if you give me a moment to shower—"

"You don't need makeup," he said, unable to hear the details of her taking a shower. "I can wait down here, listen to some sounds, if you'd be more—"

"Oh, pulleASE. Come on up, grab a beer and some plates, and we'll feast, I'll interview you while we bust a grub, and—"

"I really wasn't trying to work you all night. I—"

"Oh, I'm sorry," she said, looking down. "I didn't

mean to assume you didn't have other plans. After all, it's late, and—"

"Other plans? No, that wasn't it. I just didn't want to intrude."

Her smile returned, and it was so mellow that he was the one now looking away.

"Then, come on in. I'll only be a minute," she murmured. As he looked up at her, she did a little jig. "The man brought me ribs!"

As he hunted around the kitchen, he made up his mind. He was definitely going to invest in a soul food joint, one that specialized in ribs. The sound of the shower going on had chased him out of the parlor. His nerves couldn't take it. Smooth jazz on the stereo didn't help matters; it only made them much worse.

Her kitchen was as pristine as his—obviously they had the same routine. This was a woman who didn't stay home much, who just used an apartment to change clothes and go to work. But she'd just moved in. Then again, he remembered helping Doreetha move. Mucked-up spice bottles, all kinds of junk . . . the evidence of a good cook. And Doreetha's big behind was a badge of honor, too. He chuckled to himself, trying to shake the image of Darien's butt out of his head. They were going to talk about the things necessary for her to write her article. He was going to leave at a gentlemanly hour. They'd have a beer or two, eat, laugh, talk, and he would not think about her tender, succulent behind pulsing under black spandex. Nor would he imagine what she looked like in the shower that he could hear, with a waterfall of spray splashing her naked, perfect body, just dripping droplets all over her like diamonds running down her breasts, coursing down her belly, beading up in the silky hair between her thighs.

He slammed a cabinet door and almost crushed his thumb. He held on to the edge of the sink for a moment to steady himself. His hands were practically shaking. Dear God he wanted this woman so much it was suddenly hard to breathe.

"Did you find some plates and glasses in my new hodge-podge?" Darien asked as she bounced into the kitchen.

He straightened quickly, but just glanced at her over his shoulder. "I found the plates, but haven't found the glasses." He couldn't turn around, not now. But he wasn't sure which was worse—her hair all tussled, sweaty, with every shred of fabric clinging to her, or seeing her all shower-freshened, her shampooed hair caught up high in a tortoiseshell clip thing to show off her long neck. Girlfriend was blowing his mind as she came closer to hunt in the cabinets, wearing skin-toned leggings that gave the illusion she didn't have anything on, with a soft, white, sleeveless mohair sweater that hugged every curve she owned. She smelled like baby powder; it made him need to take a deeper breath to pull her scent in. Her mouth was covered by some sort of sheer gloss that was calling his name and her big hazel eyes were rimmed in a smoky color that made him want to just lean down and kiss her lids.

"Here they are," she said, producing them for him. "How about that beer?"

All he could do was nod.

Chapter 7

The man had actually come to her apartment. Darien pasted on her best façade of cool and strode past him. "Why don't we go into the living room? My office is set up in there, and we can kick back and eat by the fire."

What was she doing? Okay, she had to slow down and just remember that this was *the boss.* But he'd saved her . . . from much more than a teary evening alone, or having to return Mavis's voice mail, or having to check in with Cynthia, Brenda, and Louise for the fifty-fifth time. He'd made her feel good about a project she could really do well. He'd made her value family and her time, and gave her more than a pittance freelance assignment, like those she'd been using to supplement unemployment. And he'd been such a gentleman . . . had even shared his family with her.

She watched him enter the room from her peripheral vision as she set down the glasses and beer, and was surprised to see him staring at her when she looked up.

"Is here good?" he asked, waiting for her to reply before dropping the bag of ribs on the table and setting down the plates.

"It's perfect," she said, not referring to where they might eat.

He motioned toward the fireplace with his chin. "Want me to start it?"

"I really wish you would."

He didn't move. Was he hearing right, or was it his own wishful thinking that was processing everything wrong? "No problem," he said, his reply coming out lower and more gravelly than intended. "You have any tinder, anything to burn?"

She just looked at him. "Uh . . . newspaper?" She had to stop. *Did she have anything to burn?* Hell yeah . . . "Packing boxes—plenty of those."

"That'll get it started, will cause a lot of smoke, but not a real blaze. You need something solid that's gonna last longer than that." *Oh, man, he had to stop.* Maxwell thrust his hands in his pockets. "You have any matches?"

"I don't smoke, but we could light a piece of cardboard from the stove."

He nodded, needing to put some distance between them. "I'll go downstairs in the basement. I used to keep all kinds of stuff in here. Might be some wood down there."

Shoot, he'd break up furniture, if necessary, didn't she know. He made his way down to the basement, unlocking the first-floor apartment with the key on his ring, and then hurried through it to the storage area. Then it dawned on him, he needed to hand over the keys when he got back upstairs. How would that seem— the boss having the keys to an employee's personal space?

"Damn!" Maxwell punched the basement door and hustled down the steps. This mess was beyond complicated. It was insane.

But to his relief, stacked in a pile in the corner, were wrapped logs beneath a steel shelf of cleaning supplies. He grabbed two, not sure why he did, and bolted back up the steps. When he re-entered the second floor, he held out the spare set of keys. "My apologies. I wasn't trying to be funny. Things got hectic, were moving fast, and I plain ole forgot to give these to Arnetta. If you want to find your own locksmith and have the locks changed, do it and bill us, I shouldn't be in possession of these at any time—only human resources should, and ... all I'm trying to say is I wasn't trying to be funny."

She stared at him as she set down the knives and forks beside the plates. He'd had keys to her place? She accepted them from him slowly, not sure if she was disappointed or angry that he'd returned them. She stared at the keys in her palm and then again at the man who'd given them to her. He was so flustered that he'd spoken in one, long run-on apology. His eyes searched her face. She could tell his nerves were as fried as hers—it was in the way he'd swallowed hard, making his Adam's apple bob in his throat. Her heart skipped a beat, and she looked away with a smile.

"Thank you," she murmured. "But I trust you, so that won't be necessary."

If she wasn't mistaken, she was sure she heard him exhale hard.

"These ribs are the realio-dealio," she said, expertly changing subjects. "And you had the nerve to also get some macaroni and cheese, candied yams, and greens ... dang."

He walked over to the fireplace, needing a moment to recover from what could have been a disaster. He focused on starting the fire, going back to the kitchen three times with a piece of cardboard before he could get the end of it to stay lit.

He had to keep moving as Darien unpacked the food, making exclamations about how starved she was and how he'd saved her from Ramen noodles. The woman acted like he'd brought her Dom Perignon and lobster, but the fact that she was so totally appreciative was eating him up.

"Let me go wash up," he said, brandishing sooty palms. "Then, we're gonna git down."

She laughed but the chuckle hitched in her throat as he paced out of the room to the kitchen. It was in the tone of his voice, that rich, warm, Southern comfort sound, the possible way one could take the statement . . . It had everything to do with the way his jeans hugged his slim hips and the way the six-pack on the coffee table wasn't the only one he carried. In a slate-blue sweater, Maxwell Ferguson *definitely* made her wanna slap her momma. No doubt. That blue, with the slight sheen in the fine wool, just dragged her line of vision down his chest and across his shoulders, almost stopping brick by brick down his abdomen. And when the man turned around, she had to look away. His behind had to be carved out of granite. She could tell he was built when she first met him. In a suit, he was fine, but in some casual gear, her eyes were crossing.

It had been so long since she'd had some respectful and respectable male company, she didn't know how to act. Then she chastised herself. This wasn't male company—this was *the boss.*

Okay, okay, okay. She had to pull herself together. Do like Momma always said, and fix the man a plate—or was that too informal? It could be misconstrued to also be forward. Oh, forget it. They were down south, and you fixed a man's plate. But this was business, right? You didn't fix a coworker or boss a plate!

Darien's hand hovered over the Styrofoam cartons of side dishes, a serving spoon balanced on indecision. "I didn't know what you wanted, or how much," she said, an apology in her tone.

Damn . . . she was actually about to fix him a plate? Maxwell stared at her. Almost messed up and called her baby. "Uh, I pretty much like everything that's there."

He forced a smile and came over to the table and sat on the sofa. "I ain't picky." He had to clean up his comment. He definitely liked everything he saw, but he had to stay focused. However, there was just something about the way she dipped that spoon in the mac and cheese and globbed it onto his plate, then licked the excess strings off her fingers that almost made him close his eyes. The music was making him delirious, the fire was blazing, and this woman's scent was getting all confused up with the barbecue . . . Lord have mercy, and this consummate businesswoman was fixing him a plate in his old apartment, seeming like she belonged there from the very beginning . . .

He accepted the plate, took a huge bite of a rib, licked his thumb, and took a healthy swig of beer from the bottle, then set it down hard. "So, you think you can do something with this?"

She was watching his mouth, heard the words, and almost choked on her candied yams. It all started when he licked his finger and turned the beer up and looked at her like she should have also been on his plate. "I think I can do a li'l somethin'," she said between coughs.

"You know, I'm set in my ways," he said, taking another bite of rib. The fact that she'd gone into a slight coughing fit messed him up. Now he was sure she was feeling it, too—but that was too much information at the moment.

"Your ways have proven to work," she replied, seeming to have recovered. "I like what I saw in you today."

He chewed more slowly. He should have never taken her by the house.

"Your mother and father's house, with all that family standing on the porch. That's where I'm going to start the article. To me that's the most impressive."

He almost spit out his food, and he recovered by laughing, pounding his chest, and chasing it with a hard swallow of beer. "My big ole crazy family is where you're gonna begin?" He was flattered beyond measure. But she didn't need to know all of that.

"You're one helluva man, Maxwell Ferguson. Taking care of all those folks." She raised her glass of beer to him, and tipped it against his bottle. "I just have one question: Who takes care of you?"

He wasn't prepared for her direct query into his life, much less the warmth of her smile and the way the fire reflected in her pretty eyes.

"I do, I guess," he said, now picking at his plate.

"No you don't," she said softly. "Not at least from what I can see."

She smiled and sipped her beer then set down the glass with care.

"I get up every morning around five o'clock, run, do some lifting. I get my exercise, eat right, then go into the office—or out on a job site. I know enough to know that, without your health, you don't have anything." He shoved a forkful of yams into his mouth, fully aware that that's not what she was talking about.

"I also exercise and eat the best I can," she said, glancing down at her plate and then over at him with a smile. "Unless somebody tempts me."

He laughed and kept eating. Sho' she was right. He had a lot of discipline, unless tempted. Right now, he was more than tempted; he was close to drugged.

"But I want to personalize this piece," she said, merely moving the food on her plate around with her fork. "What does the real Maxwell Ferguson do on his day off? What kind of music does he like, how does he relax? What's his favorite vacation spot or sport?"

Her questions were hard to answer, so he shrugged as he gave each one thought. "I haven't been on vacation in years. I used to like the Caribbean. Nothing like blue water," he said through a mouthful of greens. "I don't get a chance to get out to the movies, or to jazz concerts . . . but, from time to time, and only because it falls on a Sunday, I do watch my football."

She picked up a rib and held it between two fingers, taking dainty bites. "Why Sunday?"

"Because after church, it's family tradition to all go over to Doreetha's for Sunday dinner—and her husband, Wilbur, henpecked as that poor brother is, demands only one thing."

"The football game be on," they said in unison, and laughed.

"You know, I'm not trying to be funny, but why don't you put on an old, raggedy T-shirt and pick up them ribs and eat 'em like they're meant to be eaten?"

"What's wrong with how I'm eating my ribs?" She laughed and set the bone down and sucked the sauce off her fingers.

He was laughing, but hesitated. He'd changed the subject to cool off the topic, but then she went and sucked her thumbs in a way that nearly made him squint. "You home, and this old country boy wouldn't tell . . . I promise," he said, beginning to not care how she took what he said. "It's just you and me in here, and I won't blow your cover."

She stood, hands on hips, gave him a jaunty expression that let him know she took no offense, and bobbed her head. "Oh, so you think I'm just some prissy sister from Atlanta by way of Philly. Aw'ight. I'ma go put on my T-shirt, and when I come back in here, it could get ugly."

She strode away, chuckling, and he wondered why he'd made the suggestion. Suddenly the ribs had lost all their appeal as he waited. But she quickly returned with a dark blue tank top on, no bra straps visible, and a pair of navy sweatpants. She plopped down on the sofa, breasts bouncing, laced her slender fingers together, and stretched her arms over her plate, and pretended

she was cracking her knuckles. She made such a pro-
duction out of the basic business of eating ribs that all
he could do was chuckle and sip his beer.

"Since we gonna be down home, I'ma saying a bless-
ing over my food," she warned, bowing her head, her
mouth moving in silence as he watched her. When she
looked up, she winked at him. "Now, it's on, brother."

He held a rib midair between his mouth and his
plate as she closed her eyes, bit into the meat that was
falling off the bone and moaned—her tongue working
rib-tip gristle, her thumb, sucking the crimson sauce off
her forefingers, using the pad of her thumb to help get
the dabs of sauce from the corners of her mouth where
her tongue tried to reach and failed. He wasn't sure
when he'd stopped breathing. It might have been somewhere between the time she'd cleaned the meat off a
bone and put half of it in her mouth and pulled it out
slowly and sighed, then went to a fresh rib, or it could
have occurred when some barbecue sauce dripped
down her cleavage and she'd sent a moist finger to retrieve it. He wasn't sure. But he was very sure that he'd
never seen ribs eaten like that, and definitely not at
Doreetha's house. There oughta be a law . . . if she was
with him, he'd never allow his woman to eat ribs in public. He'd have to shoot a nucca behind her. Watching
Darien work a rib to the bone was an erotic experience.

"Don't tell on me," she mumbled between bites. "I
don't do this in restaurants, but there's nothing like
gettin' down at home."

He nodded and took a sip of beer to wet his throat.
"You enjoy 'em like that, and I'll keep you in ribs while
you're in Macon."

"Deal," she said, not looking up or catching his drift.
"Now, what else do you like to do that you haven't in a
long time?"

Words failed him. There was only one thing on his
mind, and he definitely couldn't tell her that.

She sat back, rubbing her flat belly with her eyes closed, breathing hard. "Well? Come on, if you have to think about it that hard then that don't make no sense."

"You want another beer?"

She opened her eyes, expecting to see him smiling at her when he stood. Instead he looked at her so intently that she sat up.

"I'm going into the kitchen for a minute. You want another beer?"

"You all right?"

He shook his head no. It was the truth. He hadn't been all right since he'd met her.

"Ribs didn't agree with you?" She shot up off the sofa and headed toward the bedroom. "I have some Alka-Seltzer or something in there. See, this is what I meant about needing time to relax—executive stomach, is all it is. Brother, you . . ."

He heard her return footsteps and calmly got up and took his plate into the kitchen. He retrieved a cold beer, popped the twist-off cap, and took a slow swig, fully aware that she was standing in the doorway behind him.

"I need to go home," he said. "I'ma take one for the road and be out. That's best."

"I'm sorry . . . I didn't mean to offend you by chowing down . . . I wasn't making fun of you or anything, I was really enjoying—"

"I was really enjoying watching you, too. That's why I have to go—no offense levied, none taken. Trust me."

"Oh . . ." Darien dabbed the sticky corners of her mouth and leaned against the doorframe, partly to keep from falling.

"Now see, I didn't mean to offend you," he said, setting his beer down gently. "I really didn't . . . it was just the line of questions, with the hour, and the music, and the environment, and watching you eat . . . I don't want you to go feeling uncomfortable while you're here . . ."

"I won't." She pushed away from the wall and folded

her arms over her chest. "Okay, so the situation is a little unusual, but you strike me as a gentleman and have treated me like a lady. So, why don't we sit down, I'll get a pad, I'll get some more information, then tomorrow I'll write up what I have to, and I'll see you in the morning, sharp."

"That can work," he said, totally unsure that it would, but not exactly ready to leave. "But let's skip the questions about things I like to do and haven't for a very long time."

She just nodded and headed for her beer. Oh . . . Lordy Miss Claudy . . . he had no idea. Never in her life had a man just stood up to walk out on her from some sense of honor. Not after the kind of knot this brother had dropped to acquire her mere presence . . . and then he was trying to stay professional with an erection that wouldn't quit. Oh yeah, she was going to church this coming Sunday. Needed to fall down on her knees and get saved again. Mrs. Smith hadn't lied. Her life was changing and turning upside down.

He entered the living room but didn't immediately sit. Instead he took his time, poking at the fire embers with rolled-up cardboard before finding a seat beside her. He was glad that she'd fetched a pad and pen. That made it a bit easier to keep his perspective. But before long, she'd abandoned the pad and pen on the coffee table and had him laughing again.

"No, I'm telling you. I don't believe in no horoscopes. What does me being born in May have to do with being stubborn, as you claim?"

"You're a Taurus, and it goes with the territory."

"Now, you're going to read my palm, I guess?"

"I don't know how to do all that stuff. I just know what my girlfriend told me."

"Mavis?" He gave her a sideline glance.

"Yes, if you must know."

"I could tell y'all was tight—and she's a piece of work."

"Now what's that supposed to mean?" Darien said, but still laughing. "Only I can talk bad about my girl."

"I ain't talking bad about her, but you two seem so different."

"How so? We go all the way back to high school, brother. Don't go there."

"You have a softness about you, even when you're being tough. You care about people, seems like to me. Not that she doesn't, but she's got an edge that you don't, and I like that."

She didn't know what to say. Wasn't sure how to take the compliment. Mavis had always been the sexy, funny, outgoing one, and she was a little more subdued, but they both had participated in their share of antics.

"Don't get me wrong," he added, attempting to redress any slight he'd delivered. "But you're a keeper."

"A what?"

"See, now, I've put my foot in my mouth, but you wanted to know how a man thinks."

She genuinely did want to know how his mind worked, and she leaned forward, listening to him with every instinct within her. "I do want to know what you mean. Tell me."

"If I asked my sister Doreetha what that quality was, she'd call it grace. You're diplomatic enough for a man to bring home to his crazy family, but not to speak on their ills to his face," he said with a half smile. "If I asked Arnetta, she'd call it class without snooty attitude." He nodded, satisfied with his description. "If I asked Jovan, he'd say, *daaayum.*"

They both laughed, but she had to look away.

"If I asked my brother Otis he'd say, 'That girl's got a good head on her shoulders. Can help you build.' If I asked Monty, he'd tell me, with his country self, 'Big brother, she'd make you some purty babies.' " He laughed hard when she opened her mouth and stared at him. "If I asked Lewis, he'd say, 'What's wrong witchu, boy?' And if I had a mind to ask Odell, he'd just laugh and tell me not to look a gift horse in the mouth. The complete package—and that's the difference between you and a sister like Mavis. What more can I say?"

He was sorry that he'd made her stop laughing, but wasn't sorry that he'd told her the raw truth. At least she'd know that she was around people who thought highly of her, no matter the circumstances that had brought her to Macon.

"And, if someone were to ask you, what would *you* say?"

He was prepared for a lot of responses from her, had expected her to chuckle at his foolishness. But he wasn't ready for her serious gaze, or her eyes glittering with appreciation.

"I'd say that I wish I'd met her under different circumstances so she wouldn't ever think I had planned all along to bring her down here like a kept woman." He polished off the warm remains of his beer and set the bottle down gently, staring at the way the fire made colors shift on the green glass. "I'd say this was a woman who deserved to be courted and who deserved not to have her professionalism ever held in question. I'd say this lady was something else and had messed around and blown my mind without even trying . . . and that although, intellectually, I know that courting takes time, she's also making me think about some needs I haven't addressed since my parents closed their eyes. So, I'd say on that note, it's time to get my hat so she can write her article, undisturbed . . . and so I can remain a gentleman in her mind."

"Then I'd have to say that I'm flattered beyond your comprehension by both your definition and your discipline." She looked at him until he looked at her, noting that he hadn't stood to leave. "And I'd say that I, too, am so sorry that I met him when my life was chaotic and I'm trying my best to make amends . . . and that I appreciate the fact that he doesn't expect anything beyond business from me—and hasn't rubbed my nose in my own mess. That, Maxwell Ferguson, is a gentleman."

"You have enough for your article?" he murmured, rolling the bottle on the table between his fingers.

"Yeah."

"Then, maybe since it's getting late . . ."

"Yeah. I guess that would be best."

He nodded, but still hadn't moved. "I just enjoy your company is all."

"Same here."

He looked up at her. "You do?"

"Can't you tell?"

"I wasn't sure."

"At first, I wasn't either."

"That's fair. Neither was I."

"The more I learned, the more I liked you."

"Same here," he said quietly. "You make me laugh. It's been a long time since I really did that, too."

"Then, it's settled," she said, drawing her legs under her and leaning on one elbow. "We'll be professional, be friends, make each other laugh, and share an occasional bag of ribs."

"You're on," he said, loving the color of her skin under the low lights and fire. "But you can't keep up a professional front with barbecue sauce on your face."

She laughed hard, licked her thumb, dabbing at her chin. "Oh, where? You let me sit here all this time with my face dirty—that ain't right!" When she started to stand, he touched her arm.

"Don't go yet. Leave it. Let me get it." He reached out in reflex and found the tiny splatter mark with the pad of his thumb. Maybe it was when she'd licked her finger again that had been his undoing or the playful-

ness in her wail that had been the final straw that unraveled him.

Whatever it was, he was glad that she relaxed, sat
down easy, closer, and allowed him to run his finger
over the crusty surface of her chin. But just touching
her made his hand tremble. Her skin was like satin, the
offending splotch had to go, and before long, his thumb
had found his tongue, only to return to her chin. As he
did it, he knew it was too familiar a gesture, way too intimate a thing to do, but it was either that or draw her
in hard to kiss it off her chin—and he wasn't sure if
he'd stop there.

And just as unsure of how she'd react, he brought his
hand to her chin slowly. She simply closed her eyes as
his finger gently dabbed her chin. It was a lazy, relaxed
motion, like a window shade going down on a hot sum-
mer day. It was the kind of gesture that drew a man like
a magnet, made him tilt his head, lean in, breathe in
her scent before he found her mouth. And her lush,
smooth lips created a heat wave in his groin that somehow made his palm cradle her cheek, caress her ear, before splaying his fingers within her curly, damp tresses.

Pure silk met his hand. Every texture she owned
stole his breath, made him deepen the humid kiss until
he tasted barbecue and spicy greens, the sweetness of
her mouth candied like yams, requiring him to hold
her face with both palms, an anointed man filled with
desire, his cup running over, blessed that she allowed
him near her . . . smooth enamel surfaces and buttery
flavored soft, wet interiors, beer and mints and the
sound of a strangled moan. Her return touch did him
in. Those slender hands running across his shoulders,
then grasping the seams of his sweater, sent his hands
from her face to hold her back, to press her in close before he had to break for air.

"Darien . . . I really have to go." He sounded crazy to
himself. He was breathing hard, watching her eyes for a

sign, even though he claimed not to be a superstitious man. He could feel her chest heaving against his as she tried to regain her platonic stance. And he watched her struggle, nearly losing the battle that he'd long since lost, and it affected him deeply to know that she wanted him that badly, too.

"You're right," she finally said, but neither of them moved. She closed her eyes and let out a long sigh. "It's just been a really long time, and this—"

"Feels so good."

She stared at him as his fingers traced up and down her arm. He couldn't stop touching her, although he'd torn himself away from her kiss. It didn't help matters as he watched her eyes practically cross beneath half-closed lids upon a nod. Gooseflesh had risen on her skin, each tiny pebble on its surface making him battle not to lean her back and cover her.

He knew he was losing the fight when her hand trailed down his chest and landed on his thigh. His line of vision followed her hand, and he felt it burn where it landed, millimeters away from where he ached so badly. When she made a fist, as though fighting within herself not to take things farther, he closed his eyes and dropped his head to her shoulder.

"It's just too soon. I just really met you. I'm sorry," she whispered.

"Don't be," he told her, shaking his head, breathing in her baby-powder scent, his nose at her collarbone. "I knew better than to start this . . . it was my fault."

She shook her head, her fingers finding the crown of his scalp, stroking it gently, making him insane. "You tried to leave, but I wanted you to stay."

"I wanted to stay, too, baby . . . still do, in the worst kinda way." It was a confession that had come out on a ragged exhale. He didn't have it in him to mask his emotions or to play games. But he'd called her *baby*. Oh, man . . .

He lifted his head, knowing that the only way for this to end well was for him to leave now—and to do that, he had to get out of her face, lift his head away from her intoxicating scent, had to get his hands off her satiny skin. It was going to be like breaking a strong electric volt. He needed something to come between them that wouldn't conduct current, and right now his sole focus was on acquiring latex for the task.

The look of agony on the man's face devastated her. When he lifted his head, the seal was broken. Cold air rushed in to send a shiver of desire down her spine. His reaction had been immediate, the kiss harsh, his grip on her upper arms gentle then rough, and she ached so badly that a gasp came up from her throat without censure. She couldn't help arching against his hold, her breasts tortured by the rub against his chest, the difference of textures maddening, his thumbs passing by the place where she wanted them each time his hands slid up and down her arms.

This was not supposed to get so out of control, not like this and not so fast. She broke the kiss, stared at him, eyes seeking. Somebody had to have some sense between them.

"I can't get out of here with you looking at me like that," he admitted.

She watched his gaze travel down her face, linger at her mouth, making her feel its presence like a touch until her lips parted on their own volition, then slid down her throat, rest at her collarbone, and find her weakness. She could feel him hesitate, deciding, and her breath sped up as his thumbs tested her acceptance on her arms, then moved slowly toward the heavy lobes of her breasts. Tears were in her eyes before his palms ever covered the ache, but when his trembling fingers pulled at the hardened tips, unspent tears spilled down her cheeks, making her close her lids.

"I'm sorry," he whispered. "You're just so beautiful."

"That's not why..." She couldn't even speak as his thumbs caressed her nipples, making her dizzy with want. The sensation burned, opened her palm, flattened it against his thigh, and sent it to explore his pain.

The moment her hand slid across his length, he shuddered, arched against her touch, and captured her mouth with his own, forcing her to swallow his deep, from-the-diaphragm moan.

"I don't have anything on me," he whispered hard against her temple. "Tell me you do."

She shook her head and almost wept.

He knew that was it. The end of the night. A perfect reason to stop, cool off, let everyone regain their composure. If he could have just stopped touching her, but her stroke at his groin had ignited insanity, her bare breasts under her thin tank top making him stupid, his hand sliding down the front of her sweatpants no help... and a thong driving him mad, trying to imagine its color... until his palm slid against smooth, bare skin, all the way to the quick, not a silken strand, only swollen slickness, the stuff of fantasies, something he'd only heard of, never witnessed, always wanted, didn't believe really existed beyond video, and a voice shattering what was left of his nervous system, making him beyond foolish—reckless... not caring about a family enterprise, millions in the bank, the calamity of making unplanned babies or possibly dying young... an arch against his fingers putting tears in his eyes, strangling his voice, making him ready to beg for just one time. "I don't care, Darien... Baby, c'mon."

Everything she ever knew that was right was peeling away from her with each gentle flick of his finger. This man smelled so good, felt so good, was so good, and she knew she was supposed to say no. But he'd called her by name, called her baby in his arms, and she felt her grip tighten as her breath grew more ragged, his refrain becoming desperate, "Baby, c'mon." His touch finding her sweet spot, perfect hands, strong fingers opening her, sliding deep at just the right moment, perfect timing from wondrous hands, the rough side of his jaw pushing her shirt up her torso, his mouth claiming her nipples in shared attention, making her lose all perspective or pride and pump against the rhythmic pressure.

Her mouth found his earlobe upon a shudder, about the same time her hand tugged at his zipper, and her mind took leave and went on vacation, 'round about the time she was calling him baby. "Oh, baby, c'mon . . ." she whispered, repeating what he'd told her, acknowledging that it was too late to stop now.

A shudder ran through him as his palms cupped her behind, slid against her bare backside beneath her pants, and she'd never seen a man practically swoon from just a touch. It did something to her; she wanted to make that expression on his face last forever, yet deepen it, make it permanent every time he saw her so he'd remember . . . just like she would.

"You sure?"

Now why did he have to go and interject logic? Of course she wasn't sure! She stared at him.

He froze. She'd hesitated. *Oh, please, God—don't let her change her mind.* "When was your last period, baby? Maybe it'll be all right." Now he knew he was crazy—was reaching. *Maybe?* He sat back, closed his eyes, and breathed through his nose.

"We can't do this like this," she said and pulled down her shirt.

He nodded, unable to form the words. "I have to go, okay?" he finally said, his voice fracturing.

She nodded, unable to speak.

"You want me to come back with something?"

He stared at her, a plea in his expression.

"This happened too fast."

He nodded and zipped up his pants, standing, and

walked over to collect his jacket. "We'll let this cool down, huh?"

She only nodded and closed her eyes. Was he insane? They both needed a fire truck to hose them down.

"I'ma go . . . you all right?"

Again, she only nodded. "I can't walk you to the door," she finally murmured. "Not right now."

He nodded, thoroughly understanding, but not sure. "You ain't mad or gonna move out or anything?"

"No," she said, wrapping her arms around herself. "But if I walk you to the door, it's all over." She looked up at him dead serious.

He wavered and then made progress to leave, pulling on his jacket hard.

"You're not mad, are you?" She peered up at him, praying he wasn't.

"No. But if you keep talking, I won't have it in me to go home."

She closed her eyes and listened to his footsteps cross the floor, savoring every footfall. When the door opened and closed, she shivered. What Winn-Dixie in town didn't he own . . . or his family work at, so she could make a run for some protection? After the way he'd made her feel, and the things he'd told her from his heart, she might go to his house and throw rocks at his window till he let her in. She banished the thought as she heard his engine start. It was settled; she'd come down to Macon and lost her natural mind.

He gripped the steering wheel hard and peeled away from the curb. This didn't make no kinda sense *at all*. He could still smell her on his hands, her sweet essence permeating his car, making him drunk with the need to turn around, go back up her steps, and bang on her door. His pride was in shreds. Less than twenty-four hours in her presence and he was ready to take a risk, make a baby, didn't give a hoot about the consequences. His daddy woulda called him a fool, and his brothers woulda said the same for different reasons—now he had to work beside her and forget what she felt like?

He could still taste her sweetness in his mouth; the ache for her was profound. The drive home seemed like a prison sentence. And where was home, any ole way? Two beers under his belt, a belly full, and a gorgeous, spectacular woman in his arms . . . now *that* was going home.

As he careened up his driveway, jumped out of his car, and took the palatial front steps two at a time, there wasn't even an old hound dog to greet him. He opened and shut the door behind him with pure disgust, walked through the foyer, and mounted the stairs. When he got to his bedroom, he sighed.

If he coulda just convinced her to stay . . . ordered food in, brought her up *here.* The four-poster rice bed looked so lonely without her. He hadn't even made it when he'd dashed out that morning.

He stood very still, closed his eyes, smelling her on him. He could imagine it, vividly, what she'd be like arching under his hold, calling his name, tears of pleasure in her big hazel eyes, shuddering to every touch . . . It had been too long since he'd had that kind of night, and yet for some reason, with her, it seemed like so much more than that. She'd made him feel, had made him laugh, had made him question his priorities while also inspiring him . . . she was proud of him, but not awed, just plain old appreciative of his hard work. And she felt like no woman he'd ever touched; she was the genuine article, no fright in her voice or her spirit. She'd made him spill his guts, drop his guard, act stoopid for her, and still, he didn't care, and right now she had him wondering if he went back on bended knee with a box of condoms, if she'd have him.

He shook the thought. Too classy. By now, she'd probably cooled off, had come to her senses, most likely had changed her mind, and was probably horror-stricken that she'd let him touch her the way he had in the first place. But if she did have a change of heart, at the moment, he'd trade his right arm for it.

Maxwell went to stand by the window in the dark, looking out at all the land that bordered his house. Defeat claimed him. It had become an island, a very lonely place in the world, devoid of female laughter, a woman's touch, warmth. He'd almost made a baby tonight. He must have been missing his mind. But she would have been a pretty little thing, like her momma . . . and he would have definitely enjoyed making her.

He laughed at himself as he took off his jacket and flung it blindly across the room, thinking of Darien's graceful hands, thinking about what a nice big diamond on her finger would look like, if he, a confirmed bachelor, were so moved . . . wondering what was the acceptable courting time for a woman like her. Her bills were negligible—he didn't care about the car note anymore; she needed to be in a Jag or a Merc, anyway. If she'd let him help her, he would, but she was the kind of independent woman who would no doubt insist on working for everything she owned.

Maxwell let his breath out in frustration. He'd never met anyone like her before. What was he gonna do with this woman who was turning his life upside down? Whatever she had in credit card bills, he would gladly cover that . . . no problem. Whatever she wanted, but it just wasn't her style, he could tell.

If he wanted to truly run her out of town, all he had to do was propose something as stupid as that, and one Darien Jackson would probably slap his face for even trying to play sugar daddy. Maxwell lolled his shoulders then rubbed his face with both palms and suddenly stopped. She was in his skin. Had burrowed beneath it. She smelled so sweet . . .

The problem was going to be watching her hold a pen between her slender fingers. It was going to be next to impossible not to remember what they felt while attempting to caress away the throb that was now giving him a headache.

Yeah. This was a problem. This woman had his nose wide open, as his daddy woulda said. The only right-thinking thing to do would be to stay away from her, let her do her job, and be cool. *Sure . . .* Easier said than done. But it wasn't about making folks in the office whisper behind her back. He couldn't do that to her . . . no. But how in the world was he going to stay out of her face, just act like nothing had ever gone down? He had to figure it out before another workday rolled around because he could still smell her on him, rekindling his desire, messing up his mind, making him imagine making love to her in every room of the house—the pain of her absence making him wince till it made him wonder if settling down wasn't such a bad idea after all.

Chapter 8

As soon as the sun kissed the horizon, Darien was up and out of bed like a shot. What was the point of lying there? She'd stared at the ceiling for the better half of the night, hoping, wishing, praying Maxwell would have another lapse of judgment and return. But that wish had also put knots in her stomach. What had she just done?

Darien quickly padded across the floor. She had to get out of the now confining apartment. Had to get out of Macon. Atlanta, home, was her destination. She needed time to think, time to breathe. Something really unplanned had just gone down, and it was not a good thing, given her circumstances. Besides, Atlanta was where she needed to go to pull her feminine thang together—hair beat, nails did, feet dipped in paraffin, the whole nine. She'd almost slept with a man with barbecue sauce on her face! Girlfriend was slipping, big time.

Just as fast as the thought crossed her mind, she skidded to a stop in front of the bathroom mirror and took a long gaze. What was happening to her? Here she had what had been the biggest fish she'd ever baited on the hook, and yet, she didn't want to hook him, snag him, play him, or anything else she was used to doing to the male species. She liked Maxwell Ferguson, truly respected him. Now that was scary. The whole concept of going straight, no games, was thoroughly unnerving. What if *she* got played? What if she'd already been played?

She splashed cold water on her face and tried to shake the dual emotions that thinking of Maxwell caused. That man's gentlemanly demeanor was like a torch, burning her up from the inside out. And his integrity was like a bucket of ice water on all her normal ways of responding to a fine, eligible . . . wealthy man. She needed advice, but oddly, Mavis was the last person she wanted to consult. That gave her serious pause. Mavis was her girl, her cutty . . . but the chile was ruthless, and somehow, it seemed, Maxwell Ferguson deserved more than the normal strategy she and Mavis could cook up.

Darien's shoulders sagged. Perhaps she should go to Cynthia's, maybe do some discrete interviewing with her sisters. They'd all been married for years, seemed to be relatively happy, had husbands and children . . . had played it straight. Problem was, she wasn't sure if their path was the right one for her. The only thing she could do now was try to stay busy all week, stay out of his face, and see if Mavis might give her an extension on her article deadline. Next weekend, she was going home.

Daylight always brought a new perspective. Maxwell paced through the house in search of coffee. Sleep depravation was kicking his behind. He musta been out of his black mind last night. He didn't even know this woman, really. And here he was about to turn his pockets out, take a risk on life and limb, and even brook the possibility of becoming a baby's daddy. Too crazy!

That settled it. There was only one thing to do. Get as far away from her as humanly possible until he got his head together. He needed to stabilize. Needed distance. Today, he'd work her out of his system with a long run, lift some weights, then head into the office to clear off his desk. He'd stay away from her and out of her space, and maybe toward the end of the week, he'd go up to Atlanta and check on the real estate and chain stores. Then, he'd fly into Charlotte to put his eye on his trucking business, and then drive to Highpoint to check on the furniture operations. Mayhaps he'd fly up to Richmond that same day and check out the rest of the moving vans then drive up to DC to find out how the rest of the strip malls and retail operations were going. By the following week, at the latest, he could drive up to Philly to sit with Otis to find out how the towing operation was fairing, and might even be in the frame of mind to start opening doors to some municipal contracts with the city of Philadelphia.

"Yeah, that makes sense," Maxwell muttered to himself as he put two heaping scoops of coffee grounds in the appliance. After that, he could fly back down to Macon, chill, and have his head right. That would give him a reasonable cool-off period away from Miss Jackson. Only problem was, every time he thought about her, his chest got tight. That was *not* a good sign.

"I'm in the nail salon," Darien said, while leaving instructions for Mavis to call her back when she woke up. A week of dodging Maxwell Ferguson had made her bone weary. "I'm in Hotlanta for the day. Might buzz past my sisters', then, if you're free, maybe we can go to Justin's to hear some jazz and get a glass of wine—I'ma need it, don't know about you, girl, but phew. Thanks for the ten day deadline extension. I needed that time to do all the interviews and really understand Allied's operations."

She clicked her cell phone closed and gave instructions to the manicurist to give her an American polish job.

"What you want on your feet, doll?" The manicurist had asked the question without even looking up.

"Same," Darien said, lost in thought, but her eyes wandered over to the airbrush designs that were on the wall in a glass case.

The manicurist looked up. "You sure?"

Darien smiled. "No, I'm not really sure of anything this morning. Can I just peep at a few designs?"

"Sure," the manicurist said with a laugh, and she stopped working and allowed Darien to stand.

"I just want something different," Darien said, slowly walking around the counter to stare at the hundreds of options mounted on the wall. Each nail design that was etched on a fake, plastic nail looked more intriguing than the next. "I want something understated, classy, but . . ."

"But that will grab his attention."

Darien laughed, becoming embarrassed that her search was so transparent. "No, it's not like that. I'm trying to pick out something for my big toes, which won't be seen until spring."

"You need to put a my-love-is-like-whoa design on the big toes and put a silver toe ring on the second toe, so when the brother sees—"

"I tol' you, I'm not—"

"I've been in this business a loooong time, darlin', and I know what my customers need when they come in here." The young woman laughed with Darien, both women shaking their heads as Darien gave up the ruse.

"All right, all right, but I'm not trying to send the wrong message."

"I know," the manicurist quipped, pushing her long platinum curl off her shoulder. "They love red."

"No red. Uh-uh," Darien said, laughing harder.

"Oh. Real conservative," the manicurist said, seeming dejected. "But, trust me, those are the ones who are the biggest freaks, chile."

Darien felt her face get warm as she looked away and studied the patterns.

"He on the DL?"

"No!" Darien shouted, then covered her mouth as all heads in the salon turned and knowing grins met her. This was a mess. "Never mind. I was just tripping for a moment. Just give me an American."

"Aw, sister. Don't be like that. C'mon girl . . . try one."

Darien wasn't sure if it was the tone in the woman's voice, coaxing her to mischief, or "c'mon, girl" part of her statement that had sent a shiver of anticipation through her. But whatever it was, she still found herself lingering in front of the choices. Then she saw it—a palm tree with a sunset and blue water. "Can you put that on an American?"

"So, the brother likes the Caribbean, huh?" the manicurist said, giggling so hard that she had to hold on to the white linoleum counter. "You got you a Rasta?"

"Hardly," Darien said, playfully sucking her teeth for emphasis. "But it has been a long time since he's gone."

The manicurist whooped. "Then since it's been a long time since brother has been down there, you'd better get your legs waxed, your cha cha waxed, eyebrows did, and a facial while you're here, too!"

Getting up the mental stamina to visit Cynthia was always a process. Darien double-checked her shopping bags to make sure she had enough baubles to drop on Cynthia's two boys and two girls, Brenda's two baby girls, and Louise's three cute little monsters. The little ones were easy; it was Cynthia's teenagers who always presented a problem. But she loved her nieces and nephews more than life itself.

The moment her car pulled up to Cynthia's neat, suburban Roswell home, the door flung open, and the whole crew was running to meet her.

Amid squeals of delight, Darien passed out hugs, play taps, and kisses, presenting each child with a small token of affection.

"So, you finally decided to grace family with a visit," Cynthia said through a half smile. "And you don't need to be buying all these children no mess. You just got that job, Darien, and these children all have more than enough junk in their rooms."

She ignored her sister's cut about her finances and gave her a hug. She was glad to see Brenda and Louise standing in the doorway with open arms. Today, she would not go there with Cynthia. Today she would just visit, laugh, have fun, and enjoy the family she had.

"Now y'all shoo," Brenda teased, getting the kids out from under Darien's heels. "Give your aunt some breathing room and let me hug my sister."

Darien melted into the embrace. "I have missed y'all," she said, her heart so filled by just coming home. She turned to Louise, hugged her hard, then held her back. "Girl, you look good."

"Lost me twenty pounds," Louise said, twirling around. "You'd better watch out. I might be as skinny as you soon and come down to Macon to raid your closet."

The three women fell into comfortable banter, striding past children as they made their way into the kitchen.

"Git now, that's the last I'ma say," Cynthia warned, her body blocking the kitchen door. "We got grown folks' bizness to discuss. Y'all go find something to do with yourself."

A chorus of "Aw, Mom," filtered into the kitchen past Cynthia and wrapped around Darien like a warm blanket.

"Let 'em be, girl," Darien said, her tone gentle as she looked at all the disgruntled faces. "I miss them, too."

"You'll be here for the holidays," Brenda said, plopping down in a chair. "We don't see you much, either. I know we have a lot of catching up to do."

Louise sat and crossed her legs, and grabbed a cigarette.

"Uh-uh," Cynthia fussed. "Not in my kitchen. You take your demons on the porch."

"Cynthia, please," Louise argued, standing to go by the window. "Ain't nobody in here asthmatic."

Darien just smiled. It was good to know that nothing had changed in this part of her world. Even at this hour of the day, Cynthia was tending a stove that had smells coming from it to rival any restaurant in town. Her eldest sister had taken a stance that all of them knew by now meant she would not be moved. Cynthia's short, plump form seemed to expand and puff up when Louise struck a match, took a long drag from her cigarette, and blew the smoke out of the window with a sheepish grin. Leaning on the window like she was in a tavern, Louise's dark brown complexion caught the afternoon sun, and it lit up the mischief in her pretty almond-shaped eyes. Brenda had taken her usual position as peacemaker, sitting in the middle between where Cynthia and Louise had a standoff, her big brown eyes quietly entreating them not to start another argument.

"Whatchu cooking good, sis?" Darien asked, attempting to quell the brewing dissension.

"Nothing but the standard," Cynthia said, relaxing a bit as she took up a slotted spoon and leaned against the sink. She wiped her hands on her apron, but there was unmistakable pride in her expression as she rattled off her menu for Saturday's dinner. "Smothered chicken, gravy, rice, snap beans, and some corn bread."

"Nobody can touch you in the kitchen," Darien murmured in awe at how her sister consistently fed and tended to a full family while also marshaling over fifty nurses at the local hospital by day. "I don't know how you do it." She hoped the compliment would diffuse any inquiries to her own career and life path.

"You just have to be diligent, put your all into it," Cynthia proudly announced.

"Girl, I don't know how she does it," Brenda admitted. "I'm at the bank all day, and by the time I get home, half the time I'm ordering in pizza for me and my gang."

"That ain't no way to feed children," Cynthia said with disgust as she checked on her pots. "Can't feed children junk food."

"I know, I know," Brenda said, smoothing her new haircut. "But, working, raising children, minding after a husband who needs *everything* . . ."

"She ain't lied," Louise added, taking a long drag from her cigarette. She blew the smoke out through her nose and shook her head. "You hafta save a little space for you or else they'll bleed you dry."

Louise went to Brenda and slapped her five, ignoring the scowl Cynthia gave her for bringing the cigarette too close to her cooking. "I had to go on strike around my house to lose this twenty pounds," Louise said with triumph. "I was getting all fat and out of shape because with three younguns and a man—pulleases. They had me running everywhere, picking up everything, just slaving like I was the maid around my house, and none of them had any appreciation, so I went on strike."

"You did?" Darien said, wide-eyed, and knowing how old fashioned her brother-in-law was. "What did Douglass say?"

"What could that fool say?" Louise said, her tone and her laughter becoming brittle. "He don't buy me nothin'. I work to cover more than half the bills, and he don't take me nowhere, so . . ."

It was like a slow storm gathering in the kitchen. Darien knew Louise and Doug had issues, but hadn't been prepared to get into all of that today.

"I bet he's treating you differently, now," Brenda said

with encouragement. "Girlfriend is getting all slim, got a new 'do . . . that's why I got mine done, too. Tired of just running behind the twins with no appreciation for how hard I work."

"Damned straight," Louise snapped.

"Don't be cussing in my kitchen," Cynthia said, clearly uncomfortable by the direction of the conversation. "When you sign on to become a wife, it ain't all roses and romance. You make your bed, and you have to lie in it. Momma did."

You could have cut the sudden silence in the kitchen with a knife. Darien's gaze darted between each sister, seeking understanding.

"Momma didn't have it that bad with Daddy," Darien dared to say. But they'd made a comment that she couldn't allow to ride. They were bad-mouthing her Daddy.

"Girl, pullease," Cynthia scoffed. "You wouldn't know because you were the baby, and the sun, moon, and stars set on your every desire. Let Daddy, God rest his soul, hear it."

"Uhmmm-hmmm," Brenda muttered. "Momma worked hard, and we had chores that you couldn't believe just to help her out around the house. Ain't that right?" she added, glancing at Louise.

"Gospel," Louise said with authority. "But being 15 years younger than the next in line, by the time you came along and were old enough to help, shoot . . . you ain't hafta do nothin'. Still don't."

Okay, now it was on. Darien drew a deep breath and let it out slowly. How did it always come back to this? "I work," she said, but her voice didn't seem sure.

"Oh, pullease," Cynthia said, stirring her beans with one hand on a hip. "You work? First you had some fancy, run-to-every-restaurant-in-town type of job, and then lost it—"

"Not true," Darien snapped, defending herself. "I

was a marketing executive for a firm that merged. I didn't lose that job. I was laid off because the firm that took my company over brought in their own team. They didn't need me and the guy who had seniority, so I lost out. But I didn't *lose* my job because I was incompetent."

"All right, sore subject," Brenda said, shaking her head and going to the refrigerator for lemonade. "But you never had to do any hard-down work with stacks of papers on your desk, crazy amounts of—"

"I have deadlines, always did. Even for the year and a half I've been out of a job, I did freelance work, wrote articles for magazines, did—"

"Working for your girlfriend Mavis's magazine ain't work . . . not when you and the so-called boss go back to high school. And getting a check from unemployment while you're also getting freelance work on the side not only is dishonest and illegal, but ain't like you ever had to put your nose to the grindstone and change your lifestyle." Louise shook her head. "This chile here always lands on her feet. Steps in doo-doo and it comes up diamonds."

Darien opened her mouth to press her point, fury making her face burn, but Cynthia had beat her to the punch.

"Same thing with men," Cynthia said, her arms now folded across her chest, a huge spoon in one fist. "The rest of us went on and settled down, took husbands on faith, for richer for poorer, for better or for worse—this chile done scairt off half the eligible men who mighta married her, playing games, bleeding their pockets dry, and—"

"What's wrong with wanting to be treated nice?" Darien asked, now standing. She couldn't take it any longer. "Why can't a man have education, ambition, and, yes, some financial assets, as well as integrity? Why does he have to be broke, or boring, or just average to be considered worthy of husband material—and tell me why I, or any woman, shouldn't set her sights above average?" She hadn't meant to go that far. She hadn't meant for her hands to find her hips or her head to start bobbing with every word. The kitchen was so quiet for a moment that the only sound in it was pots gurgling.

"Now you standin' in *my* kitchen, in *my house,* and have the nerve to be talking about our husbands?" Cynthia said between her teeth. "Douglass, James, and my Ronnel are good men—even though your hoochie ass wouldn't appreciate a good man if you tripped over him."

Darien could feel her eyes narrow. Now she was a hoochie? She looked at Cynthia's dowdy beige sweat suit with cooking splatters on it and the way the polyester blend stretched over her sister's wide hips. She eyed the way her short bob haircut badly needed a perm . . . three inches of new growth showing at the roots, calling her a hoochie! Her gaze swept to Louise who'd lost weight, true, but whose nails were torn up from lack of care, her no-name jeans and cheap green blouse hanging off her because her stingy husband wouldn't allow the girl to spend money on anything but the bills . . . chile smoking herself to death out of frustration. And Brenda had some nerve with her cannonball, five-foot-two self, eating to replace the lack of attention, and the girl used to be killer fine. Outrageous!

"Number one," Darien said slowly, gathering her Louis Vuitton purse as she summoned her inner calm, "I'm not a hoochie. Number two," she added with emphasis, "I do know a good man when I see one—but I'm not ready, at twenty-five, to settle for less than I deserve." She drew in a deep breath through her nose. "Number three, like Momma always said about your husbands—if you like 'em, I love 'em. I don't have to live with them or sleep with them, so whatever goes on in your households ain't my business. But I do know this, I'm not about to give up a little romance, a little fun, a little nice treatment like a martyr. That much I do know. And, if I should make said decision, I wouldn't be hating on my sister if she made a different choice."

For a moment, it was quiet, then all hell broke loose. Talking at the same time, each sister lobbed a preemptive verbal strike. Darien's head swiveled on her neck until she was nearly dizzy.

"Ain't nobody up in here *hatin'*, Darien," Cynthia spat.

"Who you calling a martyr? I love my James. If you had a husband, you'd know," Brenda said, standing with effort.

"She *did not* go there," Louise snorted through a puff of smoke. "When you have children, you have to make some sacrifices, but if you've been selfish all your life, you wouldn't know jack about sacrificing for hearth and home!"

"She probably went down to Macon and found some new fool to work. How you get that new cushy job, anyway?" Brenda demanded.

"Not on my back," Darien nearly yelled, her voice escalating beyond her ability to keep it modulated. "How about a degree from Spelman and an MBA from Duke University? Oh, that mighta helped me land a job along with a good track record and solid references!"

"Now she's gonna start with the degrees," Louise said, throwing her hands up and dousing the cigarette in the sink.

"Miss Priss has it all worked out," Cynthia grumbled, shaking her head. "Don't y'all know that by now?"

"Has it so together that she don't need two-hundred and fifty dollars from my po' ass to keep her lights on while she was unemployed." Brenda folded her arms over her chest and glowered at Darien.

"Didn't need my five hundred, but she comes strutting in here with gifts and a designer bag, probably used it on her hair and her nails," Cynthia added, seeming satisfied by the dig.

"Uhmmm-hmmm, just like her cell phone is on my plan, but girlfriend got it all together and don't need nobody." Louise pulled out another cigarette and lit it from the stove.

"That's right," Cynthia added, handing Louise an ashtray so she could sit at the table.

They'd ganged up on her so hard that tears of hurt and frustration stood in Darien's eyes. Some of what they'd said was true—a lot of what they'd said was true—but not all of it. Yet, it had been delivered with such venom that it was hard to sort it all out. "I will be repaying each one of you the full of what I owe you," Darien said quietly, blinking back tears and standing as tall as she could.

"Tears ain't workin' on me," Cynthia said, ignoring her as she opened the oven.

"We done heard it all before." Brenda sighed. "Save it. You can pay us back when you learn how to cook or ever baby-sit some of your nieces and nephews so we can have a break instead of blowing in and out with gifts you can't afford, whichever comes first. Until then, the three of us got it handled, like we always do."

"The girl is in here acting like we did something to her, when all we did was speak the truth. Now her face is all swole up, about to cry crocodile tears because we got her game—tryin' to play us like she always played Dad. Momma knew how she was, too."

"Not impressed. You can get our money back to us when you get it to us, like you always do," Louise said through an angry drag on her cigarette. "We old bats have time, given we ain't going nowhere with our boring little lives, rowdy children, and dud husbands. Right, ladies?"

"I wish that, just for once, when I came home, y'all would be glad to see me, and that we could laugh and have fun and really enjoy one another's company." Darien hoisted her purse on her shoulder and made her way out of the house.

* * *

"So it went that well, huh?" Mavis said in blasé tone. "Them heifers ain't gonna change, so you might as well not let them upset you."

Darien twirled the long stem of her glass of chardonnay between her fingers, looking down into the translucent liquid. "I'm going to pay them back," she said quietly. "In fact, my plan is, with this job, to get straight for once and for all. I want to pay everybody back."

"That's admirable," Mavis said, sipping her cranberry juice and vodka. "So, pay their stingy behinds back and go for the big game."

"What big game, Mavis?" Darien was too weary for words and didn't have any game left in her.

"Maxwell Ferguson."

She stared at Mavis. "Him? Are you crazy? I work for the man."

"Which is why it's perfect."

Again, she stared at Mavis, wishing she'd just gone straight back to Macon to work on her article.

"You know, if you snag a millionaire, girl, all your financial woes will be over."

Darien sighed and sipped her wine. That was the last thing she was going to do—complicate her life by sleeping with the boss to gain financial favors . . . what? Just to put him in her sisters' faces. Insane? "Not this one," she said, her voice distant and barely audible over the jazz and hubbub of the restaurant.

"Why not this one? He's a perfect catch." Mavis looked at her, indignant. "Girl, did you go down to Macon and lose your mind?"

"No, Mavis. I went down there and found my mind. It's been missing in action for a long time."

Aghast, Mavis pushed back in her chair. "Somebody worked some roots on you, girlfriend. Tell me the man isn't fine—and rich, too. Pullease."

It was true. Maxwell Ferguson was all those things. But he wasn't a game to be played, in her mind.

"Mavis, he's kind, honorable, and a very nice man." Darien sought her friend's gaze for understanding.

"You slept with him, didn't you?" Mavis covered her mouth and closed her eyes. "He done blew your mind—oh my God."

"No, I haven't slept with him." Darien took a liberal sip of wine and looked away.

"You had a near miss, didn't you?"

She couldn't, wouldn't answer Mavis's charge.

"Oh my God, my best girl done slipped up, forgot the rules of the game, and messed around and fell in love." Mavis leaned forward and covered Darien's hand. "Don't go there. You cannot fall in love. Never let 'em see you sweat. You're all barracuda, the best playa in the game. You can't be allowing no man to get under your skin. Use or be used, play it to the bone. Work his pocket to a nub and—"

"No," Darien said firmly, retrieving her hand from beneath Mavis's. "He's not like that, and it's not like that. He did me a nice favor, got my career back on track, so I'm going to do a good job for him, pay off my debt, get out of the lease if I can, and get something more affordable, then come to Atlanta to pay back my sisters and try to get a job that—"

"This is terrible," Mavis shrieked. "You're talking about downsizing your lifestyle. Did you mess up and get saved? You having some sort of religious experience, an early midlife crisis? What did the man do to you, honeybird? Tell Mavis, and we'll figure this out."

"He was nice to me, Mavis," Darien said. Her voice faltered as she spoke. "He didn't ask for anything from me, and never . . . He was a gentleman."

Mavis covered her mouth. "He's all pro. Oh, shit. He turned it down, didn't he? You tried to give him some, and the man backed off . . ." She shook her head and raked her talons through her freshly permed hair. "This is bad. He's got your confidence shook—that can happen if your cashflow is jacked at the same time. What you need is a confidence booster." Mavis's gaze darted around the room and settled on a group of men engaged in conversation at the bar. "Here's what you do. Walk by them, then go up to the bar, fidget with your purse as though you're deciding, sigh, and slowly walk away. Turn on the feminine magnet and—"

"No, Mavis."

"You have to get your confidence level back to normal before it flatlines, girl. How you gonna go big game hunting when you scairt to work a drink from some fools at a bar?" Pure astonishment blazed in Mavis's eyes. "Baby, you feeling okay? You did have the flu a little while ago."

Darien smiled. "Mavis, I'm fine."

"That's why I'm telling you to get back into the game before your blade gets dull." Mavis sat back in her seat, worry replacing the alarm in her expression. "We shouldn't be paying for this lobster dinner, and we should be sipping champagne. This should not be going on the magazine's expense account. What is the matter with you?"

Darien studied the men at the bar, then her gaze swept the entire establishment. "I'm not interested. I don't even want them to buy me a drink."

Again, Mavis's hand flew up to cover her mouth. "You've got single focus?"

Darien nodded and looked down at her glass. "He's the one," she quietly admitted, almost afraid of her girlfriend's reaction.

"Oh my God . . ." Mavis leaned forward and held her hand across the table. "He kissed you, didn't he?"

Darien swallowed a smile, nodded, and took a deep sip of her wine.

Mavis sighed. "It was all that, wasn't it?"

For the first time since the conversation took the turn to Maxwell Ferguson, Darien looked up and held Mavis's gaze. "I'm messed up, girl."

Mavis giggled and leaned in closer, drinking in Darien's every word. "That good?"

Darien closed her eyes as a shiver ran through her. She couldn't even put it into words.

"Noooo . . ."

Darien nodded and kept her eyes closed. "Oh, Mavis . . ."

"You didn't give him none?"

"I couldn't . . . it was too soon."

"That's my girl," Mavis said, a hand on Darien's shoulder. "All pro. At least you kept your wits."

"No I didn't," Darien murmured, now glancing at Mavis. "Five more minutes, and it woulda been ball game."

Mavis drew away from her slowly, looking stunned.

"I think he made me call him by name . . . I'm not sure."

"What!" Mavis glanced around and lowered her voice when a few heads turned. "Just from a kiss?" She let her breath out hard and ruffled her hair. "I ain't had none like that in a long time, girl."

"I've never had any like that," Darien said so quietly that it made Mavis lean in again. *"Eva."*

"Neva, eva?"

"Neva."

"What! I'm so jealous!"

"Stop hollering," Darien said through her teeth, so embarrassed that she could have disappeared into the toes of her Pradas. But she needed to talk to somebody, even if the details remained cloaked. Then it all spilled out on the table, as though she'd knocked over her wine. "Oh, Mavis, I like him so much. There are things about him that just blow me away, and he was a gentleman, a true gentleman, and we both wanted to so bad, but we both know we have to work with each other, and he cares what his family will think about me, which makes him all the more a gentleman, and he could have, I mean, I was putty in his arms, but he got up off the sofa and—"

"Stop." Mavis put both hands up. "The sofa?"

"He brought me ribs, and we were supposed to be eating and I was supposed to be interviewing him for your deadline, and—"

"He went down home on you—brought you ribs? *A millionaire,* and sat on your sofa . . ." Mavis dissected her confession like a doctor. "Oh, brother wasn't playing fair when he came in for the kill and found your weak spot—home. Gurrrl . . ."

"I know, I know," Darien said quickly. "Then I was eating the ribs, and he got this intense look on his face, literally stood up and said he had to go, and—"

"Got shook by his own game. Girl, you *the one.*"

"I'm the what?" Darien let her breath out hard and wrapped her arms about herself. Just talking about it was giving her gooseflesh. She closed her eyes. "I'm sitting here telling you that I'm trying to figure out how to go straight, Mav, no games. I want to work with him, for him—I mean, be about the reason he hired me and not mess up while I'm down there for the next few months, but I don't know if I can keep it all straight. I'm crazy about him, and it all happened so fast. It ain't supposed to happen like that, and I'm not playing, Mav, the man is under my skin like needles, and I can't stop thinking about him in that way. But I have to—to stay professional." She opened her eyes, totally undone that Mavis was staring at her slack-jawed.

"On the sofa," Mavis whispered, nearly choking on her drink, "how intense did it get?"

Darien looked away. She was not getting into the details.

"You've answered my question," Mavis said, taking a deep swig from her drink. "And brotherman left?"

Darien nodded, but still couldn't look at her friend.

"Was he angry?"

"No," Darien whispered. "He apologized for putting me in a compromising situation."

"Oh, girl. Don't you know what that means?"

Darien stared at Mavis without blinking.

"Means only one thing, chile." Mavis let out a long breath. Her eyes became sad. "I've just lost my best friend."

"Stop playing," Darien scoffed and polished off her wine. "What would make you say something like that? We're always gonna be gurls."

Mavis shook her head and touched Darien's cheek. "Naw, baby. You got him, hook, line, and sinker, which means I just lost my roadie."

Everywhere she went and everywhere she turned, it seemed like people were losing their minds. She never thought going home to the new apartment in Macon would seem like refuge, but it was. There was no living with her sisters, and staying with Mavis was out of the question. If she'd crashed at Mavis's, they'd be up all night, analyzing an unlikely scenario that didn't need to be fantasized about, namely, a future with Maxwell Ferguson. And she dang sure didn't need to spend the whole entire night under Mavis's roof because it would be in no time that Mavis would have been able to wheedle every delicious, private detail about the incident on her sofa out of her.

And she couldn't do that, put the man's business in the street to that degree, and she couldn't even allow her mind to descend on that issue that wasn't supposed to even happen because it would mean another long, hot, frustrating night of sleepless hours, tossing and turning, and losing her mind, which might make her do something really foolish, like reach for the telephone and beg his sister for his private number. Then, how would that seem, asking Arnetta for the number to request a booty call? Then what would he think of her? It was already bad enough that things got heated, but at least she'd gotten out of that with a thread of dignity, and only because he was a gentleman.

But as she came up the front steps and saw a large bouquet of flowers set discretely on the porch, Darien held her breath. She tried to approach the vase with a huge yellow bow on it as though it were a normal occurrence.

Stooping to retrieve the floral arrangement, she balanced her purse and got out her keys, wanting to savor them and the card alone inside. The moment the door closed behind her, she bolted up the stairs and entered her apartment, nearly bumping into the door. She set the vase down carefully, pulling the small card out of the thorny spray of Cherokee roses. Her fingers gently glided over the state flower's waxy white petals, their pretty, soft yellow centers almost making her cry. In the most eloquent apology she'd ever received, the note was brief:

They have thorns, but are still perfect. The petals are pretty, but strong. I hope they'll last a long time, because they are from here—born here. I just hope you'll know that I meant no harm.

Max

She pressed the card to her chest, and when the telephone rang, she ran for it without shame. However, it took her a moment to force the disappointment out of her tone when Arnetta's voice filled the line.

"Did I catch you at a bad time?"

"No, no," she told Arnetta quickly. "I just got back from Atlanta . . . went to see some family, get more assistance with the article I'm working on." Joy seeped out and overflowed in her voice, and she couldn't help but giggle as her gaze landed on her flowers. "I also went to get my hair done."

"That's good," Arnetta said and sighed.

Darien looked at the telephone for a moment. What was up with that?

"Thank you for introducing us to Ted. He's wonderful."

Darien's mouth flew open. "Really?" she said, almost unable to recover.

"Really," Arnetta murmured. "Since the divorce, I haven't . . . He's nice, gurl. A great photographer and a true gentleman."

Combined laughter filled the line, and Darien went to the sofa and flopped on it, closing her eyes. "There's nothing like a real gentleman, Arnetta. I'm so glad he's one."

"Uhmmm-hmmm," Arnetta said, still giggling. "But I have to ask you a *big* favor, and you can say no if you want to, no pressure, but it would mean the world to me if you'd go to church with me Sunday."

For a moment, Darien couldn't answer. Arnetta had barely taken a breath as she'd rattled off the request. "To church?"

"I know it's a really big favor to ask, and I have no right, and I know, I know, it's last minute, you probably have a million things to do after already dealing with my crazy family, but I can't bring him to Doreetha's domain, have the man get shots of the Ferguson clan worshipping—"

"Ted is still in Macon? Oh, Lord . . ." Darien shot off the sofa and began walking in a circle. She wasn't casting aspersion on the situation; it was just that she hadn't expected the news, which could only mean one thing. She had to call Mavis, not to gossip, not to even tell Mavis that Ted was still there, but to get the low down on this man's information. It was not even about having her girl Arnetta possibly played.

"I know, I know," Arnetta said, her tone filled with both dread and excitement. "Please don't think poorly of me. I normally don't. It's just that—"

"No, girl, I ain't thinking like that," Darien said to reassure her. Man, could she relate!

"He said maybe he'd come to Sunday dinner at Doreetha's, too, to get a few last shots before he went back—and *all* my brothers will be there, Lord have mercy. I can't face them without backup, somebody on my side for once. Do you understand what I'm saying? Maxwell is the worst. He don't think anybody oughta be near me without putting a ring on my hand, first. Follow? Since I got divorced, all they can say is that the baby in the family don't know her own mind, and they'll act out in front of this man, girl, and I just need—"

"I gotchure back. I'll be there. 'Nuff said. What time's church—and what time's dinner?"

Chapter 9

"Let the church say, Amen," Reverend Mathis said in a deep, booming voice, standing slowly to unfurl his rotund frame from the high-back altar chair. He glanced first to his right and then to his left, nodding to his long row of deacons amid their approving "Amens," as he smoothed the front of his clerical robes, fingering the long, gold stole that swished as he approached the pulpit. "Sister Evelyn, you've been blessed with the voice of an angel, and the Daughters of the King done brought it home this morning. Amen, choir. Amen. Amen."

Darien swallowed a smile as she looked down at Arnetta's hand, which was squeezing hers so tightly it had almost lost all circulation. She could certainly understand because she must have been squeezing Arnetta's palm right on back just as hard.

Now, true, Ezekiel Tabernacle was on fire this morning, every choir outdoing the next, nearly rocking the building off the foundation. But with Ted going up and down the aisles, occasionally dropping to one knee, telephoto lens before him, matching the choirs' dramatic ensembles with theatrical camera work, magazine shutters going off like he was Hollywood paparazzi, blowing

minds and pumping egos, affecting even the good minister, what else could she do but smile?

Doreetha had a smug look of pure bliss on her face,
fanning herself, the outrageous peacock-blue plumes in
her mammoth hat jumping, but Sister Ferguson was in
her glory, do you hear. Darien bit her lower lip. Ms.
Doreetha had had a photographer from *Urban Professional*
on his knee before *her* minister, in *her* church, doing a
photo spread for *her* family—that was a stakeholder in the
church . . . shoot. Jesus might as well have come down off
the cross and anointed her himself.

Packaging. It was all packaging, how one presented
oneself, Darien thought, and just shook her head. If Ted
had taken some added liberties with Arnetta while in
town, brother was sure making good on whatever he'd
done to the Ferguson brothers' baby sister. But she'd
also never seen Ted look as completely serious, stricken
even, nervous, scared out of his mind. Dang, maybe the
boy had messed up and fallen in love.

However, she had to banish the concept. She couldn't
be thinking about love or anything else near the subject
while in church. Not! But she did glimpse down the row
of Fergusons. Every one of those brothers looked good,
wives dressed to the nines, children wiggling in their
pews. She tried to keep her gaze on the good reverend,
tried to listen to the message of faith, but her sideline
glance kept wandering to the end of the aisle.

What was she supposed to do when Maxwell had the
nerve to be sitting there looking so good, the muscle in
his jaw pulsing? French blue monogrammed shirt, gold-
and-blue paisley silk tie knotted just so, beneath a *fly*,
custom-tailored two-button navy suit . . . She thought
she'd slide out of the pew. Add the fact that when she'd
walked in there, if looks could have killed, she'd have
been dead a thousand times over. He'd barely said hello,
then had put enough distance between them to seem
unattached, which he was, but that didn't stop the fe-

male daggers and razor-eyed glances that had greeted her on a false, "Welcome to Ezekiel." No wonder he didn't deal with any of the hopefuls from Macon. Could she blame the man?

Every female in the place had cut her dead with one glare—their mommas, female cousins, aunts, all of them had looked like she'd come to town with handcuffs to shackle and drag their most eligible bachelor away to prison.

But if he wasn't dealing with anyone in town, then the alternative made her as nervous as Ted seemed to be. The brother had businesses up and down the eastern seaboard. Plus, he had locations in Atlanta—ouch. Atlanta women were awesome. Charlotte, Richmond—heaven help her, the sisters from Virginia's upper-crust rivaled Texas belles . . . DC—whoa, DC women were no joke. Professionals, upwardly mobile, she might be able to handle the stock in Philly as they didn't have southern roots, most likely—at least none that weren't a generation or two removed. But why was she even going there in church!

Maybe it was seeing Ted work so hard to make a good impression with the Ferguson clan, maybe it was the fact that she'd jumped up without a plan, taken her girl Arnetta's back, and was now committed to Sunday dinner in too-close proximity to the man she was supposed to be staying away from? Or maybe it was the fact that, in a panic, she'd driven out to the supermarket and brought Crisco and peaches, butter, eggs, brown sugar, and flour and walnuts and a cobbler pan to be able to come through Doreetha's door righteous, cobbler in hand, like her momma would have told her to do? Have mercy!

He didn't like this photographer's show off in church one bit, but it did have an amazing calming effect on his elder sister. So he'd suffer the fool who had been in his younger sister's face too much for his liking, and he would step to the man the old-fashioned way, if Arnetta had gotten played—and especially if he were the one who'd paid for the room! See, now, that wasn't right. But he wouldn't go there at the moment, not in church . . . 'cause the situation was making him wanna cuss out loud. The brother could take all the pictures he wanted, but Arnie wasn't no game, and the Ferguson boys would ride together and beat him down, if he was messin' with baby girl.

Maxwell studied Ted's expression as he took a close-up of the minister from a profile shot, noting how Rev puffed up a little and began waving his arms with more flair. Even the deacons sat up straighter each time Ted passed them by, and he thought Doreetha was gonna bust when Ted slipped behind the minister, pointed the lens over his shoulder, and took a frontal shot of the Ferguson clan sitting front and center in the packed house of God.

All he could hope was that he didn't act that way when Ted had turned his lens on him, especially not in front of Darien. But he wasn't going to look at girlfriend. Not today, and not in here. Not while she was sporting a mid-thigh high, winter-white Chanel mohair suit, hair smoothed back, Jackie Onassis or Lady Di classic style, pearls draped just so, natural-colored alligator pumps that showed off her gorgeous legs, matched her small Chanel bag and her back-kick pleated leather coat . . . smelling good enough to make him forget where he was. Pretty face made up, but not overdone. When she'd blown in the front door, he'd had to walk away. He was going to keep his focus and listen to the sermon. That was it.

But as he studied the way Ted glanced at Arnetta, every now and then, and the way she looked down at her hands, and the brother's jaw tensed, the familiarity of it all wore on his conscience. Well . . . maybe if he really liked his sister, Ted might pass muster. And, maybe, just maybe, if things had gotten a little crazy while Ted was in town but didn't go too far, he could understand it. Maybe.

Darien froze. Why was an usher coming toward her and looking at her—bringing her a microphone? *No, no, no, no no, Jesus, I know I've had unclean thoughts in your house, but do not out me like this!*

"I understand that we have two visitors from Atlanta," Reverend Mathis said. "This purty little lady can go first," he added, beaming. "Now, where's your church home."

Darien almost swallowed her tongue. "Mt. Zion—in Atlanta," she said in a very tiny voice. "Thank y'all for having me." She sat down so fast that she almost missed the red velvet surface of the pew. She glanced at Ted who seemed like he was about to hyperventilate as he gave his quick church home credentials. Her nails dug into her palms because she knew the next step was altar call.

She watched the massive choir rise. She watched the minister open his arms and lean his head back. She could hear Ted's magazine clicking. She could see deacons swaying, nurses preparing for the spirit to move people. And she had a very quick talk with the man upstairs about truly believing, but not wanting to go down to the rail, not wanting to fall on her knees, not wanting to grab hold of the minister's robes and go into a full confession in front of congregation of three thousand prayer warriors. Today was not the day to be getting' *the ghost!*

Twice she almost stood, especially when Reverend Mathis made an impassioned plea.

"Bring Him your burdens," he said, his voice straining above the choir as he implored people to get saved today—not tomorrow. "Let Him heal your wounded heart at the rail. Let His peace, which surpasses all understanding, come over you. He's the rock. When your momma is gone, when your daddy is gone, when your family just don't understand you, call Him . . . won't you come to the rail? He won't fail you!"

Darien had her eyes shut so tightly and was squeezing Arnetta's hand so tightly that she was seeing colors dance beneath her lids. Oh, no, not today . . .

"He *knows* you want to come, and you know pride goeth before a fall. He can clean up your bills, cancel your debt—because he already died to make you right and whole. He gave blood that will dry your tears! He stands for you so no one can stand against you!"

She was breathing hard. Nope. Wasn't going to no rail today. The *Amens* rang out, shrieks and wails of ecstatic jubilation, and *have mercies* rippled through the congregation. Minister was working hard today. There were special guests in the audience, and while the camera was clicking, he was going to bring a whole flock to the rail this morning. Darien steeled herself. Nope. Uh-uh. Not in front of all these folks.

"He can bring you a new attitude," the minister hollered, his voice cracking, beads of sweat now standing on his forehead as he paced. "If you've been lonely, he can bring a husband for you, a wife for you, children to the barren, health to the sick—He can lift up the load of misery and will carry your cross on His shoulders, if you will only give Him a chance this morning, hallelujah!"

Darien opened her eyes as her hand began to lift and she stared at Arnetta who'd stood, then had begun walking, holding on to her, about to drag her to the rail with her. No . . . Ted had started walking toward the minister, his lens down, tears streaming down his face. Oh, Lord . . . Maxwell glanced at her, her mouth was about to fly open when two Ferguson brothers calmly stood, got their sister by the shoulders, hugged her, and discretely sat her down.

The relief that washed through Darien almost made her call an aisle nurse. Instead she channeled the nervous energy into Arnetta's back, rubbing it to console Arnetta as much to console herself, and to keep her heart from stopping when Maxwell nodded a thank-you in her direction.

"Now *that* was church," Doreetha announced as the service concluded. She gave Arnetta a fishy glance. "Otis and Lewis probably should have let you go to the rail, *again*. But we wasn't trying to be embarrassed like that. What was the matter with you?"

"Can't be embarrassed to give it over to the Lord, now can you?" Jovan said, teasing Doreetha so she'd leave Arnetta alone as the family filed out.

Still too spent to speak, Darien just took it all in but remained mute. She simply gave Arnetta a reassuring hug as Doreetha strode past her, husband and children in tow. It was almost like walking with six-foot-tall bodyguards as the Ferguson brothers flanked all the women and children in the family, the numerous names, and which wife went with which Ferguson, all too much to absorb while walking, talking, shaking hands, and trying to recover from a near personal public spectacle—especially while remembering that she was not supposed to be looking at Maxwell.

"Girl, I almost lost it and went to the rail," Arnetta whispered as she and Darien stood in the throng waiting to greet Reverend Mathis.

"I know, chile, and almost drug me up there with you."

"I know. I'm sorry," Arnetta said, giggling. "I was moved, girl."

"You made Ted go down there and break down—whatchu do to the man?" Darien asked, not really needing an answer, but in all her years, she'd never witnessed anything like it. In just a week?

"We just bonded," Arnetta said, her line of vision leaving Darien to sweep Ted, who seemed recovered, but also appeared to now be hiding behind his lens.

What could Darien say? She nodded, wondering if a man could really bond, beyond just a sexual exploit that fast with someone he didn't know, and hoping with all her heart that a man could.

"So, another visitor from up north," Reverend Mathis said, opening his arms for Darien to fill. "Welcome." He held her back from him and nodded with approval. "You make a nice addition to Macon. I was trying to draw you to the rail today—hope you'll stay with us for a while."

"I'm here on temporary assignment," Darien hedged, glancing at Arnetta and then, oddly, Doreetha for support. "But I am very pleased to be here. You made me feel welcomed today."

"She's practically family, Pastor," Arnetta said fast, her gaze darting to her brother Maxwell. "She's coming to Doreetha's for dinner."

From the corner of her eye, Darien saw Maxwell stiffen and begin walking.

"Well, that's only hospitable, and I wouldn't expect anything less of the Fergusons." The minister gave Darien a wide smile and he glanced at Maxwell, who had conveniently melted into a throng of churchgoers. He patted Darien's hand and leaned in. "He works in mysterious ways and hears all prayer—whether you come to the rail or not."

This was not in his plans. Doreetha and Arnetta had to be out of their minds, asking the woman to dinner. It was out of order, not appropriate. Sunday was supposed to be a day of rest. And he had some fool photographer trying to push up on his baby sister, too? The man had lost his mind, went and got saved, and was now sitting on the sofa with him and his brothers in his elder sister's living room, with her husband, too—like he was family.

The knot in Maxwell's shoulders had worked its way down his back. And they had Darien hemmed up in the kitchen with the women? This was bad. He could feel it in his bones; they were plottin' and tryin' to get in his personal life, and he wasn't having it!

"Why'lln't you have a beer, Max?" Jovan said, bringing him one with a dashing smile. "Doreetha's got a ham in the oven, and I hear tell, she's got yams going, string beans, macaroni and cheese, her famous biscuits, and this might help you wash it all down while we watch the game."

Maxwell stood, accepted the beer, and walked toward the porch. "Thanks. I ain't really that hungry."

Jovan smiled, cocked his head to the side, and abandoned Ted and his other brothers to follow Maxwell. He glanced back, and broad grins met him as the men in the room shook their heads, then turned their attention on Ted.

"Hold up, Max. Can't two brothers drink a beer together?"

Maxwell sighed and leaned against the enclosed porch rail. He took a generous swig of his beer, winced, and looked out at the front lawn. He could hear football echoing through the house, mixing with the hubbub of child-produced laughter that darted between the wafting scents of good cooking coming from the back of the house.

"She brought Doreetha a cobbler, man," Jovan said in a sheepish voice.

"I know, and I don't wanna talk about it," Maxwell said in a surly tone. "She shouldn't even be here, truth be told."

"Why not?"

Jovan's wide smile was getting on his nerves.

"Because she works for the company, man."

"And? Like we don't have folks from the job to dinner from time to time? Or, we never throw a barbecue for—"

"That's different."

"Why?"

"Because it is."

Jovan nodded. "You like her that much, huh?"

Maxwell stared at his brother and refused to answer him.

"Max, she's real nice. We all like her, too."

"What does the fact that you all like her have to do with me?" Maxwell shook his head and took another swig of his beer.

"You know, if she can last in Doreetha's kitchen and through dinner, she's got the green light."

"I don't know what you're talking about." Maxwell shifted and went to the front door.

"You know I'ma ask my wife how the girl made out as soon as we get in the car, then I'ma call you to give you the low down." Jovan chuckled and went to Maxwell and punched his shoulder. "Man, she was drop-dead fine in the white suit, but then when everybody went home and changed, and girlfriend came back with the slacks and figure-hugging sweater, I thought y'all was gonna hafta call nine-one-one."

"Want me to tell Wynetta that, too—when y'all get in the car?"

Jovan laughed hard. "Man, don't even play. You know how my wife is—don't get her started. But there ain't no denying, the girl is *superfine.*" He winked at Maxwell and tipped his beer in his direction. "Thought we was gonna see you go to the rail this morning—I'da went and got saved for her."

Maxwell had to laugh. The thought had crossed his mind as he'd felt the muscles in his legs begin to push him to stand. Thankfully his brain overrode the errant thought. But Jovan needed to stop picking at the fresh scab. "Yeah, well, I'm not worrying about me getting saved," he said, deflecting the issue of Darien. "I'm worried about that photographer in there being so moved he had to go lean on the cross this morning." Maxwell nodded toward Ted and let his breath out hard. "I don't want him playing Arnie."

"I feel you," Jovan said, clinking Maxwell's bottle. "Well, if he can hang through the football game with us out there and dinner, brother might be the real McCoy. Wanna go check him out?"

"Done," Maxwell muttered, and walked back into the living room.

"I don't need no desert," Doreetha fussed as Darien set the cobbler down on the kitchen table. "I already made a lemon-butter pound cake, and Arnetta oughta had told you, I don't let nobody back here to mess in my pots but family. So, you just go on out there in the living room, and when dinner is ready, everyone will be called."

All amiable chatter stopped. Five sets of wise, wifely eyes looked up from various cooking tasks, their gaze darting between Darien, Arnetta, and Doreetha. It was as though they'd all been through the same test before, but Darien hadn't a clue about how to handle it. She glanced at Arnetta for support, but she shrugged and looked down. The silent message was clear: *I got you in, girlfriend, but you have to hold your own. If it gets real ugly, I've got your back . . . but then your position from that point forward will be a vulnerable one.*

"I understand, Doreetha," Darien finally said as gently as possible, thinking of her own sister Cynthia. A black woman's kitchen was the proving ground. "I just know that you've worked so hard all week and put so much into the church on the weekend . . . I didn't want to come here emptyhanded. That just wouldn't have been right."

Darien carefully uncovered the oblong Pyrex dish when Doreetha didn't respond. "Maybe you could just donate it to the women's guild bake sale or something because I know it doesn't hold a candle to your pound cake. That's something I never learned to make."

Doreetha's gaze softened a bit, and she waved Darien's compliment away. "Ain't nothin' to pound cake. That's easy. A cobbler takes work. Gotta baby the crust, can't play with it too much or ya jus' mess it up." Like a USDA food inspector, Doreetha sauntered over to Darien's creation and tilted her head. "You got a nice crust on here. But the proof will be when you cut it and see what's inside."

Darien felt like her legs would go out from under her. Everything that was being said today seemed as though it meant so much more than what was on the surface. "I hope it's right, Doreetha," she said, her voice soft as she looked down at her cobbler. "I tried real hard, and I did it from memory. My momma ain't here to really show me how. But if it's not what you expected, you tell me, and maybe I could learn from you some?"

All eyes were on Doreetha. Arnetta seemed like she was holding her breath. Doreetha finally sighed and nodded, and grabbed a colander filled with raw, unsnapped beans.

"Oh, if it ain't right, *I'll* be the *first* let you know— trust me. But, until we get there, you go on wash your hands, then set yourself down and help them get these beans ready for the pot. I should have done these yesterday, but had a lot of other chores to do and got behind."

"It's going to be all right, girlfriend," Arnetta whispered as they carried platters to the table. "You did fine.

Nobody *ever* got into Doreetha's kitchen on the first pass." Arnetta blew out a long breath. "Girl, if it wasn't for how you made her look good in church, I don't know if your cobbler would have got put on the sideboard today."

Darien nodded, but didn't fully understand. "I didn't bring the photographer to church."

"Shush," Arnetta warned. "That's between me and you."

Darien hurried to set her platter down without another word, taking silent direction from the other seating of the wives. She wasn't sure where to sit, but knew the head and foot belonged to Doreetha and her husband. She had enough sense to know that where each woman sat, a male went by her side. Children had been quarantined to the younguns' table. Okay. She knew how this went at Cynthia's. But Ted seemed as unsure as she did, and Maxwell offered no help or direction. There was no way to tell if he was testing her, Ted, or them both. His expression was totally unreadable, and his distant vibe was grating her nerves.

"Doreetha, where would you have us sit?" Darien asked brightly, not wanting to offend, but growing weary from the unknowable family customs.

"I made space for you and Ted at the end," Doreetha said with a wave of her hand. "Get settled so we can eat."

Interesting. Doreetha had made Darien and Ted a couple of sorts and had put Arnetta and Maxwell together.

Complying without resistance, Darien sat and noted how all the men fell in, taking seats after all the women had. She bowed her head through grace and watched Doreetha's husband carve up the ham like he'd done it a thousand times. But there was no mistaking who was the head male at the table, regardless of Wilbur's seating. From a detached place in her mind, she watched Maxwell get served first after she and Ted were given first plates as honorary guest status preempted the normal flow. Then as if by some invisible pecking order of things, each brother and his wife got served in turn.

Determined to keep the conversation light, Darien complimented Doreetha profusely—and it was no act. The woman could burn. Her yams made Darien close her eyes twice, and the butter oozing off the macaroni and cheese was ridiculous. But the ham made her stop and put her fork down.

"Doreetha," Darien said, no fraud in her tone, "if this is what you whipped up being busy, I don't know what you'd do if you had time."

"No lie," Ted added, not even looking up from his plate. "Ma'am, your cooking will make a man hurt himself trying to scarf down a plate."

Doreetha folded her arms over her chest, and a slight smile came out on her face. "It's nice to have company that appreciates what I do. These folks around here just take it all for granted."

Something so familiar echoed through Darien's mind as she looked at Doreetha. She shook her head. "All the work you do, and what you have done for the church, then prepare a feast like this . . . I'll wash *all* your dirty dishes for allowing me to sit at your table."

"I can't let you do that," Doreetha said, nearly blushing. "I don't mind feeding folks. You could put on a few pounds, so if you ever get hungry, you have a standing offer to come on and break some bread here."

Doreetha glanced at Maxwell who had a fork midair. Arnetta was coughing, having swallowed her iced tea the wrong way.

"You know, Ezekiel ain't never gonna be the same after today," Doreetha said, her chin thrust up high. "The Fergusons made history in there—Ezekiel ain't never been in no magazine. That was real Christian of y'all. Pastor like to fell out, preaching like he was a young buck again." She chuckled and shook her head, then passed the macaroni to Ted. "Now you just go on and have your fill. My brothers and my husband eat like this all the time."

Knowing it was the moment of truth, Ted accepted a heaping spoonful upon conferring a thank-you directed at Doreetha.

"Oh, so now we don't matter, Dor?" Jovan said, with a smile, motioning for the huge bowl.

That's right. Pass them snap beans down here," Otis said, seeming relieved that a good judgment on the guests had prevailed.

"Can a brother get some more ham, girl. Dang," Odell fussed.

As biscuits and yams and iced tea were passed, Darien noted how silent Maxwell had been. His comments were minimal, his focus on his plate, only occasionally glancing up to study Ted, and then returning to the task of eating. And she had to remember where she was, had to not look at him in his sweater and jeans, had to keep her eyes fixed on her hostess and on Arnetta, and make small talk with the wives. It was not about creating any wrong move that could be taken the wrong way.

"So, how long you in town for?" Maxwell asked out of the blue, his gaze boring into Ted.

Ted had a mouthful of yams, and looked like he was torn between swallowing them without chewing and accidentally spitting them out.

"Oh, uh, I'm leaving right after dinner," Ted mumbled, trying to quickly answer the big dog at the table in a timely fashion.

Arnetta blanched. There was nothing Darien could do.

"You coming back any time soon?" Jovan asked, taking a sip of iced tea without looking at Ted.

"Uh, sure—to bring everybody their contacts sheets . . . proofs from all the shots I took."

"That's why they have Federal Express," Otis said, stretching and glancing at Maxwell.

"Most of what you took is digital, right?" Lewis said, shoveling food in his mouth. "Could just e-mail them, right, Monty? You know how to open those files."

"Yep," Monty said, rubbing his belly. "Just sent a TIFF file down the wire."

"Don't see no reason for you to travel all that way, unless you have another reason to be in Macon." Odell's glance went from Ted to Maxwell, then back to Arnetta before he bit into a biscuit.

"He's going to come back so I can meet with him," Darien said quickly, trying to rescue Arnetta's date. She hadn't thought out her statement, and she immediately knew it was the wrong thing to say when Maxwell leaned forward, put his fork down, and made a tent with his fingers over his plate.

"Why?" Maxwell stared at her. The conversation came to a screeching halt.

"Because I need some shots to develop your brochures and website . . . maybe he and I will go up to your various sites, like in Atlanta and North Carolina and—"

"Yeah, next week, Mr. Ferguson. I can hang with Darien. We'll spend the night up in—"

"Not a good plan," Maxwell said flatly, and began eating, but no one else moved.

"If it's the cost," Ted pressed on, not realizing the blunder, "because of the size of this spread, I'm sure they'll cover the expense."

Maxwell pushed his plate away from him, and his gaze landed on Darien. "How long you talking about going for?"

"Well," she stammered, glancing at Doreetha and Arnetta, "we could do Atlanta with a drive, then hop over to High Point, North Carolina, press on to Charlotte. That would be one full day. Then hit Richmond and DC in a session. That would be another day," she said, tick-ing off the itinerary, making it up as she went along. "Then from there, we could drive up to Baltimore together, do that site, and finish up in Philadelphia, but that would be another day. I don't know. We could have it done by Friday, at the latest."

Maxwell leaned back in his chair, his gaze going past everyone at the table as he looked toward the kitchen. "I was planning on going to all the sites next week myself." He looked at Otis.

"You did say you was thinking about stopping by all the locations. Would make sense for you to be in every shot."

"If you're worried about getting what you want from what they do together maybe if you went with 'em, that might set your mind at ease." Jovan offered a shrug, then wiped his mouth to hide his smile.

"I might just do that," Maxwell said in a low rumble, his line of vision sweeping to Ted and staying there.

"Well, if we're gonna get good shots of each of the brothers at the various locations, and if Ted has already gotten Doreetha here in Macon . . . maybe it would make sense for Arnetta to go, at least to the real estate holdings in Atlanta and Baltimore. That way, Ted could get her in front of your first major building—the complex up there."

"I can make time in my schedule," Arnetta said fast, her eyes darting toward Wilbur for support.

"Yeah," Wilbur said, his slow, thick drawl coming from behind a yawn. "Can't leave baby girl out of the pictures for the magazines. Wouldn't be right."

As though the lid to Pandora's box had been lifted, each wife chimed in with her own endorsement for the trip.

Doreetha and Arnetta exchanged a glance. Doreetha smiled.

"Well, now that that's settled, we have some dessert," Doreetha announced.

"I'm full," Maxwell said, pushing his chair back and grabbing his plate.

"Darien brought a peach-walnut cobbler made from scratch."

Maxwell stopped mid-stride, but didn't turn around to look at Doreetha. The fact that Doreetha had put a foreign dessert over her own traditional lemon-butter pound cake was not lost on him in the least. "From scratch, huh?"

"From *scratch*," Arnetta said, with emphasis.

Jovan laughed. "Man, sit your rusty butt down in the chair and act like you know."

Dinner had been a total disaster as far as he could tell. His brother Jovan had turned on him—as did the others, even the stalwart one in the family, Doreetha, had. Wilbur wasn't any help, never was, and his nieces and nephews fawned over Darien like she was a movie star. One pimple-faced, knuckleheaded preteen had almost walked into a door when he'd seen her. Pitiful, but he could understand the boy's plight.

The entire travesty was making him lose focus as the eldest brother in the family. He'd stepped up to protect his baby sister's honor and wound up getting roped into a trip that he was supposed to be taking alone. And now he was sitting at the table, in front of family, with the best peach cobbler he'd ever had melting in his mouth, sitting next to the finest woman he'd ever been that close to.

It was taking all of his mental reserves just trying to remain as annoyed as he should have been that his personal space had been invaded. But resistance seemed futile—Darien Jackson had already invaded every sense he owned.

Her laughter was making him weak in the knees. The way she fit in so perfectly and was buzzing up and down from the table, assisting the other wives, was making him delirious. But her cobbler was beating him down. Fine as she was, and could burn, too? Had been allowed in Doreetha's kitchen? How was he supposed to stay away from her, in close quarters, maybe flying and driving together, eating together, and staying in hotels together, but semichaperoned by a photographer who needed to stay out of his sister's drawers?

But worrying about what Arnetta got herself into was becoming a very fuzzy concern as Darien flopped down on the sofa, leaned her head back, and rubbed her belly with a sigh.

"Doreetha, I'm done. Just stick a fork in me."

Doreetha chuckled and shook her head as she stood and headed for the kitchen. Jovan nearly spit out his beer but recovered before his wife saw him.

Jovan locked gazes with Maxwell for a second. "Man, enjoy your trip, hear?"

No, he didn't *hear*, and wasn't listening to a thing Jovan was implying. Ted and Arnetta were off in a cozy conversation on the porch; his other brothers were sprawled out all over the house, totally off the mission. The littlest children were beginning to show signs of fatigue—tantrums, wailing, starting to get their legs popped by overtired mothers. The preteens were in the basement with videos and computer games, loud music thumping. His brother-in-law was in a recliner, snoring. Jovan was teasing him, all out in the open, while the girl stretched out her long, lovely body, then tucked her legs beneath her, and dozed.

God, she was pretty when she slept.

Jovan nodded, as though reading his mind.

"I hear you," Maxwell murmured, not taking his eyes off Darien.

"A man's had a long day, got a full belly, and a pretty wife . . . time for me to get my hat and act like I know." Jovan stood and stretched, his gaze following behind his wife who was carrying a sleepy toddler. "Get little man down early, a brother might get lucky, if she ain't too tired." He pounded Maxwell's fist with a smile and glanced at Darien. "It ain't all that bad, you know—the state of matrimony. That's all I'ma say."

His brother loped away, and Maxwell watched him kiss his son's forehead, encircling his wife's waist from behind as she shooed him and giggled softly. Like a spectator, he sat watching each brother get collected from a chair with a gentle kiss from a wife or a tug from a child, and he watched his sleepy brothers stand, put an arm around a no longer slender waist, but their expressions contained nothing short of sheer bliss. When he watched his brother-in-law rouse himself, pushing up from the recliner with a grunt and then amble toward the kitchen, he was done. Maxwell glimpsed his baby sister. Her face was lit up as a new suitor leaned in close, the couple hanging on each other's every word.

It was impossible to keep his line of vision away from Darien as she peacefully dozed. If things had been different, he would have awakened her with a kiss . . . if they had been alone, he would have slid beside her, spooning her lush form, kissing the nape of her neck until she awakened, breathless, sated from the day and dinner, shooing him away but yielding the whole while. How did a man find a patch for his heart to cover that raw wound or find the discipline to keep his distance from something like that? And how did a man walk out the door, get into a car by himself and drive all the way home—alone—to come home to what? Work all night?

She stirred when a cool blast of air from the opening front door made her shiver. She wasn't sure how long she was out, but one shoe precariously dangled from her foot, the other one had slipped off, and as she sleepily peered around, she gathered her wits, hoping she hadn't had her mouth open.

As she looked up bleary-eyed, the last person she expected to be sitting in a chair across from her smiled. But his expression was so intense, for a moment, she couldn't move. She tried to diffuse the situation with humor, hunting for her lost shoe. "I wasn't catching flies with my mouth open, was I?"

Maxwell just shook his head, stood, and came over to her.

The man had blinked slowly. She'd heard him release a slow breath through his nose as he approached, and the whole way he walked toward her was slowly driving her nuts. This was not good. Not up here in Doreetha's house.

"Good golly, Miss Molly, your sister can cook," she said quickly, smoothing back her mussed hair. "Made the shoes drop off my feet. Now *that's* a cook, when everybody just falls out after dinner."

"It's under the couch," he said low in his throat, then got down on one knee and fished it out for her.

"Thanks," she said fast, noting that he was still on one knee holding the shoe.

It was reflex. What could he do? He looked at her pretty foot covered in a sheer stocking, the island palm trees on her toes calling his name. The silver ring had drawn his attention, but as he cupped the soft skin to slide on her shoe, he couldn't. He just held her foot for a moment, the sunset, the blue water, the butter softness of her foot burning his hand like hot Caribbean sand.

He slid his palm down her heel, under the arch of her foot, over the ball of it and looked up at her as he glided the shoe onto it. "Do you want to go home?"

The shiver the sensual touch sent through her almost made her cry out. Instead she bit her lip and nodded.

"So do I. Almost everybody is gone," he said, his tone thick and low and husky.

"I have to say good-bye to your sister and her husband, and to whomever else is still here."

He stood, nodded, and began walking. "I'll go fetch your coat."

It took her a moment to move. The desire was blatant, the intent unmistakable, and yet she knew it must have taken more than she could ever fathom for him to just step to her like that. Here.

"We're pulling out, Doreetha," he said, kissing his sister on the cheek and shaking his brother-in-law's hand.

Doreetha looked at him hard, but her gaze was soft. She opened her mouth, and then pressed one finger to her lips for a moment. "Y'all drive safe. Everybody is sleepy and has had a long day."

Maxwell nodded, his eyes never leaving Darien's. "I'll follow her home, to make sure she gets there all right."

Chapter 10

The blast of chilly night air had helped a little, as did the lingering good-bye rounds she'd made. Things couldn't just look all inappropriate, she reasoned, despite the fact that Maxwell seemed singularly focused on getting her away from Doreetha's house. They had to play it off, a little, at least. But now that she was close to her apartment, she was holding the steering wheel so tightly she had white knuckles.

Darien glanced in her rearview mirror as Maxwell's car pulled up in the driveway behind hers. Now what? There'd be this awkward moment when a decision would have to be made, or something said, so that everyone was clear . . . or . . . aw, she didn't know!

So she waited for him to walk up to her door, as she expected he might. She rolled down her window, thinking of something witty to say. "Thanks for seeing me home, Maxwell . . . that was real nice of you." She could have kicked herself as he opened the door and she stepped out. "Uh, I might still have a beer up there, from when you brought some over, if you want it." Nerves were making her run her mouth a mile a minute.

He hadn't moved, just shook his head, and had her

body blocked between him and the open door. He put one finger to her lips. "I asked you if you wanted to go home. Do you still want to go?"

She blinked twice, glanced over her shoulder to her apartment, his intense gaze almost too hot to keep looking at as she returned to it. "I guess so," she said as his finger fell away from her mouth.

"Then I'll drive you there," he said so quietly, she could barely hear him.

The man had out and out propositioned her. After they said they'd allow it to cool down. Had practically ignored her all day, wouldn't even look at her as she'd eaten at his sister's table, but was now looking at her like he could sop her up with one of Doreetha's biscuits.

"But—"

He had tilted his head so slightly, closed his eyes ever so slowly, and had come in to kiss her so gently . . . right out in the street that, anything she was about to say, she just plum forgot.

Then she remembered something really important. "I have to meet Mavis's deadline, or this is all for naught."

"When's it due?" He'd breathed the question more than asked it.

"Monday, by three P.M."

"Then you've got plenty of time." His hand trembled as he pushed a stray wisp of hair away from her cheek, then touched it, his eyes never leaving hers.

"We just committed to go to Atlanta with Ted and Arnetta . . . and I need time to write it up tonight."

"Take a laptop and write it on the drive up. I promise I won't say a word while you're working."

Was he insane? Like she'd be able to think, much less breeze into Mavis's office after being with him all night. "I don't know . . . and . . ." Her words trailed off as she stared at him.

"You gonna be able to concentrate on work tonight?"

His eyes searched hers for the truth, then delivered it on a hoarse whisper. "I sure can't."

She felt the last of her resistance to the inevitable peel away as he stepped in closer, his body shielding hers from the cold. She shook her head. "I can't think about nothin' but you."

"Then let me take you home," he said quietly. "Please. Even if just for tonight."

Her hand slipped into his by itself. Her mind was oatmeal, and her knees weren't much better as she closed her car door, depressed the alarm, and followed him to his. On what felt like a very long ride to a destination not far away, they said nothing, not even music entering their private space. Her hand rested on his thigh, and he intermittently swallowed hard, as though struggling to breathe.

When he helped her out of the car, his arm tentatively slid around her waist, and she cautiously leaned in to him, glad that he'd convinced her, although unnerved at the same time. Once inside the massive foyer, she wasn't quite sure what to do. He'd come up behind her and slid her coat from her shoulders, placing a gentle kiss on the nape of her neck. He hadn't turned on the lights, as though he'd come into this same space so often before in the dark. She heard her coat hit a chair. A gentle caress ran down her arms, his palms flattened until they enfolded her hands.

"Let's go upstairs," he murmured into her ear.

She didn't move, her body and mind needing time to process that this was going to happen, and that tomorrow there'd be no going back to the way things were before it did.

"You all right?' he asked, his kiss placed on her shoulder, his breath hot through the fabric of her sweater.

She nodded, dropped her purse, and leaned back against his warmth. "I'm all right—you?"

His arms enfolded her, and he shook his head slowly. "I ain't been all right since I met you, girl."

It was the answer she needed to hear, especially at this moment. She could feel it yield her body into a tightening embrace, made her inhale deeply, take in his earthy, male scent fused with cologne. A rough nuzzle at her neck drew a whimper, and the sound she'd made seemed to give him the courage to turn her around. A gentle kiss landed on her forehead, her eyelids, and the bridge of her nose, then sought her mouth. She could feel him peeling away his jacket, heard it drop on the floor, the more frantic the kiss became. Her hands found his back, and his traveled down hers, then his palms landed on her buttocks, and he forced her to swallow his moan.

"Let's go upstairs," he whispered hard against her hairline.

She couldn't even answer as he took her hand, drew her through the dark space, and she blindly followed him. Small hall lights greeted her when she got to the top of the stairs, and his palm lit a fire in the dip of her spine as he led her with a gentle guide forward, feeling a sense of urgency just under the surface of their skins.

Yet it felt like such a long, slow walk as he stroked her hair, kissed her temple hard, tried to continue walking without stopping, tried to keep forward progression, but seemed as though he couldn't help touching her. And her hand couldn't get enough of his waist as it slid up and down the fabric of his sweater, frustrating her fingers, which needed to touch his skin.

Nothing but moon and starlight offered illumination as her vision adjusted to the dim blue tinge of it in the room. She could make out the bed, a huge picture window seeming to frame the heavens. But even in the semidarkness, there was no mistaking the blaze of sheer desire in his eyes.

She didn't need to see it to know that it was there.

She could feel it in every agonized breath he drew, could feel it through his chest as his heart thudded loud and hard and strong. It made her step out of her shoes, and she could hear him step out of his. She could tell it by his trembling touch that cupped her behind, and how he rubbed the palms of his hands in circles against it as he nuzzled her neck. It was so very, very clear in the way his muscles moved in his back, his skin on fire, igniting hers, as he pulled his sweater over his head, almost wincing as his hands briefly left her body only long enough to pull off her sweater, and then resumed their search and fumble for the back hooks of her bra that weren't there.

He didn't need to see as her hands reached up and claimed his to help guide them to the front clasp that had evaded him. But Lord knows, he wished he could see in the dark as the sheer fabric dropped to the floor and her smooth round breasts filled his hands. His dilemma was palpable, to remove his hands so that he could finish undressing her, or to continue to cup her softness within them. The decision was too steep, too difficult a climb from where he was now standing . . . he couldn't tear himself away immediately. As a compromise upon her gasp, he bent his head, rubbed his face against the place he'd so wanted to indulge, and stripped her jeans away from her as quickly as he could.

Common sense said to slow down; her hands at his belt, tugging on his zipper shredded common sense. It made no sense at all that he couldn't catch his breath when his body slid against hers again, smooth, bare skin buckling his knees, making him lift her up and carry her forward. Long, silky legs wrapped around his waist, taking a part of his sanity in the process, making him stagger under the weight of his own desire, making him fall with her against a bed he was glad was left unmade.

He didn't need to see as his hands were torched by hot melted butter, her skin so soft that it brought tears to his eyes. He had found the islands, her island, paradise blue water lapping him between her legs, her pedicure the map to hidden treasures. And he didn't need vision, his nose was his guide, dragging him across every wondrous scented inch of her torso, her arch like a returned kiss as he found her navel, her voice a vice grip on his senses, locking in on a decibel that echoed through the room as his lips found a place that he'd wondered about the night before . . . her thong not worth the bother to remove, time being of the essence and the essence of her driving him crazy.

Sheets tangled in her fists, her voice sounding like it was coming from a woman she didn't know. She didn't require vision to have a nervous breakdown in his arms. He didn't need to see her eyes crossed, her mouth open, panting, trying to recover from the first climax before crashing headlong into the next. Tears streaming from the corners of her eyes, ruining mascara with it. She didn't care. He could see whatever he liked, as long as he didn't stop.

His name came out, sputtered. The sound of his wet, languid kisses fused with her hissing inhale . . . it was the kind of sound that a man didn't need to see to know, or to make him react, to change his direction, make him strip a gear, moving with a quickness to find the box that could end the suffering, mayhaps prolong it, he wasn't sure, as he yanked the drawer of the nightstand out, dumping contents till his hand landed on the box. And all he could see from his peripheral vision was the moonlight washing the length of her blue frosted beauty, her breasts rising and falling to the elevated blood pressure he'd produced, her legs spread, knees bent, impatient as his too-tight muscles almost made him drop the package twice from trembling hands, needing to breathe through his nose not to rush and possibly sheath himself with a rip.

But as he returned to her, blanketing her, he hesitated for a moment, now needing to see every facet of her. The moon and stars had not betrayed him nor rendered him blind. He traced her cheek, noting the tears glittering in her eyes, her thick, gorgeous spill of hair against his pillows, her lush lips parted. His hand slid down her delicate throat as his palm covered her breast, her hard arch a compliment that he returned with a kiss as his fingertips found the curve of her hip and her thigh lifted for him, her gentle tug at his shoulders a plea to not take so long.

She could see it all now, no longer blind as he looked down at her, his body covering hers, his eyes closing from desire as she lifted her backside hard so he could sink deep and fast. It was all over his face, the excruciating pleasure. She watched his head drop back, his mouth open on a low gasp, saw his arms tremble not from his own weight, but as the sensation ripped through him and tore into her. A sheen of ecstasy-induced sweat had turned his whole body into polished marble under the blue-white light of the moon.

She could barely stand to watch his expression as tears stood in his eyes then ran down his face as a shudder claimed him and his head tilted, he sharply sucked in a breath like a man drowning, and coming up for air, his gaze now leveled on her, intense. That's when she'd seen all that she needed to witness.

Her hands found the small of his back, muscles beneath taut skin grinding out a rhythm of pure work ethic, his full mouth punishing hers till her calves replaced her hands, his shoulders their new perch, a force of entry and exit so demanding that it almost lifted her up off the mattress. Her name stuttered with broken breaths let her know he wasn't playing, never had been. His grip on her gathering her body, sheets, the comforter, dragging her up and down with each thrust that sent her voice from her throat with abandon, crushed the air from her lungs, sent her fingers to rake his hair, made her lose all sense of control or inhibitions, took her to the rail, made her call on Jesus, had her losing her mind, spasm after spasm rocking her world, making her see lights beneath her lids, had her begging him to stop one moment, then in the next breath begging him not to, creating seizurelike sensations, her voice hitting notes that could shatter the window.

Moving under him like that, her voice driving him like that, hard, her breathing like that, and feeling like that, and calling his name like that, he couldn't take it. "C'mon, baby." She felt so good, like hot, liquid butter, and smelled so good, all in his arms and wetting up his sheets. "C'mon, baby, let it go for me." And her hands, her hands, Lord, Jesus, her hands, just taking him through changes with every hard pull against him.

It had been so long, but it had never been like this; he had no frame of reference, much less any discipline or control. His body belonged to her. She had stripped him of all dominion when she arched up hard, moaned deep, his name colliding with her breath, bouncing off his eardrums and dazing him. "Oh, baby, c'mon."

He shuddered so hard, and his head jerked with such a snap when the first ecstasy convulsion hit him, he almost bit his tongue. Sudden tremors followed, forcing him to simply lie in her arms, breathing hard, comforted by her soothing touch as it ran up and down his spine. Rivulets of sweat coursed down his temples, his shoulders, his chest, and his back. He couldn't move. Wouldn't have wanted to if he could. The pleasure she'd unleashed in him came from way down in her delta, there was no escaping it, even if he'd tried. This woman was the essence of Deep South.

With great effort, he tried to roll off her and gave up by simply pulling her limp body on top of his. It was too painful to pull out—too soon, he couldn't do it. He wanted to stay there, marinating, fused to her, feeling her muscles twitch and contract around him till new tears rose in his eyes.

He pet her silky, damp hair, loved that all the pins had dropped from it, loved that she was rag weary, and was too pleased that she could barely lift her chin. He kissed the crown of her head as she snuggled against him; her body fit against his so perfectly, her cheek finding that just-right spot on his chest. Oh, yeah . . . he wasn't playing, never had been. This was *the one*, and he wasn't even afraid to admit it at the moment. This is what he'd been missing in his life—she was like air, a requirement to live. Darien was a necessity. His priorities shifted right then, just as she'd shifted her weight.

"Baby, you all right?" he murmured

"Yeah . . . you?" she whispered soft and low.

"Yeah . . ." he murmured from way down in his throat. "Girl . . ."

"Uhmmm-hmmm, but I don't think I can write that article tonight. Tomorrow is dubious, at best."

She kissed his shoulder, his chuckle deep and slow and vibrating through her skin. She leaned up and found his mouth, and his response was almost frightening. She'd expected to brush his mouth and doze, but instead his gaze became intense, he leaned up, and pulled her beneath him.

"If you're going to miss your deadline, might as well make it worth the trouble, right?"

Her eyes opened wide as his hand slid down her body and back up again. "But . . ."

"I know," he said in a tense whisper. "I don't know what's the matter with me, but I can't get enough of you."

Stunned speechless and flattered silly, she smiled as he leaned over toward the light, his hand resting on the lamp switch.

"Can I?"

"You're gonna turn on the light . . . now?" She dabbed her eyes, knowing smeared makeup had turned her into a raccoon.

He kissed her nose, then nuzzled her neck. "Yeah, I wanna turn on the light. Don't you know how beautiful you are?"

He could feel his pulse quicken as her thighs tightened around him.

"I'm not sure my eyes are ready for the glare," she said, her breath a hot, whispered plea against his ear.

His mouth went dry, and he quickly nodded. Forget the light. "Make you a compromise," he said, finding her ear to whisper his message into it as he moved against her slowly. "Stay until morning, have breakfast with me . . . make love to me when the sun comes up, too."

Her hand found his cheek as a shudder ran through her. No man had ever asked her to stay beyond dawn, and definitely not like that. "I'll stay as long as you like, even though I know we have to be discreet."

He couldn't bring himself to stop moving, although he knew he eventually had to. The box on the floor was beckoning him, but so were her smoky hazel eyes sparkling in the moonlight. "Then stay for permanent," he heard himself say, no judgment left to argue with his heart. A pleasure spike was crawling up his back one vertebra at a time, making it near impossible to think and talk and move against her or garner logic while her body worked. "I don't care what people think," he heard himself say. "Darien, just tell me what you want, and it's done." His face was burning up, her fever all-consuming as it raged through him.

What was he saying? She couldn't think while he was moving against her; she could halfway catch her breath. Stay permanent, did he say? He didn't care what people thought . . . "Maxwell, we have to . . ." Her voice was breaking up, just like any coherence she once had. "What do you want?"

"You, baby," he murmured hard and pulled out.

He braced himself on the bedpost, his breathing ragged as he grabbed the box on the floor and found some tissues. She stared at his profile in the semi-darkness, his serious expression seeming pained as he put on a new layer of protection. He glanced up at her for a moment before coming back to sink against her warmth, but when he did, his touch was so gentle that it was as though he were handling fragile glass.

"I want a family," he murmured hard against her cheek, "somebody to fill this house up with laughter, to fill my life up, and I don't wanna play games, deal with drama, or be a bachelor all my life. I want to put my arms around you after dinner . . . I want to tuck our children into bed and then savor every inch of you." He let his breath out in a rush, his voice catching in his throat. "Oh, girl, I'm so tired, you can't even imagine."

Although his words were terrifying, she nuzzled his neck and kissed his face, her hands tracing the thick ropes of sinew under his skin, reveling in his back as he moved against her. The morning would shed light on all that had been said and had been left untold. For now, she banished her conscience and her worries, and just let his touch speak for them both, knowing exactly how he felt.

At first light he heard water running. The vacancy beside him and cool air gave him a chill. He sat up slowly, honoring his fatigued muscles, and smiled. "Oh, yeah, definitely . . ."

He followed the sound, his mind in a trance as his body obliged forward motion. Entering the first section of the master bathroom, he was glad she'd shut the adjoining door that led to the shower and tub, running water opening his internal faucets . . . damn, it was just like being married, all illusions stripping away. He hurried to finish and wash up, lathering her scent away from his hands with a sigh, splashing cold water on his face, finding a glob of toothpaste, yet not wanting to chase away the taste of her just yet.

Maxwell gently opened the inner door and saw Darien bending over the deep tub, stirring shower gel bubbles in it. The sight of her was paralyzing. Sunlight kissed her supple spine; her firm, smooth behind glistening from the previous night; hair tossed over her shoulder, a golden, bronze, auburn mane; lithe arms dangling in a profusion of foam . . . She tilted her head, glanced at him, and smiled. He nearly held on to the doorframe to keep from passing out.

"Good morning," she said softly. "I just wanted to take a bath."

His jacuzzi belonged to her. Was made for her. He couldn't even muster a smile as he watched her slip beneath the churning surface, lean her head back on the tiles, and groan.

"My body hurts," she said, her eyes still closed, her smile serene.

"So does mine," he said, more to inform himself than her. "Mind if I join you?"

"Sure, but you know I do have to write this morning . . . at some point."

"No problem," he said hoarsely, crossing the room and remembering her deadline. "You want to use my office downstairs?"

She opened her eyes and chuckled as he began lathering her back, his hands melting against her skin. "I already did, remember?"

"Yeah . . ." He remembered. How could he forget? His chair would always have her presence affixed to it whenever he sat, a mirage, a sweet vision of her straddling his lap, her hands clasping the high back of it, her sensual moans renting the air, chasing the work off his desk, bending his mind, altering his will. He shivered and moved closer to her.

"I tried to go down there last night, but somebody wouldn't leave me alone," she said teasing him, turning in to his touch.

"I couldn't help it," he murmured against her neck, his hands coming down her shoulders, her soap-slicked back sliding against his chest as his lathered hands covered her breasts. "Lord knows, I couldn't help it."

How could she argue her point while he was doing that? She knew she had work to do, but . . . oh, God . . . the man felt so good. She'd tried to break away, get her mind to find its way back into her skull, but every time he breathed into her ear, moaned, "C'mon, baby," she forgot all about everything but the sound of his voice.

Her escape last night had been worthless. The kitchen offered no buffer to his attentions, only evidence of where he'd cornered her again, made her knees jelly, stole her determination to save some of her for later. His chest now covered where her spine had hit Spanish tiles. Her butt felt like every muscle in it had been stripped. He was supposed to take her to her apartment and wound up in a compromising position against an unopened door. They were gonna let things cool off a bit, but the living room got christened instead. They were gonna eat, but as she came into the dining room bearing food and much-needed fuel, one intense glance from him had made her set the plates down, made her cross the room to fill his arms . . . dinner at that table would never be the same.

Darien sighed, whupped, but her hands clutched his thighs as she leaned her head back against his shoulder. "Just one more time, then I have to . . . oh, God . . ."

He loved to hear her voice do that. It made him crazy, irrational, take unwarranted risks. But in the water, the blue porcelain making the deep tub look like the Caribbean ocean . . . the sun coming through the skylight and windows, bathing her beautiful skin the range of reds and copper it owned, her pulsing grip, the water, the water, made everything slippery, made his mind slip, made his body slip into hers, and the shock of wet sliding made him lose his mind.

On his knees, he couldn't think. On her knees, she was devastating. Her back dipping, water churning, the sound of it splashing, slapping skin—deafening, her cries mind altering, her sensations breath robbing . . . the doorbell be damned. It felt so right, so natural, so incredibly, audaciously good. He was hollering, getting this, regardless. Gettin' it righteous, for the first time in his life, *oh yeah, jus' like that . . . uh-huh . . .* sweet sugar-coated woman, he'd be her suga daddy. Just call him by name. "Oh, Darien, girl, yeah . . ." A key in the lock was a non-issue. Darien's flat belly held tight under his palm was causing delirium. He didn't care if she got pregnant, he'd marry her for sure—just don't stop. Then she jerked, moved, and turned sharply.

"Did you hear that?"

"Hear what?" All he could hear was his heart thudding in his ears.

"The door. Somebody's in the house."

He knew it as true, but looking at her glistening breasts, the ache of incompletion was making him stupid. "Huh?"

"Maxwell, somebody's downstairs!" she hissed.

"Don't worry about it," he said, unable to think as he reached for her again. *Please baby, don't worry about nothin' right now.*

"I *am* worried about it," she said, standing. "And . . . and . . . you don't have anything on."

Guilty as charged. The latex was long gone. He stared up at her, water cascading down her body. "I know, baby, but . . ."

"Uh-uh. It could be Doreetha or one of your brothers,

or . . . oh, Lord, have mercy. They can't see me like this. And we can't be having *unprotected sex*. What were we doing!"

He couldn't offer protest as she hopped out of the tub, bolted toward the room in only a towel.

He stood, the erection killing him. He grabbed a towel, fury at the intrusion kindling. He'd flushed the house of invaders, his sanctuary had been breached, his invitation to her naked body rescinded, cold air cutting him, his voice about to explode in a sonic boom. "Yeah!"

"Mr. Ferguson," an elderly voice called out. "It's me, Maybel. Didn't mean to wake you, sir, but good morning, just the same."

He peered down the stairs, saw his housekeeper glance around at the clothes on the foyer floor, and almost died a thousand deaths as she picked up Darien's jeans with two fingers and carefully put them on a chair.

"I can come back a little later . . . can run some grocery errands and stock the cabinets . . . I didn't know, uh, I didn't mean to be a bother."

"No bother, ma'am, at all. Thanks, Maybel," he said, trying not to stare into her eyes, shame making his face hot. "That would be a big help."

She just nodded and slipped out the door as quiet as a mouse. He went to hunt for Darien, but the groove was totally blown. He found Darien wrapped in a sheet, frantically winding her hair into a bun, her eyes darting around the room as though seeking a quick place to hide.

"My clothes are downstairs," she whispered.

"I know," he said and sat down hard on the edge of the bed. "Miss Maybel is gone."

"Miss Maybel? Oh, no, not Miss Maybel."

He just nodded and tried to will himself flaccid.

"But she goes to your church," Darien said, covering her mouth with both hands.

He just nodded and closed his eyes, pain lacerating his groin. "Half of Macon goes to my church."

"That's terrible . . . oh, no, this is not happening. Maxwell, please, you have to take me home. You have to go down and get my clothes!"

He nodded, his chest constricting. "Give me a second. I can't make it down the steps, right yet."

"Stop playing," she said through her teeth, her gorgeous eyes wild, her slender hands urgently gesturing, her wet bun unraveling, her wavy tresses now on her shoulders, the sheet coming loose right before his eyes.

"I'm not playing."

"Then get my clothes. If she doubles back and catches me, I'll die."

He could barely watch her as she worked herself up into a frenzy, the sight of her burning the saliva away from his mouth. He stood with effort and forced his legs to move. He'd actually felt her for a few seconds . . . raw, wet—it was a heart-stopping experience. He held on to the banister and staggered down the steps, totally through. Just one more time before reality set in. One more go-hard, lose-your-mind session, that's all a man asked for. He grabbed up her purse and her rumpled clothes in one deft motion, and slowly made his way back up the stairs, glancing at the clock—ninethirty.

"It's nine-thirty," she announced. "You haven't called in. They must be thinking . . . wondering . . . I have to check my cell phone. Doreetha is probably having a coronary. Arnetta, oh, no . . . I know she knows, and, this is so tacky. Maxwell, we can't be rolling like this. We have to be a little more discreet, have some semblance of dignity, some pride . . . I don't want people down here to think of me this way. I don't want folks looking at me sideways when I come into the office."

He nodded. That's all he could do as he watched her drop the sheet and cover one of the natural wonders of the universe with a sweater and jeans. It was such a sad moment when she put on her clothes that he simply had to turn away and hunt for his own.

"I'll take you to the apartment. Maybe, say, by noon, one o'clock at the latest, we can drive up to Atlanta with Arnie and Ted, deliver your outline to Mavis, and keep on pushing."

"That makes sense," she said quickly, collecting her shoes. "No hanky-panky on the road, though." She looked at him without blinking. Her hands were on her hips. "I mean it. I don't want anyone talking about me, or your brothers thinking I'm just some hoochie."

"No chance of them thinking that," he said in all honesty.

"Still," she protested. "I mean it."

He knew she did, but have mercy. "All right, you're right," he finally said.

He let his breath out hard, not sure how he was ever going to adhere to the impossible and keep his hands off her.

Chapter 11

She couldn't look at him as she hopped out of his car and raced up her apartment steps. There was no time to think about what had happened, had almost happened, or how any of it might look. She dropped her keys twice, but finally managed the locks. She stripped her clothes like they were burning her, showered, and came out of the bathroom brushing her teeth in a whirl. Her laptop was calling her name—she had a deadline. Her hair was wet, her bags needed to be packed. *Make time stand still for just a moment, oh Lord.*

She dressed like a speed demon, brushed on makeup fast, and plopped herself down to write about one man's life. Her fingers flew across the keys, green and red word-processing flag lines of spelling and grammatical mistakes be damned. The ache that he'd left was making her story come up from her soul. Her thighs still burned from his touch, her body still ached from his down-home good lovin'. The man had practically asked her to marry him. She didn't need to consult her notes. She knew Maxwell Ferguson by heart.

* * *

By eleven o'clock, he was in his office, bags packed, his gaze sliding away from Peg's as she handed him telephone messages with inquisitive glances. He tried to keep his tone even, authoritative, in control. Even Doreetha had enough sense to back off—he wasn't playing.

"You pulling out soon?" Jovan asked, putting his head in the door.

"Uh-huh," Maxwell said, not looking up from his desk. He could feel Jovan still hovering, knew a too-wide smile would be on his face. Maxwell focused on his voice mail, his mind scattered by Darien's touch.

"Got a second?"

"I really don't," Maxwell muttered. "Is it urgent?"

"I don't know, brother. You tell me."

Maxwell looked up and let his breath out hard. "Not today, man."

Jovan ignored the warning, came into his office and shut the door behind him, and then sat down. "So?"

"Baby brother, for real. Not today."

"I'm just—"

"In my business. Back off." Maxwell stood.

Jovan rubbed his chin and laughed. "Whooowee. Okay. It's like that."

"Yeah. It's like that." Maxwell gave him his back to consider while he stared out the window. Family got on his nerves.

"You figured out how you gonna take her to all the sites without her bumping into your *past life*?"

Maxwell slowly turned around and stared at his brother.

Jovan nodded and stood. "C'mon, playa. You might have been out of circulation for a while, but the females you had in your face . . . Atlanta . . . need we discuss Richmond, Charlotte . . . have mercy, aw, brother, DC—"

Maxwell held up is hand. "I get your point." As much as he hated to admit it, he was glad Jovan had brought this potential disaster to his attention. The thought of other women had never crossed his mind. Up till now, they weren't an issue. But if Darien got the wrong impression . . .

"You'd better make sure she knows she's the one, bro, or she could get cold feet, think you're playin' her, feel me?"

His brother was making him nervous. In his own brain he'd claimed her as the one, but to hear it said out loud by another man, made reality set in. He leaned on the windowsill, his thoughts sliding slowly into the hot tub, and he closed his eyes. He'd gone skinny-dipping . . . he'd lost his natural mind!

"It's not what you think," Maxwell said, defending his shaky position and Darien's privacy. "She's here on business, and it's too early to tell if anything more might develop." He pushed off the windowsill and went back to his desk.

"You need to stop playing with this and with yourself," Jovan said, his tone teasing.

"I'm not playing anybody." Maxwell looked at his brother hard.

"You playing her?"

"No."

Jovan stared at him with a smile. "Then she's the one, right?"

Maxwell walked away, rubbing his jaw.

"You know Miss Albright seen y'all outside her apartment last night . . . all in the street, man."

Maxwell turned and stared at his brother.

"Phones 'round Macon been lit up like a Christmas tree . . . then the boss walks in floating, wearing soft clothes, all casual, dragging a suitcase, late as shit when he normally comes in here at seven-thirty before everybody else. New sister in town is AWOL. Miss Maybel is at the market shopping for you like it's the holidays . . . had to call Doreetha to get a larger than normal check authorized, said she had to set up your household proper, *now*, since you was keeping lady company, but you didn't hear her tell it. That's how I know, and Doreetha came busting into my office wantin' to know when you'd taken leave of your mind."

Maxwell closed his eyes. Macon was too small and way too familiar.

"I tol' Doreetha," Jovan pressed on, "that you'd snapped, probably about eight o'clock after dinner . . . right about when you was putting that girl's shoe on in Dor's living room, like the chile was Cinderella. Man, she is definitely a princess, can't blame you. Told sister it was the look on your face. You was practically drooling on yourself. I asked big sister to be gentle since we ain't neva seen you look like that before. Doreetha is worried. Arnie is about to do back flips. Otis and them told me to tell you you's one lucky mother—"

"Jovan, I can't deal with this right now. I'm serious. It's all speculation and gettin' misconstrued the wrong way."

"Hey, I'm not bringing a bone to carry a bone, I'm just telling you the word on the streets—as your marketing director, it's my business to know talk around town."

Maxwell's nerves were coiled so tight that he could almost hear his spinal discs crack. "Squash all the noise about Darien, all right? She deserves respect. Nothing happened, and I don't want people talking about her like that."

"I'll do what I can to kill the noise," Jovan said, "but I'm your brother, and I know you. How you gonna lie to me?"

"Thanks," Maxwell said, not addressing Jovan's question.

"She's incredible, ain't she?" Jovan's hope-filled expression sought an answer.

Maxwell nodded and he raked his fingers against his scalp. "I don't know what I'ma do, man."

"Daayum," Jovan murmured and stood slowly. "She blew your mind like that?"

Maxwell's gaze sought the window. He didn't like the sound of it, but it was the truth. "Things go right, I might put down some foundation."

Jovan had crossed the room, his hand landing on Maxwell's shoulder. "I'ma kill the gossip as best I can. You worryin' me, though. Ain't this kinda quick?"

"Yeah. Too quick."

Both brothers stared at each other.

"That's a serious move, man," Jovan said in a quiet voice. "Ask me how I know."

Maxwell nodded.

"You gotta take it slow, let this thing burn down, then decide."

"Sho' you right." Maxwell stared at the floor, feeling like a fool.

"Happens to the best of us, man. Remember Pop used to say, even iron wears out. You just tired, and she's so fine . . ."

"She's so fine, she made me stoopid," Maxwell admitted, trying to force himself to laugh.

Jovan laughed with him and gave him a quick embrace. "That's the brother I know. You'll be all right, playa. Girlfriend just took you to the rail, and you ain't been to church in a long time."

"Tell me about it. It was a religious experience."

They laughed hard, and Maxwell tried his best to regain his perspective.

"Try to keep your head on the road, man—seriously."

"I know. I am," Maxwell said, his voice unsure. "My focus is on making sure Arnetta is all right."

"Yeah, yeah, yeah," Jovan said, moving toward the door. "That's what we all say."

* * *

She'd e-mailed a very rough draft of her article to Mavis and couldn't stop yawning. Her eyes burned, her legs were like rubber, each step a wobbly effort. If she could just lie down for an hour . . . but that was impossible. She heard cars pulling up in the driveway and began locking her door.

Arnetta's bright smile greeted her. Ted was beaming. But Maxwell was hanging back a bit, leaning on his car. What was that about?

Darien pasted on her best smile and rolled her suitcase forward. She watched Maxwell slowly approach as though he were willing himself to measure his strides.

"You ready?"

"You?"

He nodded and took her suitcase.

"Where to first?" Arnetta asked, her voice chipper.

"I have to buzz up to *Urban Professional,* drop the cleaned-up article on Mavis, and then we can head to the chain stores and shoot the real estate," Darien said in a weary voice through a yawn.

"Yeah, I have to check in with Mav, too," Ted said, his voice heavy with fatigue. "Need to be sure she didn't double-book me—only got her voice mail all weekend."

"Then let's do this," Maxwell said, his back straight, his eyes masked by sunglasses, the muscle in his jaw working. This was such a bad idea.

She was grateful that he drove in silence. Only the click of her nails against the keyboard filled the car as she put the finishing touches on her story. It was a masterpiece, if she had to say so herself. She only hoped the family would like it. Darien stopped typing—did she say family, without mentally prefacing it with the Ferguson family?

She had to get herself together.

He had to get himself together. There were too many

unanswered questions in the bright light of the day. Who was this guy who had been stalking her? Did he need to get strapped to take her from city to city? How did they hook up? Where did she meet him? What was the brother's name?

And who was her family? He needed to meet the Jackson sisters. There were so many things about her that he just didn't know. And now it disturbed him that he'd neglected to understand, how did she make it for over a year on unemployment alone? At that lifestyle? Didn't add up.

A lot of things didn't add up, as she stared at her laptop. Okay, sure, he didn't mess with anybody in Macon, so she was told. But a man like Maxwell Ferguson who loved to make love like he did, couldn't have gone for very long without some woman somewhere. And what about all his holdings, all his business locations? There was surely some sister tucked away, and plenty gamin' going on. His approach was too smooth, too professional, too skilled. A brother didn't get that way falling off the back of a turnip truck—uh-uh.

Now, true, he'd blown her mind royal, but she wasn't no fool. And she'd seen his kind before, albeit not as handsome, wealthy, or suave. And the business he'd started had a missing element. Fact one, his mentor Bill Jones had given him his first contract, and that had been parlayed into an empire, but how did that first contract come about? She had questions that needed answering, especially after a near-miss. Skinny-dipping? Was she mad?

This time when she pushed the elevator button, there was no trepidation within her, just determination. She had to figure this out, figure out her life, and stop wanting the man beside her so much. The visit would be brief. She was on a mission. It was getting near time for her to pack her bags, get her hat, and be out. She could feel it in her bones.

"Hey, Mav," Darien said when her girlfriend crossed the lobby.

Mavis stared at Darien and the group who'd come into the lobby with her. Mavis coolly appraised Arnetta, but smiled. Her eyes briefly scanned Maxwell and Ted before returning to Darien's. "Hi. You have my story?"

"E-mailed it this morning," Darien replied, all business. "Here's the polished draft. Edit away at will, I just want it in this issue."

Mavis accepted the folder as Darien produced it. She scanned down the page. "The draft was excellent. This is superb." She glanced at Ted. "I liked the prints you e-mailed. But how did the Fergusons get to hijack my best photog for a week?"

Ted smiled and looked down at his shoes. "You know I hang loose, Mav. I'm a freelancer. A brother has to do what a brother has to do."

She let her breath out in a long sigh. "Stay in touch while on the road. You might have to parlay your time between them and me if I have a critical shoot. Understood?"

"Yeah, Mav, I got you," Ted said. "It's all good."

Mavis narrowed her gaze on him, but smiled. "It had better be all good." She looked at Darien. "Is it?"

Darien swallowed a smile as Maxwell looked away. "I think so."

He only wished that his sister would stop talking. His brain needed space and rest, and his body was sore. The photo shoot at the development was wearing him out. He was hungry and irritable, and Ted's attention to his sister was getting on his nerves. Darien's quiet presence wasn't much better. She was like a constant, nagging ache that couldn't be fulfilled.

After hours of driving, setting up, breaking down camera equipment, watching Arnetta giggle and pose, he knew he didn't have much latitude in his attitude. Plus, the fact was, he didn't need to be here at all.

"We can go back over to Peachtree Road and have dinner," Maxwell said. "Need to get a hotel, catch some z's, then tomorrow, I might let you all push on without me. I really can't take this much time away from the business, playing around taking pictures."

Arnetta looked as though she'd been slapped. Ted froze. Fury burned Darien from the inside out.

"Yeah, let's eat," Darien snapped. "We're all tired and need some rest. If you have to go back, fine. Understood. But please don't refer to what Ted and I are trying to accomplish on your behalf as *playing.*"

"My apologies. I'm just cranky because I'm hungry." Maxwell sighed and leaned against his car. Even angry she was beautiful and turning him on.

"The Imperial Fez is nice," Arnetta offered, appearing to try to keep the peace.

"Yeah, whatever," Maxwell said, getting into his car, not even waiting for Darien. "Y'all decide. My brain is fried."

He sat staring at the menu, listening to the three of them talk. He didn't feel like eating anything eclectic, exotic, or spicy. He wanted something basic. Regular. That, and a shot of Jack Daniel's. Maxwell rubbed his jaw, five o'clock shadow grazing his palm.

From the minor part of his brain that was still functioning, he heard Darien answer a cell phone call that had made her voice grow strident.

"I swear! Family. Every time I'm in Atlanta, they think I'm supposed to drop whatever I'm doing and come run to Cynthia's or baby-sit." Darien shook her head. "I'm sorry y'all."

Arnetta laughed. "I know how family can be. Will drive

you out of your mind." She glanced at Maxwell. "They all think because you're the baby that one, they have the right to tell you what to do all the time, and two, that you don't know your own mind."

Maxwell glowered at Arnetta over his menu, signifying that she was not helping his mood. But as the conversation wore on, and Ted joked about his own family, concern threaded its way through Maxwell's system.

"Well, Darien, if you can't beat 'em, join 'em."

Everyone stopped talking and looked at Maxwell.

"Pardon?" Darien's gaze was locked with his.

"If that was your sister who called, why don't you invite them here to dinner? We'll get a larger table—they might be able to accommodate them and any husbands and kids. My treat."

Half of her was elated, and Arnetta agreed with a whoop. Part of her was cautious. It was all in the way he'd said it; his tone wasn't right. What did he mean by *if* that was her sister? Hmmm . . .

"It's short notice. They might not be able to make it to turn on a dime."

Maxwell set down his menu very carefully. "You won't know till you try. Call her back."

Defiance was making her palms tingle. This wasn't about a spur-of-the-moment treat; this was a cell check. Maxwell was testing her. He obviously didn't trust her. She didn't know what wild thoughts were running through his head. She couldn't stand a jealous man, wasn't having it. He'd been short with her all day, and this was the final straw.

"Another time," Darien said evenly, then picked up her menu.

"Yeah, all right," he said, his tone cool. "Another time. Right."

"Aw, girl," Arnetta fussed. "Go on and call your family. What's the matter with you? Big brother is buying;

we all are flying. C'mon. If you could stand my crazy sister, Doreetha, I'd love to meet yours."

"Hey, lady," Ted said with a grin as he sipped his beer. "Everybody got crazy folks in their family, mine ain't no exception. So, if that's all you're worried about," he added, glancing at Maxwell, "however they act ain't no reflection on you. Is it, Max?"

Maxwell lowered his menu and his guard. He'd never even considered that Darien might feel awkward with her family around him—now being both her lover and her employer. And then, too, as proud a woman as Darien was, already feeling indebted, and probably nervous about having spent the night with him, he could fully appreciate her not wanting to add to her personal tab, even though he'd long since stopped running one. He could almost feel her cringe when he'd made the offer and could see the wheels in her pretty head turning.

"Ted and Arnetta are right," Maxwell said, his voice mellow. "I was just trying to kill two birds with one stone. You're here, so are we, so is your family . . . I know what it's like to be stretched in several directions. But I'd like to meet them, and they are more than welcomed to join us—if they can make it."

Darien sat back and studied him, unconvinced. She wasn't crazy. She'd heard *a tone*. But as the others jumped in, adding their two cents and pleas, she could feel her body relax. "All right," she finally said. "But I wouldn't be surprised if they can't come."

Maxwell let his breath out in very slow increments. Relief made him hail the waitress for another drink. He'd almost messed up bad, almost offended Darien in a way that might have been relationship terminal. And it messed with his mind that he'd even referred to what was between them as a relationship. He was in deep.

But he couldn't help smiling as he listened to her fuss. Arnetta rolled her eyes as the familiar struggle-with-family conversation ensued. Ted tipped his beer to Maxwell's glass. "Can't live with 'em, can't live without 'em."

Maxwell nodded with a smile, softening to the idea of Ted as a possible brother-in-law. It was all in his easy manner, the way he looked at Arnetta with a gentle expression, and it had everything to do with seeing his baby sister laughing and chattering away like he hoped Darien might be before long.

Darien snapped her cell phone closed and sucked her teeth.

"The verdict?" Maxwell asked, his attitude much improved.

"They're coming—all slow and full of drama, but leaving the husbands, who are working and the kids because they have a neighbor who can sit."

"Girl, I know," Arnetta said, laughing, picking at her appetizer.

Darien had to laugh, despite being peeved. But it warmed her to no end to hear Maxwell's deep rich laugh come up from his insides. The sound of his voice rushed through her till she had to glance away.

And there was something so genuine about the way he finally listened to Ted, heard the brother's dreams about becoming a filmmaker one day. She could see the wheels turning in Maxwell's mind, saw him occasionally glance at his sister, and give her a slow, discreet nod of support that said everything and nothing. Darien was sure she could almost hear Max's deep baritone murmur gently, "If you like him, I love him . . . baby girl, it's gonna be all right."

That's whom she wanted in her life—someone who was open, accepting, forgiving, and kind. Mistakes could happen to anyone. She just hoped the man across from her had a forgiving spirit. Right now, he seemed to possess that and so much more.

A sudden peace filled her as she just watched this man function. Every moment she spent with him she learned so much about how he operated. Adding the new awareness to her memory of the previous night, she felt her body warm under his gaze.

"I think your people are here," he said with a smile, hating to break the trance Darien had caused.

She glanced over her shoulder. "Live and in living color. Brace yourself," she warned, standing. "They're a trip."

Darien tried her best to quell the noise as her three sisters talked at once. She did her best to make introductions all around while the waiter added a table to theirs.

Curious glances passed between her sisters, and as expected, Cynthia was the first to speak up.

"So, my sister works for you, huh?" Cynthia said, her line of vision riveted to Maxwell.

"Yes," Maxwell said carefully, wondering what he'd been thinking when he launched into this misadventure. "Arnetta is over personnel, and Ted is assisting with a photo shoot for *Urban Professional*. That's why we're in town. Glad you could join us."

She listened carefully. Maxwell had gone into corporate-speak, although she wasn't sure why. Then it dawned on her: the man was nervous. She almost giggled.

"Ain't that Mavis's magazine?" Brenda asked, her mouth twisting as she peered at her menu.

"Yeah, gurl," Louise said, her gaze sweeping the table.

Maxwell watched Darien stiffen. He knew exactly why, had had it done to him so often growing up that he could spot it a mile away.

"We were fortunate that Darien had the inside track over at *Urban*. When she told us about her friend Mavis, we all met her and were sold. Mavis Williams is a dynamo, like your sister, and we're glad she's on our side."

He let his gaze settle on Darien for a moment, hoping she could read his mind from a mere glance. Yeah, baby, it doesn't matter that Mavis is a close friend—that's how business is done. They hatin', trying to minimize your accomplishment, but I'm not. "Darien is going to put Allied on the map."

Maxwell smiled as he watched the wind go out of her sisters' sails. Not in his presence was he going to allow Darien's spirit to be crushed. Ted jumped in, and he was thankful for the reinforcement. The brother was all right—he'd have to let Jovan know it was cool.

"Yeah, Mavis is all that," Ted said. "Gave me my first break. You saw the cover stories last year? That was me. But Darien ain't no slouch. The girl has PR in her blood."

"She can sell anybody anything," Cynthia said, perusing the menu. "You got that right."

Ted fell quiet, his gaze searching Arnetta's.

"That's so true. You should have seen her wear down my elder sister, Doreetha," Arnetta said, her smile strained and her eyes blazing with quiet rage. "Darien brought a peach cobbler in there to Sunday dinner and just melted Doreetha on the spot—right in her kitchen. Darien is—"

"Darien cooked?" Louise gave a hard and brittle laugh.

"Helped Doreetha break beans and everything," Arnetta said, her eyes sad as she tried to help.

Darien sat up tall. "I did."

"It was good, too," Ted said, trying to step into the line of fire.

Maxwell nodded with a grunt. This brother was very cool.

"Oh, pullease, girl," Cynthia said, ignoring Ted and laughing, but the tone in her chuckle was rigid. "You lucky they didn't put you out for trying to poison the family,"

"Mr. Ferguson, if you value your life or your family's, don't let her go there too often. Up here she's banished from Cynthia's pots," Brenda said, her easy banter containing venom.

From the corner of his eye, he watched Darien wind the napkin in her lap around her fist. Her sisters were pissing him off in the worst way. And the nicks and slices to her confidence were delivered with smiles, up close from family, Roman style. It reminded him so much of the type of crap his father used to do to him that he almost turned the tables over.

"You know what," Maxwell said, slowly, his line of vision capturing Darien's. "You have quite a baby sister there." He looked at Cynthia, the ringleader, the message in his glare unmistakable. "I like her cooking. Like her style. And I like what she's done for my corporation, thus far, and trust her not to poison my family." With that he smiled and hailed the waitress. "Everybody ready to order?"

She could barely eat or keep her hands from shaking. The man had cowed her sisters, had stepped to them on her behalf—in front of his family—and never missed a beat. Oh, Lord, this was *the one*. Please, Jesus, let the dinner be over soon. She knew her sisters, they were furious, all smiles aside. They'd cut Arnetta dead and had only given Ted patronizing responses to his attempts to neutralize the topics with filmmaking conversation. She wanted to wring their necks as they sat there taking pot shots at everyone, everything, commenting on people at other tables, their whole vibe one morass of negativity. But Maxwell's occasional glance, while professional, sent her quiet support that she deeply appreciated.

"Well, I'ma tell you the truth," Cynthia said, having

eaten and drank her fill. "I never heard of no Allied States, LLC."

Darien almost dropped her glass. Arnetta and Ted looked away. Maxwell smiled.

"No, I'm sure you haven't," His tone took a weary, patronizing dip, "but that's why I hired Darien."

"Well, it's nice that you hired our sister into your little company. That's real nice," Louise said, smiling into her glass of wine.

He watched Arnetta bristle, saw Ted begin playing with silverware, and just shook his head. It wasn't worth it. But what he hadn't noticed was Darien gathering storm clouds.

"Louise," Darien said, her voice as smooth as honey, "his *little* company is worth ten million annually—and this man has helped his siblings each become millionaires before they were thirty. That's why *Urban Professional* is doing a spread on them." Darien sat back and sipped her wine, twirling the glass between her fingers. "So, while you all don't follow business news much, please do not embarrass yourselves in front of my client, especially when he's paying for your dinner."

Maxwell almost choked on his after-dinner coffee. She'd sliced her sister so quick and with such precision that he knew Louise didn't know she was bleeding till the poor girl dropped from the cut. All pro. And she'd done it for him, because they'd attacked what he'd built. Aw, yeah, Darien was the one.

"Well, we can pay for our own dinner, if that's a problem," Cynthia said, folding her arms over her chest. "Had we known . . ."

"Ladies, please," Maxwell said, trying not to smile. "It's all good. We invited you to our table. It's been a long day. Everyone is tired and winding down. Let's order some dessert."

"We have to be getting back before the babysitter pulls

her hair out," Brenda said, her smile tight. "We thank you, though, so much."

"It was a pleasure to meet you," Louise said, standing first, shaking hands with Maxwell and Ted when they stood, then Arnetta as an afterthought.

"Yeah, a real pleasure," Cynthia said, rummaging in her purse for her car keys without making eye contact.

"Darien, you know that cell bill is running high this month," Louise said as a parting shot. "Call me later."

"Wait." Maxwell was on his feet when Darien stopped breathing. He looked at Darien. "Your sister's right. Give her the telephone."

His gaze bore down on Louise without a filter, wiping away her smug expression as the three sisters stopped walking. "You shouldn't be running up her phone bill on business calls for Allied. Order whatever top-of-the-line model you want so you get clear reception, and I'll have Doreetha put it on the expense account . . . and since you'll be traveling, you'll need your own American Express card—and come to think of it, you shouldn't be clocking extra miles on the Diamante lease. Tell Doreetha what you need in the way of a vehicle and select one from my fleet, hear?"

He was glad that his sister was there as a witness because he'd just lost his mind. But it was a matter of principle. Arnetta was nodding. Good. Darien's mouth had dropped open. Good. Ted was shaking his head. Damn right—*this,* brother, is how you handle your bizness. And them three heifers standing in front of him coulda been bowled over with a feather. Excellent.

Wait till he put the rock on girlfriend's finger!

Chapter 12

"I don't care what he said, Arnetta, or how sweet it was that he did what he did, I can't let him do that." Darien kept her voice to a whisper as she confided in Arnetta in the ladies' room.

Arnetta's hands went to her hips. "Why not?" she whispered back. "You saw how they were just dogging you."

"Yeah, but it's been that way for years, and it's not his place to fix that. *I* have to fix it."

Both women paused as another woman entered the powder room. Once establishing that she was an unknown, the heated debate continued.

"But you saw how my brother looked at you. Girl, he's crazy about you!"

"That's why I can't let him do this, Arnie. He's already covering the apartment, my car note, my—"

"No. Be clear," Arnetta said, her finger up, wagging with a big smile. "You are paying for that. Wait till you see your first check."

"Okay, okay," Darien said, unwilling to relent. "But to pay for my cell phone, give me a credit card, and a freaking car? Oh, no, girl—over the line."

"Let's put it this way. If you were working for some big company, like IBM, don't they give their marketing people expense accounts, pay mileage reimbursement, have a fleet, and cover their business cell phone expenses, and any other equipment-related expenses that go with the individual doing their job?"

"Yes, but—"

"And, if my brother thinks highly enough of you to extend the same courtesies to you that he gives all his top-level executives in the firm—"

"But—"

"What's the problem, Darien?" Arnetta's hands were on her hips, and she was no longer smiling.

Darien looked away. "I don't want to feel like a prostitute."

"A what?"

The look of horror on Arnetta's face made tears begin to form in Darien's eyes.

"Arnie, listen . . . I don't want him to come up there one day, put the key in the door, put me out, tell me how I ain't shit . . . strip me of that credit card, take the keys to the car, stomp on my cell phone because it's really his . . ." She covered her mouth and walked toward the sink, needing air. "I don't want to ever be that dependent on no man."

To her astonishment, Arnetta's hand touched her shoulder. "You've already slept with my brother, haven't you?"

Darien closed her eyes, unshed tears wetting her lashes. "It happened so fast, Arnie. I swear to God, I'm not playing him. If he were a major corporation, I'd jump for joy and accept everything he's offering as a perk to go with the job, but I slept with the corporation, and I am scairt to death. When he changes women like he can probably change his wardrobe, I'm old news and I'm out. I know how this works."

Arnetta opened her arms and gave her a gentle hug.

"My brother ain't like that." She held Darien back and smiled sadly. "No more."

They both chuckled as Darien sniffed. "Ah . . . the qualifier."

"I know it's scary to trust, girl. You think I ain't scairt?"

Darien searched Arnetta's face.

"Ted is making me jump out of my skin, and it all happened so fast, so furiously . . . there was so much passion all bottled up, and we'd been through so much." She sighed and sat on the edge of the sink. "I've had a brother stomp out, break up stuff, take back gifts. Only difference was, I was paying for it. My first husband couldn't deal with how my brother took care of us better than he ever could. He used to burn up money, do dumb-dumb junk to keep me broke, and it made him angry that Max could always come to my rescue. Then he went beyond the financial and got physical and started also having affairs. That's when we all had to put him out. I thought Maxwell might go to jail."

The insight Arnetta offered was profound, and Darien nodded and spoke quietly. "Had the first love of my life offer for me to move in with him while I was at Spelman. He was a little older, my parents were hysterical, and he took care of mostly everything. So I had my double life going—my room at school, and my home away from home with him. Then he found somebody new and took everything back . . . said things, did things . . ."

"Is this the guy who was stalking you?"

Darien looked at Arnetta and willed her heart to start beating. She'd forgotten all about the terrible lie. "No," she said in a near whisper.

"Well, I know one thing for sure, my brother's crazy about you—and he don't hit women, never did." Arnetta forced Darien to look up. "You don't have to accept the perks of the position, if you don't want. But while we're on the road, I can put a full list in your folder as part of

your compensation package. There are some benefits
to knowing somebody on the inside."

"Thanks, Arnie, but y'all have done enough." Darien
leaned on a stall door, unable to look at Arnetta or herself in the mirror.

"You may not believe this," Arnetta said, carefully
enough to draw Darien's attention away from the floor.
She held Darien's gaze. "I've *never* seen him act like this
before. Me and Jovan are like, she's the one."

Darien smiled. "It was just—"

"No. I'm serious." Arnetta wasn't smiling as she folded
her arms over her chest. "The man is acting all impul-
sive, moody, laughing . . . jumped up and defended you
in front of your sisters. Is so agitated, trying to keep up
this front that nothing is going on, he's all evil and
surly . . . girl, please give that man some more."

This time they both laughed, even though embar-
rassment claimed Darien. Then, in a mercurial flux of
emotion, words rushed past her lips in a flood.

"Oh, God, Arnetta," she said covering her face. "He's,
he's . . . like no one I've ever met before. I like him so
much, his family . . . y'all, are more than I've ever had,
even while my parents were living, but I don't want to
cross the line, don't want to take advantage, or seem
like I am. I want this to be right. Last night was never
supposed to happen."

"Last night was really the first time y'all hooked up?"

Darien held on to the stall for support and nodded.

"No, wonder . . ." Arnetta walked over to Darien.
"Okay," she said flatly. "I'ma tell you this, but you could
have probably guessed." Arnetta folded her arms over
her chest. "My brother had a lot of women, up and down
the coasts, chile. Tall ones, short ones, girls with big
butts, girls with no butts, ones from rich families, some
that was so hoochie you'd squint. Wherever Maxwell
was working, he drew 'em like flies. You might meet

some on the road, but I want you to hold your ground. Doreetha put her eye on you, and so, girl, you the one."

Darien didn't say a word as Arnetta walked in a small circle, talking to her like she were a prizefighter and Arnetta was her cut man.

"Now, here's the thing," Arnetta said firmly, "and you can do with it what you want. My brother *never* came to work late behind some stray tail. Eva. Maxwell Ferguson always handled his business." Arnetta counted the charges on her fingers as she spoke. "Second off. He never, ever, *ever* brought them home, through the business, or turned over any job or enterprise function to them wannabes. He didn't have them at Doreetha's, that's for sure—and more importantly, never walked any of them into his board room. Fact is, he never brought any of them into Momma and Daddy's house, which is where he lives now. He kept everything separate, very separate. He might have dropped a bracelet here, a pair of earrings there, peeled off a knot, took her to eat, then rolled."

Arnetta sighed and threw up her hands. "He was acting crazy before you even slept with him, ask any of us, later . . . we'll tell you. So I don't know what you did to him, but I'm glad you did it."

No words were necessary as she hugged Arnetta hard. But she really wanted to convey just how dear a friend she'd become. "I'm not gonna do your big brother wrong, I promise," she whispered.

"Relationships are funny; men are even funnier," Arnetta said, holding her back. "If y'all don't work out, and it wasn't because of something slimy, then me and you always gonna be friends. You had my back when it counted, like I have yours—so, we gurls now, hon."

It was like she'd known Arnetta all her life, and the tears just ran as they both laughed.

"Go 'head," Arnetta said through her giggles. "Fix

your face. We done solved the problems of the world in the ladies' room."

"I appreciate what you're saying, Ted," Maxwell replied as he signed the check. "I think you're a good man, but Arnie is my boo. Just don't mess over her. She's been through a lot."

Ted nodded and toyed with his empty beer bottle. "She's . . . she's what I've needed all my life, man. I know I'm an artist, and this sounds flaky, but I'm not playin'."

"It don't sound flaky," Maxwell said, looking up. "Things can happen to a man fast."

Ted motioned with his chin in the direction of the ladies' room. "That was some cold-blooded chivalry I saw go down, brother. Hope one day I'll be able to stake a claim like that and do for mine like you do for yours."

"It ain't about—"

"No," Ted said, interrupting him. "It's about caring about somebody, having her back, not allowing anybody to squash her spirit. You love that girl, man. A blind man can see that, which, to me, is so cool. You've done your running, hit this place in your life where it's about quality not quantity . . . hey," he added with a nod, "go for it."

Ted's assessment was too simplistic; maybe it was just too real. He wasn't ready to fully acknowledge it nor could he deny it. After being a player, hanging loose, freelancing all his life, the prospect of going to the next step terrified him. He'd seen too many men go down, lose everything they'd built, all because they made a wrong choice. So, rather than fully commit to the charge, Maxwell just smiled and told Ted, "We'll see."

But as they left the restaurant and checked into the Doubletree, four rooms for the sake of appearances, Maxwell had to wonder.

Darien didn't seem as distant as she'd been earlier. Crazy thing was, he was more remote than ever before.

And as everyone conveniently went their separate ways, his brain fought hand-to-hand combat with his body, sending him to his room alone while his thoughts stayed with her.

However, fatigue had a way of dropping the most worthy contender to his knees. As soon as Maxwell got into his room, he crossed the floor and sprawled on the bed, not even changing his clothes.

The ringing phone woke him out of the partial coma. If he could just get five minutes more . . . It stopped, he dozed back off, then it started again. Pulling himself to the edge of the bed, a familiar voice roused him.

"Can we talk?" Darien asked, her tone mellow.

"Yeah . . . wanna come down here, or want me to come up there?"

"I'll come down," she said. "See you in a few."

He was already at the door when she knocked.

His first reflex was to just pull her into his arms, but there was something tentative in her expression that made him hesitate to do that.

"You got a minute?" she asked, glancing round the room.

"Yeah, c'mon and have a seat."

"I've done a lot of things in my life," she said quietly as she sat staring at her hands, "that, frankly, I'm not proud of."

"We all have," he murmured, sitting on the edge of the bed facing her chair.

It was clear that he didn't understand where she was heading. After what Arnie had told her, she knew he thought she was talking about men, when she was talking about money. The stalker thing had been a lie, a big ruse to throw a repo man off her trail. But she never knew that it would wind up being a secret kept from a man she cared about. And even though it was a relatively small thing, she wanted to get it off her heart.

"Maxwell, for a lot of reasons, even though I appreciate it, I can't accept all the stuff you offered me while you stepped up to my sister Louise."

"Baby, listen, you should have those things, and I don't care about the money. It ain't that much, really, and if you're traveling, you need a phone, a decent car, and some plastic. That's basic."

He was making this so hard for her, the more she stared into his intense brown eyes. And the way his voice got all deep and mellow when he called her *baby* . . .

"Listen, Maxwell, seriously. One's boss shouldn't be calling her baby while offering corporate perks—you know the two get real murky, and if things don't work out . . ."

"Yeah, I know," he said, standing to go to the sliding glass windows. "It's just that when I heard Louise digging at you, it made me remember."

She stood and went to him, touching his shoulder. "Remember what?"

He let out a long breath. "My father used to pick at every little victory I had and just crush it in his fist. Any of his other children could do no wrong, but me . . ." Maxwell shook his head. "Then I hooked up with Bill Jones, my mentor, an older brother who showed me things, exposed me to things, and my father hated it. Anything I did with Bill was wrong, every business idea I had was destined for failure. What your sisters were doing was one in the same in my eyes—you wanted more than the food they offered and the shelter and hated having them give you things with strings attached."

"Everything they've ever done for me has come with a deep personal cost."

"Yeah. I hear you. That's why he and I bumped heads all the time because unlike my sisters and brothers, I said, screw it, I'll go for my own and will not be manipulated by the lack of resources. He was going to act like we had a business deal instead of a father-son relationship, then I'd go find someone to step in and provide those emotional things he couldn't—with no strings attached. That's who Bill Jones is to me. The man gave me a lot more than money, Darien. That will always mean something."

His tone was so somber, filled with so much repressed rage that all she could do was look at him for a moment.

"I don't ever want to be perceived as using you, Maxwell. And I also don't want to be in a position . . ." she couldn't find the words.

"Darien, when I give someone something, I cut strings right then and there. If we have an agreement, then, yeah, I expect you to hold up your end, but I have never put a woman in a position where my sleeping with her was traded for anything. So do not confuse the two. What comes with the job is very separate from what goes down between us. I hate strings attached, too. Like I said, my father used to hold things over people's heads, dangle his authority, or if he gave you anything, you'd hear about it for the next twenty years. That's probably why he died of a heart attack . . . the man had a hard heart and half killed my mother with his spirit every day he was with her. I don't ever want to do that to any woman. My mother cooked and cleaned and washed and scrubbed and had baby after baby for him in stair steps until she wore out and died thinking she owed the man for keeping a roof over her head. That was bull."

He stared at Darien a long time, stopping his confession just short of the truth about Bill Jones. After all he'd told her, how could he explain to her that his daddy had called his mentor a crook, and how could he even express how his mentor had made some mistakes—bid tampering, they'd called it? Contracts went to certain people, regardless of the lowest cost bid. Bill had slid him one of those inside deals trying to help him get his feet on the ground, to get established—just like any father would risk for a son he loved. The first contract made the first loan possible. From there, he'd never looked back—until his father died, vindicated, and had told him from his sick bed that the only reason he'd made it further than him was because he'd had an unfair advantage.

And how could he look into Darien's big hazel eyes and tell her that at the very foundation of his firm there'd been some shady dealings? She couldn't interview Bill Jones for her story, and he was glad that it was already in. He hated the media, what they'd done to a good man, and he hated politics even more. Bill Jones had done no less than what the big boys did over golf.

"When I saw Louise stepping on your self-esteem, I couldn't take it, Darien," he admitted after a long pause. "I can't see someone just beat on a person for no reason. I ain't got it in me . . . especially don't ask me to stand by and watch that happen to my woman."

He turned away from her. It didn't matter that most of America's top businesses had a little insider trading going on. It didn't matter that he worked like a mule, day and night, to try to pay back his jump-start and prove his father wrong. All that mattered was that he never wanted Darien to look at him with distrust in her eyes.

His woman? She touched his shoulder. Did he hear what he'd just said? And yet, he'd told her all of that in the most profoundly honest, open confession she'd ever heard.

"Maxwell, the guy who I said was stalking me—"

He whirled on her and held her by both arms. His kiss crushed her mouth. "Don't worry, baby, if you saw him or he called you, it'll be all right."

"No, Max, it's . . ."

"It's the past, and you've had men, I've had women. Unless you're at risk, I don't wanna know about no other man."

His fingers traced her cheek and forced her to close her eyes.

"You called me your woman, and—"

"Are you?"

She looked at him, her stomach aflutter, her heart so full she could barely speak. "Am I?"

He nodded. Was she crazy? "Let's stop playing with this."

"We're both on emotional overload," she said, trying to get enough space between them so she could tell him what had to be said.

But the look in his eyes when he nodded and his lids closed slowly made her stomach clench.

"I've been on emotional overload since you waltzed into my boardroom. Thought I could keep my distance, but I was playing with my own mind." He closed the small gap between them and breathed into her hairline. "Then I kissed you," he said, his nose trailing down her neck. "And I touched you," he whispered, rubbing her back. "And I made love to you," he said, his breaths becoming labored. "And all day I swore that I could shake it, could back off, stay away from you till it cooled down."

His arms encircled her as her hands slid up his back. "And all day I couldn't stop remembering what you sounded like and felt like and smelled like and tasted like till I could barely eat dinner, couldn't stand the wait for this moment tonight. Then I've just told you something I've never told another living soul . . . yeah, in my mind, you're my woman—and it ain't got nothing to do with money. Am I making sense?"

He was making so much sense she was about to sob. Her mouth found his to keep from blurting out her confession. Her hands raked his body as she remembered the night before, the agony of the separation, all the fear, and worry, and doubt . . . everything that his sister had told her, everything that she'd just heard came together as she gave herself to him fully.

Her skin caught fire as his bonded to hers, his hot breaths battering her senses. He'd stood up for her, had claimed her, had brought her out in public, respected her, said she mattered and proved it, and this was all she had to give in return.

Every inch of him she'd cherish as she led him over to the bed and undressed him. When the truth came out, he might leave. But for now, she wanted to show him how wrong his father had been. He deserved pleasure, deserved to enjoy the fruits of his labor . . . his labor was worthy, held a family upon broad shoulders. She kissed his shoulders until he gasped, found his chest, laying her palm over his heart, pet it, stroked it, licked it until he arched. Yes, she would be good to his heart, this man of iron ethos, she would. And she peeled away her clothes as she dragged her nose down his abdomen, revering each brick of it, her hair dusting a trail behind each deep, wet kiss, honoring all that he'd stomached, all the pain that he'd sucked up and swallowed for no reason at all.

Her hands slid against his spine, her fingers splayed under his backside, the soft side of her cheek a velvet stroke that promised more. He deserved so much more, and her tongue slid against steel that quivered, his gasp as though she'd cut him, her mouth a molten sheath to heal the pain, her hands holding his hips, stroking his thighs, aiding her in his release from self-denial.

The crown of his head was dug into the pillows, every deep plunge of her mouth making him arch up to meet her. He couldn't bear to watch her, but had to open his eyes. What he needed was in the suitcase, halfway across the room. It felt so good, his vision was blurring. He pushed up on his elbows, unable to catch his breath. As he stared down his body at her, a hard shudder coursed through him.

Her auburn hair billowed over his stomach, her fluid

movement, her shoulders working, her graceful curves
in repose. Jesus . . . he was so close to the edge, it didn't
make sense.

He couldn't speak, just touched the top of her head.
She looked up, her mouth swollen, face flushed, knowing.

Without a word she left him, went to his bag, and
rooted through it. He couldn't even tell her where to
begin, much less breathe. But she mercifully returned
with speed, and covered him while he remained as still
as possible, her gentle touch unfurling a long, deep moan
as she rolled protection down on him. The change of
textures was disorienting, but at this juncture, he was
beyond the fine points.

Yet, he'd been prepared to sit up and was stunned
when she took the lead. Her kiss was so aggressive that
he almost strangled on his own spit. Her body was like
hot wax against his, and her mount was so hard, so immediate that he sat up from the sudden sensation. Arms
enfolded his shoulder, her kisses covered his head, slender fingers raked his hair, and her voice with the rhythm
of her hips beat him down.

"You're such a good man," she murmured. "Oh,
Maxwell . . . I'm crazy about you."

There were no words as she whispered sweet noth-
ings that right now meant everything.

"Oh, baby, what did they do to you? I'll be there," she
promised, her voice trailing off with his shudder, then
dropping an octave as he drove against her harder.
"Give it to me . . . all the hurt . . . get it out."

He was sobbing and cumming, and spasms were col-
lapsing his spinal column, her voice pulling everything
out of him that had been trapped inside for years. Tears
stung his nose; he was choking as he called her name.
Her fragrant hair was plastered against his wet face, his
hand unable to pull her hard enough or fast enough

against him, each pleasure spike bulleting through his groin . . . had him rocking her like a baby, his head dropped back, battling for air.

She sat with her legs wrapped around his waist for what felt like a long time, until he could breathe again, until the intermittent jerks had stopped. Until the tears had stopped. He hadn't been prepared for that.

"You all right?" she murmured against his hairline, flinging her hair over her shoulder and kissing his cheek.

"No. Not at all," he said and smiled as his head dropped to her shoulder. "My mind is all messed up, woman. What'd you do to me?"

"Just cared about you, that's all," she whispered gently, petting his back. "Somebody has to care after you, don't they?"

The woman said she cared after him. He took in a deep, shuddering inhale willing his eyes dry. She cared after him. "Oh, God, don't say that, girl."

"I can't help it," she whispered, rubbing his hair with her cheek. "I care so much about you, Maxwell . . . I'll give you my best. That's all I have to offer."

He looked up to the ceiling, the stuccowork on it becoming blurry. "That's all I ever wanted anybody to give me."

"That's all I've really ever wanted, too."

His mind had been made up before his feet hit the floor. In Highpoint, he'd figure out her taste in furniture. When they got to Charlotte, he'd tell the boys to move it back to Macon and set it up in the house. Maybel would need to stock the joint with champagne and roses in every room. When he got to Richmond, once he saw what style of properties she liked, he'd make a call— start construction. Rebuild what had been a shrine to his parents and get it ready for his wife. In DC, he'd walk her past some stores, get the sense of her taste in rocks. When they hit Baltimore, it was about finding girlfriend a car. In Philly, they'd relax, do dinner, then walk around the galleries and let her show him the art she might like.

Oh yeah . . . he was a man on a mission, and time waited for no man. She was the one; sistah got game . . . but so did he, and he would bring it on strong.

She practically crawled back to her room and was almost too tired to see the blinking light. All she wanted was a shower, to brush her teeth, a few minutes alone to get ready for the ride. But she'd just turned in a story. Mavis flashed through her mind as she reached for the telephone. Wonder of wonders, that's just who called.

"Mavis," she said weakly, once the call connected.

"Girl, what happened to your phone? They said it had been disconnected."

"Long story. I have to get a new one. Soon as I do, I'll holler."

"Cool, but I got a call from some old dude wanting in on the story. He said he needed to talk to you, but didn't want to let Maxwell know he had a comment. I wouldn't give him your number, but told him I'd give you his— just in case this was some long-lost relative with drama wanting in on your piece."

"Bill Jones, by any chance?' Darien sat down quickly and snatched the message pad.

"Yeah. How'd you know?"

"I have wanted to talk to that man . . . and folks kept giving me the runaround about him, then things got crazy."

"Yeah, well . . . I sorta started doing my own digging," Mavis said, her tone filled with concern. "Seems that his name splattered the Macon-Bibb County papers several years ago for some state contract mess. It even showed up in *The Atlanta Tribune*. What's his deal?"

"An old friend of the family," Darien said, casually, alarm coursing through her. She set down the pen slowly next to the pad.

"Girl, don't have my magazine caught up in no mess. If the Fergusons have some yang with them, we kill the story now. You hear me? I cannot tell my boss that I've plastered these folks on the cover as some upstanding family, and they've got skeletons rattling around in their closet."

Darien closed her eyes. "I won't, Mav."

"I don't like the sound in your voice."

"I'm fine. I was just out all night with everybody, and I'm tired. His old man isn't going to be a problem."

"Good. Let me know his deal. I have to run. Here's his number," Mavis said, rattling it off quickly. "The issue will hit the stands in two weeks. Luv ya. Ted's shots are da bomb."

Da bomb . . . Darien repeated to herself. What was gonna blow up now? Trepidation made her dial the number slowly. No answering machine came on, and no one answered. Old folks were adverse to technology, that she knew. But she tried the number again, hoping for some answers. But another part of her really didn't want to know. What if this man was going to try to hurt Maxwell or try to blackmail him for some cash? What if this old man whom he loved like a father had a slimy agenda? A chill ran through her as she stood, dropped the number into her purse, and headed for the shower.

Darien feigned calm the best she could during breakfast. Maxwell looked so happy, like a man with the weight of the world lifted from him. He was almost like a different person. His easy manner matched his casual ivory cable sweater and olive slacks. He was so loose that it was almost scary.

Arnetta kept giving her knowing glances, and she

passed off her unusual quietness for pure beat-down tired. In sly giggles, Arnetta claimed the same excuse, but it hurt Darien to know that their reactions were for totally different reasons.

As though sensing something was wrong, every now and again, Maxwell would cross the invisible public line and hug her in or peck her cheek. Then it seemed that he just gave up all façade when they got on the short flight to North Carolina, threading his fingers within hers as they sat side by side.

"You sure you're okay?" he asked softly, touching her cheek.

Darien nodded and kissed his nose. "I'm fine, just wore out."

He sat back in his seat and sighed. "Yeah . . ."

She could only hope that would satisfy him—for now.

Chapter 13

"So, tell me, what's your favorite color?"

Darien glanced at Maxwell as he asked yet another off-handed question.

"For furniture?"

"Yeah. I'm trying to decide what the new lines might look like . . . can incorporate a little change—somebody who has an eye for décor might be able to make some suggestions to the team down here."

"Well," she stammered, not wanting to offend him. "While the period pieces are nice and strong sellers, on a personal level, I prefer the clean lines of modern . . . a few artsy pieces with a splash of color. I would take a knobby natural linen, put a mud cloth throw on it, then maybe put a stylized orange leather chaise longue opposite it."

He gave her a look like she was speaking Greek.

"Soho, New York—loft action. No knickknacks and stuff like that, no doilies and frillies, colors bold, cultural, art infused. I don't like traditional, at all." But she cleaned up her response when his expression became crestfallen. "But I love what you've created here."

He smiled. "Then it's all good."

Again she watched him pace away. He walked around the furniture warehouse, slapping five and introducing everyone, knowing each employee by name. Ted was having a field day. Arnetta looked like she'd keel over from a love jones, and Maxwell was so chipper, the man seemed to be walking on air.

"Don't like traditional things, huh?' he said, teasing her in a private moment as the group moved through the building to the showroom floor. "But you'd mix and match, some old, some new to be what you said, eclectic?"

She laughed as he nodded toward the beds.

"Any of those work for you?"

She laughed harder and moved away from him.

"Not even the four-poster?" he whispered in her ear discretely and then found the managers to talk to.

As she stood in the midst of the hubbub, his palatial estate came to her mind. The rice bed was magnificent; it was the walls that were the problem. The whole house didn't seem lived in at all. No art, no books, no plants to speak of. Just expensive and out-of-place furniture without any kind of connecting theme.

"You know," she said, one finger on her lip. "I had an idea—might be a bad one for business, but hey."

"Talk to me." He folded his arms over his chest, his expression serious, his eyes fixed upon hers.

"Like, what would happen if you kept the beautifully carved wood frames, and put heavy, bold fabrics on there—like upholstered them with exotic fabrics from the motherland, India, Turkey. I mean tapestry-type fabrics—some solids, some patterns, or a wild mix? Kept the traditional stuff for the base you've already built, but I bet your market could expand to black urban professionals and yuppies in the fast cities, like New York, LA, DC, you know?"

She walked over to a gorgeous oak sleigh bed and ran her hand down the headboard. "Take this piece and put Adinkra symbol stencils in black stain across the top . . . use the heart-shaped Sankofa, since it's a bed and do a black-and-white mud cloth pattern comforter with it—da bomb." She pointed out a traditional French armoire. "Do the same with that, or cover a Queen Anne chair with Native American, hand-woven blanket material. You could do a small test, throw a catalog up on the web, and see what happens."

"Okay," he said, beaming.

She stared at him. "Okay. That's it?"

"Yeah. Done. I like it. Different. Adds new life."

His mood was so unexpectedly jubilant that she almost didn't know how to take him. Arnie had even begun teasing her and had told her to check him for fever. He was the same way in Richmond, asking her about real estate and crazy junk—façade style improvements and whatnot.

Repeatedly she kept warning him that all she was offering was an opinion, not a consultation on how to run his business, which seemed to tickle him to no end. He'd been successful all these years, doing what he was doing, so the last thing she was trying to do was mess up his profitable operations with her wacky tastes.

And she was really worried when he got involved in the intimate details about her choices of tiles, and listened with total focus when she began explaining color schematics that could go with Moroccan tiles, which would then go with the whole cultural effect, but his properties were development white boxes for residential rentals and commercial strip malls. It wasn't about funking them out—that would be up to the tenants.

But she did tell him in DC how much the brownstones

were her favorites, which oddly seemed to make him sad. He didn't appear to get himself back in sorts until she explained that it was the woods and space within them, the high windows, skylights, spiral staircases because they had the height. He listened intently as she described what could be done with recessed lighting, then all was well. It was the strangest thing.

However, she stopped him dead in his tracks when he casually proposed going in a jewelry store along the way. That didn't have anything to do with business, and she was not indulging in one of her all-time weak-nesses—jewelry. Nor was she coming back to Macon with some fancy bracelet or something, and was not going to have Doreetha set hounds on her behind it.

"Maxwell Ferguson, as I live and breathe," a tall, im-peccably coifed sister said as she sauntered to their table.

"Oh, Lord," Arnetta murmured.

Darien's radar went up, and the sister who was dressed in a magnificent Ellen Tracy taupe wool sashayed over to the table. Her short, jet-black hair was layin' and looked like velvet. Her coffee-brown skin, flawless. Her exotic eyes were rimmed with charcoal that gave them a dreamy, drink-you-in appearance. She flashed a brilliant, cos-metic-dentistry-has-worked-on-me-baby smile. Her per-fect boob job made Darien nearly faint. Her legs, which were two inches longer than Darien's, were expertly waxed, covered in silk—Victoria at work. Her fingers were sporting French tips, wrist flashing much ice, feet covered in real crock, bag by Fendi. The woman looked so good that Darien had to suck it up and give respect where it was due. This was a high-maintenance diva, if ever she'd seen one. She knew DC would be a prob-lem.

She watched Maxwell stand, his smile easy, his manner too fluid for her liking.

"Veronica, how are you?"

"Wonderful," she said, pecking his cheek. "How's business going?"

"Good," he said, a bit of strain in his voice, but just a hair. "Things at the law firm going well, I hope?"

"Made partner," she murmured. "We should do lunch and celebrate."

He smiled but didn't answer her. "Let me introduce you to Arnetta James, our vice president of human resources. Ted—"

"Oh, I know Ted from *Urban Professional*. He does the DC circuit quite often. Arnetta, Ted, it's a pleasure." Veronica draped her hand down and gave each one who reached up a careful shake. But her gaze smoothly shifted to Darien.

"Darien Jackson, public relations," Maxwell said, his gaze now going between both women. "She's coordinating an entire firm overhaul. That's why Ted is here, too, because of the spread that's going in the magazine."

Darien watched him. Maxwell was explaining way too much to this witch. But, she would not go there. Nope. She pasted on her best corporate smile and extended her hand. "It's a pleasure."

Butter softness met butter softness, manicure for manicure, they were an even match. Veronica smiled, as did Darien. *Step off. You had your shot.*

"So you're the woman who actually got *the* Maxwell Ferguson to agree to a magazine exposure? I'm impressed," Veronica crooned. "Do you have a business card . . . since you're only there *temporarily*, as a *consultant*, my firm might be interested in your skills."

Oh, shoot—trumped! Over a business basic, a card. Arnetta cast an apologetic glance at Darien.

"No, I don't," Darien said, the words oozing off her

lips. "We've been traveling all around the region, but when our FedEx arrives tomorrow, I can have a courier drop one at your office, if you give me yours."

Veronica smiled. Her nod said *touché*.

"I'm fresh out. Did a conference today, but Maxwell knows how to reach me." Veronica leaned in to him and brushed non-existent lint off his sweater. "If you're going public, you ought to call me before you make any sudden moves with your enterprise." She cast him a sexy wink, waved a half wave to everyone at the table and moved away, purring, "It was a pleasure."

Ouch. All right. She would have to let it ride.

Maxwell sat down and immediately picked up his fork.

"I'm not going to ask who that was," Arnetta snarled.

"Good," Maxwell said through a bite. "Don't."

This was what Jovan had been warning him about— his old past on the open road. Okay, what was done was done. He just wished Darien would offer more than one-word answers. The only thing she'd been very vocal about was not staying overnight in DC.

True Baltimore was no more than an hour away, but everybody was tired. However, push on he would. Maybe once they got settled into the hotel, all the misunderstandings would cease.

He could understand where she was coming from, though. Veronica was fine, no question about that. But what Darien didn't understand was there were thousands of Veronicas out there. Either a man had gotten his run out or he hadn't. Some brothers just couldn't pass up the eye candy—true, he'd been like that once. But then something happens inside and a realization hits: all of the women he'd had were high-maintenance drama queens, totally neurotic. He was not trying to go there or start a family with one of them. Veronica was the kind of woman to bleed a man to bankruptcy in divorce court, or take his children to Paris because she didn't like the maid he'd hired.

He glanced over at Darien. Naw, his baby didn't have a thing to worry about.

She was shook. It had been a while since she'd been this messed up by a competitor, but facts being what they were, she was shook.

Veronica was not only leggy and fine, but she had the education thing going on, too, along with what seemed to be inbred pedigree. Darien let her breath out hard. She'd never had that, never would. Her gaze scanned the horizon of I-95 North. What was the point?

She'd picked up tips on class and style by imitating those around her from social echelons just beyond her reach—and it had landed her in debt up to her eyeballs. She'd learned to dress like them, talk like them, act like them, play games like them. The realization made her sad. At Spelman, she wasn't fourth-generation elite. And she'd had to learn as much as humanly possible in the corporate arena. If it got ugly, say at a cocktail party, and she had to go up against a Veronica, the woman would have decimated her. Art, culture, novels, politics, world events, foreign films, she knew Veronica probably possessed those skills—the DC sisters had that culture thing down.

"I can only take you so far, Maxwell," she murmured, looking out the car window.

"What are you talking about, you can only take me so far?" His gaze swept her as the car swerved, and he returned his attention to the road. He checked the rearview. Ted and Arnie were still behind them. He hated rental cars!

"As a PR consultant, I only have the skills to take the company so far. Then you're going to have to get somebody who's out of my league, and I understand that. There's no hard feelings."

"I don't know what you're talking about, Darien. Out of your league? Girl, stop."

"Mavis is the next rung up, sorta. She's more into the life, the whole buzz-buzz, wine-and-cheese circuit convo thing, but we both have the same background. When your firm starts getting serious ink, there will be opportunities coming your way, folks you'll need to circulate with to go from ten million to a hundred million, and I can't get you there. That's Madison Avenue level, at the very least, DC's finest can network you in. Maybe Chicago or New York types, you understand?"

He heard her. "Veronica is a very old flame who is very needy and very insane. Drama. I'm done with that."

He hadn't heard a word she'd said. "It's not about her, specifically. It's about what she represents, who she knows."

"She's shallow, and yes, knows people, but those folks are like crabs in a barrel, fronting with no real connections worth all the headache that goes with the interaction."

Damn, he'd heard her.

"Okay, Maxwell, point taken on some of them, but there are a lot of—"

"Frauds out there," he said firmly. "I've got the genuine article, and when the firm is ready for Madison Avenue, I'll take the one I trust—you—up there, and we'll sit down at a meeting, together, with you as my public relations advisor, and we'll hire the next-level talent we need—together." He glanced at her. "I don't want to talk about Veronica any more than you want to talk about the crazy guy who you have yet to name for me."

Phew. Okay. That was deep. It messed her up, made her sit back and seal her lips. Brother was not playing. She hadn't heard that tone in his voice. It was more than direct; it was final. But the last part of what he'd stated just made her close her eyes.

"Maxwell, all my life I've been gaming."

He didn't say a word, just drove.

"I've been a fraud, have been fronting, buying stuff to make myself feel whole . . . like I could compete with women like Veronica."

"All the material possessions in the world and all the gloss, Darien, isn't what a brother is looking for at the end of the game. Not when a man is ready—before then, yes. But not after he's ready, end of story."

His comment stole her voice for a moment. "I'm just now seeing that because I've found somebody like you."

He smiled, his glance at her tender. "I ain't so bad for an old country boy, am I?"

"You're perfect."

"Good." He sighed. "Look, I already told you that, back in the day . . . yeah, the flash would have blinded me. A lot of brothers go through that phase, but it don't last—nor do those relationships. When things get real, you've gotta have a woman who can deal with the ups and downs. You've gotta love her if she's fat or skinny . . . if her hair is done or not. And she's gotta love you if you're having a good year or not, if you can buy her a big house or not, and if you get fat, dumb, and happy with a beer belly or not." He chuckled and slapped his stomach. "One day, baby, all of this might go to pot. Hope you'll still love me. Will ya?"

She became very, very still. He was talking about growing old and getting potbellies . . . was talking about love, that four-letter word that was to remain unspoken.

"If you'll love me when my butt gets as big as Cynthia's."

He laughed. "It can get as big as Doreetha's . . . shoot, I might like that." He winked at her. "Long as you don't stop doing what you did to me in Atlanta."

She looked out the window and chuckled. "I didn't do nothing to you in Atlanta."

"Stop playing."

They both laughed.

"For real, though," she said, needing to wipe her slate clean. "I brought clothes, jewelry, went here and there, trying to compete and keep up with the Joneses and got myself into hock."

"So, we'll get you out of hock. When you know better, you do better, Bill used to tell me all the time. He gave me a shot. I've messed up a few early deals, trust me, but somebody helped me. I didn't do *everything* all by my lonesome."

There it was again, the dual issues that had been stabbing into her brain; what did Bill Jones want, and she had to tell Maxwell there was no stalker.

"Max, I'm going to work off my debt."

"Have it your way," he said in a weary tone, "but I can help, and there's no strings attached. I'm crazy about you, want to see you have nice things . . . I don't know, Darien. I don't know what is 'politically correct,' " he said, making little quotes in the air with one hand. "This is the age of the independent woman, but still a man ain't nothin' if he don't do for her. What's a brother to do?"

"Just love me for now and let me sort this all out."

He became very, very still. "I do love you, you know that, right?"

She became very, very still again. Then the floodgates opened. Words poured out in nonsequiturs. "I love you, too. That's why I can't have you thinking some brother was stalking me when he wasn't. I can't let you pay bills that really came from foolishness, and too-high pride that made me freelance for a year, thinking I was going to land—in the middle of a recession—back into the cushy corporate post I had before, and all because I couldn't back down from a lifestyle that was prefabricated and ridiculous—that's pride, foolish pride. I will not work you like that, not after all you've done and been

through, Maxwell. I may not be much, but I do have
some decency. And, at first, I thought you were just the
repo man, and yeah, yeah, I was ready to game to the
max to keep my stupid car! But, then, Jesus, you were so
genuine and nice and just . . . aw, Lawd, brother . . . just
the one, and I couldn't even think to do that to you—
and you keep giving, and in the old days I would have
burned your plastic up, but I don't roll like that anymore."

She covered her face. Her ears were ringing. She felt
nauseous. He hadn't said a word. They drove like that
for miles. Her breathing hard, him looking straight
ahead.

"So, you lied to me?"

His question felt like a slap in the face, timed after
fifteen agonizing minutes of pure silence. She couldn't
even look at him.

"Yes. But only about the guy."

He swallowed a smile. "But, see, woman, if you'd lie
about something as serious as that, then how would I
ever be able to trust you?"

"You wouldn't," she whispered thickly.

"But I appreciate that you told me. That means something." He glimpsed her from the corner of his eye.

"I'm glad it does, even if that's all we have left. I just
hope you'll know that everything else I did was for
real."

Why were women so melodramatic? Maxwell shook
his head.

"You played me, girl."

She swallowed hard and nodded. "But not all the
way."

"That's like being a little bit pregnant."

"Technically . . . yeah, you're right." She let her
breath out hard.

"Darien," he said. "Look at me, honey."

She shook her head. "I don't want to see the disappointment in your eyes."

"That's not what you'll see," he said softly, touching her arm.

She glanced at him and only looked away when his focus went to the road.

"We all make mistakes. Like I said, I have my mess with me, too. But sometimes a mistake can come up roses."

She looked at him and saw a half smile.

"I thought some fool was chasing the *finest* women I'd ever laid eyes on . . . who dropped a mink in a lobby with only a red teddy under it—bare feet, running from the law and a stalker. A brother was messed up, I tell you." He chuckled. "So, I said, Maxwell, my man, for this one you might hafta bend the rules and let the car note slide. Sleep on it, but that's the thing, I couldn't go to sleep after I'd seen you. Otis read me the Riot Act. He was right, I was wrong, but, dang, girl, *yous fine.*"

She slapped his arm and laughed hard, incredulous. "You said you didn't go in for flash anymore, so how you gonna tell me about my teddy!"

"I said I was recovered, not dead." He laughed hard, hoping that one day he could demonstrate the courage she just had in the name of love. So he tried to tell his story in a fable, the way old folks down in Macon were wont to do. Maybe, when it all came to light, she wouldn't think ill of him.

Maxwell let out a patient breath. "Lotta people make decisions like that every day. The police might let a ticket slide because the person he pulls over got a long story. Gas man might go to your house at the end of the week, when you say you'll have the money, instead of the day you don't. You know, there's a window of opportunity where personal discretion is involved. And, some folks get used to having that done for them all the time because they think they're entitled. Me, I was always grateful when a little slack got cut my way."

"I hear you," she murmured, snuggling against his shoulder. "I love you."

If Ted and Arnie weren't behind him, he would have pulled off at the next exit to find a motel.

"I love you, too, girl. So, I'm glad you jump-started my competitive nature—among other things," he said, stroking her hair. "Men, we go through that. Size a brother up, try to see how much he's worth. All I could imagine was some polished, corporate debonair fool had you, then snapped when you left him, but figured you were used to a classy guy who could roam the circuit with authority. You know, the kind who stops traffic when he walks in the room—*bam.*"

"And, you're not that? Pullease . . ."

He leaned over and kissed the top of her head, warmed by her compliment. Dang . . . he'd told her he loved her, and she'd said it back.

"Then, I got to play knight in shining armor, a little bit," he said, chuckling. "I loved it."

She peered up at him and shook her head, smiling. "You're a mess."

"Aw, girl, you don't know. It felt good. And the more you said no, the more I just wanted to do. And because you were struggling against help so, I knew you weren't playing. If you had tricks and games, you would have been all on it, snatching and grabbing. Then my sisters put their eye on you—Doreetha nailed it, said ya had home training. My brothers were laid out since they saw ya, and Arnetta has already claimed you as kin." He kissed her head again, this time letting the kiss linger. "See, sometimes a mistake can work out, but don't let me fool you. I've seen enough game players in my day to spot 'em real quick."

"I'm not playing now," she murmured, rubbing his arm.

He swallowed hard. "Neither am I, and I'm glad you stopped and told me such a fish tale that I had to walk away scratching my head."

She laughed, but it came out low and sexy from her throat. "How long till we get into Baltimore?"

"I don't know," he said on a short breath. "Maybe a half hour."

"We should have spent the night in DC."

"I know, girl."

"Think we should get separate rooms?"

"What's the point?"

"You're right, you're right. How long did you say?"

He glanced at her. "Fifteen minutes, tops, if we stay at a hotel in the Inner Harbor."

"Let's do that, then. I don't think my nerves can take driving much farther north."

Christmas seemed so far away. He'd never be able to hold out till then, especially not when her need to be with him had come down hard and fast like it had—just like his.

"What's your favorite stone?"

"Besides diamond?"

They laughed.

"I can't even think about it right now."

"I'm trying to neutralize the subject. Tell me shape."

"Oval," she murmured, closing her eyes and tracing his thigh.

"Size?"

"Large," she said with a deep, sexy chuckle.

"I meant . . . never mind." He had to do better than that. That would have given it away.

Her hand was dangerously near his groin. "Girl, stop. I've gotta keep my eyes on the road."

"I'm not doing nuffin'."

"Stop," he said, hoping she wouldn't.

"Tell me what you want, first, when we go upstairs."

He almost swerved off the road. He hadn't seen this side of her, but the more comfortable she got with who they were, the sexier she became. He loved that about her, the fact that he could bring that out, and it wasn't just there on the surface for any ole body to have. He liked having to work for it. "I can't even talk about it at this point."

"Then I know what it is."

He almost closed his eyes, but then remembered he was driving. "Stop. Ten more minutes."

"All right, but I'm gonna tell you the same thing when we get upstairs."

If she was working him, so be it.

He didn't care how it looked, or how early it was. He left his sister and Ted standing in the lobby dumbstruck. No, he didn't need no concierge to bring up the bags or interrupt his flow. He needed this woman immediately in his arms, behind a locked door, stripped. His needs were basic. Very plain at the moment. He hoped hers were. Because when he opened the room door, it was over.

Bags hit the floor; she was in his arms. Her sweater almost ripped as he yanked it over her head. The seal between them was only broken as layers of clothing got removed. There was nothing suave about it. If the hook or button didn't give, it got damaged.

"Stop."

"I can't."

"Get it out and on now before you start."

She was the only one making sense.

"All right. Don't go nowhere." He pulled away from the wall and unzipped his suitcase.

She got on the bed, all the lights on. She was breathing hard; so was he. He had the box in his hand. She studied it.

"How you want it?"

"Without this."

She smiled. "Not tonight."

"Then marry me."

She opened and closed her mouth. "Stop playing."

He chuckled. It was not supposed to come out like that. "My bad."

She scooted away from him. "Put it on. I don't trust you."

He sat on the edge of the bed and worked fast. She had every right not to trust him. He had definitely lost his mind.

But when he came to her again, all playfulness had gone. Her gaze was serious, her breathing ragged, like his. He could tell by the look on her face, no foreplay was needed; she was good to go. She nodded, as though she'd read his mind. He complied, thanking her with a deep kiss.

In a frenzied, unvarnished, give and take, they were one. Her moans trailing his, chasing them through his chest until hers cornered it. Her uplifts, meeting his down strokes, synchronized, guttural—no terms of endearment; no easy, gentle touches. Hands found an anchor and held on. No past existed. Only the present mattered. The future was too far away to worry about. The storm was too torrid for the mind to travel that far.

He could feel her sliding, coming toward the brink, and it pushed him over. He couldn't even utter her name.

His mind went blank. Cleaning the slate of all that had come before her but had enough reserves to know none would come after her. Winded, he lay on her breathing, eyes shut tight. The light was now too intense. He hoped she was all right; he was for damned sure.

The last of the shudders abated in slow retreat. She took in air through her mouth, her eyes closed, knowing. Her body reverberating his rhythm all through it.

For richer, for poorer, business boom or bust. Scrambling to make ends meet or drinking champagne by the sea. Fancy dinners in swank hotels or chitterlings done down home. Big belly, flat belly, no babies or ten. It didn't matter. This was it. The end of the line.

If there had ever been any question before, she knew—this was the one.

Chapter 14

Maxwell stretched and smiled with his eyes still closed. It never ceased to amaze him how women could always seem to wake up first and commandeer a bathroom first. It had to be something in their DNA.

The previous night of outright passion had made every muscle in his body feel like lead. He could barely stand as he trudged across the floor and nearly tripped over Darien's purse.

Bending with a grunt, he shoved the contents back inside it—then stopped as his eye caught a glimpse of something that gave him serious pause. What was Bill Jones's name and number doing on a piece of notepaper from the Atlanta Doubletree? Hadn't he asked her not to follow up with Bill? Didn't they have an understanding that he'd wanted to let sleeping dogs lie? The worst part was, if the number was on that particular hotel stationery, it meant that she'd been in contact with the man during their trip . . . something so recent— and had done it all the while professing that she was bearing her soul, coming clean, starting anew. Why didn't she tell him she'd spoken to Bill?

Maxwell put the note back where he'd found it and righted her purse against the wall. He listened to the shower. Just moments ago it had been his intent to join her to savor an early-morning interlude. Only hours ago, in the heat of their private night, he'd thought of her as the one, someone he could trust . . . someone to be his wife. But with this standing between them, she might as well be in another room, if not another state.

Perhaps Jovan had been right. It was time to slow down, gain perspective, and make very wise decisions.

"Good morning, sleepyhead," Darien said brightly, bouncing into the room with only a towel on. "I would ask you how you slept, but since I already know you didn't do much of that," she said, laughing, "I'll ask, how you feelin'?"

"I'm all right," he said, his tone controlled. "You done in the bathroom?"

She just stared at him for a moment. "Yeah." Her voice was a mere whisper as she studied him hard, confused. "What's the matter?"

"Been wasting a lot of time, girl. But we've had fun. Now it's time for me to get back to work." He crossed the room and slipped into the bathroom alone.

Even though she wanted him to have all the success in the world, she secretly hoped that something had gone wrong with the business—and prayed that nothing was wrong between them. His responses were serious, cryptic, and aloof all through breakfast. Arnetta couldn't even draw him out, nor could Ted. Each time Arnetta discretely inquired, Darien could only shrug. She'd gone as far as to even tell Arnetta how he'd been before she came out of the shower, which was anything but cool. They'd slept cuddled up like paired spoons.

He'd been positively morose during the Baltimore photo session, so much so that Ted gave up and just focused on the other employees and his brother Montrose who'd come up just for the session. Monty wasn't able to get to the bottom of it, either. And Darien found herself in the position of being an outsider. Ted was offered more conversation than she.

The silent drive up to Philadelphia was nerve-racking. For the duration of the journey, Maxwell kept what little conversation there was strictly business. All she could do was watch him maneuver in traffic and return innumerable business calls on his hands-free telephone unit.

Her hopes of finding out what was wrong were dashed when Otis couldn't draw him out, and the Fergusons seemed to mysteriously close ranks on her. The tension was horrible. No one was talking, there were no plans to go eat together, just the cold shoulder.

Darien sifted every fact in her mind, reviewed, and rehashed every waking moment they'd been together, and drew a blank. It didn't make sense. If there was something he didn't like about her, or he'd had a change of heart, or he was angry about making the commitment to give her a cell phone or any other perk, he should have just flat out told her. That would have made more sense than this!

By dinnertime, insecurity began to really set in. It had entered her pores, was washing through her bloodstream like the flu. Anger and tears were just beneath the surface of her skin. All it would take was a nick to make it surface and turn into a full-blown event. If he wanted to get with Veronica or a woman like that tramp, then he should have been man enough to just say so. But to string her along, lead her on, then just dump her by being nasty . . . making her be the one to break up or to do something as a reaction to his treatment that he could then cite as the reason things wouldn't work between them . . . men! She'd thought Maxwell was above that, was better than that, and had more integrity and courage. This was childish! And he said he didn't play games, right!

"I need to stay up here in Philly for a day or so after you all go back, then I'll rejoin you all Monday," Darien announced. "I have a few things to do up here."

"I bet you do," Maxwell said, not looking up from his Palm Pilot.

Arnetta glanced at Ted, who shot a troubled look over to Otis.

"What is *that* supposed to mean?" Darien kept her voice modulated and set her menu down slowly. That's all she'd need was for heads to turn within the posh environs of Zanzibar Blue. No, she had to be cool, let the soft jazz and upscale after-work patrons surround her and keep her grounded.

Maxwell looked up slowly, his gaze lethal, but his voice so low and even it could have cut cement. "It means that I *know* you have a lot of business to handle— *so handle it.*"

Otis hailed a server as he polished off his tumbler of Chivas. Arnetta studied her menu so closely that it was only two inches from her face. Ted sent his gaze to the jazz combo that was performing. Darien's nails dug into her palm. Oh, now, it was on.

"If you've got a problem with me staying in Philly for a couple of days to work the press and to get an East Coast trail of newspaper ink happening, then you need to say that, rather than signifying your discontent."

"I never signify, Miss Jackson. If I don't like something, I'll tell you straight with no chaser. Handle your business."

Now she was Miss Jackson? Complete disbelief swept through her. Oh yeah, and she wasn't Miss Jackson last night when he was hollering and calling her baby!

Ted choked on his water. A server arrived and stopped the timer on the bomb that was about to go off. Arnetta rattled off her gourmet entrée choice so fast and with such detail that the veteran server had to actually write it down. Otis was so flustered that he couldn't decide, and when the waiter turned his attention to Maxwell, he simply waved him off.

"Ladies first," Maxwell said in a rumble. "I'm not hungry."

"You ain't eating?" Otis asked, glancing around the group, astonished.

Maxwell shook his head. "Just Jack Daniel's, black, straight up."

Arnetta let her breath out in a slow stream that almost produced a whistle. "Darien, uh, whatchu having, girl?"

"Given that I've just lost my appetite, too, I'll go with a small bowl of lobster bisque." Darien shut her leather-bound menu hard, but handed it to the server with a forced smile.

"Maybe an appetizer, sir?" the server asked, his voice so smooth and diplomatic that one could tell he'd seen this scenario before.

"Thank you, but I'll pass on everything," Maxwell muttered.

Darien just looked at him. She was so angry that her ears were ringing. She wanted to reach across the table and slap his face, but thought better of it. All right, so if that's how he wanted it, fine. No one else at the table had done a single thing wrong to her, and she wasn't going to allow Maxwell's negative vibes to ruin the evening. She'd go back to the Ritz Carlton, to her own room—alone—and would get her press releases ready. She didn't have to take this from him—boss or not, lover or not!

* * *

Dinner was a disaster. As good as the food looked, and as rich and well seasoned as it smelled, she couldn't taste it. Rage and hurt had deadened her senses. Whatever the group had been talking about, she hadn't a clue. Her focus was on her wineglass, and would occasionally drift over to the musicians.

She made a laundry list of the thousand errands a woman who was about to be given the boot needed to run. First stop, go to 1515 Market Street up to Consumer Credit Counseling Service and consolidate all bills into one payment. That way, once she slapped the boss's face and resigned, or he fired her, whichever came first, she'd have a manageable, single bill to begin healing her credit so she could perhaps one day have her own credit card. She'd give him his damned cell phone back and go get a prepaid one, with ten dollars worth of minutes on it from the 7-Eleven convenience store.

You could run but you couldn't hide. It was time to pay the band because she'd danced her natural butt off. Fine. So be it. She'd even call up the student loan people, fall on her sword, and get an unemployment deferment, then when that ran out, she'd get a hardship deferment—this time she'd do the paperwork, would just sit down and address the details instead of running from the feds. Although the car was going to be an issue, she'd let the dealer just take it—maybe get a hooptie? She wasn't quite sure what to do about that. Perhaps the folks on Market Street at the counseling service would know.

As Darien twirled her napkin in her lap and intermittently sipped her wine, oblivious to the strained attempts to conduct civil conversation going on around her, she wanted to kick herself. How had she allowed herself to get into such a mess in the first place? she wondered. If she had done all the things that she had to do on Friday, years ago, she'd be out of hock, a free woman, with consolidated debt that she could handle, her own apartment, a regular car—nothing flashy, but something to get her from point A to point B—and would have probably been employed somewhere, even if it wasn't her dream job.

She stifled a sigh. Okay, it was time to handle her business. Maybe, even if Maxwell was being a hard ass, maybe one of his brothers would relent and at least agree to ship her things up north. Maybe Arnetta would allow her to pay the moving costs on a sort of layaway plan, which she'd honor to the bone because Arnetta had been nice to her—they were girls. Plus, she had to call Mavis and see if she could dredge up some freelance work to tide her over while her things were in storage and she looked for a new apartment and a job. This time, no swank joint. Basics. An efficiency, perhaps, near one of the more than twenty-two Philadelphia college campuses—as long as it was clean and in a relatively safe campus police–reinforced zone, she could hang.

Although her pride was stung and she was hurt to the bone, she had to go back to Macon and at least make it till payday. A sigh crossed her lips, and she could feel her shoulders sag. There was no family up in Philly, no good friend's sofa to crash and burn on, and the last place she was going to go was one of her old suitors' apartments. No. She had some connections up here, freelance workwise. She had to start where she at least knew the terrain a little bit. Once she got financially stronger, she could branch out. Right now, though, it was best to keep her cards close to the vest and play it safe, conservative, for once.

Her family and Mavis crossed her mind, and she instantly banished the thought. This was a solo mission, and Atlanta was out of the question. Not that there wasn't opportunity there, but she couldn't bear to have her sisters rub this very personal failure in her face. And,

Mavis . . . she didn't think she could deal with being laughed at and called a fool.

She could sit there looking pitiful all she wanted and could sigh till the cows came home. The woman had lied. She'd taken the most sacred part of his trust regarding a person he cared about so dearly and was playing games with that. Intolerable. He'd thought better of Darien Jackson . . . had messed around and allowed her to blow up his head. But that was just the thing—he might have been born at night, but not last night. Uh-uh.

So girlfriend could take her fast-talking, city-walking, fine self on. He wasn't trying to play or be played. Matter of fact, he'd let her get her run out, give her as much rope as she needed to tangle herself up and bust herself. The truth always came out, and when it did, there were no words.

Only problem was all the mess he'd started. Not just with her, but he had his whole operation in the middle of it. And he was caught in this very tricky position now, all because of her. He had furniture being reupholstered, damned Spanish tiles en-route, art from galleries in DC on the way, Miss Maybel buying up liquor store shelves and cleaning out florists. Maxwell rubbed his jaw and looked at the band. He knew pride went before a fall, but to stop all that motion now meant he'd have to admit he'd done it all for a woman. Never happen.

What the hell was he gonna tell the construction crew? Oh, I changed my mind, don't want the skylight, or the recessed lights? Was he supposed to just say that he didn't want 'em to paint the whole house over? How was he gonna explain all the details he'd been exacting about on the stains for her armoire and vanity—he had women's stuff coming into his house! Pots and pans and dishes and such. Yeah, like he could say he just had a change of mind. Sure, his brothers would believe that he'd torn out the fountain and replaced it with some crazy five-thousand-dollar modern art thing all on a whim—they'd commit him! He almost groaned out loud thinking about the pool and tennis court he'd approved with a wave, telling the fellas, "Just do it."

This woman had no idea, no concept what he would have done for her, if she'd just been real. He took a swig of his drink and set it down so hard on the table that all conversation stopped. He didn't care.

"Otis," he said, unable to stand it any longer, "cover the bill with your card and turn in the expenses. I'm done."

All eyes were on Maxwell as he stood. He refused to look at Darien.

"You're gonna just leave and go back to the hotel without any of us?" Arnetta asked, her gaze tearing around the group.

"I've got things to do back in Macon. Something came up that I need to address. I'll see y'all tomorrow."

"You're flying out tonight?" Otis leaned back in his chair and wiped his head.

"Yeah. Like I said, brother, I'm done." Maxwell allowed his gaze to linger on Darien as he began moving away from the table.

"But your photos, man . . . uh, what do you want me to—"

"Give them to Darien," Maxwell snapped at Ted. "She'll know what to do with them. She has the best game in town."

If she hadn't been so mortified, she would have wept out loud. Everybody was trying to act like nothing out of the ordinary was going on, chitchatting nervously about every insignificant thing they could scavenge to talk about. In their attempt to salvage her dignity and appear as though they had no concept that she had been sleeping with the boss, it only made the humiliation burn more.

It didn't help that Arnetta rubbed her back during the entire short walk to the hotel. Nor did it help that Otis who'd previously been her worst critic, kept mumbling parables in his own, inept male way.

"You know, Darien, the Lord works in mysterious ways," Otis said, as though trying to deliver a sermon on the palatial white marble front steps of the Ritz Carlton.

Darien inwardly cringed, nodded, and smiled. "It's all good," she said blithely, hoping to escape.

"We gonna look back on this and laugh one day, girl," Arnetta assured her. "The boss gets moody sometimes, but don't let it scare you off, hear?"

"I got plenty of good shots that should chill him out," Ted said, petting his camera. "Great stuff you can use for the campaign, feel me?"

"Thanks, Ted," she said quietly, "but somehow I don't think that's the issue."

There. She'd said it. They could all stop pretending like they didn't know what the real subject matter was. Now would they please just let her go up to her room to grieve alone?

Otis shook his head, and the group tightened around her, imparting platitudes like one would tell a mourner at a big family funeral.

"It's a long road that has no turn," Otis said, nodding. "Jus' keep yo' eye on the sparrow."

Darien closed her eyes. She would die a thousand deaths on the steps of this five-star hotel.

"Uhmmm-hmmm," Arnetta said.

Darien was just glad the woman hadn't said *amen*.

"It'll be aw'ight," Ted said. "It's all good."

"Uh-huh," Darien said, fishing for her plastic room key. She was out.

Darien ruffled her hair as she stood at the gate at Philadelphia International Airport waiting on her Southwest Air flight. Things did happen in mysterious ways, she had to admit. Even Mrs. Smith said that when she'd popped in and gave her a hug—and how needed that hug was—and that hug had turned into a confession, which brought out Mrs. Smith's black book of available apartments. Darien closed her eyes. All she had to bring was the first month and last month's rent down upon Mrs. Smith's good word, and she'd be in a cute little efficiency not far from Drexel U.

The orange-and-blue patterns on the planes, and the fluorescent lights in the building made Darien squint. Winter was here, but the ground was still dry. The holidays were pressing near. It was supposed to be a happy time of year, and she'd accomplished a lot in short order. Why did she feel like crying?

She had a good plan for once in her life and had taken the first solid steps toward rebuilding her credit and getting out of debt. She'd made good on her promise to Mrs. Smith—had gone as straight as she knew how to, albeit with a small passion-induced detour, but still . . . She owed the world beyond student loans just a little under ten grand, and ironically, because she'd landed a cover story, Mavis could pay her three dollars a word for a thirty-five hundred-word piece. Go figure.

Ten thousand five hundred dollars was on its way to her, all because Mavis loved Ted's photos and her story. Yet it irked her that the reason Mavis's boss went for the high freelance payout was because all of Ted's expenses on the exclusive had been covered by Allied, which meant there was a little fat in the budget to pay the writer. And it bugged her to no end that all the media contacts she'd spoken with were interested in doing a piece only because it would tie in with a spread about to hit a national mag that they could piggyback off. Fine.

However, this time, there'd be no shopping. Christmas this year would be homemade cookies, cobblers, and love. The whole chunk of money on the way was going to pay off her debt. Her paycheck, the one and only she'd most likely draw from Allied, would get her into her apartment. Anything left over from those two checks might buy her some bus tokens and food until she got another freelance gig and a job, which she reasoned wouldn't be impossible, now that she had a cover story soon to be in her portfolio. The mink had to go, too— that would wipe out the balance due on the car lease, maybe, and might let her get a five-hundred-dollar used clunker. Darien sighed.

But it kept coming back to Allied States, LLC, and the maverick behind it. Everything she was going to leverage to fast-forward her life came from there. She hated that fact. Then again, she didn't. That's what was supposed to be the deal when they'd met. He would help her get on her feet, she'd do good work for his firm, and that was the end of the transaction. She'd done her part; he'd done his. So what, they'd had a mad, crazy, intense fling in the process. They were both grown, both players to the bone. So why did she still feel like she wanted to cry?

The late afternoon sun bathed her apartment as she stepped into it and quietly shut the door. She'd told herself she was over it. Had repeated that to herself over and over on the plane. Had reminded herself to be realistic when no Lexus pulled up to collect her from the airport on a bright, sunny Saturday afternoon. She'd told herself this was the way things were as she'd climbed aboard a Macon-Bibb County Transit bus alone, bumping the suitcase up the steps without aid to stand holding a metal pole. So there was no reason for tears to even try to run down her face when she spied the dead spray of white Cherokee roses on the counter.

Breathing hard, refusing to sob, Darien crossed the room and attacked the offending flowers. "In the trash, you are dead," she said, her voice faltering, and she winced when a thorn bit into her finger.

That was it. The nick that drew blood and every repressed emotion up with it. She rushed to the sink and turned on the cold water. She watched as the running tap washed the little red droplet away, a tinge of pink hitting the porcelain. And she wasn't sure why that made her bawl, or why it made her bend over and nearly vomit. She didn't know why she was thinking about ribs and a man slamming his finger in her cabinets. And she didn't know why he had to give her those dumb flowers, any more than she knew why she'd kept the card and one of them pressed in her journal.

Darien covered her face with her hands. She didn't want to look at the now shriveled petals that were once fragrant and waxy and fresh . . . oh, why was she thinking about how she'd gone to the salon and gotten waxed just for him? She scrunched up her toes in her shoes, remembering putting a special design on them for him.

"Stop it," she shouted to herself. "You will not go there." She quickly dried her face with a dishtowel. Yeah, okay. She might be pretty, but she had thorns, too. She'd pack this joint up and blow out of town so fast that his head would spin. She could get a job! She could pay her own bills! She had a career, and a life, and friends, and family, and could find a way to get a car! She had somewhere to live and connections, knew people, too! No strings attached . . . yeah, she'd cut the cord and cut his ass dead. In a little while, she'd have credit again, and she didn't need him for any of those things!

Darien drew in a deep, steadying, cleansing breath through her nose and let it out through her mouth. This was war. She dragged her suitcase into the bedroom. Today and tomorrow she was packing. Monday, she was resigning. As a consultant, there was no such thing as two weeks notice! She'd live like a hermit till Monday—one spoon, one fork, one plate, and a cup left out, plus toilet paper, soap, and toothpaste, that was it. Everything else was going in a box to await a state of readiness to move. When the mail came from *Urban Professional*, she'd be on her way to the check-cashing agency, would wire the cash to her Philly bank and then get out of town. Allied could simply forward her the one and only check she'd accept from them.

She noticed the sun about to drop beneath the horizon as she set out the single fork, cup, and spoon next to the plate. She glanced around the apartment with purpose, glad that she still had boxes in the basement, glad that she'd been so otherwise consumed that she hadn't fully unpacked anyway.

Otis's platitude jumped into her mind. "Yeah, all right, Lord, you work in mysterious ways, I know . . . had to bring me all the way down here to break my pride—that's done," she said bitterly, talking to herself. She snatched up her pocketbook and dumped the contents on the bed, and searched for a huge satchel that she could stuff all her necessities into. "Good thing I didn't unpack all the way, but you didn't have to make him so fine, did ya?"

Sorting with care, she sat down beside the pile, tired and defeated. She took out the corporate credit card, Allied's cell phone, and roughly shoved them aside. Then she began sorting receipts to turn in for her expenses on the road, growing weary just thinking about the conversation she knew she'd have to have with Arnetta.

But as she saw the note with Bill Jones's number on it, she sighed and closed her eyes. "Lord, have mercy . . ." She had to call the old man back. Even angry with Maxwell, she wasn't trying to have her magazine article and any press she'd drummed up ruin the man's business all because some elderly blackmailer from the sticks had an agenda. She at least owed his brothers and sisters that much. No matter how wrong Maxwell was, the rest of the Ferguson clan were good people.

She stood with purpose and punched in the number on her cell phone and waited. When the line connected, she let out an impatient breath of relief.

"Mr. Jones, Darien Jackson here. You called?"

"Why, yes, ma'am," he said in a cultured, old south croon. "Why, it's a pleasure, and I thank you kindly for taking the time from your schedule to do me the honor."

Her hand clenched the telephone. This was an old time player, for real. His attempt at southern charm grated her to the last hair on her head. "I don't mean to be short, Mr. Jones, but I'd like to understand the nature of your call."

"Of course. I do understand you young folks have things to do, places to be, and people to see. But I heard tell, through my good friend Reverend Mathis, that you were the young lady about to set Macon upside down. That's how I came to call yo' magazine, and they wouldn't allow me to acquire your number, which is understandable, but I am glad you called."

"Why didn't you want Maxwell Ferguson to know you'd been in touch? I'm sure the good Reverend must have told you that I'm on temporary assignment at his firm—you could have contacted me there."

Deep, baritone laughter filled the telephone, and it made her uneasy.

"Just like a good reporter—wanna get the facts, right?"

She liked nothing about his tone or the unspoken implication in it. Her nerves tightened the muscles at the base of her spine. This old man was going to be a problem; she could feel it. A swath of protectiveness toward the Fergusons cut through her personal issues with their family head and made her voice become tight.

"The facts that I have gathered so far, sir, are that they are a fine, upstanding, noble family who have worked hard for everything they have. *That's* what's going into my article."

"Only fittin'," he said with a deep sigh. "That's why you and I need to talk."

Darien paused. She wasn't prepared for the way his voice had become tender.

"All right. I'm leaving soon . . . to uh, take on another assignment. So, I can't—"

"What about tomorrow, after you go to church?"

Darien paused. "I don't go to church. That was a special occasion to accompany a photo shoot."

"Well," he said slowly. "I can't argue with that. I don't rightly attend much myself these days on account of my health. But Rev comes to see me and check on me from time to time."

Looking at her watch, she knew it was too late to go by Bill Jones's house tonight. "What about tomorrow morning. Will that work for you?"

"Do you prefer coffee or tea?" he asked with a smooth chuckle. "Been a long time since I had a lady by here."

He knew it was foolish, but he kept glancing around the sanctuary hoping she'd come to church. Now what had possessed him to even go there was beyond him. But his head still swiveled each time the big double doors in the back opened.

"She's probably on the next thing smoking back to Philly," Arnetta hissed, her jaw set hard as the choir rocked.

"I don't know what you're talking about," Maxwell grumbled. "I ain't looking for her."

"You need to apologize, man," Jovan said under his breath. "Otis told me you acted the park ape up there. You can't be treating no woman you trying to court like that in a restaurant, boy—you crazy?"

"First of all," Maxwell whispered hard, leaning in toward Jovan, "yo' ass wasn't there, and second—"

"You are *not* cussing up here in the Lord's house, Maxwell Ferguson," Doreetha hissed. "You best go to the rail today, boy!"

"That's what I told him," Arnetta said, her head bobbing.

"Apologize, man," Otis muttered, leaning over a pew to get near Maxwell's ear. "Po' chile was almost in tears on the hotel steps."

See, this was why he didn't do church, didn't let family in his business, and definitely didn't let no woman under his skin!

Darien stood on the porch of a gray clapboard house that needed great repair, her eyes making a financial assessment as she waited. She tried to gauge how much the old buzzard ambling to the door would try to soak from the Ferguson family.

A sense of responsibility set her jaw hard. A sense of indignation pushed her shoulders back and lifted her chin. But as warm, kind eyes set in a brown, tired face opened the door, it was hard to keep the daggers in her glare.

"Aw, now, ain't you just as lovely as I imagined you would be," Bill Jones said, holding the screen door out for Darien to enter.

She just smiled and didn't verbally answer him, but allowed her gaze to settle on the tattered furnishings as the smell of mildew and old age entered her nose. However, home training took over, jutted her arm out and gentled her expression as she shook Bill Jones' hand then followed him to sit on a beat-up blue floral sofa. She looked at the Dollar Store coffee mugs he'd set out on a plastic platter with a can of condensed milk beside it near a sugar bowl that was half empty. A sad knowing overcame her as she graciously accepted his humble offering.

"Well now, since you pressed for time and came all the way here to the edge of Macon to see me, the least I can do is git to the point." Bill Jones stirred his coffee slowly and sipped it loudly, setting his mug down on the table with care. "Doctor says I should give it up at my age, but force of habit, like most things, I can't."

She nodded, fully understanding the stark truth in his comment. Darien took a sip of the lukewarm coffee and tried to keep an open mind. But a hundred questions leaped in to flood it as she stared at what she could tell had once been a refined gentleman. It was in his ruddy, freshly shaven face, his close barbered shock of silver-gray hair, and the odd choice of a golf outfit—green plaid pants, highly polished shoes, lemon-yellow sweater, strange. So much could be told by his tall, lean carriage, his little mannerisms of speech . . . it was in his eyes, and his hands, that were tapered, not calloused, a bit bent by arthritis and yet strong.

"Ah, to the point," he said with a sad smile when she hadn't joined him in polite banter.

She wished she had, but frankly didn't have it in her to beat around the bush.

"My Maxwell," he murmured, again stirring his coffee.

Darien bristled at the ownership. The man had a father.

"That boy is like a son to me," Bill Jones said in a far-off voice.

Darien sipped her coffee very slowly to keep her eyes from narrowing. This old man, true, needed money, and she knew Maxwell enough to be sure he would give him the shirt off his back, but not like this, not by being leveraged, and not by playing the violin strings of family attachment.

"Me and his daddy used to be fast friends—that's how I came to take Maxwell under my wing."

"That's nice," Darien said without emotion. "Was real decent of you to watch out over a good friend's son with no strings attached." She hoped her message would be subtle enough, but clear enough, to get through while allowing Bill Jones to save face. If he'd back off, she'd back off, then things could go on without a hitch.

"No strings," he said, looking at her squarely. "He probably didn't tell you, because some things are hard for a man to say out loud, but his daddy had a hard spirit, especially when it came to Max."

She nodded. So far, so good. She'd heard as much already.

"Good. I'm glad he told you that. You must mean a lot to him to give up that hurt."

She looked down into her coffee mug. This wasn't about him interviewing her. The old goat had it twisted.

"Problem always was, his daddy was jealous."

"Jealous?" She'd meant to let Bill Jones ramble, then say her peace about not using people, then get up and leave. But the question had bumped into the tidy speech she'd prepared in her mind and simply fell out of her mouth.

Bill Jones nodded. "Uhmmm-hmmm. It was horrible

to watch. Started when Maxwell was a baby. He was first born, a beautiful, healthy, smart little boy—and his momma doted on him. His father was jealous, lotta men in the world like that." Bill Jones sighed and shook his head. "The man used to put that boy down at every turn. And each baby she had, still none compared to her first, and less time and less time was there for his daddy with all those chillen. Then, Maxwell started getting tall, got strong."

"Oh . . . Mr. Jones . . ." She set her mug down as she closed her eyes. She could just see it.

"Yep," he said, in a flat voice. "What child don't bring home every accomplishment and stand there waiting on a hug or a compliment?"

Darien swallowed hard as she listened, her heart breaking.

"And the taller he got, the smarter he got, the madder his daddy got at him. So, I stepped in, trying to help."

"You took him to the baseball games and stuff?" she heard herself ask beyond her will not to.

"His daddy was always working, you see. That was his excuse anyway. Could make it to the other children's events, mind you, but not Maxwell's, so I went. I clapped. I took him for that pop afterward at the diner. I taught him how to drive my car, alls so he didn't have to go to his daddy and beg." Bill Jones sat up tall. "His momma thanked me, but that became problematic after a while, too, and ended a friendship. She would always throw my help in her husband's face, even though I told her not to."

Darien sipped her coffee fast. This was too much information, and she wasn't sure where it might lead or turn. If Maxwell's mother had stepped out, she didn't want to know—TMI, too much information. She hated journalism.

"Wasn't like that," he said, chuckling and shaking his

head. "Although people speculated from time to time. Got so bad in Macon, folks thought I'd sired the boy."

She held her coffee cup in midair.

"No, I didn't."

She covered her heart with her hand. She couldn't help it.

"Believe half of what you see, and none of what you hear, darlin'." He smiled, seeming flattered, and then began toying with the sugar bowl. "But, I didn't care. Wouldn't have minded if that were the case—even though it wasn't. But what I didn't like was a bright, capable young man getting his self-esteem beat to nothin'. So, as he got up in years, I took him with me. I used to work high up in the state. Had contracts and contacts, state dinners, political affairs to go to . . . took him with me to everything to show him the way it was done, how to handle his business one day."

She was leaning forward so far hanging on Bill Jones's every word that, if a breeze blew, she would have fallen on the floor. The distrust of politics . . . the disdain for the media . . . the need to work like a packhorse to measure up . . .

Bill Jones's gaze slipped from hers and sought the window across the room. "I didn't have sons, didn't have any children. My wife . . . well . . . that's another story, and you didn't come here to hear all of that. Point is, I doted on him, watched him bloom. But I had me a little tumble from grace. Got in a snag, close to the time I was about to retire. Administrations change, allegiances change, so goes the world of politics." He smiled a sad smile and glanced at her for acceptance. "You're from Atlanta. You know how politics go."

"I do, sir. That's why I stay away from them."

He chuckled. "You sound like Maxwell. Must be why he's so sweet on you."

"He talked about me?" Her gaze caught Bill Jones's and held it.

"In a round-about way, being he's a gentleman and fairly closed mouth."

She smiled and glanced away.

"Before you came down here, he started asking me all sorts of questions about when it might be a good time to settle down. Asked me a lot of questions." Bill Jones held up his hands. "Didn't name no names, but had the kind of questions he never used to have for me."

Darien chuckled and easiness slid into her countenance. Her guard lowered with it, and she reached out and touched Bill Jones's arm. "I'm glad he had you to help him grow into who he's become."

A warm hand covered hers. "And I'm glad he got knocked over his head by fate and bumped into you as a lady reporter instead of those sharks that could tear him to pieces. That's why, after Rev put the word on you, I decided to call."

"I don't want him hurt," Darien admitted quietly.

"Neither do I, baby girl."

Companionable silence rested a spell on the sofa between them. She now understood the magnetism of Maxwell's mentor. There was a depth and wisdom that went far beyond the surface.

"I called you over here for two reasons," Bill Jones finally said. "I'm an old politician, and I don't do anything without an agenda."

This time when he spoke, she didn't tense; her smile was genuine.

"I figured that, for one, I had to see this girl from up north who blew the lid off Ezekiel Tabernacle and had gotten herself invited to Doreetha's house for Sunday dinner on the first pass." He laughed a deep, resounding laugh that came up from his belly. "I had to know who'd flustered Reverend's whole flock with a camera man going to the rail."

"They told you all that?"

"I don't go to where tongues wag anymore, which for me, at my age, happens to be church. But in the supermarket aisles, I learn a lot."

They both laughed.

But after a while, his eyes became so sad and his smile faded like a slow sunset.

"Miss Darien Jackson, Reverend came to me because we go way back, too. He was all excited about the cover story you were writing, and wanted to know my opinion. We wanted to be sure that what you wrote would separate my past from Maxwell's. He's worked hard for everything he has. I won't let him give me a dime because I don't want it said there was some kickback paid to me." He stood and walked over to the fireplace and leaned on the mantel, but held her gaze.

"Five years short of retirement, I had gotten tired of seeing the good old boys send their sons to Harvard and Yale, and feather their starter homes from unfair advantages. So, I decided, I was almost good as gone, so I was gonna help a few of my own." He lifted his chin. "I ain't shamed of it. Yes, I did what I did. Paid the price dearly, too. Lost my job, my pension, my wife moved back to her people in Texas . . . they talked about me like a dog in the press, and everybody I helped couldn't remember my name—scared of the repercussions to their good, safe lives. But their children went to good schools and their wives wore fur coats."

Bill Jones raked his fingers through his hair. "It was a garbage contract—hauling and removing dry rubbish from state office buildings. Had a prime contractor, but needed a minority subcontractor, was a huge job. I knew how much the state would let the contract go for. I didn't outright tell him, so as not to get him in trouble if things ran aground. I didn't tell him things like I did the others who were used to playing the dirty politics game. Maxwell was an innocent, too young to get down in the mud and woulda never wanted to know. But I made suggestions as he struggled with the paperwork. He just so happened to come in the lowest cost bidder, then he and his brothers had to work like fools to meet the conditions, 'cause their first time out bidding, they'd barely put enough profit in it to live on."

Darien wrapped her arms around herself, imagining the disappointment, all the heartache Maxwell must have internalized once his beloved mentor fell from grace. And she couldn't even begin to fathom the unwarranted fears he harbored about ever being found out. His entire family standing on his shoulders, sisters and brothers who probably never knew how he truly came to land the first big deal, the bottom possibly dropping out at any moment, with a father sitting there, smug, waiting for failure, and the press making loose associations, innuendo stoked by community murmurs about his mother and Bill Jones and him, then his good business fortune, even an investigation that she was quite sure he must have had to endure for years.

"Oh, God, it must have been terrible for him . . ."

"It was. Tore me up." He stared at her, leaned forward and flattened his palm on his chest. "But they got the job done," he said in a proud whisper. "Got their feet on the ground, their name out in the world, and once the dust settled, more contracts came that brought more trucks in different cities that didn't care about Macon's mess, and those contracts leveraged building purchases, and he was on his way."

Bill Jones sauntered around the room forcing Darien to follow him with her eyes. "So, do I care that I'm old and tired and dying of cancer and broke? No. Not one wit. *We won*. They mighta got me, but another generation got through, was passed over. They hung me up on the tree, but my boy and his brothers got away. Now look at all them children and wives, seeds planted in my mud, but coming up roses and rich!"

He stopped walking. "My friend was a stubborn fool. He even rubbed that boy's nose in my dirt at the very end, unable to see the big picture. That's when I knew he wasn't just jealous of Maxwell, he'd always been jealous of me, too, and his son carried the double load, just because he'd clung to me for a little respite."

"And to think I came here to argue with you because I thought you wanted to dish some dirt or cut a deal to keep what you've told me out of the media, just so . . . oh, Mr. Jones, I am so terribly, utterly sorry."

He leaned his head back and closed his eyes, his strong melodic voice filling the room. "I'm from the old south, baby girl. I remember the days . . . So, I figured, while I still had position and breath in my body, I would tip the scales just a little to let a few get some of that American dream pie now, rather than in the sky once dead."

He straightened himself, smoothed the front of his sweater, and looked at her hard. "I needed to put my eyes on you, tell you this story, reason with ya, make sure you didn't get too ambitious and decide to tell the side of this tale that shouldn't go in print because some of you new younguns with new, fancy jobs and what have you do not respect the fact that ain't nothin' changed since the beginning. I couldn't have you do an exposé, wouldn't allow you to just ruin a man to further your career. No, indeed. I had to speak on it."

"I'm glad you did," she said, standing and going to hug him.

A pair of old, warm, strong arms enfolded her. "Tell your story, darlin', and tell it right. Don't give up on that boy."

"I won't," she murmured, his hug so familiar it could have been her own daddy's. She squeezed him tight and rested her head on his shoulder for a bit to soak a little of him in.

"I'm so glad you came in here ready to fight me, Miss Darien, angel from up north, 'cause now I know for sure he picked a good one."

Chapter 15

She knew she was out of order, hadn't been invited, but her car was on autopilot. She didn't have a dish in hand, an acceptable Sunday offering, or a good excuse. He wasn't even speaking to her for some odd reason, but she knew it had something to do with fear.

So she swallowed her butterflies whole, got out of her car, and took a deep breath. Her gaze scanned the cars in front of the house and in the driveway until she spotted a navy Lexus. This didn't make any sense, but right then, it made all the sense in the world.

Yeah, she'd only known him for such a short time, but her hand still found the bell. She took another deep breath as Doreetha answered the door.

"I'm sorry to bother you during dinner, but I really need to speak to Maxwell for a minute."

The shock on Doreetha's face almost made her turn on her heels and bolt for the car, but a woman-to-woman silent exchange went down, and Doreetha held her elbow firm.

"That's right," Doreetha said, nodding. "You go on in there and set yourself down at the table and c'mon and eat. You family."

The hospitality gave her courage; Doreetha's conviction gave her faith. But the thought of entering a place where she wasn't wanted by the man she wanted gave her acid stomach.

All the laughter and food passing stopped as she entered the dining room. Glasses of iced tea were slowly set down while forks were held in state between midair and male mouths. Children craned their necks to see what was going on at the grown folks' table. Darien held her ground, but her voice was very soft.

"Hi, everybody."

"We missed you at church," Doreetha mercifully said, busying around the table as though expecting her all along. "Set yourself down, chile, and eat."

"How was your stay in Philly?" Arnetta asked, talking a mile a minute. "You got everything done you were gonna do with the newspapers? We're so glad you came back . . . uh, before Monday. Ted went back to Atlanta to turn in his photos Friday night."

"Good to have you back," Jovan said, glancing at the other brothers and their wives. "Ain't it nice to have her back so soon?"

Murmurs of assent danced around the table. Darien held her breath. Until she got a nod from Maxwell, she could not, would not, sit down.

"Uh-huh," Otis said, his eyes on Maxwell. "Real good."

Maxwell sipped his iced tea and quietly chewed his greens, never looking up.

"It's all good," Lewis said. "Ain't that right, Odell?"

"Yeah, girl. Sit down. Monty, pass her a plate."

"You want white meat or dark meat?" Doreetha's husband asked, his nervous gaze darting from Darien to Maxwell. "Doreetha put her foot in this bird."

Darien moved forward slowly, watching Maxwell's smoldering expression. All she wanted to do was tell him that he had nothing to worry about from her regarding Bill Jones. If he wanted to break it off, that was fine, but he had to know that. Darien held onto the back of the chair, but still didn't sit in it.

"I don't want to invade your space or wear out my welcome, Doreetha."

"Too late for that," Maxwell muttered under his breath.

Again, the table went still. She looked at him, their eyes met, fury kindled within her as his stare pulled away.

She wasn't sure if it was the sarcastic comment or the look in his eyes that made her bold, but she'd had enough. "May I speak to you for just a moment, Maxwell?"

"I'll be in the office, Monday . . . if you call Peg—"

"It won't wait till Monday, and I'm not making an appointment with Peg to talk to you."

Even the children stopped eating.

"Then what is it?" Maxwell pushed his plate away from him and leaned back in his chair, eyes blazing.

"I'd rather discuss it in a more—"

"This is a family business." Maxwell looked around the table. "Everybody here is an officer of the firm, save the kids. Now, if you've brought the office into my personal space, my sister's home, while I'm eating on a Sunday afternoon, and it can't wait till Monday, then I guess it's urgent enough for every executive in here to hear it, since we're talking strictly business."

Darien felt her head tilt on its own volition. She chuckled and looked away. She was hoppin', spittin', fightin' mad. She could feel his brothers begin to pull back in their chairs. Doreetha had set a platter of cut turkey down real gingerly on the sideboard. Arnetta put her napkin beside her plate. It was all happening in slow motion, even as she told herself that she would not cause a scene.

"I will not be in the office Monday because I resign."

"Now hold on a minute," Maxwell shouted, standing fast. "You come into my sister's house and—"

"I asked you nicely, professionally, and politely, but your stubborn ass wouldn't have the decency to get up from the table! And I was trying not to put your business across Doreetha's table, but since you went there—"

"What!" Maxwell bellowed, rattling glasses as his fist found the table. "I went there, *I went there?* You defied a directive and—"

"What directive, negro?" Her hands were on her hips. Maxwell's sisters gasped.

"You were not supposed to get Bill Jones involved in the article! I told you not to call him. I forbid it, but you went behind my back anyway and called the man! Don't deny it—I saw his number in your purse when it fell, and you were in contact with him while we were in Atlanta together and didn't tell me!"

"Oh, girl, you didn't . . ." Arnetta breathed into her palms.

Doreetha sat slowly and took a sip of tea. Two of the wives stood and began clearing the table, three more went to hustle the youngest children out of earshot as the Ferguson brothers shook their heads and looked away. Doreetha's husband just sat with his mouth open as older children gaped wide-eyed.

An unstable, very volatile element within Darien bubbled up and came out on a breathless sentence. "The man called me," she shrieked. "Call him now and ask him!" Darien's hand slapped the table.

Appearing stunned for a moment, Maxwell backed up, but there was much less thunder in his voice. "Then how come—"

"Don't you interrupt me, dammit." She wagged her finger as she lobbied her complaint, not caring what came out of her mouth. "He called *Urban Professional* magazine, got Mavis. He wanted to talk to me before the story broke, understood, and we all know why. Mavis gave me the message when I got back to my room, and we both know there was no time while I was in *your* room for me to sneak any call to no Bill Jones!"

She walked in a hot line between the archway and the chair. She didn't care what they thought, didn't care that all their eyes were wide or that Maxwell looked like he'd collapse from an aneurysm. He'd offended her integrity—attacked it outright. Intolerable.

She spun on him, hands on hips, neck bobbing with each word. "I was trying to keep from upsetting you—I don't know the man from a can of paint, and working in PR, you see all sorts of nasty things done. I didn't know if he wanted to blackmail you, soak you dry, and I knew you loved the ground that man walked on, so yeah, I was gonna call him and read him the Riot Act."

"You went to bat for me like that?" Maxwell said, his voice losing all bluster.

"Yes!" Darien shouted, holding on to the back of a chair to keep from hurling a glass at him. "I drove to his house because he gave me directions. While y'all were in church, my plan was to find out his angle, try to reason with him, and if he started some mess, I'da beat that old man down with some very well-connected folks in the spin business. I would have buried him in negative press—if he went for you."

She was breathing hard, had to push away from the chair, had to look up at the ceiling. "I got there," she said, folding her arms over her chest, willing herself not to cry. "We both came out swinging." Her voice dropped to a reasonable pitch from sheer exhaustion. "He was protecting you, I was protecting you. I stepped to him about this family, and we wound up hugging."

"Dayum . . ." Jovan murmured.

"Tol' you you should apologize to her," Otis said, punching Maxwell's shoulder as he got up from his seat.

"You stood for the Fergusons, just went to battle for us, like that?" Doreetha shook her head, amazed. "Told you you shoulda went to the rail today, big brother."

"See, I knew my girl wasn't like you thought, Max. What's wrong with you?" Arnetta got up and indignantly brushed by him to stand at Darien's side.

"Look, Darien, I didn't know that—"

"No. I'm done," Darien snapped. "If, after all we've been through . . . if you think I'd do something like that to you, then there is nothing I have to say to you." She turned and looked at Doreetha and Arnetta. "I want to thank you for all you've done for me. The article will be nice, front page, and we've got some great shots in there at Ezekiel. The newspapers are carrying different scaled-down versions at all your site cities. You should start to see some very nice clippings—tell Peg to get 'em—over the next few weeks."

"Darien, listen—"

She held up her hand, ignoring Maxwell and cutting him off. "I'll have a formal consulting engagement termination on his desk Monday, nine A.M. sharp. My bags are packed, my apartment is packed, my expense report will be turned in, and I'll make arrangements to have my furnishings trucked to Philadelphia Monday."

"Wait, wait, wait," Jovan said. "This is getting way out of hand. Why don't we all sit down, finish dinner, and take some deep breaths . . ."

"Chile, we ain't running you out of town on no humble," Doreetha exclaimed, wringing a dishtowel in her hands.

"Neither is our brother. You work for the firm, not him," Arnetta said, glaring at Maxwell. "We will close ranks so fast and freeze his stubborn behind out, you don't know."

"That's right," Doreetha's husband said "They will. Seen it done plenty times."

"Now, I can get the trucks free," Otis said sadly. "Not

that I'd want to, but it's only right that we make sure
your things are returned proper."

"Me and Monty can see after any odds and ends you
need," Lewis said, "make sure you got food stocked in
your refrigerator when you get back home. Odell will
help with the move, just like before."

He wasn't sure if it began when Darien started walking away or just listening to the family close ranks to as-
sist him for her . . . or if it was the knowledge that she'd
fought for him that was just now sinking in. Maybe it
was just the sheer knowing that she would have gone up
against even his mentor, or maybe it was because it had
taken him this long to calm down, to de-escalate, and
get it all straight in his head, but when Lewis said he was
going to help her go home, something fragile in his psy-
che snapped.

"She *is* home!" Maxwell rounded the table and
stopped Darien's retreat with the sound of his voice.
"She's already where she needs to be."

She shook her head and began walking again.

"Girl, I'm sorry. I didn't know. That's a real sore spot
for me and—"

"How many other sore spots you got like that, that
might hurt me bad or scare me? Huh? I'm done,
Maxwell."

She brushed past him and made her way through
the house.

"You know like I know, you'd better go git 'er," Jovan
said, no nonsense in his tone.

"Handle your bizness," Otis warned, "before loneli-
ness handle you."

Darien was on the porch by the time Maxwell caught
up to her. He tugged on her arm. She stopped and
looked down at his hand. He removed it, panic making
his shirt stick to him.

"Baby, listen, I didn't know, and I don't have to call
Bill to believe you, and—"

"And my bills are paid. I made arrangements, legitimate ones, on my own while I was in Philly to consolidate my debt, on my own, without your help—no strings attached, remember? I did what I was supposed to do, you did what you promised you would, it's just business, no strings attached, so I'm out. And I haven't played you, okay."

"It has nothing to do with that!" He could hear his voice ringing through the house, every word convicting him, being misunderstood. He'd always been a private person. This was way too public. They needed to talk, alone. This was so over the top. It was killing him, massacring his pride.

Maxwell took a deep breath, tried to touch her arm again, but she flinched away, tears and fury glittering in her gorgeous hazel eyes.

"We need to talk, privately . . . sort this out . . ."

"No!" she shouted, a new decibel of rage in her voice, despite the fact that his was mellow, low, and humbled. It was a matter of principle. "When I wanted to talk privately, wanted to tell you what happened with me and Bill, you gave me your arrogant *be*hind to kiss. You've embarrassed me in public, showed out at a restaurant, gave me the blues, the cold shoulder, had me weeping my eyes out in my apartment—correction, *your apartment*—not even knowing what I did wrong, then you hollered at me across your sister's table, just flat blasted me, flagged me so hard I can never look your family in the face again, uh-uh. I don't have to be treated like that. Why? 'Cause you think you can buy me! And you say I'm the one who plays games? Oh, we can talk, right—so you can get all up in my face and talk low and sexy and try to make it all right?" She flipped her wrist, opened her palm, holding it up to back him off. "Pullease."

"Darien, I know nothing I say is gonna—"

"No, it's not!" Full-fledged drama had a chokehold on her. She couldn't help it. Everything she'd ever wanted to tell a man who had hurt her feelings, had made her feel less than, became a heat-seeking missile issued from her mouth. Maxwell Ferguson had a target on his forehead and she was not playing. "There is *nothing* you can say to me now, not a thing. There is nothing you can do for me now. I'm through, done, finished. I have never been so humiliated in all my born days!" The tizzy was making her stomp her feet, wave her arms, and had her hair wild. "There is noth—"

His sudden, hot kiss and grip on her upper arms stopped every charge she was firing.

"I have men digging up my yard for you, woman! I have furniture on its way from High Point with your color scheme and stains. I have all my furniture being ripped up at the upholsterers, Spanish tiles being flown in and grout all over my kitchen and bathroom floors! Don't tell me I don't care, Darien," he sputtered. "I have a back hoe out there digging up an acre for the tennis courts and pool, art I don't even know why it costs so much laying against the walls waiting for you to pick out custom frames!"

He dropped his hold on her and walked in a circle. "I messed up, yeah. But damn, give a brother a break. I listened to what you said you wanted . . . I-I thought I knew . . . and . . ."

"Wait," she said, her voice so quiet that he looked up. "You did all that for me . . . When?"

"Every day, when I'd walk away from you, I'd make a call. You were supposed to come back home. I wanted to surprise you, but you're so stubborn and ornery . . . the roses probably done wilted by now, all them plants I sent Maybel to put in there . . ." He let his breath out hard and rubbed his face with both palms then shook his head, his gaze traveling off into the distance. "I couldn't even get you to give me a straight answer on what kinda rock you might like without an argument, girl."

"What kind of rock?"

"Yeah," he muttered, walking away to seek refuge deeper into the house. "A rock," he said, yelling the response over his shoulder. "A ring kinda rock. An I'm-serious kinda rock. An I-ain't-playing-and-I-want-every-brother-who-runs-up-on-you-to-know-you-got-somebody-at-home-who-can-handle-his-business-so-they-need-to-step-off-kinda rock!"

He didn't care that the whole family was standing up as he passed them to go into the kitchen. He needed a beer, needed some space. His whole life was on public display, splattered there by a public relations expert. She might as well have taken out a front-page ad in The *Wall Street Journal*. Outrageous.

"That boy got a helluva way to ask a woman to marry him." Jovan shook his head.

"But he definitely is handling his bizness," Otis said, slapping fives all around.

Darien stopped in the archway. She had to pass all of them to get to Maxwell, and she wasn't sure her legs would carry her in a straight line.

"You still moving?" Doreetha asked with a sly half smile.

Darien shook her head.

"I don't need to draw up any paperwork on Monday, right? You ain't quittin' are you?"

She looked at Arnetta and shook her head. Hell no she wasn't quittin' on this man.

From her peripheral vision she could see smiling wives who she'd have to soon get to know. She glanced at young, eager faces, aware that soon she'd have to become adept at rattling off their names, knowing all their favorite things, treating each one as the special gift they were.

She shyly picked her way past the clan and found Maxwell standing with the refrigerator door open. His back was to her, rigid with fury, as he sipped a beer and then slammed the door with a vacuum-sealed thud.

She didn't say a word, just ran her hand up his spine nice and slow, the way she knew always unraveled his nerves. It made him turn around and kiss the top of her head, and she filled his arms and kissed him deeply. "I ain't going nowhere," she murmured.

"Then, you need to stop playin' with me, girl."

"You wanna go home?" she asked, kissing his neck.

He swallowed hard and glanced toward the dining room. "Yeah, but now how would that look in front of my family after all this commotion?"

"Do you care, right through here?"

He shook his head. "You?"

"Uh-uh . . ."

"There's construction dust everywhere, holes in the wall . . ."

"You did all that for me?"

He nuzzled her temple. "Would raze and level the place for you . . . wasn't nothin' without you but a shell, anyway."

"Wanna go back to my place?"

He chuckled. "Oh, so now it's your place."

She laughed low in her throat. "Yeah, now that you're treating me nice. But everything's in boxes."

His hand slid to her waist then found the sway in her back. "You was really gonna move, weren't you?"

She leaned against him. "In a New York minute."

"I'm glad you're already packed. Won't be no issues for the fellas to go get your stuff and bring it home."

"You said something about a rock." She giggled.

"I might have. Was it oval?"

She smiled and kissed his chin. "You know that's what I said."

"They've got this real nice bed-and-breakfast in town . . ." His voice had become a ragged whisper into her hairline.

"I don't know," she said in a way that made him give her a worried look. But her smile chased it away. "Why don't we go where we can make a lot of noise—and where nobody will be putting a key in the door."

"Yeah . . . and why don't you call in sick on Monday? The boss won't mind."

She chuckled and sucked his earlobe. "Okay," she whispered on a light gasp as his hand traced her bottom. "You gonna follow me over to my place?"

"Uh-uh," he murmured.

"Your place?"

He shook his head.

She pulled back and looked at him.

He smiled and tilted his head, and motioned to her feet with his chin.

She stared at him in confusion.

"I had come by these tickets to St. Lucia, being so inspired by a design I saw somewhere . . . was gonna take a sister there while all the dust and construction was going on, if a sister would just act right and stop playing."

Epilogue

One year later . . .

She was watching the wedding video; he was watching her. What was on the screen didn't compare to witnessing the low lights and fire dance across her hair and skin. He fished the strawberry out of his champagne and offered it to her, just to get her to turn in a little closer to him. He wanted to watch her bite it, see the color stain her mouth, watch her eyes close slowly the way they always did when she ate from the edges of his fingers.

"It's sweet," she murmured, then licked her lips and brushed his mouth.

"So are you," he told her, his hand caressing her hair.

"Aw, didn't Ted do a nice job with the video?"

He nodded, but wasn't looking at it. "Yeah . . ."

She chuckled, thoroughly engaged with the big day. He didn't care that the television had her attention, as long as it was making her smile.

"Cynthia looks like she's walking to the gas chamber though."

He glanced at the television and chuckled and shook

his head. "Aw, now, don't be too hard on 'em, baby. They're crazy, but they're family." He was so mellow and felt so blessed that he didn't have it in him to hold a grudge.

"If Doreetha hadn't insisted that she needed them to walk beside your brothers—humph. Them heifers didn't have to be in it if they were gonna look like that."

His gaze went to the television, but he saw so much more than she did on their first anniversary. She probably saw sleeveless dark blue velvet dresses with a profusion of orchids and paradise blue pansies. He saw a woman who'd chosen his mother's favorite colors to surround them, even though it was not necessarily her taste. She probably saw a well-orchestrated event that seated five hundred; he saw his bride who'd graciously compromised time and time again to give his elder sister the reigns to coordinate everything, and he also saw his bride take his mentor's arm and proudly walk with Bill Jones toward him.

That had been a defining moment. Nieces and nephews were somehow all incorporated. Initially he'd balked at the runaway plans, thinking it was an unnecessary extravaganza. But as his attention swept to the big screen, he saw his brother Jovan at his side, his sister Arnetta, and his wife's girlfriend, Mavis, at hers as maids of honor. Darien had brought his life full circle, completing it, leaving no one out of her wide embrace. Yeah, he could see it all clearly now.

"You're awfully quiet. You all right?"

He nuzzled her cheek. "Yeah . . . you?"

"Uh-huh," she said softly, snuggling against his chest.

"You sure you aren't disappointed? I mean, we could have gone away somewhere nice." He breathed into her fragrant hair and spoke into it with ardor. "If you don't like anything, you tell me, baby. I can change it as well as me."

She glanced around the living room he'd redecorated just for her. He probably only saw a house; she saw a home. As a man, he probably only saw the things he'd brought to fill it; she saw someone who'd moved heaven and earth to make her happier than she'd ever dreamed. What would she ever want or need to change?

"We are somewhere nice," she said softly, brushing his chest with a gentle kiss. "I'm somewhere perfect . . . with someone perfect, made just for me."

He hugged her and kissed the crown of her head. "I know Macon is a little slow, doesn't have the pace of the big city . . . if you ever get tired of being here, we could go up to Atlanta or Charlotte and build where there's more to do."

She shook her head. "Family's here. You're here. This is right where I've always wanted to be."

"But Arnetta's gone off to LA to be with Ted . . . Mavis is up in Atlanta; your sisters are there, too. I figured you'd want to be where it's more cosmopolitan. I'm working all the time, and I figure you might get bored, after a while, and—"

"Shush," she said gently, putting a finger to his lips. "I told you, baby, I'm home."

The touch of her finger at his lips that stopped his clumsy tumble of words burned him. Her eyes said it all, much more than what she'd said out loud. *She was home.* He could feel it. He was blessed, and for the first time, truly knew it. There was no place in the world he'd rather be.

Her hot gaze made the burn at his mouth travel down his throat, light up his chest, set fire to his abdomen till it clenched, and then stoked the embers in his groin that had been smoldering for her all afternoon.

She set down her glass, then removed his from his hand, and carefully set it beside hers on the coffee table. She stared up into his intense but gentle gaze. She touched his face, felt the tips of her fingers tingle. She could barely catch her breath when his stopped briefly and got trapped inside his chest.

"This house is missing something though," she whispered. "Something that I don't know if I can live without anymore, Maxwell."

He opened his eyes and caught her hand within his, kissing her palm long and slow. "Name it, and I'll order it tomorrow. Just turn off the TV and come to bed."

She smiled. "It doesn't come out of a catalog or off a showroom floor, though. Then, again, these days it might."

Her smile widened. His head tilted. He didn't care what she wanted to buy, as long as she came to bed right now.

"If it's custom made or a one-of-a-kind piece, I can cover it. Go ahead and get it." He reached for the remote and clicked off the television. Next New Year's Eve, the black sand of Maui would be her mattress.

"It's a huge investment, Maxwell."

He kissed the bridge of her nose. "Girl, don't offend me. You know I'll work hard for whatever you want."

"I know . . . that's why I want one . . . custom made, by you."

He leaned back a bit and stared at her in disbelief. Was she saying what he thought she was saying? Ready for . . . he had to be sure.

"Maybe it's wishful thinking," he hedged, not wanting to spoil the evening. "I know you have your career . . . we've only had a year together, and I don't want you to feel rushed." She had to understand that he never wanted to steal her zest for life or wear her beautiful body out or make her weary and age fast, dropping babies too quickly like his mother had. He couldn't be the cause of that.

"Whenever you're ready, I am," she said in a near whisper. "But I don't want to rush you to commit. It's a lifelong investment in time and patience and love."

As much as he wanted to fill her with life, he had to really consider if he was ready to share her so intimately with another human being. And in that moment some of his old rage against his father began to quietly fade. He cupped her cheek, the softness of it radiated warmth through his palm, ran up his arm, and threaded around his heart.

"What if I get jealous and can't bear to share your lap?" he murmured. His question was honest as he searched her eyes for understanding and found it.

"What if it's a little girl, and you shower her with so much affection that I feel like second fiddle?" She drank in his gaze, the thought giving her pause as well as wisdom. Then she laid her old struggle with her mother to rest, just that fast.

"You'll always be my first baby," he whispered, suddenly unable to tolerate even the smallest space between them.

"And you'll always be my truest love," she whispered, yielding to his embrace. "Maxwell, let's really fill up this house."

Grab These Other
Dafina Novels
(mass market editions)

Check Out These Other
Dafina Novels

Sister Got Game
0-7582-0856-1

by Leslie Esdaile
$6.99US/**$9.99**CAN

Say Yes
0-7582-0853-7

by Donna Hill
$6.99US/**$9.99**CAN

In My Dreams
0-7582-0868-5

by Monica Jackson
$6.99US/**$9.99**CAN

True Lies
0-7582-0027-7

by Margaret Johnson-Hodge
$6.99US/**$9.99**CAN

Testimony
0-7582-0637-2

by Felicia Mason
$6.99US/**$9.99**CAN

Emotions
0-7582-0636-4

by Timmothy McCann
$6.99US/**$9.99**CAN

The Upper Room
0-7582-0889-8

by Mary Monroe
$6.99US/**$9.99**CAN

Got A Man
0-7582-0242-3

by Daaimah S. Poole
$6.99US/**$8.99**CAN

Available Wherever Books Are Sold!

Check out our website at www.kensingtonbooks.com.

Look For These Other
Dafina Novels

If I Could
0-7582-0131-1

by Donna Hill
$6.99US/$9.99CAN

Thunderland
0-7582-0247-4

by Brandon Massey
$6.99US/$9.99CAN

June In Winter
0-7582-0375-6

by Pat Phillips
$6.99US/$9.99CAN

Yo Yo Love
0-7582-0239-3

by Daaimah S. Poole
$6.99US/$9.99CAN

When Twilight Comes
0-7582-0033-1

by Gwynne Forster
$6.99US/$9.99CAN

It's A Thin Line
0-7582-0354-3

by Kimberla Lawson Roby
$6.99US/$9.99CAN

Perfect Timing
0-7582-0029-3

by Brenda Jackson
$6.99US/$9.99CAN

Never Again Once More
0-7582-0021-8

by Mary B. Morrison
$6.99US/$8.99CAN

Available Wherever Books Are Sold!

Check out our website at www.kensingtonbooks.com.

Grab These Other
Dafina Novels
(trade paperback editions)

Grab These Other
Thought Provoking Books

Adam by Adam
0-7582-0195-8

by Adam Clayton Powell, Jr.
$15.00US/$21.00CAN

African American Firsts
0-7582-0243-1

by Joan Potter
$15.00US/$21.00CAN

African-American Pride
0-8065-2498-7

by Lakisha Martin
$15.95US/$21.95CAN

The African-American Soldier
0-8065-2049-3

by Michael Lee Lanning
$16.95US/$24.95CAN

African Proverbs and Wisdom
0-7582-0298-9

by Julia Stewart
$12.00US/$17.00CAN

Al on America
0-7582-0351-9

by Rev. Al Sharpton
with Karen Hunter
$16.00US/$23.00CAN

Available Wherever Books Are Sold!

Visit our website at www.kensingtonbooks.com